Miss Julia Renews Her Vows

Also by Ann B. Ross

Miss Julia
Renews Her Vows

ANN B. ROSS

VIKING

VIKING
Published by the Penguin Group
Penguin Group (USA) Inc., 375 Hudson Street, New York, New York 10014, U.S.A.
Penguin Group (Canada), 90 Eglinton Avenue East, Suite 700, Toronto, Ontario,
Canada M4P 2Y3 (a division of Pearson Penguin Canada Inc.)
Penguin Books Ltd, 80 Strand, London WC2R 0RL, England
Penguin Ireland, 25 St. Stephen's Green, Dublin 2, Ireland
(a division of Penguin Books Ltd)
Penguin Books Australia Ltd, 250 Camberwell Road, Camberwell,
Victoria 3124, Australia (a division of Pearson Australia Group Pty Ltd)
Penguin Books India Pvt Ltd, 11 Community Centre,
Panchsheel Park, New Delhi – 110 017, India
Penguin Group (NZ), 67 Apollo Drive, Rosedale, North Shore 0632,
New Zealand (a division of Pearson New Zealand Ltd)
Penguin Books (South Africa) (Pty) Ltd, 24 Sturdee Avenue,
Rosebank, Johannesburg 2196, South Africa

Penguin Books Ltd, Registered Offices: 80 Strand, London WC2R 0RL, England

First published in 2010 by Viking Penguin, a member of Penguin Group (USA) Inc.

1   3   5   7   9   10   8   6   4   2

Publisher's Note
This is a work of fiction. Names, characters, places, and incidents either are the product of the author's imagination or are used fictitiously, and any resemblance to actual persons, living or dead, business establishments, events, or locales is entirely coincidental.

Library of Congress Cataloging-in-Publication Data

Ross, Ann B.
Miss Julia renews her vows / Ann B. Ross.
p. cm.
ISBN 978-0-670-02155-0
1. Springer, Julia (Fictitious character)—Fiction.   2. Married people—Fiction.   3. City and town life—North
Carolina—Fiction.   I. Title.
PS3568.O84198M569 2010
813'.54—dc22
2009042561

Printed in the United States of America
Set in Fairfield
Designed by Alissa Amell

For Claudia—beautiful, courageous and full of grace.

Miss Julia Renews Her Vows

Chapter 1

"Mr. Pickens," I'd said in a tone that demanded his full attention. And to make sure he listened, I raised my finger to him. "Mr. Pickens," I said again, "if you break Hazel Marie's heart, you will answer to me."

This little lecture occurred right after he'd resigned himself to the fact that he couldn't wiggle out of it this time. He was roped and tied, and I intended to make sure he knew it.

He clasped my finger and moved it aside. "Be careful where you point that thing." Giving me that lopsided grin that told me he wasn't taking seriously a word I said, he went on. "You can stop worrying, Miss Julia. My heart-breakin' days are over."

"Seeing is believing, and with your marital history—which you've taken no pains to conceal—I have every reason in the world to worry. Three wives, Mr. Pickens, and not a one of them took. Marry 'em and leave 'em, that seems to be your motto, and I'm telling you now, I am not going to have Hazel Marie treated in that fashion."

"Now, Miss Julia," he said, while those black eyes danced in his head. "I didn't do the leaving. Every one of them left me, so, see, I am innocent on all counts."

"Huh," I said, glaring at him. "If that's true, it just goes to show that you were doing something wrong or not doing something right. I remind you, Mr. Pickens, that you have responsibilities now, and your carefree days of coming and going as you please are over."

"My goodness," he said, grinning at me, "looks like I can't win. But," he went on, sobering up just slightly, "I am well aware of my responsibilities. You don't have to remind me that Hazel Marie's having twins."

"*Hazel Marie's* having twins! Stop right there this very minute. *She's* not having them. *Both* of you are, and I'll point out to you that what you say and how you say it are fairly good indicators of how you think. So you just might take a good hard look at your own attitude toward those babies—they are *yours*, Mr. Pickens, and you are just as responsible for their existence as Hazel Marie is." I gave him a sharp nod of my head to punctuate the statement. "And don't you forget it."

∿

We'd had that little conversation the morning of his and Hazel Marie's wedding, although to call that hurry-up, practically last-minute civil ceremony a wedding made my skin crawl. Dashing down to the clerk of court's office for a license early on a Monday morning, then making the drive to a magistrate's office for legal sanction with no notice to friends or announcement in the *Abbotsville Times,* Hazel Marie in a skirt half zipped up with a safety pin to hold it on and crying because she wasn't walking down an aisle with a cathedral train trailing along behind her, and Mr. Pickens gritting his teeth to get through it—well, I wouldn't classify that as anybody's idea of a proper wedding, even though it did get the job done. Thank the Lord.

I was also thankful that our state did not require a waiting period, because we didn't have a minute to lose getting those two married. We did, however, have to wait for Mr. Pickens to drive over to Asheville to get all his divorce decrees out of his lockbox. Seems you have to prove you're unattached before getting reattached. Then Sam, Lillian, Lloyd and I went with them to the courthouse and waited out in our car while Hazel Marie and Mr. Pickens went in to get the license, and I was just as glad not to have seen the clerk's face when Mr. Pickens spread out all three decrees like a losing hand in gin rummy.

I must say at this point that Mr. Pickens had shown some forethought by stopping at a jeweler's and buying a wedding ring on his hurried trip to Asheville. It was only a plain gold band, but it was a wide, thick one, which with the cost of gold these days was no minor purchase. Of course, there was no engagement ring because there had been no engagement, but that could be rectified in the future, on an anniversary, perhaps, if they stayed married long enough to have one.

⌒

When they came out of the courthouse and got in Mr. Pickens's car for the trip to an out-of-town magistrate's office for that travesty of a ceremony, we followed them. Going to Waynesville for the civil ceremony had been my idea, in order to forestall the *Abbotsville Times* from making a public announcement as to the exact date of legalization. If the Waynesville paper printed it in their public notices, more power to them because no one in Abbotsville would see it. Sam and I were to be the official witnesses, for which I was glad because I intended to make sure the whole thing was done up good and tight, so nobody would be able to talk his way out of it.

Lloyd was the happiest of the entire wedding party, and I'm including the bride and groom. In fact, he could hardly sit still, for he was at last getting the daddy he'd never had and he loved Mr. Pickens to death. And to give the devil his due, Mr. Pickens felt pretty much the same way about him. Which was all the more reason to make sure that Mr. Pickens toed the line and kept his shoes under the right bed.

Lillian was with us, too. She'd been at the house the day before, even though it was a Sunday, when Mr. Pickens came waltzing in with the announcement to all and sundry that he was marrying Hazel Marie the following morning. With a whoop of joy, she'd immediately started preparing dishes for the wedding luncheon.

Lillian was another one who'd fallen under his spell, so he could do no wrong in her eyes. She gave him a lot more credit for good intentions than I did.

She'd shown up on that Monday morning dressed in her Sunday churchgoing clothes: a solid white nylon dress with a red patent leather purse the size of a weekend suitcase and red patent leather heels that she could hardly walk in. And on her head, she wore a wide-brimmed red hat with silk anemones and a veil on it.

That meant that Lillian was the only one of us wearing white, a fact that kept Hazel Marie in tears of recrimination at her own precipitous fall from grace, so obviously apparent from the size of her midsection.

It got worse when Lillian happened to mention that Latisha,

her great-granddaughter, had wanted to go to the wedding, but Lillian had left her with the neighbor lady. Hazel Marie really started crying then, because she couldn't stand leaving Latisha out.

"Just hold on," Mr. Pickens said, showing remarkable self-control under the circumstances. "I'll go get her."

"Well, you do that," Lillian said, "an' I got to set here an' braid her hair for a hour or two, 'cause she can't go lookin' like she do now."

I had to step in then because any further delay in the wedding plans would make a nervous wreck out of me. "Go by and get her afterward, Mr. Pickens. She can come to the wedding luncheon. And Lillian, be sure to give her a handful of rice to throw."

"Yes'm, that do the trick an' she won't know the diff'rence."

⌒

So we got them married and those two rapidly growing infants legitimate. And when all is said and done, that was more important than a properly formal and traditional ceremony, although I was heartsick at the secrecy and the haste with which it had to be done.

Chapter 2

❧

I was heartsick over more than that, though, for now came the need for explanations and cover-ups and outright lies that in the long run no one would believe. In truth, however, I didn't care whether anyone believed them or not, just so they acted as if they did.

Part of the problem was that this time I had no leverage by which to elevate Hazel Marie to a respectable position in the town. The first time, that time when she showed up at my front door with my recently deceased husband's little son in tow, I had steeled myself to stare down the gossip and rumors, the whispers and the titters at how my pillar-of-the-church husband had betrayed me. I did it by accepting Hazel Marie and Little Lloyd myself, and, furthermore, by compelling the town to accept them, too. I was able to do it, too, because half the town owed money to Wesley Lloyd Springer's estate and I announced that I was calling in the notes because I was sick and tired of my houseguest being snubbed. There must have been a number of heart-to-heart talks between husbands and wives all over town after that, for all of a sudden, Hazel Marie was invited to everything anybody was giving and to some things they'd just decided to give. The women, who are undoubtedly the worst when it comes to excluding people and standing on principles they don't require of themselves, quickly decided that Hazel Marie was a lovely, if slightly countrified, young woman, and that with a little Christian charity on their part, she would fit right in. Their husbands breathed sighs of relief as I extended their loans at lower rates than Wesley Lloyd had been gouging them with.

But this time, in spite of the fact that Hazel Marie was respectably married for the first time in her fortysomething years, there was nothing I could do to prevent people from ostracizing her after they counted on their fingers the length of time between wedding and birth dates.

On the drive back from the magistrate's office, Lloyd rode with his mother and new daddy. They would go by and pick up Latisha while Sam, Lillian and I went on home to prepare the bridal luncheon.

With Lloyd out of our car, I was free to discuss the next problem facing us, so I did. "Sam," I said, "how are we going to explain this?"

"Explain what?" he asked as he merged onto the interstate.

"Why, this hurry-up marriage without benefit of clergy and wedding invitations and parties and all the usual and expected festivities of a proper wedding. And explain, also, the fact that those babies are going to be born long before the normal nine-month span is up."

Sam, with his eyes on the road, smiled. "There've been a number of hefty premature babies born around town, Julia, so ours won't be the first."

"That excuse won't work in this case, because near as I can

figure, Hazel Marie is already about four months along, and no way in the world will anybody believe five-month-premature babies can weigh six pounds each."

"I think of that, too," Lillian chimed in from the backseat. "An' 'sides that, twinses is known for comin' early, so that don't give us much time to play around in."

"Oh my goodness, Lillian, I hadn't even thought of that. You're both going to have to help me figure out what to do. I mean, what to say, because you know the first thing people're going to ask is when did they get married. Especially when Hazel Marie announces her marriage wearing a maternity dress."

Sam glanced at me. "*We* should announce it, Julia. In fact, I think we should have a party—a big one at the country club, maybe, invite everybody and announce it there. And," he went on with a grin, "dare anybody to say a word."

"They wouldn't say anything, anyway," I said with a sigh of despair. "They'll be as nice as can be to my face and to hers, but then they'll snub her as if she has leprosy. Strike her right off their dance cards. Their invitation lists, too."

Sam reached over to stroke my hand. "I think you're worrying too much about it. Hazel Marie's going to be so busy, she won't notice what anybody else is doing. Or not doing."

"She sho' will be, Miss Julia," Lillian said, straining against her seat belt to lean up closer to the front seat. "She gonna be so full of bein' married to Mr. Pickens, she won't even want to go to no parties, an' she not even see them give her the evil eye when she go to church. She gonna be so happy, she won't care nobody else happy for her. And 'member this, twinses take up lots of time an' she be too busy to worry 'bout what yo' lady friends sayin'."

"Well, that's another thing," I said, recalling Hazel Marie's announcement of her intentions the day before. "Maybe I shouldn't tell this, but she told me yesterday that she intended this marriage to be in name only. Have you ever heard of such a thing?"

Sam's eyebrows went up and Lillian put her head back on the seat and murmured, "They Lord, what she gonna think of next?"

Then Sam laughed. "You believe that, Julia?"

"I don't know if I do or not. She seemed pretty determined at the time. But then she acted real thrilled when Mr. Pickens showed up, so who knows what she'll do. But she said she wasn't going to put up with somebody who was just putting up with her because he was forced into marrying her. And I can't say I blame her, except I don't know if I can handle a quickie divorce. I'm not doing all that well with a quickie wedding."

Sam was a steady and trustworthy driver, so I didn't have to watch everything he was doing. I could put my head back and listen to the hum of the tires on the pavement. But that respite didn't last long, for I thought of something else to worry about.

I sat up straight. "Sam, where're they going to live? I couldn't stand it if they moved to Mr. Pickens's house in Asheville."

"I've already talked to him. They'll live in my house, at least till the babies come and Hazel Marie's back on her feet." Sam was referring to the lovely old house where he'd lived for many years before we married. He still kept the house up, using it as an office for his retirement activities. And also using it as an excuse, in my opinion, to keep James employed. Sam had an unusually soft heart.

"Well, that's a relief," I said, "but I'm a little surprised that Mr. Pickens agreed to it. He's so independent, you know, and stubborn about some things, like accepting help from anybody."

"He's worried about Hazel Marie," Sam said, as he pulled out to pass a car. "I think he wants to keep her close to you." As I mentally preened at being needed and appreciated, Sam went on. "And to Dr. Hargrove."

"Miss Julia?" Lillian strained against her seat belt. "I don't know as she oughta be that far away. Mr. Sam's house almost four blocks from us, an' if she get in a bad way when Mr. Pickens at work and Lloyd in school, what she gonna do?"

"Oh my," I said, thinking of the bad scare we'd already had with Hazel Marie. "She really needs somebody with her all the time. Lillian, do you know anybody who'd like a steady job with good pay and benefits?"

"No'm, not right off. Most peoples I know like to work at McDonald's or out to that big plant what's hirin' 'bout everybody that come in. You can't hardly find no baby nurses no more."

"Well, what do new mothers do?"

"Law, I don't know, Miss Julia. Them doctors send 'em home the next day an' tell 'em to get lots of rest an' don't do too much. Make you wonder what them doctors thinkin', don't it?"

"I should say it does. Well, Lillian, I guess it'll be up to you and me. We're the only family she has, so we can tend to her and those babies during the day and Mr. Pickens will have to take up the slack at night."

There was dead silence in the car for a long minute as we all thought of Mr. Pickens dragging out of bed in the middle of the night—not once but several times—to change diapers and feed one or both of those babies. I could just picture him stumbling around, half asleep, heating a bottle and rocking a nursing baby. And just as he got that one down and crawled back in bed, the other one would flare up.

Sam started laughing and Lillian and I joined in, all of us enjoying the same thought: Mr. Pickens's rambling days were over.

"Well," I said, wiping my eyes, "I don't know that we ought to leave it all up to him, especially right after they come home from the hospital. Think about this, Sam. What if we encourage them to stay with us for a while longer. Hazel Marie's already in our downstairs bedroom, which would give them plenty of privacy, and also keep her from going up and down the stairs as Dr. Hargrove told her not to do. You and I could continue on in her room upstairs and, in the meantime, furnish the sunroom, where Coleman used to stay, as a nursery. Then when the babies are born, we could exchange rooms with them. That way, their whole little family would be on one floor together because Lloyd would be right across the hall, and you and I would be available to relieve them."

"Relieve them?" Sam asked. "You mean, get up at night and feed them? I'm not sure I know how."

"Why, there's nothing to it," I said, convinced that we'd have no trouble, even though I'd never done it myself. "Lillian can show us and we'd take turns. But let's not worry about that now, because Hazel Marie may not be out of the woods yet. Dr. Hargrove told me that this is a high-risk pregnancy and she needs somebody with her all the time in case of an emergency. She simply cannot live anywhere by herself."

Struck with sudden inspiration, I grabbed Sam's arm. "Sam! Etta Mae Wiggins is who we need. She'd be perfect. Hazel Marie's known her for years, and she's a nurse. Well," I went on, somewhat chastened by a second thought, "not exactly, but more of a nurse than any of us."

Sam, glancing at me, smiled. "Sounds good to me. Maybe she'd be willing to live in for a few weeks. Sure would save wear and tear on us."

Lillian leaned forward again. "That Miss Etta Mae a hard worker, an' real nice. But you better figure out where everybody sleep, so they all under one roof and nobody four blocks off by theyselves. An', Mr. Sam, don't you worry. Once you try it, they's nothing sweeter than a tiny baby full up from a bottle an' goin' all slack asleep on you. Even if it in the middle of the night an' you half asleep, too."

"You know me, Lillian," Sam said, glancing at her in the rearview mirror, "I'm pretty much up for anything. You show me how to do it and I'll be rocking with the best of 'em. And Julia, you won't have any trouble making the case for them to stay on with us. Pickens still has some follow-up work to do in Charlotte, so he'll be leaving in a day or so."

"*Leaving!* Why, he just got married. What about a honeymoon? What about taking care of his wife? What does he mean, taking off two days into married life?"

"Well," Sam said, "he didn't exactly take all that into account when he accepted the Charlotte job. He has to close up the apartment he rented and finish what he started, which, I remind you, he cut loose from just to come up here and help me."

"I know," I conceded, recalling how Mr. Pickens had dropped everything to investigate the break-in at Sam's house and ended up not only solving that but discovering the reason for the larceny of the files that Sam needed for the book he was writing, as well as uncovering what proved to be a jaw-dropping scandal. Of course, Mr. Pickens had a great deal of help in doing so.

"Well," I went on, "I guess I should just be thankful for the marriage and not concern myself with how they conduct themselves in it."

"They'll work it out, sweetheart," Sam said, taking my hand with his free one. "We did, didn't we?"

I smiled and nestled my hand in his, content in the happiness we'd found in each other. Now, if only Hazel Marie and Mr. Pickens could find even a smidgen of the same for themselves.

Chapter 3

I won't go into all the details of that mockery of a bridal luncheon, but we all made an effort toward exhibiting a celebratory spirit. Sam toasted the newly wedded couple with a glass of iced tea, sweetened and lemoned, and Lloyd, giddy with joy at having Mr. Pickens and his mother married, laughed at everything anybody said. The boy was supposed to have been in school—it was the first day of the fall term—but this marriage had been a long time coming and he more than deserved to be a part of it. Latisha sat, fairly silently for her, overcome with awe at being at a real live wedding, a misconception about which nobody disabused her.

Later, I heard her ask Lillian, "Is that all there is to it? Just settin' around eatin' chicken salat and drinkin' ice tea? Look like they'd be doing something else 'sides that."

I hadn't lingered to hear Lillian's explanation of a real wedding, because she'd taken the time to impress on the child the importance of a church function with her whole family present and happy for her—trying to forestall, I supposed, any rash spring into marital congress when Latisha got old enough to make the leap.

But even later, after Latisha had apparently mulled over the difference between what she'd seen and what she'd been told, she said to Lillian, "I guess the reason Miss Hazel Marie and that big ole black-eyed man didn't walk down no aisle is 'cause they too ole to make it down there, don't you?"

Lord, I'd have to tell Mr. Pickens that, and Hazel Marie, too, when she was in better spirits. For as soon as we finished lunch, Mr. Pickens insisted that she lie down for a while, and he did it just before I was about to suggest the same. She looked drained, as if the morning activities had sapped all her energy. As likely they had, for she'd hardly been out of the house, much less the bed, for several weeks.

I must say I was heartened by Mr. Pickens's concern for her and hoped it was an indication of more to come.

While Hazel Marie rested, Lillian sent Latisha outside to pick the last petals of the late-summer roses as a substitute for slippery rice. That kept her entertained while Sam and Lloyd went with Mr. Pickens to Sam's house to transfer his belongings to our house. Mr. Pickens had meekly accepted our plan for them to stay with us, but he'd hardly had an argument against it because he was already making phone calls and setting up plans to leave.

That was probably one reason Hazel Marie took to her bed again. The whole episode was so far from her long-held dream of a splendid wedding that it was no wonder she was dispirited. Why, as far as I knew, there was not even a honeymoon on the horizon, nor any plans for one.

I'll have to say here that when I calmly thought over the events of the previous day and of the morning, I had to admit I was not all that displeased with the way things had worked

out. We'd gotten them married, which had been my unyield-
ing intention from the minute I'd learned of Hazel Marie's
condition. If, on the other hand, there'd been no compelling
reason to hurry up and marry and Mr. Pickens had proposed
and provided a ring and an engagement had been announced
and the church reserved, what in the world would I have done
to dissuade Hazel Marie from wearing white satin with a veil
and having half a dozen attendants? The thought of it was so
unsuitable for a first-time bride with an almost teenaged son as
to give me a throbbing headache.

When the phone rang that afternoon, I hurried to pick it up
for fear the noise would disturb Hazel Marie.

"Julia?" LuAnne Conover, my long-standing friend, said as
soon as I answered. "You won't believe who's back in town."

"Who?" I asked, but with little interest. I knew I should tell her
what we'd been up to that morning, but I couldn't bring myself
to do it. I would have to work up my courage to tell anybody,
much less LuAnne, that Hazel Marie was now a properly married woman, although with an improperly advanced pregnancy.

"Francie Pitts!"

"No!" I said, my interest suddenly engaged. "What's she
doing back here?"

"Well," LuAnne said, settling in for a juicy discussion, "she's
moved into Mountain Villas. You know, that new retirement
complex on the other side of town? But no little apartment for
her. No, ma'am. She has a cottage all her own, and you know
what they cost, and guess what?"

"What?"

"She's by herself!"

"You mean she left her husband?"

"I should say she has. Left him in the ground! He's dead, Julia, can you believe that?"

"Oh my," I said, thinking over Francie's numerous forays into marital bliss, most of which had quickly turned into mourning periods.

"And get this, Julia," LuAnne went on. "She's not even going by Francie Pitts or Sanders or any name we know. She's Francie Delagado or Delano or something like that. At least that's what Arley Hopkins said, and she lives out there, too, so she knows. See, Arley said that when Francie moved to Florida after marrying What's-his-name, Herb Sanders, I think, well, he died down there, and she married this other person and then *he* died and now she's moved back here."

We were both silent for a minute; then I said, "How many does that make?"

"Well, let's count 'em up. She was a Pitts for the longest, remember? But who knows whether he was the first? Anyway, he died about nine or ten years ago while they were living here, and we all went to the funeral. Then she married Ray Hooper, but he was already on his deathbed, so that didn't last long. Then she up and married the Sanders man and they moved to Florida, and after that came somebody Welton or Walton. That makes four we know of, and there could've been more."

"I think you left out one, LuAnne, because I remember hearing about her marrying somebody who lived on a yacht or a houseboat or something on the water. Seems like he had a foreign-sounding name."

"You're right! That must be where the Dela-something comes from. So that makes *five* husbands, and every last one of them dead and buried. And you know something else? Arley said that Francie is already eyeing every man who lives at the Villas."

"My goodness, they're all on their last legs already. I'd be tired of going to funerals, if it were me."

"Julia, you're not getting it. I tell you, I think something weird is going on. Tell me this, how many people do you know who've racked up five dead husbands over a ten-year period?"

"Well, not any, come to think of it. But LuAnne, you can't mean you think she had anything to do with those deaths." I paused to let the idea soak into my mind. "Can you?"

"I wouldn't put it past her," LuAnne said darkly. "But if you tell anybody I said that, I'll deny it to my dying day."

Promising that I'd never quote her about such a thing, I went on to ask, "What should we do, LuAnne? I mean, do we include her in everything again?"

"I say we don't. Everybody who lives at the Villas seems to get all wrapped up in the activities out there, so she may not even have time for us. Or want any, either. That would get her off our backs, but just in case, I think we ought to ignore her. I mean, she's been here at least six months and who has she contacted? Nobody, that's who. So as far as we know, she's still in Florida."

"That's true. But I find it strange that she's not called any of us. You know how she is, always so confident that nothing can go on without her being a part of it."

"I wouldn't call it confidence," LuAnne said. "I'd call it high-and-mighty arrogance. Just because Wilbur Pitts was a diplomat in some country nobody's ever heard of was no reason for them to retire here with their noses stuck up so high they were in danger of drowning when it rained."

"He wasn't so bad, LuAnne. In fact, I thought he was quite

nice. A little shy, perhaps, which I thought a bit unusual for a diplomat, but maybe that's why they retired him."

"Well, *she* wasn't shy. She came sailing into town like a queen, and you know, Julia, we all kowtowed to her. We just let her lord it over us as much as she wanted to. Her and those awful hats. And that simpering laugh, remember? Even when you didn't see her, you always knew when she was around. Oh, and I forgot to tell you. Arley said Francie doesn't have a wrinkle on her face, and Arley thinks she's had *work* done on it, because she's started wearing pancake makeup like you wouldn't believe. Probably to hide the scars."

"Oh my," I murmured, trying to picture Francie's overly powdered face realigned and made up.

"Anyway," LuAnne went on, "I say that what she's been up to these past ten years cancels out any need for us to get tangled up with her again." LuAnne paused, then said, "I never liked that woman to begin with, and I think we ought to let sleeping dogs lie."

Agreeing that we had no social obligation to seek out Francie Pitts, or whoever she now was, especially because she'd made no effort toward us, we ended our conversation to await developments.

But I couldn't get Francie off my mind, maybe because it was such a change to have something besides Hazel Marie's situation to occupy it. I'd never understood Francie's overweening self-possession. It was as if the idea that she'd be unwelcome anywhere by anybody never entered her head. LuAnne had been right: queenly was the correct word for her. It was not that she'd been pushy, exactly. She'd just accepted inclusion as her proper due.

But the strange thing about it, especially our allowing her to get away with it, was that she was such a nonentity. She was a short, dumpy little woman, one of those whose figures was a solid block with hardly the hint of a waist. And there was not a bit of comeliness in her face. It was full with stubby features and small eyes, none of which she took any pains to disguise with makeup, other than a little lipstick—that orange Tangee kind—and a great deal of powder. The only striking thing about her was her hair, which she dyed red. No, it was more orange than red, but either way, you couldn't miss it.

Well, there was another striking thing about her: her clothes. I don't know whether she thought she was a leading fashion icon or what, but she had all her clothes handmade by some seamstress in Atlanta. And she made sure that we knew they were of her own design. As if we couldn't tell. She liked voile and other filmy fabrics that flipped and swayed with every swishing step she took, and in the winter she topped them with wool jackets and furs. And every last outfit I'd ever seen her in had a matching hat—either a turban in the same material or a brimmed hat trimmed with matching fabric.

And her personality was nothing to write home about, either. She didn't have any. I'd never known her to make an effort to engage anyone in normal conversation. She simply sat and waited for others to come to her, and even then, her conversation was no more than a litany of complaints.

How she'd attracted so many husbands was beyond me, but, hearing Hazel Marie stirring in her room, I put Francie aside and went in to speak to the new Mrs. Pickens.

Chapter 4

Tapping on Hazel Marie's door and hearing her response, I breezed in, determined to be bright and cheerful. "How're you feeling, Hazel Marie? You have a good nap? How're you liking married life?"

"Well, so far," she said, covering a yawn, "it's pretty much like single life. Where is he, anyway?" Hazel Marie had gotten out of the pinned-up skirt of her wedding outfit and put on another of her sweat suits, or whatever they're called. They were the only thing she could comfortably wear because they had elastic in the waist, but elastic can stretch only so far and sooner or later other arrangements would have to be made. It was a marvel to me that she had so many workout outfits, because Hazel Marie was not at all athletically inclined. But they had certainly come in handy as her waist continued to expand, seemingly on a daily basis.

"He and Sam and Lloyd are over at Sam's house, packing Mr. Pickens's suitcase to move over here. But goodness, they've had plenty of time to get back, so I don't know what they're doing. Probably sitting over there talking to give you some quiet time."

I sat down in an easy chair by the window and waited to see what her mood was going to be. Expectant mothers are at the mercy of their hormones, don't you know. She should've been filled with happiness, for she'd wanted to marry Mr. Pickens almost from the first day she'd met him, and that had been some while ago. But now that she had him, she didn't seem to be taking a whole lot of pleasure in it. Mr. Pickens had been a hard man to pin down, and with good reason. As I've said, he was gun-shy when it came to taking a fourth wife, which in my opinion spoke well of him because it indicated that he was able to learn from his mistakes. The reason he'd given for resisting marriage—and this in spite of so obviously adoring Hazel Marie—was Lloyd's sizeable inheritance from Wesley Lloyd Springer. Hazel Marie greatly benefited from it and would continue to do so until Lloyd reached maturity, and even then I couldn't imagine that the boy would allow his mother to live in penury.

Mr. Pickens, to his credit, did not want, in the first place, to live off another man's wealth, and in the second place, he would not consider being supported by a stepson. That commendable mind-set would certainly create problems, because Hazel Marie had become accustomed to benefiting from the Springer estate and, let's face it, a private investigator's income would hardly equal the income from the boy's inheritance.

But it was their problem and I determined to leave it to them to figure out. At the moment, I had more pressing matters to deal with.

"Hazel Marie," I said, watching as she scooted up in bed and propped herself against the headboard. "We need to think of some way to announce your wedding. In fact, the longer we put it off, the worse it will be, so we need to come up with a plan. Sam has suggested that we have an announcement party, sort of a belated wedding reception, which a lot of people do, especially when they have small family-only weddings, and it's often done weeks after the honeymoon."

As the horror on Hazel Marie's face registered with me, I stopped and held up my hand. "But I don't think that's such a good idea."

"Me, *either*," she said. "Oh, Miss Julia, I couldn't face a big party with everybody looking at me and knowing we had to get married. It would be awful."

"Oh, I agree. I wouldn't put you through that for anything. But here's what I've come up with, because one way or another, we've got to let people know that you are now Mrs. J. D. Pickens. I mean other than just seeing him come and go, then gradually realizing that he's moved in for good. And, of course, seeing your condition."

She began to cloud up then, so she reached for the Kleenex box on the bedside table to have it near to hand.

"Now wait, Hazel Marie. I think I've come up with a solution. See what you think about it. Why don't I have a luncheon and invite eight or ten of our closest friends and just announce it there? I mean," I quickly added as she began shaking her head, "without your being there. Just think about it for a minute. Every one of those women will go home and tell at least a dozen others and before nightfall everybody in town will know that you two are married. The word will get around without us having a big party and putting you right out in front on display."

"I don't know," she said, wiping her eyes on her sleeve, in

spite of having a handful of Kleenex. "They'll still know that
we, well, kind of jumped the gun. I mean, I can't hide anymore,
so they're all going to know and they'll despise me for it."

"No, they won't. They might guess but they won't *know,*
because I've thought of that, too. What I'll do is tell them that
you and Mr. Pickens got married in San Francisco when you
were there back in the summer, but given the weird goings-on
in California, I wasn't sure that this state has reciprocity and
I insisted that you do it again. That would take care of things
if anybody gets wind of the ceremony this morning." I waited
a few minutes for her response, but didn't get one. "What do
you think?"

"I wouldn't have to be there?"

"No, it'd be better if you're not. See, I can make it like it's
a big joke on us. Maybe tell them that we'd thought of having
a—oh, I just thought of something! I'll say you'd planned to
have a renewal of vows and a big reception, maybe at Christmas; but you two got ahead of us and turned up expecting
twins, so we had to renew your vows at a magistrate's office.
Just to be on the safe side, see? In case there was any question as to the efficacy of a California wedding. How does that
sound?"

Hazel Marie bit her lip, considering what I'd said. "It sounds
pretty complicated. I'm not sure it'd work."

"Doesn't matter if it would or not." I waved my hand at the
thought. "All we need to do is give them a reasonable explanation, one they can accept without thinking too hard about it,
and it'll work. Everybody thinks the world of you, Hazel Marie,
and those who know you or even know of you will give you the
benefit of the doubt—if they're given a good enough reason.

And I intend to give them reason enough to believe whatever I tell them."

"When would you do it?"

"As soon as possible. This week, because we don't have a minute to lose. You need to be able to get out of this house and go about your business with your head held high. And as a married woman who everybody *knows* is married, you can do that. I'll start calling this afternoon. If you agree."

She leaned her head against her knees, then finally looked up at me. "I don't know what else to do. But Miss Julia, I am so sorry to put this on you. It'll be you who'll have to sit there and tell your friends one big story after another, and all because of me. I just hate that I've done this to you."

"Why, Hazel Marie, I don't mind a bit. I am so happy to have you married and those babies you're carrying taken care of that stretching the truth a little is a small price to pay." I sat for a minute, running over in my mind whom to invite and just exactly how I was going to make the announcement—when the entrée was served or perhaps over dessert?

"There is one other thing, Hazel Marie," I said, bringing up a more worrisome matter. "You have got to tell Lloyd about the babies. He may already suspect that something's going on just from looking at you, and remember, he can count as well as the next person. I'll leave it up to you what you tell him, but he might hear that I've told about a San Francisco wedding, so you might want to mention that."

"Oh, I hate to tell him such a story, but I was planning to tell him about the babies this afternoon, anyway. That was one reason I took a nap, putting it off as long as I could, I guess. J.D. said he'd do it for me, but I think I ought to."

"I do, too. You and that boy have been so close for so long. He deserves to hear it from you. I'll send him right in to you as soon as they get back."

"Ask J.D. to come in, too, if you will. I think," Hazel Marie said, "maybe it'd be better if we both tell him."

"I think so, too, Hazel Marie," I said, agreeing with anything she said just to get the matter taken care of. "It'll be your first little family conference and a token of things to come. That boy is so thrilled right now at having a real family that he won't question a thing you say."

When the men got back from Sam's house, Mr. Pickens went straight into Hazel Marie's room with the one suitcase he'd brought from Charlotte, and I sent Lloyd in behind him. I hurriedly and quietly told Sam and Lillian what was taking place, and Sam said he'd recuse himself and go help Latisha denude the rosebushes. Sam frequently lapsed into legal terminology, which got him out of a lot of tight spots because nobody understood what he was saying.

I took myself upstairs, trying to get my mind off what Lloyd's reaction would be as he was told that his brand-new nuclear family was about to explode into five members. I'd spoken to Lillian about the luncheon and we'd decided that Thursday would be a good day to have it.

⌣

"Let's do chicken à la king," I had said, "over those little puff pastry shells. And maybe a fruit salad."

"You gonna need something green," Lillian had told me. "I might can find some asparagus."

"Oh, just open a couple of cans of English peas. Nobody's

going to notice what they eat. Not after they hear what I have to say."

I spent the next hour or so telephoning the people on my invitation list. Because the luncheon was such a spur-of-the-moment affair, several already had plans of one kind or another, but I told them that I had a momentous announcement to make and they should drop everything and come. LuAnne was sure that I was going to announce Francie Pitts's return, so she assured me she wouldn't miss it for the world.

"I can't wait to hear what everybody says," she said with an anticipatory giggle. "They're going to rake her over the coals."

I didn't correct her, simply saying that we'd certainly discuss Francie. Actually, Francie's return was a godsend for me because, with luck, it would divert attention from Hazel Marie's hasty nuptials.

At the dinner table that evening, Hazel Marie made a gallant effort not only to eat a decent meal, but also to appear content in her new status as a married woman. Mr. Pickens, sitting next to her, kept cutting his eyes in her direction and reaching over to touch her. He even held her hand under the table as we waited for Lillian to serve dessert. Hazel Marie, however, seemed to give him little encouragement, refusing to meet his eyes and concentrating instead on her food. At least, though, she didn't shrug him off or break down in tears. So that was a good sign.

Lloyd, on the other hand, seemed to be in a daze. He hardly said a word, just sat there playing with his food and gazing off into the distance with a look of starry-eyed wonder on his face. I had no doubt that he was thrilled with the marriage, but how he was handling the news of his incoming siblings was another matter. I think the news of their imminent arrival had left him stunned and unable to comprehend the ramifications—a perfectly normal state of affairs, if you ask me. I'd suffered through the same reaction.

Lillian came in proudly bearing a fresh coconut cake, which she sat in front of me along with a stack of dessert plates. How she'd had time to do all that baking I didn't know, but she was doing her utmost to make this wedding day a festive one. And so was Latisha, who'd strewn rose petals all around the kitchen. I'd brushed several out of Sam's hair and later found one in the basket of rolls.

Mr. Pickens took one look at the cake and said, "Lillian, if I wasn't a married man, I'd come courtin' you."

Lillian laughed. "Look like you a day late an' a dollar short, 'cause you done missed yo' chance with me."

Lillian's pleasure in the day's events served to release the tension at the table and to divert all of us from thoughts of what this long-awaited wedding should have been like.

Later, not long after supper, when Mr. Pickens went into Hazel Marie's room and closed the door behind him, I had to scurry around, keeping myself busy in order to do some diverting of my own. Their wedding night! And right under my roof. Of course, their sleeping together was nothing new for them, but it was for me and I had to scramble to keep my mind off it.

On the other hand, I reminded myself as I went upstairs, if Hazel Marie kept to her stated resolve, there would be a wide space in the bed between them tonight and a grouchy Mr. Pickens in the morning.

Chapter 5

Lloyd's door was open and his lights still on, so I stuck my head in before going to our room. He was sitting up on the bed, still in his shorts and polo shirt—his wedding attire—with his knees bent as he played with something electronic.

"Lloyd?"

He looked up from the cell phone he'd been tapping, his face lighting up with a brilliant smile. "Hey, Miss Julia. Come look at this." He held out his phone so I could see the tiny screen. "Here's a picture of Mama, and here's one of J.D. and this one's of both of them."

"Well, my goodness, what won't they think of next?" I took the phone and looked at the picture of Hazel Marie and Mr. Pickens smiling out at me. "It sure is small, but just as clear as a bell. Show me how to get to the others."

He did, showing me how easy it was to snap a picture, then to run through the album, so to speak. "You just aim it and press this button. And you've got a picture."

Amazing, and I hadn't even mastered a throwaway Kodak.

"Guess what else I'm doing," Lloyd said, and went on before

I could. "I'm texting everybody I know to tell them about my new daddy and my new . . . whatever they are."

Well, I thought, maybe I hadn't needed to have a luncheon after all. Lloyd would have the word out long before I could announce it. Except no one I knew would recognize a text message if it jumped up and bit them.

I sat on the side of the bed and smiled at him. "So you're feeling all right about it?"

"Miss Julia," he said in that serious way of his, "this has been the happiest day of my life."

"What did you think when they told you about the new babies?" It had crossed my mind that the boy might suffer from suddenly having to share the limelight with two little intruders. He'd been an only for so long, you know.

"Well, at first I couldn't figure it out," he said, frowning. "I mean, Mama and J.D. just got married this morning and the day wasn't even over and here they were saying twins were on the way." He looked at me, wide-eyed. "All I could think of was 'Boy, that was fast.'"

My stomach knotted up and a powerful urge gripped my chest, as my face contorted with the effort to contol myself. I had to exert every fiber of my being not to roll on the floor, laughing.

"But then," Lloyd went on, "when they said they'd really gotten married in San Francisco, I thought, 'Whew.' Except I wondered why they hadn't told anybody. Especially me."

I didn't know how to respond, but for his sake I said, "They didn't tell me, either."

"You know why they didn't, don't you?"

I shook my head, afraid I'd say something different from what he'd been told.

"It was because they felt so bad for doing it when I wasn't with them." Lloyd beamed. "They planned to do it all over again anyway when I could be there, but then Mama got sick and first one thing and then another happened and this is the way it worked out."

"Well, it's something we can laugh about for years to come, isn't it?" Actually, I was about to choke already from holding myself back. I had to get to my feet and get out of the room. "It's been a busy day and tomorrow's another one. School, you know, so you need to be in bed."

I hurried across the hall to the room that Sam and I were sharing until Hazel Marie could go up and down stairs again. I quickly closed the door and hurried to our bed, where Sam was reading.

"Sam," I said, gasping from the laughter that I could at last release, "you'll never guess what Lloyd thought when they told him about the babies."

After telling him between ripples of laughter what Lloyd had said, I could finally laugh as long and as hard as I wanted to, so I put my head on Sam's shoulder and did it until I cried. And kept on crying until I ended up in deep sobs and floods of tears, with Sam murmuring, "Julia, Julia, it's all right."

Straightening up and drying my face with the edge of the sheet, I said, "I don't know what brought that on. I thought I'd strangle myself, trying not to laugh, and here I am crying like a baby."

"Stress, Julia," Sam said, running his hand up my arm.

"That's what it is. You've been under a lot of it here lately, and now you can let it go. It's a wonder you've been able to bear up."

"Well, the way I feel now, I could just cry all night and turn into Emma Sue Ledbetter."

Sam laughed and drew me to him. "Cry all you want to, but stay Julia for me. And listen, we've got them married and they're still with us, with no plans to move off with Lloyd, so you can rest easy now."

"Yes, well, I guess. I still have to get through the luncheon and all the tall tales I'll have to tell. But I'll make a vow to you, Sam, I am not going to get myself in a situation like this again. I have never in my life done so much storytelling as I've done during all this. And now," I said, struggling again to speak as more tears cut loose, "and now I'm wondering if we did the right thing. What if they're both miserable? What if they should've never married? I'll never forgive myself if I've pushed them into something neither of them wanted."

"Julia," Sam said, wrapping me in his arms, "you have to stop taking on everybody's problems. Hazel Marie and Pickens are both adults, and you didn't push them into anything. They've done what is right and, if it doesn't work out, why, nothing's been lost and a father to those babies has been gained."

"You're right. I know you're right. I keep forgetting about those babies, which is the strangest thing. It's the *expecting* them that's worried me, not the two little real people who'll be coming. That sounds silly, I know, and I'm as bad as LuAnne, being so concerned about appearances, but I so wanted to protect Hazel Marie and Lloyd."

"And you have," Sam said. "Nobody could've done more,

and they love you for it. And I do, too, but if you keep comparing yourself to Emma Sue and LuAnne, I'm going to have one nightmare after another."

"Oh, you," I said, laughing while I untangled myself from his arms and got ready for bed.

Once I was beside him and snuggled up close, I had the strangest recall of certain events in the early days of my first marriage. Not knowing any better, I'd slip closer in the bed to Wesley Lloyd, wanting, I expect, some reassurance that he was happy with me. "Move over, Julia, you're crowding me," he'd say. Or "Get on your side of the bed." It was off-putting, to say the least, and I quickly learned to keep my distance. Learned it too well, if you want to know the truth, for Sam had proved to be just the opposite and I was having to learn all over again the joy of touching the one you loved.

I was almost asleep when Sam said, "Julia?"

"Hmm?"

"Larry Ledbetter dropped by the house this afternoon." Sam was speaking of his house, probably while Mr. Pickens was packing his suitcase.

"What'd he want?" I mumbled, not particularly interested in a pastoral visit, unusual though it was.

"Wants us to participate in a few study sessions he's dreamed up. We'll meet on Monday nights for about six weeks, just to see how it goes. He wants us to provide a stabilizing influence, whatever that means. I said we would."

My eyes popped open. "A stabilizing influence for what?"

"For young couples in the church. Seems it's to be an enrichment course mainly for them."

"Spiritual enrichment?"

"No." Sam let a second or so pass, as my eyes began to close. "Marriage enrichment."

I sat straight up in bed. *"Marriage* enrichment? Marriage *counseling?* Is that what it is? Sam, how could you? I don't want to be counseled about anything, especially our marriage. What does Pastor Ledbetter know about it, anyway? He's no expert. All you have to do is look at Emma Sue to know that."

Sam drew me back down beside him. "We're not going to be counseled, Julia. If anything, we'll be there to help counsel the others. Give them the benefit of our experiences. Besides, Ledbetter won't be the counselor. He's got somebody lined up who knows what he's doing. A Christian psychologist, he said."

"That does not reassure me," I said, lying stiff beside him. "I don't trust psychologists as far as I can throw them, and anybody who has to tack his Christianity onto his occupation is somebody to stay away from. 'Go into thy closet and pray in secret,' or something like that. But don't *advertise* it just to get clients. I mean, you don't go to a Christian barber, do you, expecting to get a better haircut?"

I could sense Sam smiling in the dark. "I agree with you, sweetheart, but let's humor him. We haven't done much in the church lately, and I thought this would be easy enough. We can drop out anytime you want to."

"What about now?"

Sam laughed. "Look at it this way. We might pick up a few pearls that would help Hazel Marie and Pickens. Of course, the sessions would be ideal for them, but it's a little early along to be suggesting it."

The possibility of helping them get a good start in their marriage put a different light on it, and I relaxed, thinking I could take notes on salient points and pass them on to Hazel Marie. I wouldn't dream of attempting to counsel Mr. Pickens, even from a safe remove.

I turned over and scrooched down, ready for sleep. "Well, okay, but I'm taking it one Monday at a time. You might end up going by yourself and see what kind of model that would be."

Sam laughed and put his arm across my waist. "I'll risk it."

Chapter 6

As I walked down the stairs the next morning, I heard a chorus of voices and laughter coming from the kitchen. I glanced at my watch, thinking I was running late. But no, if anything I was a little early, but obviously others were already up and stirring.

Pushing through the kitchen door, I saw Mr. Pickens, Lloyd, Latisha and Lillian filling plates, looking for backpacks, laughing and carrying on as if they were in Grand Central Station.

"Hey, Miss Lady," Latisha sang out. "I'm gonna go to school today, 'cause I had to go to a wedding yesterday an' couldn't make that ole school bus."

"Good morning, Latisha. I'm sorry you missed the first day of school, but we were glad to have you with us. Aren't you in the first grade this year?"

"No'm, I'm goin' in that ole kindygarden, an' it don't matter if I miss a day or two, 'cause I already know everything they gonna say, anyhow."

Lloyd laughed and helped her pour milk on her cereal. "Just wait, Latisha. Next year, you're gonna blow that first-grade teacher away."

"Miss Julia," Lillian said, "you want eggs this morning?"

I nodded and drew a chair out from the table. Mr. Pickens came over with a heaping plateful and sat beside me.

"Sam not up?" he asked.

"He'll be down in a minute." I cast a careful eye in his direction, trying to read his expression to determine just what, if anything, had taken place during his wedding night. "How's Hazel Marie this morning?" I asked, then could've bitten my tongue off. Knowing him, he'd put the worst possible spin on my question.

And he did. He looked up at me from under those black eyebrows, grinned, and said, "Blooming like a rose. I think married life agrees with her. It sure does with me."

I rose from my chair like it had a spring in it. "Here, Lillian, let me take that." Meeting her halfway across the kitchen, I practically snatched a platter of scrambled eggs from her.

Hazel Marie, in another sweat outfit, came in then from the back hall at the same time that Sam entered from the dining room, their appearances adding to the noise level but relieving me of responding to Mr. Pickens. The man was beyond belief, giving me that smug, self-satisfied grin of his, as if all Hazel Marie had needed was him.

From the looks of her, though, he may've been right, for she did seem more at peace than I'd seen her in a long time. Her eyes were clear and her complexion had lost the blotches that all that crying had etched on her face. Mr. Pickens gave her a kiss as she sat down beside him, then they whispered together for a few minutes, a rudeness that I overlooked given the circumstances.

"Well, I'm on my way," Mr. Pickens said, getting up from the table. "Come on, kids, I'll drop you off at school."

He shook Sam's hand, thanked him again for all his help,

then came around the table to me. "Look after her for me, Miss Julia. I'll be back sometime Friday."

He picked up his suitcase and hanging bag, which had been in the corner, kissed Hazel Marie again and herded the two children out. As he, Lloyd and Latisha left, the kitchen began to return to its peaceful state. I smiled at Sam, poured coffee for him and gave thanks in my heart for what was looking like a good beginning to Hazel Marie's marriage. Except, of course, for the fact that the groom had left after one day of it.

"Miss Julia?" Hazel Marie said, as she took another piece of toast. "I have got to go shopping and find something I can wear besides these sweat suits. I'm so afraid somebody'll see me, though, before they know I'm married. I'll really need some for next week, because J.D.'s made reservations for us at the Grove Park Inn. Will that be all right? I mean, to leave Lloyd with you?"

"Of course it will, and I'm glad to hear it. At least it'll be a semblance of a honeymoon for you, but are you sure you ought to go out of town? Dr. Hargrove wants you close by, doesn't he?"

"Yes, ma'am, but that's why we're just going to Asheville. And I have an appointment Thursday morning, so I'll make sure it's all right."

"Why, that's perfect, Hazel Marie. That's the day I'm having the luncheon, and you need to be somewhere else, anyway. Why don't you go to the doctor's, then go on over to Asheville and do your shopping? By the time you get back, everybody will know and you won't have to slip around and hide anymore." That seemed the perfect solution, until I stopped and thought about it. "No, that won't do. You can't be driving off by yourself and walk all over that mall alone. You haven't been out of bed that long. What if something were to happen?"

"I'll take you, Hazel Marie," Sam said. "If the doctor says it's okay, we can leave from his office and go right on over. To tell the truth, I've been thinking of going to the mall anyway. They've opened a new Reel and Gun store, and I want to see what they have. While you're trying on maternity clothes, I can be trying out a new rod. Would that work?"

Hazel Marie smiled. "That would work just fine."

I declare, Hazel Marie almost ran me ragged all that day and the next. I don't know what had happened on her wedding night, but some kind of energizing change had come over her. Her appetite picked up considerably and she couldn't sit still for two minutes. Always had to be up and doing, wandering around the house, asking Lillian what she could do to help, making out lists for her shopping trip and wondering when she could go to Velma's.

"Velma!" I cried as soon as she mentioned the woman's name. "I have got to invite Velma to the luncheon. I'll call her right now."

"You're inviting Velma?" Hazel Marie asked in wonder. "You've never had her before, have you?"

"I've had her for large events, but never anything as intimate as this. But Hazel Marie, if we want to get the word out that you're a settled married lady, who better to tell than the hair-dresser to the stars?"

Hazel Marie laughed, looking and sounding like her old self, with the exception of a few extra pounds and a couple more inches around her waist. "I expect you're right about that.

But what will LuAnne think? Or Mildred, even? You know how particular they are about appropriate guest lists."

"I know, but they'll just have to put up with it. Besides, it's already a mixed group, because I'm not having this luncheon for entertainment purposes. I have serious business on my mind."

"Who all are you having?"

"Well, let me see. LuAnne and Mildred, of course. And Emma Sue and Helen Stroud. Oh, and Tonya Allen, Tina Doland and, you'll like this, Hazel Marie, Etta Mae Wiggins. Margaret Hargrove and Binkie. And now, Velma. That's a good group, don't you think?"

Well, no, she didn't. She stared at me, her eyes slowly filling up. "You're going to tell all of them? I don't think I can stand it, Miss Julia."

"Now, wait, please don't get upset. We agreed that this is the best way to do it. When they leave here, all they're going to know is that you and Mr. Pickens have been married since back in the summer and that now you're expecting twins. And I'm going to tell them that we didn't announce it earlier because you came down with some kind of flu and we were afraid you'd lose the babies. They'll understand that *nobody* announces anything under those circumstances."

"Won't they think it's funny that I'm not here?"

"I'll just tell them the truth. I'll say that you're a little embarrassed that you got pregnant so fast and, besides, you had a doctor's appointment. What could be more truthful than that?

"And listen, Hazel Marie, I've covered all the bases. Emma Sue, Mildred and LuAnne will take care of everybody in the Presbyterian church. Tina Doland will spread the word among the Baptists, and Etta Mae will do the same all over Delmont. Margaret Hargrove will tell the Medical Auxiliary, Binkie'll take care of the legal community and she'll tell Coleman, who'll pass it along to all the law officers, and Velma will tell everybody who puts a foot inside her shop." I stopped and thought for a minute. "I need an Episcopalian and a Methodist. Think, Hazel Marie. Who else can I invite?"

"Velma's a Methodist, I think."

"Oh good. That'll take care of them, then."

"Who's Tonya going to tell? She's about stopped going to church, hasn't she?"

"Well, who can blame her?" I said, thinking of Mildred's lovely daughter, who not so long ago was a delightful, if slightly unstable, young man, a transformation that many in the First Presbyterian Church of Abbotsville couldn't seem to come to grips with. "I think she spends most of her time in New York. Probably feels more at home there, where she's not so unique. Anyway, can you think of anybody else I should ask?"

"Well, counting you, there'll only be eleven at the table, so you need one more. What about Miss Mattie Freeman? Didn't she used to be a Methodist?"

"Yes, she was, until she got mad about something and moved to the Episcopal church. So she'll cover them, and I might be nipping something in the bud at the same time. After she fell that time on our front steps and had to be taken to the emergency room, I was afraid she might sue us. But she wouldn't dare after accepting a luncheon invitation. Besides, she wasn't hurt and it wasn't our fault anyway."

"You know, Miss Julia," Hazel Marie mused, "I just keep learning how to do social things all the time. I mean, you have to be so careful about who you invite and why you invite them and who sits by who, and all kinds of things. It's so involved, I don't think I'll ever learn it."

I reached over and patted her knee. "Of course you will. One of these days, you'll have your own home and be doing your own entertaining. And that reminds me, Hazel Marie, we need to order you some calling cards. Nobody uses them anymore, except to enclose with gifts, but they're nice to have. And some informals, too. You'll use them a lot for thank-you notes and such." One must do what one can to make the best of adverse circumstances, and having engraved stationery would elevate Hazel Marie's current circumstances.

With the luncheon plans finalized, I hurried off to phone the rest of the invitees, apologizing to each one for the lateness of the invitations but promising a stupendous announcement that they wouldn't want to miss. With a promise like that held tantalizingly before them, I would have a full table, each one eager for the latest news.

After hanging up the phone from the last call, I sat for a few minutes going over my mental notes for the luncheon. Then I called the Flower Basket for a centerpiece to be delivered early Thursday morning. That was it, then. Everything was well in hand, unless Dr. Hargrove told Hazel Marie she couldn't go shopping. If that turned out to be the case, Sam was to entertain her until the luncheon was over—take her to his house, have James give them lunch, take her for a ride, anything to keep her out of the house while the representative ladies of the town learned of her new status.

Counseling! The thought sprang suddenly and full blown into my mind, rushing into the space that the problem of Hazel

Marie had so recently occupied. *Marriage* counseling! A cold shudder ran down my back.

Why had Sam agreed to attend and, even worse, promised the pastor to take me with him? Was it his gentle way of letting me know that something was missing in our marriage? Was he unhappy? Regretting his choice of me? And, I asked myself, why shouldn't he regret it? He'd known from the first that Hazel Marie and Lloyd were part of the package, but now Mr. Pickens and two infants were being added to the mix. Maybe they all were more than he wanted to take on. He'd lived alone for so long after his first wife passed, his days quiet and orderly, and now the poor man could hardly move without stepping on somebody. Maybe he was seeing these counseling sessions as a way not to enrich but to enlighten, so that I'd learn how I was ignoring his need for a harmonious life.

I closed my eyes and bowed my head, overcome with the thought of baring our souls and the intimacies of our marriage to a perfect stranger, regardless of his qualifications, Christian or otherwise, much less sharing our experiences in front of younger couples who'd snicker at the idea of elderly marital congress. I couldn't bear the thought.

But I had to bear this one because there was no getting around it: Sam *wanted* us to go into marriage counseling. If he felt the need of some kind of enrichment, then that meant he also felt that something was lacking.

Well, I said to myself, so be it. I'd try it, but as I'd told him, the minute we stopped being role models and became subjects, I was hightailing it out. If he didn't have the courage to tell me to my face what was wrong, I didn't intend to hang around to hear it in front of a dozen other people.

Chapter 7

Thursday was a clear but nippy fall day, perfect weather to reach into the winter closet for a wool suit. Sam and Hazel Marie left about ten-thirty for her appointment with the doctor, after which they planned, with the doctor's approval, to go on to the large mall in Asheville. Hazel Marie was noticeably agitated, knowing what would take place around the table in her absence.

"Put it out of your mind, Hazel Marie," I told her as they headed for the door. "By the time you get home, the word will be on the street and you won't have to hide anymore. Just don't tire yourself out shopping. Sam," I said, turning to him, "don't leave her in that maternity shop for hours. Make her stop and rest now and then. She ought to have a glass of orange juice by midafternoon, too."

"Yes, ma'am," he said as they both laughed at me for being a mother hen. "We'll be fine, Julia. Come on, Hazel Marie, let's get out of here before the ladies descend on us."

And descend they did, almost all of them appearing at the same time, talking and laughing as they called out greetings and swarmed into my living room. I noticed a few raised eyebrows as they eyed one another, wondering, I assumed, about my choice of luncheon guests. It wasn't long, though, before a few began to ask about Hazel Marie, why she wasn't there, was she still sick and so on. Wanting to put those concerns to rest, I merely said she hated to miss seeing them, but she had a conflict.

As they mingled and caught up with one another, I realized that everyone was there except Etta Mae Wiggins. Her lateness was holding up everything because I'd told Lillian not to prepare anything to serve before the luncheon. My plan had been to rush them to the table, let them eat, make my announcement, then get them out the door as quickly as possible.

So where could she be? It wasn't like Etta Mae to be late, especially because she'd been so excited to be included in a do at my house. Glancing at my watch, I hurried to the kitchen just in time to see Lillian hang up the phone.

"That was that nice Miss Etta Mae, callin' from her car. She say she got held up by a patient, but she on her way. She say don't wait on her—she be here in ten minutes."

"Well, of course we will wait for her, but Miss Mattie Freeman's stomach is growling, so she better hurry."

Finally, Etta Mae came rushing in as I held the door for her. A pungent, though not unpleasant, aroma of flora and fruit wafted in with her and settled around both of us when she drew up short to catch her breath. With hair flying and face red and flustered, she began apologizing all over the place as she explained about some patient she couldn't leave until a sitter got there, but finally she just did. I assured her that it was perfectly all right, although it wasn't. Still, the poor thing was so upset that her hands were trembling as she put her huge tote bag on a side table.

After introducing her to those who didn't know her, I began herding them toward the table, hoping to get my announcement over and done with because by that time I was wondering if another way wouldn't have been better. I had no idea what other way there could've been, so I took myself in hand and got ready to do what I had to do.

LuAnne pulled at my sleeve as we drifted toward the table. "Julia?" she whispered. "Let me tell them, okay? I've got something even you haven't heard."

"You mean about . . .?"

"Well, yes," she said, as if I were a little slow on the uptake. "Francie Pitts, of course. But what I don't understand is why you invited some of these people. If they know her, she must've really gotten around before she moved away."

I didn't respond to that, only saying, "Just jump right in, LuAnne, anytime you want to. I'll be glad for you to tell them."

I hurried away and directed Emma Sue to the place at the end of the table, opposite me. As our pastor's wife, she expected it, and most of us honored the expectation. Quickly moving around, I edged Mildred Allen to the place at my right, not because she was the honored guest, but because I knew she'd be supportive when it came time for my announcement. And also because Mildred needed the extra room that an end seat would give her.

I had not bothered with place cards, hardly knowing how to seat such a motley gathering—some didn't even go to Velma and most of them had never met Etta Mae. Some hostesses, and I was usually one of them, put a great deal of thought into *placement,* as the French say, but as we say in Abbotsville, whom to seat by whom or, more generally, whom to keep away from whom. On this occasion, except for Emma Sue and Mildred, I let them fend for themselves.

Lillian had prepared our plates in the kitchen, so as soon as we were seated, she began serving them. The plates looked lovely, as did the centerpiece, and as I passed a basket of rolls I was pleased with the general air of companionable conversation that was taking place. I'd been right about the wool suits, for that was what most of the women were wearing. All except Etta Mae Wiggins, who was wearing a long-sleeved dress with an almost equally long slash of cleavage. Yes, I know it's the current style, but I could do without seeing what shouldn't be shown, especially when I'm eating.

But I was glad to see her—she and I had been through too much together for me not to appreciate what a stellar person she is, in spite of her taste in fashion, men and a number of other things. It pleased me to see that Binkie Enloe Bates, my sharp little attorney who looked like a high school cheerleader, had taken Etta Mae under her wing and was engaging her in some mile-a-minute conversation.

"Okay, ladies," LuAnne sang out as soon as I lifted my fork, "here's what you've been waiting for. You'll never believe this, but Francie Pitts is back in town, and she's looking for her *sixth* husband!"

Emma Sue, Mildred and Helen Stroud immediately looked at LuAnne, their attention fully engaged. Everybody else frowned because they didn't know Francie and had no interest in what she was doing. I expect they were wondering why in the world I'd invite them to a luncheon to hear such a thing. Just wait, I thought.

"It's true," LuAnne said, having gotten their attention and holding it as she took a bite of chicken à la king. "You may not know this, but she's buried five husbands in ten years, and everybody at Mountain Villas says that no single man out there is safe. And they're getting worried about the married ones."

After answering several questions as to where Francie had been and why she was back, LuAnne glowed in the spotlight. "But here's the thing," she said, trying to appear concerned but inwardly delighting in such delicious news. "The last I heard, which was just this morning, was that the Coral Gables police want to talk to her about her next-to-last husband. Now don't get me wrong, they're not calling it a suspicious death, but they are looking into it. But *I* think," she said, then pausing for maximum effect before going on, "they're considering her a *person of interest*. She certainly is to *me*."

Well, that created a buzz of talk, even among those who didn't know Francie from Adam, and LuAnne reveled in being the bearer of bad news.

The topic of Francie entertained everybody throughout the meal, as those who knew her supplied interesting tidbits of her life to those who didn't. In addition, her hats came in for an inordinate amount of discussion.

After Lillian cleared our plates, she brought in a lemon chiffon pie and a stack of dessert plates, placing them before me for serving. As she came back in, bearing the silver coffee pot, she leaned close and whispered, "You better get to it if you goin' to."

I nodded, knowing the time had come. When each guest had a slice of pie in front of her and after they'd seemingly exhausted Francie as a source of wonder, I drew a deep breath and announced, "Well, I know you'll all be interested to know that our sweet Hazel Marie is now a married woman and—"

That was as far as I got, for Etta Mae squealed with unmitigated delight and there was a sudden chorus of exclamations of astonishment and questions of when, where and who.

Raising my hand to quiet them, I went on. "Of course, she married Mr. J. D. Pickens and—"

I had to stop again to let the cries of wonder and more questions die down.

"And to tell it all," I said, trying to express some small amount of outrage, which they would expect from me, "those two got married *in secret,* would you believe? Back in the summer when they went to California, and didn't tell anybody, not even me or Lloyd, because they were ashamed of themselves for doing it without any of us being there. Their plan, which I only recently learned of, was to get married again—well, I guess more along the lines of renewing their vows—at Christmas and have a big reception at the club. In fact, Hazel Marie had already started on the guest list. And also," I said, trying to get in every excuse I could think of, "they didn't tell anybody because they were afraid they'd hurt Lloyd's feelings for leaving him out. So," I went on, daring to look around the table to see how they were receiving the news, "that would've worked if Hazel Marie hadn't gotten sick, which was all the more reason for them to keep the secret—she wasn't able to enjoy married life or even to move in with Mr. Pickens. And besides, he had a commitment in Charlotte and couldn't look after her, so they just kept quiet about it. And now," I said, planting a big smile on my face, "and now, or rather, just recently, they've learned that she's expecting. So," I hurried on, "they have renewed their vows in a quiet, family service because they wanted Lloyd to be a part of it and because I wasn't sure that an out-of-state ceremony would be binding." I smiled again and tried to look a little embarrassed. "I really think they were just humoring me, and it was actually for Lloyd's sake. Of course he's just thrilled to death. You know how much he thinks of Mr. Pickens, and to have him as his father, well, it's really been an extraordinary time for all of us." I trailed off, because every woman sitting there knew exactly who Lloyd's real father had been, and I could've put a sack over my head for reminding them of it.

"Julia!" LuAnne demanded, "why didn't you call me the minute you found out?"

"Well, I—"

"She's expecting?" Etta Mae Wiggins asked, wiggling with excitement. "When is it due?"

"Where're they going to live?" Helen Stroud asked. "They aren't moving away, are they?"

"Where is she, anyway?" Mildred asked. "Why isn't she here?"

"Oh," Tina Doland said, "I can't wait to tell everybody. It's so romantic."

Emma Sue was frowning. "I thought she was taking a job in Florida."

Tonya Allen said, "That poor girl. Getting married and pregnant and sick all at the same time."

Velma said, "I've been wondering why she hasn't been in the shop. I bet she really needs color by now."

"Who're we talking about?" Miss Mattie Freeman asked, swiveling her head from one speaker to the other.

"Yes," LuAnne said, picking up on Emma Sue's remark, "what about that job she had?"

"Oh, well," I said, hoping to sidetrack her, "she's had to turn that down. As you can imagine with all this going on."

"Well, I don't understand," LuAnne said, frowning. "Didn't she know she was married when she took it?"

"They were thinking of moving to Florida, LuAnne," I said, with some firmness so as to put an end to that line of questioning. Then, raising my voice to get the attention of the others, as well as to give them something else to chew on, I said, "Now for the really big news, something that I know you're going to rejoice about with us. They're expecting *twins!*"

That about brought the house down. I'd never heard the like of *oohs* and *aahs* and other expressions of joy and wonder—so many, in fact, that they completely overwhelmed any lingering suspicions in the minds of a certain few.

"Twins!" Etta Mae shrieked.

"No wonder they had to tell it!" Tonya said. "I wouldn't wait till Christmas, either."

"When did you find out, Julia?"

"What does Lloyd think?"

Miss Mattie peered around through her thick glasses. "Who're we talking about now?"

"I bet her new husband's surprised!"

"Oh, I bet *she* is!"

By this time, they were all laughing and the questioning glances were being ignored, so I was breathing somewhat easier—until Mildred said, "But why isn't she here, Julia? We want to congratulate her."

"Two reasons, Mildred," I said, and everybody stopped talking to hear what they were. "Number one, she had a doctor's appointment that I was unaware of when I set this date, and number two, she's a little embarrassed at getting pregnant so fast."

"Oh, honey," Mildred laughed, as she lightly slapped my arm, "she shouldn't be! At her age, the faster the better. But don't you dare tell her I said that."

⌇

By the time they'd left, still talking and laughing, some with real joy for Hazel Marie, I felt purely drained. But it was done, and I was reasonably pleased with the way it had gone.

"Lillian," I said, pushing through the swinging door into the kitchen, "I hope I never have to go through something like that again. Pour us some coffee, and I'll tell you about it."

"I hear most of it already."

"Yes, but you didn't see all the frowns and sidelong glances. I just hope to goodness I answered the main questions." I took a cup from her and sat down. "Actually, though, I pretended I didn't hear half of them."

Chapter 8

It wasn't fifteen minutes later that the phone rang and LuAnne said, "All right, Julia, I want the *real* story. You know it won't go any further."

Well, of course I didn't know that, so I assured her that she already had the real story and repeated it all again. She seemed less than satisfied, but I stuck to it by refusing to add or subtract anything from it.

"Uh, uh, uh," Lillian said when I was finally able to hang up. "You gettin' good at all that storytellin'."

"Well, I should hope so. I've had to do enough of it. But Lillian, I'd do the same for you if you got in a similar situation."

She started laughing, finally saying, "I like to hear some story you tell about me. Talk about miracles, you be yellin' 'Hallelujah!' all over town."

As Sam, Lloyd and I slid into our usual pew on Sunday morning, I reached for the hymnal to look up the hymns that were listed in the bulletin. Not that I intended to sing any of them, especially because hardly anybody but Sam and the choir could sing them, but I did like to participate in the service by being on the right page.

It was both a pleasure and a relief to begin taking up our weekly routine after so many upsets and worrisome occurrences. Mr. Pickens had come walking in with a little more swagger than usual on Friday afternoon, acting full of himself and carrying on with Lillian and Lloyd until I'd about had enough of him. But Hazel Marie was packed and ready—wearing one of her new maternity outfits—to go on their close-to-home honeymoon at the Grove Park Inn in Asheville. She was excited about going, but she tried to hide it, telling me earlier that she was trying to be a proper married lady with good manners and a sedate outlook. She said she didn't think it was appropriate to get all giddy and excited about things now that she was the new Mrs. Pickens.

"Hazel Marie, honey," I'd said, "marriage does bring change to your life, but don't feel that you have to totally redo yourself."

So off they went, and the house had settled down to a semblance of the way it once was. I told Lillian to take the whole weekend off and everything had gotten so quiet that I hardly knew what to do with myself.

Of course, I had to face the members of the Lila Mae Harding Sunday school class that morning and was inundated with questions about Hazel Marie—a clear indication that the word had gotten around. I had my story down pat by then and just rattled off the same reasons, excuses and explanations that I'd been giving, so easily by this time that I'd almost come to believe them myself.

When Pastor Ledbetter rose up behind the pulpit, he gave me a hard look, even while he was welcoming visitors and announcing the first congregational hymn. I had counted on Emma Sue's telling him the news because I hadn't been able to bring myself to lie to his face. I suppose I'd been guilty of skirting the truth to him before, but never on the scale that this instance would have required. So I knew from his stare and tight lips that his feelings were hurt because he hadn't been asked to do the remarriage or the renewal or whatever it was that Hazel Marie and Mr. Pickens had. I couldn't return his look, nor was I able to give him any assurance of my continued respect for his office, if not for him. As a matter of fact, I was feeling just a little shame that I'd gone to such lengths to make sure that he would have nothing to do with helping Hazel Marie in her plight. He was, underneath it all, a man of good heart, which, however, could not compensate for his also being a man of rigorously held views as to what was right and what was wrong. Even worse, he made sure that everyone knew just what those views were, and woe betide any of his flock who stepped over the line.

While the choir sang the anthem, I looked through the bulletin to catch up on the announcements of the various activities that were offered to church members. The Every Member Canvass was coming up soon, so we were urged to prayerfully reconsider the amount of our tithes and offerings because the church was in dire need of a youth minister. The Knitwit Group would be meeting in the Fellowship Hall for a demonstration of some new stitches. The Young People's Group was making plans to go to Carowinds in Charlotte, and they needed a few more chaperones, plus any donations anyone wanted to make. Canned foods for the hungry were being collected in a basket located in the narthex. A marriage enrichment program for at-risk couples was starting Monday evening in the church parlor, and there was a sign-up sheet in the secretary's office for anyone wanting to attend. I sniffed and read on.

Then my eyes nearly bugged out. The enrichment sessions, called Stoking the Embers, were to be facilitated by Fred Fowler, BA, MA, PhD, a Christian psychologist with thirty years of experience in rekindling the flame of Christlike love in limping marriages.

I swallowed so hard that I almost strangled myself. *Dr. Fred Fowler!* Could it be the same Dr. Fred Fowler who'd been part and parcel—and instigator—of the most shameful moment of my life? How could the pastor have brought that redheaded fool back to the church? What had he been thinking?

Oh, I knew what he'd been thinking. And it certainly hadn't been about *my* feelings. In fact, it was a slap in the face. It was all I could do to sit there, stiff as a board, and endure the rest of the service. Just as the pastor began his sermon, Sam put his arm around the back of the pew, encircling my shoulders, as was his custom. I couldn't even look at him. Did *he* know about Dr. Fred Fowler? Did he know about Dr. Fred Fowler and *me*? I wouldn't put it past Pastor Ledbetter to have told him. But no, I reassured myself, Sam knew nothing about that episode in the bridal parlor. He would've said something, asked me about it, indicated in some way that he knew what had happened. Sam wasn't a man to close up and silently suspect the worst. And there'd been no change in him or in his attitude—no narrowed eyes, no snide remarks, nothing except a willingness to fall in with the pastor's plan of getting us to a marriage counselor who, to my certain knowledge, was a sneaky, underhanded and pitifully poor excuse for a leader, guide or facilitator of any kind of an enrichment program.

Just see if I ever had the pastor do anything for anyone in my family ever again. I no longer felt even a smidgen of regret for bypassing him during our recent troubles. He'd be lucky to get the merest greeting from me ever again.

I sat there stewing and simmering, getting more and more agitated as he droned on and on about whatever his sermon topic was that Sunday. I couldn't tell you a word he said or any one of the three points he made. All I could think of was how quickly I could get out of the church and what I could do to forestall a meeting between Dr. Fowler and Sam. For even if the pastor had held his tongue, would Dr. Fowler?

Finally, that interminable sermon was over and we rose while the choir and the pastor sang their way down the aisle during the recessional hymn.

"I don't feel well, Sam," I said, as the congregation bustled around, gathering themselves to file out of the church. "I'm going out the back." I pushed Lloyd out ahead of me and, going against the flow of exiting congregants, headed for the back of the church.

Sam could go out the normal way and shake the pastor's hand if he wanted to, but not me. The only way I could get out of that counseling session the following night was to get sick and stay sick.

"What's the matter, Miss Julia?" Lloyd asked, hurrying to keep up with me as I headed around and past the apse and down the back stairs to the Fellowship Hall. "You got the flu like Mama had?"

"I expect I do, so don't get too close. I don't want you catching it." Out the back door we went, Lloyd trotting along beside me as I sailed past the cars in the parking lot, around that brick monstrosity of a Family Life Center, across the street and finally through the door of my house. "I'm going to bed, Lloyd. You and Sam can fix your own lunch."

"We'll fix you some, too."

I glanced back and saw Sam crossing the street, a worried frown on his face. Hurrying up the stairs, I called back to Lloyd, "Don't worry about me. Tell Sam that all I need is to get in bed and not be disturbed."

I didn't just lie across the bed, I undressed and got in it, determined to be too sick, too weak, too something to go get counseled. As I pulled the covers up almost over my head, I remembered the reason that Dr. Fred Fowler had been so attentive during his first foray into our church. I sprang straight up, gasping for breath as the recall struck with full force—Pastor Ledbetter had primed him to evaluate my mental capacity in the hopes that I'd be declared too incompetent to administer Wesley Lloyd Springer's estate. And it had been during his evaluation, of which I'd been completely in the dark, that I'd been enticed to make a spectacle of myself in the bridal parlor of the church. Oh, how close I had come to being made a ward of the state and having every cent of Wesley Lloyd's estate in the hands of Pastor Ledbetter and his handpicked elders.

If it hadn't been for Sam and Binkie and a scrap of paper scrawled on by Wesley Lloyd that changed everything, who knows what would've happened? Sam stood up for me then, but would he once he knew how I'd closed my eyes and thrown myself at the most repulsive man in the Western world?

Hearing Sam's footsteps on the stairs, I flung myself back down and pulled up the covers.

"Julia?" he whispered as he tiptoed to the bed. "Are you all right?"

"I'm fine," I groaned. "Just a little stomach upset. And some dizziness and an awful fatigue. And a scratchy throat, and I'm aching all over." I couldn't think of any more symptoms and hoped those would do.

"I'll call Dr. Hargrove."

"No," I said, more strongly than I'd intended. Then, modulating my voice, I whispered hoarsely, "No, Sam, all I need is some rest. I'll call him tomorrow if I'm not any better."

"Well, can I bring you a bowl of soup?" Bless his heart, he sounded so worried.

My stomach growled, giving credence to my claim of an upset digestive system, but in reality making me aware of how hungry I was. "Maybe just a cup," I whispered pitiably, "and a soft drink to settle my stomach."

"I'll be right back."

"And plenty of ice, please."

Hearing him leave, I threw the covers back and wondered how long I could keep up the pretense of illness to my trusting and concerned husband. Through tomorrow night, at least, I told myself. Then I could legitimately drop out of being counseled on the grounds of having missed the introductory session. And if Sam felt the need to get psychological help in order to stoke his embers, why, he could just get it by himself.

Chapter 9

Of course, the best outcome of all would have been if Sam had decided not to go, either. But he felt an obligation to support the pastor because he'd been specifically asked to be there. It was the same with anything anybody came up with—the Kiwanis, the Rotary, this fund drive, that fund drive—ask Sam Murdoch; he'll support it. All I could do was hope that he'd feel enough concern for me to want to stay home.

Hearing Sam's footsteps coming up the stairs again— thank goodness for that one creaky tread—I quickly rear-ranged myself in bed. He came in, bearing a tray with a cup of soup, some crackers, a can of ginger ale and a glass filled with cracked ice.

Setting it on the bedside table, he reached over and felt my forehead. "You're a little warm, Julia. I wish you'd let me call the doctor."

I wanted to tell him I was warm because my embers were glowing, but I just moaned and assured him that all I needed was a little time in bed. "It's just a twenty-four-hour bug, Sam. I'll be better tomorrow. Maybe the next day."

"Well," Sam said, as he prepared to draw up a chair and

watch me eat. "Lloyd's worried about you, but he's a little disappointed, too. He wanted to go to that dog show, the field trials over at the fairgrounds, remember?"

"Oh, that's this afternoon, isn't it? I'd forgotten, but you two go right ahead."

"I can't leave you alone, Julia. Not with you sick like this."

That was exactly what I wanted to hear, but tomorrow night, not today. "That's sweet, Sam," I said, reaching for his hand. "But really, do go on and take him. All I'm going to do is sleep all afternoon, so there's no need for the two of you to sit around here while I do it."

After a little more encouragement, he finally agreed to leave me to suffer in peace. "I'll lock up good," he said, "but I don't feel right about going. If Lloyd hadn't been looking forward to it so much, I wouldn't. We won't stay long, though."

Finally, they left. I heard them go out the back, heard car doors slam and the car back out of the driveway. With relief, I sat up on the side of the bed and devoured that meager lunch. Then I put on a robe, went downstairs to the kitchen and fixed a sandwich, being careful not to leave any crumbs lying around as evidence. I had left the tray in the bedroom, too, for appearances' sake.

But after wandering around the house for a while, I got bored and went back upstairs. What was I going to do with myself for twenty-four hours? Well, for one thing, I thought as I got back in bed, I could try to sort out my feelings. So far, my thoughts had been bouncing from one side of my head to the other, and I couldn't tell which was causing me the most distress.

Number one, I began, as I leaned against a pile of pillows,

Sam was altogether too willing to go to a psychologist to have our marriage enriched. Was it, as he claimed, only because he wanted to cooperate with the pastor? Sam was an amiable soul and readily disposed to put himself out to be helpful, even if he had little use for counseling by committee or by a self-styled expert. Still, I couldn't discount the possibility that he sensed something wrong with, or missing in, our marriage or, heaven forbid, me. The thought of Sam's being unhappy made me ill, and I mean really ill.

Number two, I was constitutionally unable to submit to discussing my needs, feelings or the state of my marriage in front of other couples, Dr. Fred Fowler facilitating. Furthermore, I felt no need for any kind of counseling, whether to help or to placate the pastor. I was happy and content in my marriage and didn't want anybody meddling in it, especially to stoke embers that as far as I was concerned, were sizzling along just fine. In fact, if they blazed up any higher, I wouldn't be able to stand it.

Number three, how in the world could I face Dr. Fred Fowler under any circumstances? Shame washed over me at the very thought. And come to think of it, how could he face me? Because, let me tell you, it was only because of *his* words and *his* actions that I lost my head in that bridal parlor, in spite of what he told Pastor Ledbetter. He'd acted the innocent, saying that I'd attacked him when all it was was a bereaved and neglected woman responding to a little perceived kindness. The man was a menace.

Number four, Pastor Ledbetter. What was his purpose in all this? Why did he want Sam and me in the sessions? Was he out to deliberately embarrass me? Or did he have some ulterior motive concerning the state of my mind? But what good would that do him now? The Springer estate was tied up as tightly as it could possibly be, and there was no way he could get his hands on it. Besides, the Family Life Center, which was the reason he'd wanted access to the estate, was already built, even though there was still a hefty mortgage on it.

I gave up after number four because they were all running together by this time. What it came down to was this: whatever was going on, I wanted nothing to do with it. Actually, I could put a stop to it immediately if I could bring myself to tell Sam about that awful episode in the bridal parlor. My face burned with shame at the thought of admitting and describing the need that had been so overwhelming as to blot out the repugnance I'd felt every time I looked at Dr. Fowler. I'd had to keep my eyes closed.

My excuse for what happened was that I had been *lonely,* lonely to the depths of my soul. Having lived with Wesley Lloyd Springer in a barren marriage for more than forty years, then discovering what he'd done—kept a mistress and had a son— I'd been more than ready for a few sweet words whispered with gasping breath, even if it was in a church setting. And Dr. Fred Fowler had been more than ready to provide those words, enticing and provoking an unhappy, unloved woman into a compromising position on a green velvet love seat—all in an effort to prove me incapable of looking after myself and the Springer estate.

Talk about needing psychological help! *I* wasn't the one who needed it, and he called himself a *Christian,* too.

Of course, there was another option. I could simply get some backbone and tell Sam straight out that I wasn't interested in being counseled by anybody at any time, and that as far as I was concerned, any enriching that our marriage needed could be done in the privacy of our home. I could just tell him that I wasn't going, period.

Yes, and what if he thought we had a real problem? Would my recalcitrance tell him that I was refusing to face the facts and didn't care whether he was happy or not?

Leaning my head against the pillows and staring at the ceiling, I wondered if we should've renewed our vows at the same time Hazel Marie and Mr. Pickens said theirs for the first time. Maybe that would have reassured Sam that our marriage was alive and crackling along just fine. For the life of me, though, I couldn't see how repeating a few words that we'd already said could stir up his fire, or anybody else's.

Lord, what a mess. I threw back the covers and tried to think of something else. How in the world had Hazel Marie spent days upon days in bed? After only a few hours of it, I was about to lose my mind.

When the telephone rang, I eagerly reached for it, then hesitated before picking it up. If it was Sam checking in, I needed to sound pitiful, but it might be someone who would help me pass the time.

To be on the safe side, I answered as neutrally as I could—let whoever it was make of it what they would. "Yes?"

"Miss Julia? I'm sorry to bother you, but I don't know who else to call. Do you know where Binkie is?"

"Who is this?"

"It's Etta Mae. Etta Mae Wiggins. Miss Julia," she went on, her words spilling out in a rush, "I really need to find Binkie, and nobody answers at her house and she's not in her office because it's Sunday and I don't know what to do." She ended on a sob that sent a jolt of concern through me.

"Etta Mae, what's wrong? Where are you?"

"I'm in *jail*! And they won't let me make any more phone calls and I think they're going to lock me up and I've never been in jail before and, please, Miss Julia, please find Binkie for me. I need a lawyer real bad and I don't know anybody else that would come. Please, please, don't let them lock me up. I didn't do anything—I promise I didn't."

By this time, I'd swung my feet out of bed, sitting there gripping the phone for all I was worth. "*Why*, Etta Mae? What're they accusing you of?"

Etta Mae swallowed a sob, trying to get the words out. "It's a client, a patient, one of the ladies I visit every week. They say I stole her gold bangle bracelet, and I didn't, Miss Julia, I swear I didn't."

Etta Mae worked for the Handy Home Helpers, functioning, as near as I could make out, like a visiting nurse. But because she wasn't a professional nurse—I think she'd had a few months of night school at the community college—she was more of a combination nursemaid and housemaid who did minor cleaning, ran errands, drove clients to the doctor and in general gave a helping hand to shut-ins and the elderly who couldn't do for themselves.

"Well," I said, "if you didn't do it and you don't have it, how could they arrest you?"

"I think because," she said in a quivering voice, "they think maybe, well, probably because they think I tried to kill her, too."

"*Tried to kill her!* Etta Mae, forget about the gold bracelet! That's the last thing to worry about. Now, where are you?"

"At the sheriff's office. Downtown in Abbotsville. The Delmont deputies picked me up at my trailer and all I was doing was reading the Sunday paper. They brought me here, and they keep asking me where I was on Thursday, and I was there. I mean, she was on my schedule that day and I visited her right before I came to your house for the lunch party, but she was fine when I left. I promise she was. I didn't even know there was a problem until today. Oh, Miss Julia, they're going to lock me up, and I don't know what to do."

"I'll tell you what you do," I said, beginning to come out of my gown. "You don't say another word to anybody. I'll be right down there and we'll get this straightened out in short order. The idea, arresting you! Stop worrying, Etta Mae, I'm on my way."

I left a scrawled note for Sam on the kitchen table, tried to call Binkie one last time and had to leave a message, as I assumed Etta Mae had, too, and left with a racing heart and a firm determination to stand up for Etta Mae Wiggins, as she had stood up for me so many times before.

Chapter 10

The first person I saw when I walked into the Abbot County Sheriff's Office was Lieutenant Peavey, wouldn't you know? He was just turning away from the officer at the front desk, heading back into the depths of the department. Before he got very far, I marched right up and planted myself in front of him. He'd have to go around or through me, and I wasn't sure which he'd do.

Ignoring the way he towered over me and craning my neck to look straight up into those cold blue eyes that were usually hidden by dark aviator glasses, I said, "Lieutenant Peavey, I'm Julia—"

"I know who you are."

"Well, yes, I expect you do. But I'm here on behalf of Etta Mae Wiggins. I'd like to see her, please."

"She's being interviewed."

"Interviewed! Without a lawyer? You can't do that!" I bit my lip, considering. "Can you?"

"I said she was being interviewed, not interrogated. And I didn't say she was responding."

"Well, good. I told her not to, you know. But I want you to

know that I think it's a crying shame that you would arrest some-body on a Sunday—the Lord's day, a day of rest, a day when lawyers are out of town. How could you do such a thing?"

"One day's as good as another in my line of work."

"Well, if that's the case, I feel sorry for you. But look, Lieu-tenant Peavey, sir, you can't really believe that Miss Wiggins had anything to do with stealing anything, much less trying to kill someone, whoever it was."

"Her patient," he pronounced, as if the mere words were an accusation. "The one she was supposed to be taking care of. We're talking to everybody who had any contact with the victim that day, and Miss Wiggins did."

"That doesn't matter," I said, waving my hand. "As far as I know, she had contact with the woman every week, and if she'd planned to steal from her or kill her, she had plenty of time to do either one long before last Thursday. Besides, I can personally vouch for Miss Wiggins, because she has an alibi. She was having lunch at my house."

Lieutenant Peavey gazed down on me from his great height. "How do you know when the attempt was made?"

"Well. Well, I don't. But I just can't imagine that anyone would try to kill a person and then come to a luncheon and eat chicken à la king. Can you?" I kept my eyes trained on his, not allowing him to intimidate me any more than he normally did. "Tell me this, then. Just what time was the attempt on the woman's life made?"

"That information hasn't been released."

Well, that just frosted me good. How could a person defend herself if she wasn't told the crucial time? I'd hate to have to account for my time every minute of the past day, much less

the past week, and I was sure that Etta Mae was in the same
fix. But then I realized that she would have a daily schedule of
the clients she had to visit, so maybe she would have an easier
time of it.

"Then tell me this," I said, "has the information about when
I can see Miss Wiggins been released? And just where is she?
And how is she? I'm holding you responsible for her welfare,
Lieutenant, and I want your assurance that she is being well
treated."

I thought he wasn't going to answer, so I stood there, using
every fiber of my being not to back down under his unrelent-
ing gaze.

Then he said, "Have a seat in the lobby. I'll see if she's ready
to go."

He turned away and, I declare, I almost crumpled to the
floor as relief flooded through me. I wobbled to a molded plastic chair and seated myself, prepared to wait as long as it took
to get Etta Mae out of the clutches of the law.

It was a good thirty minutes before Etta Mae appeared,
and I hardly recognized her. She was in her usual jeans and
T-shirt, both as tight as they could be, but nothing else was
as usual. Her face was white and mascara smeared, her hair a
mass of tangles, and she was so shaken that an officer held on
to her arm.

I came to my feet and hurried toward her. "Etta Mae, honey,
are you all right?"

"Oh, Miss Julia," she said as a gush of tears came spurting
out of her eyes.

I had an urge to hug her, but that's something I rarely do,
as she well knew, so I gave the officer a cold stare and took her

arm from him. "Do I have to pay any bail? If so, tell me when, where and how much."

"She's not under arrest," he said, his eyebrows lifting. "At least, not yet. Besides, it's Sunday and the bail bondsmen are closed."

"Who said anything about a bail bondsman? There's a checkbook in my purse and I don't mind using it. Bail bondsmen closed, indeed! I guess that's just another reason you pick on a poor, defenseless woman on the Lord's day, isn't it?" I turned away and started for the door. "Come on, Etta Mae, let's get out of here."

As we started out the door, I glanced back and saw the desk officer, the officer who'd accompanied Etta Mae and two others in the hall, all with small, appreciative smiles as they gazed at Etta Mae's tightly wrapped figure. I glared at each one in turn and stepped behind Etta Mae so that all they could get was a good view of my beige cashmere coat.

Etta Mae almost stumbled going down the steps, so I held on tight until we reached my car. She got in the passenger seat and sat, trembling, with her hands clasped between her knees. "Put your seat belt on," I said as I closed the door and went around to my side.

"Now, Etta Mae," I said as I started the car and turned onto the street, heading for Delmont, where Etta Mae's single-wide trailer was hooked up in the Hillandale Trailer Park, "I don't understand any of this. Why in the world would they think you had anything to do with whatever happened?"

"Because I was there that morning," she said, looking straight out the windshield. She took her bottom lip in her teeth, then went on in a trembling voice. "I got there about eight-thirty, my usual time, because I have another client to see before her on Mondays and Thursdays. And she's the worst patient I have. Nothing ever pleases her and she's overweight and won't try to help herself. It's all I can do to move her." Etta Mae turned to me with a pleading look. "And that's the truth, Miss Julia. I couldn't any more attack her than I could fly. She could swat me down with one swing of her arm if she wanted to."

"I believe you, Etta Mae. But what happened that morning?"

"Well, she was in a bad mood when I got there, but that wasn't unusual. But that day, her sitter hadn't come in, so she was more upset than normal. I got her cleaned up, checked to be sure she still had enough of her medications, got her out of bed and her foot elevated—she has gout—and then she started accusing me of taking her gold bangle bracelet. I just laughed it off, because I'm not a thief and I thought she'd just mislaid it. Then she told me to call the sitter, Evelyn somebody, and tell her she'd better get to work or she wouldn't have any work to get to. That's the way she said it. 'Tell her to get herself over here now or don't bother coming at all.' And she told me not to leave until Evelyn got there. Well, I waited and waited. Then I called Evelyn again on her cell and found out that she was on her way, but she'd stopped at the grocery store. So she wasn't in any hurry to get there, and I don't blame her, but I told her I had to leave, that I had another appointment. And she told me to go ahead, she'd be there in fifteen minutes anyway, and the client would be fine by herself. And if Evelyn says any different now, why, then she's just not telling the truth." Etta Mae stopped, drew a rasping breath and went on. "So that's why I was late getting to your house, Miss Julia. I'd had to wait and wait, then run home and change clothes. I was just beside myself, because I didn't want to miss your party."

"I appreciate it, Etta Mae, and I'm glad you made it." But even as I said it, I recalled how agitated and flustered and breathless she'd appeared when she got to my house. Was that really because she'd been running late or was it because she'd just committed one crime and attempted another?

Lord! What was I thinking? Not Etta Mae, no way in the world would I ever believe that. Why, she'd been collecting rent for me from the trailer park residents for years, and not a penny had ever been missing.

"And I swear, Miss Julia," she went on, "I swear on a stack of Bibles a mile high that I didn't touch that woman. Well, except to give her a sponge bath and change her gown and the sheets on her bed. But that's all, and as soon as Evelyn told me to leave, I was out of there. So I couldn't've been the last person with her. Her own sitter, who she'd brought from Florida with her, was practically on her doorstep."

"I expect they're questioning everybody who saw her that day," I said soothingly. "It sounds like you're in the clear, so I wouldn't worry any more about it. Except, why do they think somebody tried to kill her?"

"I don't know! They wouldn't tell me a thing, and Miss Julia, they treated me like a criminal—took my picture and everything. And all they told me is that Mrs. Delacorte's in the hospital after some kind of assault—the aggravated kind, even. And I don't know if she's accused me or if Evelyn has or anything at all."

"Well, we'll get Binkie on it. You need somebody to protect your interests. I expect she and Coleman are just gone for the day, maybe taking the baby to the dog show or something. We'll keep trying to reach her."

By this time, I'd turned into the Hillandale Trailer Park—one of the less desirable assets of Wesley Lloyd's estate that Lloyd and I had inherited—and was driving down the graveled road that ran through the middle of it. I'd engaged Etta Mae some time back to manage it for me, and she'd done an excellent job getting rid of the riffraff and demanding that the residents keep the place clean and free of litter. Her own little trailer looked neat and inviting, if you cared for a residence sitting on cement blocks. There were two pots of chrysanthemums by the steps leading to the door and a couple of plastic chairs under the awning.

"Will you be all right by yourself?" I asked, as I parked beside her recently acquired red car.

"Yes'm, I guess. Just so they don't come back for me."

"I'll walk in with you and see that you're settled. You need to take it easy, Etta Mae, and try not to worry. I'm sure Binkie'll be around by tomorrow and she'll take care of everything."

Etta Mae pushed open the door to her trailer, hissing through her teeth on finding it unlocked. That alone should've prepared us for what we saw. We weren't, though, because who would've been prepared for their home to be in complete disarray?

"Who did this!" Etta Mae cried as she stood just inside the door and looked at the cushions on the floor, the drawers pulled out, food staples opened and spilled out into the sink and on the counter and books splayed out in front of a little two-shelf bookcase.

"Oh, my word," I said, but by then Etta Mae had run down the narrow hall, stopping abruptly in the door to her bedroom.

"Look at this!" she shrieked. "Just look at this!"

I followed and looked over her shoulder into the back room and saw every scrap of clothing she owned, including her lacy underwear, piled up on the bed or flung onto the floor. All the drawers in her dresser had been pulled out and emptied, shoes had been thrown out of the closet and the whole place looked as if it had been gone through with a fine-tooth comb.

"Oh, Etta Mae," I said, patting my chest. "Have you been robbed?"

"No. Oh no," she said, her face red with anger and her fists clenched. "I've not been robbed, I've been *searched*! This was *police* work, and I'll bet anything it was those dang Delmont deputies who did it!"

"They can't search without a search warrant, can they?" I asked. Then, seeing the despair on her face, I went on. "Unless you gave them permission to do it."

"Well, I guess I did," Etta Mae said, her shoulders slumping. "They asked if they could look around, and since I knew there was nothing to find, I said they could. But I didn't expect them to tear up everything while they did it."

"But why would they even want to search your home? And leave such a mess, too?"

"Looking for that blasted gold bracelet, I guess, and they didn't care what kind of mess they left. They wanted me to know they'd been through my things. I tell you, Miss Julia, they like it when people are afraid of them."

"Oh, I don't know, Etta Mae," I said, trying to calm her down. "I haven't found that to be true with the deputies I've met."

"Well," she said through gritted teeth, "you haven't met the ones in Delmont. This isn't the first time they've had their fun with my underclothes." She turned and stomped back to the little kitchen area of the living room. Standing there, surveying the disorder, she said, "I'm gonna sue 'em. I'm gonna sue every last one of 'em, see if I don't."

"I don't blame you, but talk to Binkie first." I walked to the sink and looked down at the mixture of flour, cornmeal, sugar and who knows what else. "Why in the world would they ruin food like this? They've just poured everything out with no thought of all the starving children in Africa."

Etta Mae was seething, standing by me surveying the contents of the sink, breathing hard. "It just shows you how they think, or *don't* think. Because who, I ask you, would be dumb enough to hide a gold bangle bracelet in a box of grits?"

My goodness, I thought but didn't say, I would've thought a box of grits would be a good hiding place. But what did I know about criminal behavior?

Etta Mae whirled around, the soles of her boots crunching the grains of sugar and grits that were scattered across the linoleum. "I'm so mad I can't see straight!"

"Pull yourself together, Etta Mae, and let's make a start on getting this cleaned up. Then you get a few things together, because you're not staying here by yourself. You're going home with me."

Chapter 11

She didn't want to do it, declaring at first that nobody was going to run her out of her own home. But as we began tackling the cleanup, I kept on at her.

"Just for tonight, then," I said. "You can't stay here after your home has been invaded like this. We'll get the worst of it today, then we'll come back with Lillian tomorrow and really clean this place up."

She began dipping out the mess in the sink, filling a trash bag with cornmeal, sugar and the rest, muttering to herself the whole time. "What if the drain got stopped up. Where would I be then?" In a few minutes, she cried, "Somebody poured syrup in first. How disgusting!"

I busied myself straightening the living room, which was part of the kitchen, or vice versa; who knew? I put the cushions back on the sofa and the easy chair, then drew up an ottoman to sit on while I restacked the books in the particleboard bookcase. Interested in her reading choices, I noted one book on home care for invalids and another called *Professionalism on the Job*—both textbooks. There were a couple of books by J. A. Jance, a new paperback by Charlotte Hughes and several secondhand looking Sue Grafton paperbacks. In fact, most of her library, if one could call it that, consisted of paperback editions, but at least she was a reader, and that said a lot.

"Etta Mae," I said, rising with difficulty from the ottoman, "I'll go back and start separating your clothes. I'll just fold and stack them, then you can put them where they belong."

"You don't have to do that," she said, as she scrubbed the counter. "I'll be through here after I sweep."

"I don't mind at all. The sooner we finish, the sooner we can leave."

She didn't dismiss the idea, so I figured she'd come to terms with leaving the trailer, even if for only one night.

Walking into her bedroom, I glanced around, realizing how much I was learning about Etta Mae Wiggins's private life— as, I assumed, the deputies had, too. The books one reads and the state of one's bedroom can certainly tell a tale. And what struck me most in that room was not the mattress on a frame with no headboard or the cheap dresser with drawers hanging out or the pitifully small lamps on the floor, but the elegant étagère on the far side of the room. A beautiful French—or maybe French-inspired—piece made of fruitwood with carefully detailed inlay and a glass bow front.

I had to go over and touch it, my breath catching in my throat as I ran my hand over the fine wood. But it was so out of place I couldn't help but wonder how and where she'd gotten it. Then I saw the reason it was in a single-wide trailer on the outskirts of Delmont, North Carolina. One of the slender, gracefully curved Queen Anne legs on the back side had been replaced with a straight stick of wood. Damaged goods, I thought, then my heart gave a compassionate lurch as I realized that Etta

Mae had attempted to match the finish by painting the stick with brown shoe polish.

I had been so taken with the piece of furniture that it was only then that I took notice of what was on the shelves in the étagère. Barbie dolls! Each one was arrayed in the finest apparel and displayed one after the other on the three shelves. Of all the things in the world to collect, I thought, who would want Barbie dolls?

Well, obviously, Etta Mae Wiggins, and who was I to criticize? I turned to the bed and began separating sweaters, underclothes, skirts, uniforms, T-shirts and blue jeans. Actually, it wasn't a difficult job, once I started, for Etta Mae didn't own a large wardrobe. Now, if it'd been Hazel Marie, I'd have been folding and hanging clothes the rest of the day and into the night.

I heard Etta Mae's boots stomping down the hall as she came back to the bedroom. "I still can't get over this," she fumed. "They did it on purpose, I know they did."

"I'm beginning to believe it," I said, handing her a pile of folded underpants and brassieres. "Here, I don't know which drawer these go in. But I'll tell you this, Etta Mae, I am going to report it to Lieutenant Peavey. If he has a bunch of vandals in the sheriff's department, he needs to know it and do something about it."

"Lotta good that'll do," she grumbled as she put a stack of T-shirts in another drawer and slammed it shut. "It's me, Miss Julia. I know you don't believe it, but they wouldn't do this kind of damage to somebody like you. Or to anybody who was somebody. But they know they can get away with it with me. I don't have a daddy or a husband or, looks like, a lawyer, either. They know I have to take whatever they dish out."

"Oh, Etta Mae, I don't think that's true." I almost tripped

over a sandal that had been slung from the closet, then said, "But I could be wrong." Then, in an effort to distract her, I went on. "I couldn't help but notice your lovely collection of dolls, Etta Mae. You have them beautifully displayed."

She looked up from folding a pair of jeans, fear etched on her face. "Are they all right?" She ran around the bed to look closer. "If there's the least bit of damage to any one of them, I'm gonna sue the whole department, I swear I am."

"They look fine," I assured her. "I don't believe they've been touched."

"Well, thank goodness," she said with some relief. Then she took the hem of her T-shirt and rubbed away a smudge on the glass. "I keep it locked, so I guess if the glass isn't broken then they didn't put their nasty hands on them."

"I'm glad the deputies showed some restraint. Your dolls really are lovely."

She turned to me, a smile lighting up her face. "I just love to look at them. Did you see the Winter Queen Barbie? That may be my favorite. But I'm saving now to get the Empress of the Golden Blossom Barbie. It's new and so beautiful, and I can get it with four easy payments, though I guess they won't be so easy now."

"Don't worry about that now, Etta Mae. But I'm glad to know that you have a hobby. Collecting is fun, isn't it?" I said, wondering what my hobby was. Collecting young women in distress, it looked like.

After packing a few items of clothing, Etta Mae locked her trailer and we went to our cars. Saying that she'd need to be at work early the next morning, she followed me in her little red car. I'd had to offer no other reasons for her to leave, maybe because she feared to sleep alone in a place that still bore the trace of strange footsteps and the reek of unknown men.

She was thrilled with the sunroom when I took her upstairs at my house and explained that it was where Deputy Bates, now Sergeant Bates, had lived before marrying Binkie. She looked around, somewhat in awe, although to my mind it was a simply furnished room with lots of windows.

"It's just like a motel room," she said, and I had to stop myself from remonstrating with her. A motel room, I realized, was the height of luxury to her, and therefore the comparison was a compliment to me.

Hearing Sam and Lloyd come in downstairs, I urged her to go down with me. "Sam needs to hear what's happened. Though he's not practicing law anymore, he hasn't forgotten anything. He can give you some good advice."

She was hesitant about seeing him. "What will he think about me being here? He might not like it."

I laughed. "Sam will love having you here. Now come on and let's go see him."

Of course, Sam was surprised and pleased to see her. He had always had a soft spot for Etta Mae Wiggins, so much so that at one time I had feared for my own place in his heart. But I had learned that in spite of her free and easy manner and her laughing and flirty ways, Etta Mae was essentially of high moral character. Right then, though, she was subdued and overwhelmed with the troubles that she was facing.

Lloyd was delighted to see her, rattling on about Mr. Pickens and his mother, about the wedding and their honeymoon, about the field trials they'd just seen and, in general, talking a blue streak, all of which seemed to put her more at ease.

I started a pot of coffee, sliced a pound cake that Lillian had left and had us all around the table for a legal counseling session.

"I didn't do it, Mr. Sam," she said, after we'd recounted the afternoon's events, including her interview by the deputies, her attempts to find Binkie, my driving her home and the state of her trailer when we got there. "I didn't take that bracelet— I've never even seen it—and I certainly didn't physically attack her." Then, with a nervous giggle, she said, "Though I've felt like killing her a few times. She's so awful."

"Well," Sam said with a smile, "I don't believe I'd admit that to Lieutenant Peavey."

"Oh!" Etta Mae said, jerking upright in her chair. "I may've already done it. Before you told me not to say anything, Miss Julia. But I didn't mean anything by it. It's, you know, just something you say when somebody's so hard to get along with. You reckon they'll think I really did try to kill her?"

"I doubt it," Sam said soothingly. "But you should be careful from now on, at least until we learn more."

"Like what, Mr. Sam?" Lloyd asked. "What else do we need to know except that she didn't do it? I don't see how anybody could think she did."

Etta Mae put her hand on his and squeezed it. His was one more voice in her favor.

"Well," Sam said, "the first thing we need to know is exactly when the alleged attack occurred. Then if you can account for your whereabouts at that time, Etta Mae, you're off the hook." Sam stopped and studied a minute. "Since they have you in their crosshairs, I'm assuming the attack took place between the time you say you left and the time her sitter got there. But we don't know that. If it occurred later in the afternoon and the sitter wasn't there for one reason or another, you'll have to be able to prove where you were."

"Well, I was here from a little after twelve till, I guess, about two o'clock, don't you think, Miss Julia?" I nodded, trying to remember when the luncheon had been over. "Then," Etta Mae went on, "I stopped at Ingles on my way home to pick up something for supper. I don't know if I can prove it or not, but I didn't get home till a little after three. And, oh! I called Lurline—she's the owner of the Handy Home Helpers—to see if she wanted me to make a visit to anybody that late in the day. She didn't, thank goodness, so I just stayed home and paid bills and watched the news and fixed supper and I guess that's all."

"I expect this Lurline can confirm your phone call," Sam said. "I don't suppose you kept the grocery receipt, did you? It would have the date and your checkout time on it."

She shook her head. "I always throw those things out." She turned to me, her eyes misting up. "You don't keep yours, do you, Miss Julia, just in case you need an alibi?"

I shook my head.

"Okay," Sam said, as he filled in a time line on his yellow legal pad. "So you had no contact with anybody after about three-thirty?"

Etta Mae shook her head.

Sam put down his pen and sat back in his chair. "Then let's hope that's not when the attack happened. Now, you said they told you that the woman's in the hospital. Do you know if she's badly injured?"

"No, sir, they wouldn't tell me a thing."

Lloyd and I had been listening to the back and forth, taking

it all in and hoping that the attack had taken place in the middle of the day when Etta Mae had been sitting at my table—an
airtight alibi if I'd ever heard one.

Then Sam brought up something else. "One other thing,
Etta Mae. What is the woman's mental condition?"

Etta Mae frowned. "Well, she's pretty sharp. I mean, she
knows what she wants and how to get it, if that's what you
mean. She's not suffering from any kind of dementia or anything. She just has gout in her big toe. The left one."

"Okay, that's important. Because if she's claiming that the
attack took place during the morning, *while* you were there,
then we have a real problem. Your word against hers."

"But she was fine when I left!" Etta Mae cried, then buried her face in her hands. "Oh, Lord, what if she swears I did
it while we were alone together? How am I going to prove I
didn't? Everybody'll believe her and not me."

"I won't, Etta Mae," Lloyd said.

"Nor me, either," I chimed in.

Sam patted her shoulder. "Let's wait till we hear her story.
Binkie will find out the relevant time and the nature of the attack.
Then we'll know where you stand and what we're up against."

Etta Mae looked so lost and scared that Lloyd was moved
to say, "You probably need to stop thinking about it, Etta Mae.
Why don't you come up to my room and watch the football
game with me?"

As she followed him out of the kitchen, Sam turned to me.
"Now, Mrs. Murdoch, I want to know what you were doing
running around town when you're supposed to be sick."

Chapter 12

"I expect I'll pay for it tomorrow. In fact," I said, leaning my head on my hand and sighing pitifully, "I think I'm beginning to already. But, Sam, I couldn't *not* go. That poor girl had no one to turn to, and she needed help. The least I could do was rise from my sickbed and go to her aid. But now," I went on, getting unsteadily to my feet, "I think I'd better get back in it."

Sam quickly came around the table and took my arm. "I'm worried about you," he said with a concern that shamed me. "I wish you'd let me call the doctor."

"I'll be all right. Really, I will. I just need to sleep it off. Besides, I'd hate to disturb the doctor on a Sunday evening." Hated to disturb him anytime, if you want to know the truth. The last thing I wanted to do was see Dr. Hargrove, who took every opportunity he could get to do a complete examination. Why, I'd gone in one time with a sore throat and ended up in stirrups, would you believe? With that kind of meticulous attention to a minor complaint, it wouldn't take him long to learn that there wasn't one thing wrong with me.

As Sam and I walked toward the stairs, his steadying arm

around me, I said, "Why don't you take Lloyd and Etta Mae out for supper? I'll be fine by myself."

"Nope, I'm not leaving you alone again. No telling what you'd be up to. Don't worry about supper. I'll fix my famous pancakes."

I managed a weak laugh. "That's fine then. But I don't think I can face butter and syrup." Actually, though, pancakes with melted butter, warm maple syrup and sausage links would've hit the spot, but depriving myself of pancakes was just another sacrifice I'd have to make because of my foolish behavior in the bridal parlor.

⌒

The sacrifice became even sharper a little later on when I was lying in bed listening to the three of them laughing and talking in the kitchen. I could hear Lloyd's delighted giggles and Etta Mae's voice teasing him and Sam's deeper one as he flipped and served pancakes. They were having fun while I was upstairs alone, feeling sorry for myself. And I had another twenty-four hours to endure just so I could get out of being enriched.

There was only one thing for it: Dr. Fred Fowler had to go.

So what could I do to get rid of him? I put my mind to the problem, trying to ignore the happy sounds from downstairs. It seemed that Dr. Fowler was here for six weeks at least, and longer if there was enough interest for a second round of enrichment sessions.

What if a rumor about some dark and devious misdeeds started floating around town?

I turned over in bed, briefly mortified at the thought. I wasn't the kind of person to deliberately ruin someone's reputation. Yet the man was dangerous. Just think of all the widows in the church,

I reminded myself, lonely and needy widows, just as I had once been. Why, he would have a field day if he took a mind to woo one, or several, of them. Think of the damage he would do!

The more I thought about it, the more I began to realize that I had a duty to warn people of his propensities toward mature women. Maybe I wouldn't be starting a baseless rumor. I could be helping to avert a multitude of personal tragedies. Maybe I would be preventing some other desperate woman from suffering years later because of one little misstep, as I was now doing.

"Miss Julia?" Etta Mae whispered as she tiptoed into the room.

She scared me half to death, for I hadn't heard the creak of that stair tread because she was so light on her feet. Thank goodness I was in the bed and not up walking around the room.

She leaned over me, concern on her face. "Do you feel like eating something? I brought you some broth and toast."

I sat up in bed, thanking her and looking skeptically at the tray she set on my lap. Clear broth, dry toast and a cold drink—just what a sick person needed.

"Thank you, Etta Mae," I said. "I'll try to eat a little. Are you settled in all right? There're fresh towels in your bathroom, but if you need anything else, just let Sam know."

"Oh, I'll be fine. Don't worry about me. I don't want to be any trouble. But can I do anything for you? I can call Lurline and tell her I'm nursing you and can't come in tomorrow."

"No, don't do that, though I thank you for the offer. Lillian will be here, and Sam's in and out all day. You don't need to disrupt your schedule for me."

"Well, I'd be glad to do it. But I do have to see Binkie tomorrow. I just hope she has time for me."

"She'll make time, Etta Mae. And I think, if I were you, I'd sit down tonight and write down everything you did last Thursday, and the times you did them."

"That's what I'm going to do while my mind's halfway clear. I'll tell you, Miss Julia, when those deputies were leaning over me, breathing down my neck and asking one question after another, I couldn't think straight. But Mr. Sam's going to help me remember, hour by hour, everything I did the whole day long."

"Well, good," I said, but with a pang of envy—or was it jealousy?—at the thought of those two working alone together.

"Yes, and Lloyd wants to help, too."

"Even better," I said.

Urging me to call her during the night if I needed anything, she started to leave but turned back. "Oh, I wanted to tell you, I'll be up and gone early tomorrow. I have a client way past Delmont who wants me there by seven every Monday morning. I won't disturb you before I go, so I'll just thank you now for everything, especially for getting me out of jail."

"You weren't exactly in jail, Etta Mae, but I'm glad you felt you could call on me. Now, I do want to hear what Binkie says, so come by when you finish with her. And remember that the invitation to stay here as long as you want is still open."

She flashed her brilliant smile and left me to wallow in a lonely bed of my own making.

⌐

Etta Mae did, indeed, leave early the following morning, just as everybody but me was stirring. I heard Lillian come in downstairs while Sam was shaving, but I stayed where I was.

"You feeling better?" Sam asked as he came back into the room, buttoning his shirt.

"Not really. I was up and down most of the night with an upset stomach."

"I'm sorry, honey. Why didn't you wake me? I didn't hear a thing."

Well, of course, he wouldn't, because I'd slept like a log. "I didn't want to disturb you."

"You can disturb me anytime you want," that sweet man said. "Now, listen, if you're not any better today, I want you to call Dr. Hargrove. And if you don't, I will."

"I will. I promise. I can't take much more of this." Actually, it was the bed itself I'd had enough of, but surely I could manage twelve more hours of it—just long enough for Dr. Fred Fowler to start enriching, then I was going to have a miraculous recovery.

⁓

Sam and Lloyd had barely gotten out the door downstairs—one on the way to school and the other to the office at his house—when I heard Lillian climbing the stairs. There was more than one creaky tread under her.

"What you doin' in that bed?" she demanded as soon as she appeared in the room. "What's the matter with you? You not s'posed to be sick."

This was Lillian's way of expressing concern, and if she'd been kind and solicitous, I'd have felt I was on my deathbed.

"Just an upset stomach, Lillian. It's made me feel a little weak and trembly. I think if I stay in bed today, I'll get over it faster."

"Well, you do look a little peaked. You feel like gettin' up an' lettin' me change the sheets?"

"That would be lovely." The thought of getting out of that bed even for a few minutes made me throw back the covers and swing my feet to the floor. I had to remind myself to slow down and sway a little when I stood up.

I felt guilty when she took my arm and led me to one of Hazel Marie's pink velvet chairs beside the front window. She tucked an afghan around me, then proceeded to strip the bed for a change of linens. I could hardly meet her eyes, I felt so bad about what I was doing—though not quite bad enough to stop doing it.

"Miss Julia," Lillian said as she snapped a sheet over the bed, "Mr. Sam, he tell me 'bout Miss Etta Mae an' her troubles, an' I been frettin' over it ever since. How anybody could think that little woman could hurt anybody is beyond me. You reckon them police gonna come back an' get her again?"

"They certainly shouldn't," I said. "She's as innocent as the day is long, and I'd like to know whether that patient of hers has actually accused her or not. I'm hoping they took her in simply because she'd been to the woman's house and they're questioning everybody who'd been there. It beats all I've ever heard, though, Lillian, that somebody would walk into a person's home, steal a bracelet, then try to kill the owner. Be sure all the doors are locked. I wouldn't want it to happen here."

"Law, me neither."

When I was back in bed, propped up against a pile of pillows, and Lillian had gone downstairs to fix a bowl of oatmeal for me, I wondered what I could do to pass the time. I was supposed to be too sick to want to read anything, much less do any handwork, so the day stretched out interminably before me.

When the phone rang, I snatched it up, hoping for some time-passing word from anybody.

"Miss Julia?" Etta Mae's trembly voice said. "I just thought I'd call and let you know that if you need any nursing care, I'm available."

"Why, I thought you had a full schedule of patients."

"No'm, not any longer. I just got fired."

"*Fired!* Etta Mae, what happened?"

"Well," she said, then stopped to blow her nose. "Lurline said she couldn't have somebody with a cloud over her head working for her. Her clients wouldn't stand for it. They'd all be afraid I'd do the same thing to them."

"But you haven't done anything to anybody! What do they have to be afraid of? I hope you told that Lurline woman that you're innocent and she has no right to fire you."

"Oh, she knows it. She's just worried about appearances and about losing clients. I expect she's right. They'll all be afraid of me because I'm practically a jailbird."

"Now you just stop that kind of talk right now," I said. "You are certainly not a jailbird. You and everybody else that was in that woman's house last Thursday have to be questioned. It's a perfectly normal thing for the investigators to do and doesn't at all imply guilt. And you need to stop thinking that way." I drew in a deep breath. "Now listen, Etta Mae, I don't think your employer has any right to fire you under these circumstances. You might discuss it with Binkie. I expect she can get your job back for you under a fair hiring act or something. Have you seen her yet?"

"No'm. I have an appointment at one o'clock, but Miss Julia, I don't think Binkie can do anything about Lurline. Lurline never pays any attention to anything the government comes out with. She says they don't know what she has to put up with and if they don't bother her, she won't bother them."

"Well, they just might bother her if she's fired you without cause. But look, Etta Mae, you go on and see Binkie, then I want you to come back here. I want to know everything she says and I want you to be sure to tell her about losing your job. I'm going to look for you this afternoon, and you come prepared to stay here with us."

"Yes, ma'am, I'll come by, but I guess I better not stay over. I thank you anyway, but I ought to go on home and try to think of somebody who might hire me. I need the work."

"I know you do," I said, and I did. I already employed her to manage the Hillandale Trailer Park, but her only remuneration for that was a rent-free space for her single-wide. "So I'm hiring you to look after me until Hazel Marie needs you." I heaved a sign. "I'm not well, you know, and I could use your expertise. So you just pack your suitcase and plan to do some twenty-four-hour nursing care."

"Really? You really mean it?"

"Yes, I really do. This has happened just at the opportune time, when I'm laid low and you need a job. I'll look for you this afternoon."

With that settled, I hung up the phone, lay back on the pillows and wondered what I had done. I hadn't planned on being sick much past eight o'clock that night—just long enough for the marriage enrichment session to start without me. But with a live-in private-duty nurse on her way, I was going to have to think of something that would keep me sick enough to need her, but not sick enough to keep me in bed the livelong day. Maybe walking pneumonia would do it.

Chapter 13

With Lillian's encouragement—she said it would make me feel better—I got up later in the morning and took a bath. It helped fill the time, but after I got into a fresh gown and bed jacket, there was nothing for it but to crawl back in bed and stare at the four walls. Whoever said that resting in bed was good for you had never spent much time in one. All it gave me was restless legs syndrome.

A little after two o'clock, Etta Mae Wiggins came by after her appointment with Binkie. I was relieved to see her, not only to find out what Binkie had had to say, but to have something to think about other than the long afternoon stretching out before me.

"What'd she say?" I asked as soon as Etta Mae walked into the room. "Pull a chair up close, Etta Mae; I want to hear everything you talked about and everything Binkie told you."

"Well," she said, clasping her hands in her lap to keep them from trembling. Her face was deathly pale, maybe because her makeup had faded. "Well," she said again, "I told her what all had happened, and she was surprised. She said she usually hears things like that around town before a client comes in, but in this case she'd not heard a word. Anyway, all she could do was tell me to call her if the deputies pick me up again. And not to say anything until she gets there."

"That's all?" I couldn't believe that Binkie had had no more to say on the subject. Why, it was no more than what *I*'d told Etta Mae.

"No'm. Binkie's going to find out exactly what the client has said; who she's accused, if anybody; and just what line of investigation the deputies are working on. Oh, and what Mrs. Delacorte's condition is—how badly injured she is and so on."

"That's your patient or client or whatever she is? Mrs. Delacorte? I don't believe I know her."

"Probably not. She moved into one of the cottages out at the Mountain Villas Retirement Center only a few months ago."

Still thinking I might have heard of the woman, I asked, "What's her first name?"

"Fran is all I've ever heard. Mrs. Fran Delacorte."

"Good Lord!" I said, throwing back the covers and springing out of bed. I stood up so suddenly that my head began to swim and I had to clutch at Etta Mae to keep from falling.

"Miss Julia!" she cried, holding on to me. "What's the matter? Are you ill? You need to go to the bathroom?"

"No, no, I'm all right." I sank back onto the edge of the bed and tried to get myself under control. "It's just . . . well, I think I've just put two and two together. You said she was from Florida, too, didn't you? So tell me, Etta Mae, this Fran Delacorte, is she a short, heavyset woman with a lot of strange-looking hats?"

"I guess, though I wouldn't call her heavyset, exactly. I'd say she's just plain overweight. And she does have a lot of hat *boxes*, though I don't know what's in them. And she's as short as I am, maybe a little shorter. I'm not sure because she's always in bed or sitting in a chair with her foot propped up when I've seen her. That big toe of hers, you know, where she has the gout? Well, it sure keeps her off her feet."

My eyes narrowed as I gave it some thought. "She have a queenly sort of attitude? As if everything you do for her is only her rightful due?"

Etta Mae gave a short bark of a laugh. "I'll say. That woman's never once even said thank you. Not that I expect it, you understand, because after all, she is paying for the service. But she's not the easiest client I have by a long shot."

"She have orange hair?"

"Well, it's mostly gray now, but the ends are orange. She tried to get me to give her a dye job, but I wouldn't touch that with a ten-foot pole. She'd have my hide if it didn't turn out right."

"Etta Mae," I said, coming to a conclusion, "I think I know who she is."

"Yes'm, I do, too."

"No, I mean I think I *really* know who she is. I think she's Francie Pitts, and if she is, you could be in more trouble than you know."

"Oh, don't say that! I already know I'm in trouble." She sprang up from her chair and began pacing the floor, wringing her hands in agitation. "How much more could I be in?"

"Wait, Etta Mae, I didn't mean it that way. Come sit back down, and let's talk about this." I could've kicked myself for overstating the case and increasing her anxiety.

She slid back into her chair but remained tense and visibly upset. "Do you know her? You know what she might say about me?"

"If this Fran Delacorte is the woman I know as Francie Pitts, then, yes, I do know her. But I can't be sure without seeing her. The thing of it is, Etta Mae, the one I know has been married and widowed a half dozen times and has that many names she can call herself. And the one I know has also just moved here from Florida and is living now in a cottage at Mountain Villas. LuAnne Conover told me all about it, because Francie used to live here in Abbotsville and we all knew her then. But I haven't seen her in several years, so really it could be somebody entirely different."

But I didn't think so. My mind was running in overdrive, trying to think of what it would mean to Etta Mae if her patient was the same woman who'd buried so many husbands and, if LuAnne's report was correct, was even now being viewed as a person of interest in the death of one of them.

But if Etta Mae's patient and the woman I knew as Francie Pitts were one and the same, why would she draw attention to herself by falsely accusing Etta Mae just when the Coral Gables police were looking so closely at her?

Uh-huh, and maybe that was the reason. Maybe she thought that by appearing the wounded victim of a theft and a vicious attack, she would elicit a little sympathy and put the Florida investigators off the track.

"All right," I said, making up my mind. "Here's what we have to do. First of all, we have to find out if it's Francie Pitts we're dealing with. Then we have to find out if she's specifically accusing you." I thought for a few minutes as Etta Mae waited with anxious eyes for whatever I'd come up with. "And I guess we should find out how badly injured she is. The Francie I know is entirely capable of exaggerating anything that happens to her. Why, for all we know, she's lying up in bed, enjoying all the attention she's getting."

"Well, I don't know, Miss Julia," Etta Mae said with some skepticism. "From what the deputies let slip, she was knocked out cold and was still not fully coherent three days later, which is why it took 'em so long to come after me. That doesn't sound too good."

"No, it doesn't. But I'm telling you, Etta Mae, Francie Pitts could dramatize anything. Everything she talked about and everything she did was always bigger, better, more unusual or worse than anybody else's experiences. I wouldn't put it past her to be making more of this than there actually is."

"Well, but," Etta Mae said, "it might not even *be* Francie Pitts. It might be Fran Delacorte and she's really been hit over the head and now has brain damage that'll keep her confused and crippled for the rest of her life. And it looks like she's telling everybody that I'm the cause of it!" Etta Mae's hands were about to be wrung off her wrists, the way they were twisting in her lap.

"Well, there you have it," I said, trying to give her some hope. "If she's confused from a blow on the head, what good is her testimony? No court is going to take that kind of testimony as irrefutable evidence of guilt."

"Oh, don't talk about going to court! I can't stand this, Miss Julia, I just can't. I'll never be able to work in this town again if patients can't trust me. And to be accused and tried, even if I got off, why, it would ruin me forever."

"It's not going to come to that, so just get it off your mind.

Look, Etta Mae, we need to know more than we do. And I know who can tell us. I'm calling LuAnne Conover and putting her on the case. If she can't find out, nobody can. And there's one more thing we can do—or *I* can do. If it is Francie Pitts, and LuAnne will know if it is or not, I can visit her in the hospital."

"But, Miss Julia, you're sick. You can't be visiting anybody."

"Oh pooh, I'm going to be well in a few hours, don't you worry about that." I glanced at the bedside clock, relieved to see that it was almost four o'clock. Eight was slowly approaching— the time when Sam had promised the pastor to be at the counseling session.

A sudden sinking spell flew over me that had nothing to do with Etta Mae's problem and everything to do with that meeting. I could just imagine Dr. Fowler with a smirk on his face, sidling up to Sam and intimating that he knew his wife intimately, or even flat-out telling him of that shameful episode when I'd lost all sense of myself.

But one thing was clear: I couldn't suddenly recover my health at one minute past eight o'clock. I'd have to watch the clock and be back in bed with a relapse by ten o'clock when Sam came home. Surely a caring husband wouldn't demand an accounting from a woman so obviously ailing.

Chapter 14

After sending Etta Mae home to pack a suitcase for several days of in-house private-duty nursing, I telephoned LuAnne.

Dispensing with the usual social niceties, I plunged right in as soon as she answered the phone. "LuAnne, what's the latest word on Francie Pitts?"

"Oh, Julia, I was just about to call you. You'll never guess, but Arley Hopkins told me that she's in the hospital with a huge bump on her head and a concussion. Somebody attacked her! And Arley said she even has bruises on her neck where somebody tried to choke her. And I mean right in her own home on the grounds of Mountain Villas. And you know they advertise how safe it is out there."

"Oh my," I said, my worst fears for Etta Mae confirmed. "Do they know who did it?"

"No, but Arley said they have their eye on somebody. All they need is a little more evidence, then they'll make an arrest. And it can't come too soon, as far as I'm concerned. Imagine, Julia! Somebody's walking around town who's capable of such a thing. Makes me shiver to think about it."

"So she's really injured? I mean, she's not just putting on, is she? You know how she is."

"Well, Julia, I would think that a bump on the head and bruises on her neck qualify as real injuries. But I know what you mean. She would certainly make the most of whatever happened to her."

"Well, let me ask you this, LuAnne, what's her condition now? Can she have visitors?"

"I haven't the slightest. Arley didn't say, but who'd *want* to visit her?"

"I might. Just to be neighborly, if nothing else."

"You know what you'll get, don't you? Thirty minutes of moaning and groaning and feeling sorry for herself and poor-little-me carryings-on. I wouldn't recommend it, Julia, I really wouldn't. She'll hang on to you like a leech if you do. And she'll make you feel obligated to be at her beck and call from then on."

"You may be right," I said. "I'll have to give it some thought before doing anything. I'm a little under the weather myself, so I probably won't." But I probably would if making a hospital visit was the only way to find out what Francie was saying about Etta Mae.

"I'm sorry to hear that," LuAnne said. "Does that mean you won't be at the counseling session tonight?"

"Oh, I couldn't possibly," I said, making myself sound a whole lot worse than I was. "I've been in bed for two days almost. But are you going? I thought it was mainly for the young marrieds."

"Well, here's the thing. Pastor Ledbetter called this morning and asked Leonard and me to come. Seems they didn't have the reponse they thought they'd have—hardly anybody signed up for it, and he's afraid of hurting that doctor's feelings if nobody's there. So I said we'd be glad to attend. I'm hoping that Leonard will benefit from it. If anybody needs enriching, he does."

I couldn't disagree, but LuAnne seemed not to understand that the sessions were for couples, not just for half a couple—my own husband showing up alone notwithstanding. Of course, what she'd told me about a lack of congregational response to Dr. Fowler's offerings thrilled me. Maybe he'd lose heart and go back where he came from.

"Sam's planning to be there, too," I told her. "The pastor asked us to attend, but I'm too wiped out to get out of bed."

"Well, you know, I might just stay home, too. It's the men who need something like that. Maybe with just Sam and Leonard, they'll decide to make it a men-only course, and we'll see some changes around here."

As soon as I hung up the phone, it rang again with Sam on the line, asking how I was feeling.

"Not so well," I said, hating to be less than truthful, but every time I thought of facing Dr. Fowler, I felt decidedly unwell. "I was so hoping to be able to go to that meeting with you tonight, but, Sam, I'm just not up to it."

"Well, I've decided not to go, either. I'm staying home to look after you, and I just called Ledbetter to let him know that we won't be there."

My heart took flight at that announcement, and I sat straight up in bed. What could be better than neither of us in

Dr. Fowler's line of sight and subject to his possible reference to a certain episode?

"Oh, Sam, you don't have to do that," I said, but quite pitifully to confirm how badly I needed him. "But I'll be so glad to have you home." My voice got a little quavery. "I've missed you today, especially since I've felt so bad."

"Did you call the doctor?"

"Uh, well, I have a call in now."

"That decides it, then. I'll be home in a little while. You need anything from anywhere?"

"Just you," I quavered, hung up the phone and lay back in blissful relief that Sam would be spared a potentially humiliating and marriage-damaging revelation.

⟿

It was barely an hour later when Etta Mae returned, bearing a suitcase that Lillian helped her lug upstairs and deposit in the sunroom. And only a few minutes later both of them showed up in my bedroom, Etta Mae in white nylon pants and top with white running shoes on her feet and a clipboard in one hand and a black doctor's bag in the other. She was taking her new position seriously, which portended bad news for me.

Lillian pulled two chairs close by the side of the bed, sat down in one and said, "Now you got somebody know what she doin' to look after you, so we gonna get to the bottom of this. Go ahead, Miss Etta Mae."

"Okay, I'm ready." Etta Mae clicked her pen and poised it over the clipboard. "Now, Miss Julia, when did your symptoms first present?"

I frowned, wondering how closely she intended to question me. "You mean, when did I get sick?"

She nodded. "I need to know everything so I can chart your progress. That's what a private-duty nurse does."

"Oh, okay. Well, it was yesterday, just as the pastor started his sermon, that I suddenly felt unwell."

She jotted that down. "And how did you feel? Nauseous? Dizzy? Weak? Did you have any kind of stabbing pain or did you just feel faint?"

"Yes."

"Yes, what?"

"All of what you said."

"Where did you have the stabbing pain?"

"Uh, in my stomach."

"In your actual stomach or was it lower down in your abdomen?"

"Both."

"What about vomiting or diarrhea?"

"Yes, I've had that, too." Well, I'd certainly had both at one time or another.

"Okay," Etta Mae said, pulling out a plastic tube from her doctor's bag. She unsheathed a thermometer and put it under my tongue. "We'll see if you have any fever, and I'll check your pulse and blood pressure, too."

When those procedures were done and she'd charted the results, she said, "I think you may be on the road to recovery. Everything's normal, and that's a good sign."

"Well, I don't know, Etta Mae," I said, turning my head away. "I still don't feel too good."

"You don't look too good, either," Lillian said, studying my face intently. "You look a little liverish to me." She turned to Etta Mae. "See how bilious her face is?"

"It is not!" I said, indignant at the thought. "There's nothing wrong with my face or my liver. Besides, it's the lamp bulb. It turns everything yellow."

Etta Mae reached over and pulled down one of my lower eyelids. "Her eyeballs are nice and white. I don't think there's any liver involvement. Yet, anyway."

Etta Mae then leaned back and tapped the nonworking end of her pen against her mouth. "I think you just picked up a bug, Miss Julia. The intestinal upsets indicate that, so it'll take a while to feel like yourself again. Have you been taking anything?"

"Taking? Oh, you mean medicine? Let me see, I took some aspirin yesterday."

"Well, let's not take any more of that. Aspirin can irritate the stomach lining and cause some of your symptoms. Has your doctor prescribed anything?"

"Uh, well, I didn't want to bother him, because I think you're right, Etta Mae. I think I just have the twenty-four-hour flu. Maybe the thirty-six-hour kind. Besides, it's too late in the day to be calling him, so let's wait and see how I feel tomorrow."

"I guess we can because you don't have a fever. But if it spikes up tonight, I'm going to call him. Now, Lillian's made you some nice Jell-O, and I want you to eat that along with some soup and crackers. We need to force the fluids, too. Are you sleeping all right?"

"Fairly well, I guess, if I don't have to get up to use the bathroom."

"I might need to stay here in the room with you tonight. I'll ask Mr. Sam if he'll sleep somewhere else, and I'll doze in one of those easy chairs."

"Oh no, Etta Mae," I said, seeing my situation taking a turn for the worse. "There's no need for that. I don't want you to sit up all night. I'll call you if I need anything, and besides, I wouldn't rest well without Sam."

"Okay, then," she said, finally putting aside the clipboard. "But if that fever goes up, we'll have to rethink things. Miss Lillian," she went on, turning to her, "I'll help you fix a tray for her."

They stood up, preparing to leave, while I hoped that I'd given enough right answers to keep me ailing past eight o'clock.

"Where's Lloyd?" I asked. "I haven't heard him come in."

"He stop off at Mr. Sam's house," Lillian said. "He called when he got out of school to let me know. I think I hear 'em coming in now."

And so did I, for the sound of doors opening and closing and Sam's deep voice along with Lloyd's higher one drifted up from downstairs.

"I better get down there," Lillian went on. "I got to put supper on the table. They be starved to death."

"Thank you both," I said, as I heard Sam's footsteps on the stairs. "I really think I'm getting better, although it still might take a while."

My heart was beginning to beat a little faster, as it always did when Sam approached, but at the same time, I was trying to appear tired and weak and constitutionally unable to attend a meeting that night.

Chapter 15

I could hear the three of them discussing matters as they met on the stairs. They spoke softly, but I could pretty much figure out Sam's questions about my condition and Etta Mae's responses. After a little more back and forth, with Lillian chiming in occasionally, Sam's footsteps continued on to our room, where I awaited him.

"Well, sweetheart," he said, as he approached the bed, "I hear you're expected to live. And now that you have expert nursing care, I hope to see some rapid improvement."

"Oh, Sam, I hope you don't mind my employing her. I really don't need expert nursing care, but she's in a bad way and I had to do something."

Sam took one of the recently vacated chairs and, smiling, leaned over and took my hand. "You're a good-hearted woman, Julia, and," he went on, "I'm glad to have her here. I was beginning to get concerned about you, so it relieves me to have a professional on the job."

"Really, though, all I need is you. And Lillian, of course, but did Etta Mae tell you what Binkie said?"

"Apparently she didn't say much because she didn't know

much. I talked to Binkie myself this afternoon, and all she knows is that the woman is still in the hospital with a blunt-force injury to the head from the impact of a large flat object, which they've not identified. She has a multitude of other complaints, as well. Sounds like she'll be there for a while."

"Oh my word, that's not good." I sat up in bed to look him in the face. "You know who she is, don't you? It's Francie Pitts, remember her? And Sam, I wouldn't believe a word she says. What else did Binkie say?"

"Honey, what I just told you was all she knew, and she got that from somebody in the sheriff's department. She's not been allowed to interview the woman yet. Seems the doctor says she's too traumatized to submit to questions."

"Uh-huh, she's too traumatized to submit to questions, but well enough to leak a few hints to steer the investigation toward Etta Mae. That sounds just like something Francie Pitts would do—get her mind set on something and no amount of logic or proof or evidence will get her off it."

"Well, I don't know, Julia. It doesn't seem that she's named anyone, because apparently whoever it was came up behind her." Sam turned my hand over, then squeezed it. "I don't think I know this Francie Pitts. Binkie said she used to live here."

"She did, about ten years ago, and Sam, she went to our church. When she went, that is, because she wasn't very faithful and ended up an Episcopalian, I think. I expect you'd know her if you saw her. Her husband, I mean her husband at the time, was supposed to have been in the diplomatic service before retiring. I think he was in Panama at one time or another."

"I vaguely recall hearing something like that. But no, I guess I didn't know them."

"Good thing you didn't. As soon as she buried that husband, she hooked another one. And because you were available at the time, she might've set her sights on you."

Sam laughed. "I doubt it. Besides, I already had my eye on you." His eyes sparkled as surprise lit up my face.

"Oh, Sam, you know not. Wesley Lloyd was still alive and well then."

"I know it, but I figured sooner or later you were going to have a great awakening. I planned to be there when you did."

Not a great awakening, but a great joy filled my soul as Sam revealed that he'd cared for me long before he'd declared himself. Can any woman resist a man who has loved her from afar? I couldn't and, obviously, hadn't.

We talked on about this and that, covering the possible outcomes of Etta Mae's problem and discussing Francie's checkered marital history, as reported by LuAnne.

There is nothing in the world like talking over things with a man who listens and responds and adds his opinion and wants your thinking on all sorts of matters. I was the most fortunate of women, and I looked forward to a long, pleasant evening in the company of my husband.

Just then Etta Mae came in, bearing a tray and calling out, "Knock, knock. Supper's here."

Sam hopped up and moved his chair out of the way. "Come on in, Etta Mae."

Etta Mae put the tray on my lap and stood back. "Try to eat all of it if you can. I didn't give you a whole lot, because you don't need to overdo it."

Looking down at the quivering slab of Jell-O and the steaming soup, I said, "I certainly won't with this. Thank you, Etta

Mae. I'll do my best to get it down. Now, you and Sam go on and have your dinner. I'll be fine."

Etta Mae smiled at me. "I'll come back for the tray as soon as we finish. Then I want to help you get a bath and give you a back rub and get you ready for a good night's sleep. How does that sound?"

Not so good, actually, though I didn't say it. My plan was to spend the evening with Sam and provide some enrichment for our marriage, proving thereby that he didn't need to get any from anybody else. Etta Mae was taking this nursing business entirely too literally.

Before I could say anything, though, Sam announced, "Looks like you two will be pretty busy, so I think I'll go on over to the church after dinner. I'd just be in the way here, anyway, and Ledbetter will appreciate my showing up. Might as well make some points while I can."

The bottom just dropped out from under me, and I wondered if I could work up a seizure or something to keep him home. But no, not with Etta Mae around, who would either see right through me or call the ambulance on me. There was nothing I could do but appear undisturbed by Sam's decision.

"I'll miss you, Sam," I managed to say around the lump in my throat. And without any effort at all, a few tears filled my eyes.

Sam apparently didn't notice, for he leaned down and gave me a kiss. "I'm leaving you in good hands."

And away he went to eat dinner with Etta Mae and Lloyd, and then to spend a couple of hours in the company of Dr. Fred Fowler, sneaky seducer of lonely women.

Left alone, I looked askance at that meager meal on my lap,

realizing that I'd not had a decent one since Sunday afternoon—
which hadn't been all that filling to start with—and here it was
Monday evening. So let's say since Saturday night, and I was
about to cave in. But I could hardly eat the little that was there
because I'd so quickly gone from the high of Sam's decision to
bypass that meeting to the low of his change of mind. Sudden
emotional peaks and valleys can wreak havoc with one's appetite, even when one's stomach is empty.

I ate what I could, so Etta Mae and Lillian wouldn't fuss
at me, set the tray aside and tried to calm my agitated nerves.
How I was going to get through the next few hours, knowing
that Sam and Dr. Fowler would be near each other, I didn't
know.

After the meal was finished downstairs, Sam came back up
to see me. By that time, I was so on edge that I wanted to fling
myself at his feet and beg him to stay home. But I restrained
myself to a few pitiful sighs, without giving away my deepest
concern.

"Sam," I said, after he leaned over and kissed me good-bye,
"I want to caution you about that counseling session. We were
only supposed to be there as role models, not active partici-
pants. And just remember that Dr. Fowler is not a *medical* doctor, so you don't have to believe everything he says."

Sam laughed. "The wool doesn't get pulled over my eyes too
often, sweetheart. I practiced law too long for that. Now you
have a nice evening, and I'll be back in an hour or so."

And off he went, and there wasn't a thing I could do about
it other than have a major relapse, which I'd already waited too
long to pull off. But at least I'd kept myself out of that enrichment session, and that's what I'd started out to do. The thought

of having to make eye contact with that redheaded fool of a marriage counselor made my stomach turn, so I'd spared myself that humiliation. Now all I could do was hope that Dr. Fowler wouldn't know who Sam was and that Pastor Ledbetter would hold his tongue and not tell him.

Soon enough, though, Etta Mae was back in my room, ready to get me bathed, redressed, combed and rubbed down. She was quite efficient, obviously from having a lot of practice with weak or ailing patients, of which I was neither but had to pretend to be.

After she had me back in bed, she gave me a dandy back rub and finished off with a dusting of talcum powder. It did feel wonderful, since I'd begun to worry about developing bed-sores from my day and a half of lying around. Then Lloyd stuck his head in the door to ask how I was feeling.

"I'm much better, honey," I assured him. "I fully intend to be up and doing tomorrow."

Etta Mae raised her eyebrows. "We'll see about that."

Ignoring the cautionary tone of her voice, I asked Lloyd about his day at school, especially what extracurricular activities he was planning for the new school year.

"I'm thinking of going out for soccer," he said. "Except some of the kids began working out before school started when I still had the tennis clinics. They'll be ahead of me, but I don't mind sitting on the bench if I don't get to play."

"That's a good attitude, but I'll be surprised if you have to sit on the bench for long. Just remember that very few people are good at every sport—think of Michael Jordan when he was playing baseball. Tennis is probably your game."

"I think so, too. But boys' tennis at school is not until spring, and I want to do something to stay in shape."

Well, bless his little heart, he was so serious about everything he did, and because he wasn't a natural athlete, all I could do was encourage him in his efforts. I feared he was doomed to soccer disappointment, but perhaps he'd shine at tennis in the spring.

When he left to do homework, Etta Mae said, "Would you like to try to sleep now? Or do you want to watch a little television?"

"Neither one. I've already slept too much today, and there's nothing on television. Oh, except *Antiques Roadshow*. You can turn that on if you want." Maybe looking at all those old things would keep my mind off what was going on in the church across the street. Etta Mae turned on the television set that Hazel Marie had hidden away in a French provincial gilt-encrusted cabinet that had most certainly not been intended to house a television set, seeing that television hadn't been invented when the cabinet was made.

Etta Mae puttered around, straightening jars and bottles on Hazel Marie's dressing table, cleaning the bathroom and in general trying to earn her money.

"Etta Mae," I said, "please sit down and rest. You're making me nervous." That wasn't all that was making me nervous, of course, because just as soon as Sam returned, I knew I could have a major marital crisis on my hands. It would all depend on how willing Dr. Fred Fowler was to preserve a respectable woman's reputation and her good name. To say nothing of her marriage.

Chapter 16

Not quite two hours later, we heard Sam entering the front door and locking it behind him. Etta Mae hopped up, asked if I needed anything, then excused herself to head for the sunroom.

"Call me if you need me during the night," she said, with a last smoothing of my sheets.

Lying alone in the bed, I heard Sam walking through the house, turning off lights and, finally, climbing the stairs. He stopped by Lloyd's room and spoke to him for a while, then, loosening his tie as he came, appeared in our room. I held my breath, as I searched his face for some sign of his mood—had he been enriched or had he been enlightened?

Neither, it seemed, for after inquiring about the current state of my health, he proceeded to ready himself for bed, just as he did every night.

"Well," I said, unable to stand the suspense any longer, "are you feeling any richer? Maritally speaking, that is."

He twisted his mouth, frowned a little, then said, "Can't say that I am, now that you mention it. You would've been bored silly, Julia. Dr. Fowler, whoops, I mean Dr. Fred, which is what he wants to be called, spent the whole time telling us what he's *going* to do but no time at all on *doing* it."

Dr. Fred? I mulled that over, thinking it sounded awfully close to the name of a certain television counselor, which in my opinion was no coincidence. Maybe Dr. Fowler had visions of enriching millions of marriages in one fell televised swoop.

"Anyway," Sam went on, "we heard about his background and his experience, and the reason for having the sessions." Sam stopped and yawned. "I think I was bored silly myself."

That certainly did my heart good, though I was careful not to let it show. "I expect he's only having the sessions because Pastor Ledbetter asked him to, plus he's getting paid for them. But what did *he* say his reasons are?"

Sam smiled. "To hear him tell it, he's been entrusted with God's plan for marriage, and his aim is to put more fun and romance into this most intimate of relationships. And get this, Julia, he's going to identify the twelve insidious love busters and teach us the twelve love kindlers that will transform any marriage, no matter how little a given couple has in common. And believe it or not, he guarantees that his plan for stirring the embers will put the spark back in a marriage in only six weeks. Now, aren't you sorry you missed it?"

The slightly ironic tone that Sam was taking as he recounted the good doctor's plans reassured me, and I was gradually able to relax. So far, so good.

"Who all was there?" I asked, as Sam went into the bathroom to brush his teeth.

After a while he came back and climbed into bed. "Let me see. The Conovers were there, though Leonard looked half asleep. And Ledbetter, but not Emma Sue. He made some elaborate excuse for her, said she wasn't feeling well and needed to stay in bed. Maybe the two of you caught the same bug."

My eyes darted around, thinking about that. "Maybe we did," I said, but I couldn't help but wonder if Emma Sue had the exact same symptoms I had, which is to say, none.

"And," Sam went on, as he switched off the bedside lamp, "the Comptons, remember them? We went to their wedding last year."

"Oh, she's Elsie and Ben Landrum's daughter, isn't she? My goodness, I wouldn't think they'd need any rekindling after such a short time."

"Well, you never know. Then there was Mack Grover and his wife, both of them looking a little embarrassed to be there. I guess it was kind of like admitting publicly that something's wrong with your marriage."

Exactly, I thought, and wondered again why he'd been so willing to attend.

Sam turned over and put his arm around me. "You're feeling better?"

I nodded against his chest.

"Dr. Fowler said that he's often called a love doctor, but I don't think we need one, do you?"

Indeed, I did not.

⌒

Bright and early the next morning—well, as soon as Sam left for the office at his house—I was out of bed, fully dressed and on my way downstairs, just in time to meet Etta Mae coming up with my breakfast tray, an aromatic aura of eau de cologne and oatmeal surrounding her.

"Miss Julia!" she cried. "What're you doing up? You need to be in bed."

"No, I don't. Just turn around and let's go to the table. I'm tired of that bed and tired of having nothing fit to eat."

Issuing cautionary advice to my back, she followed me into the kitchen, where I had to endure the same warnings and dire predictions from Lillian.

"Both of you, just hush," I said, taking my place at the kitchen table and unfolding a napkin. "I am perfectly all right now and ready for some real nourishment. There're things that need to be done today, and the first one is to visit Francie Pitts. If Binkie can't get in, maybe we can." I paused to accept a plate of scrambled eggs and grits from Lillian. "Well, maybe not you, Etta Mae, because Lieutenant Peavey might not look too kindly on that. But I can certainly call on her. Lillian, put some bacon on this plate, please."

Lillian put her hands on her hips and pronounced, "You don't need no greasy bacon on yo' stomick, sick as you been."

"That's right," Etta Mae chimed in. "You have to be careful what you eat for the next several days. If you're determined to be up, then Lillian and I are determined to see that you eat right. Lillian," she went on, turning to her, "just bland, non-greasy foods for her."

"Now listen, you two," I said, straightening up from my plate. "I am not sick, but I'm going to be if I don't get something filling to eat."

"Yes'm," Lillian said, "but you *been* sick, an' you can't go eatin' jus' anything. It'll tear yo' system up good."

"You should listen to her, Miss Julia," Etta Mae warned.

"You don't get over all the digestive upsets you've had in just one night."

"But I'm telling you," I said, reaching for another biscuit, "I am not sick."

"Maybe not now," Etta Mae said, "but you do need to go easy so you won't have a relapse."

"Will you two listen to me?" I said, deciding that I'd better own up to what I'd been doing if I wanted any peace. "I am not sick now, nor have I been sick. I hate to admit this, and if either of you let on to Sam about it, I'll deny it to my dying day. But the fact of the matter is, it was the only way I could see to get out of going to that meeting last night. So there. Now, Lillian, will you please bring that plate of bacon over here."

They stared at me for a good minute, then Lillian flapped a dish towel and said, "They Lord. I been worryin' myself to death about you, an' you been playactin' all this time?"

"Well, yes, and I'm sorry. But I *thought* I was sick, especially when I read that announcement in church Sunday morning. I almost threw up all over Judge Peeples, who was sitting in the pew right in front of us. And Lillian, I wanted to tell you, but I was afraid you'd give me away. Without meaning to, I mean. And besides, my stomach kept on clinching up every time I thought about going to that marital enrichment class. So, see, I wasn't telling too much of a story."

Etta Mae sat there with her mouth open. She closed it, then opened it to say, "I'd love to go to something like that if I had a husband to go with. Why didn't you want to?"

"Well, if we're being honest . . ."

"'Bout time," Lillian snapped.

"Wait, now don't get upset with me. I had a very good reason for not going, but it's not one I wanted Sam to know about. Lillian, you remember Dr. Fred Fowler, who came around not long after Mr. Springer passed?"

Lillian squinched up her eyes and frowned, thinking back. "He that runty little redheaded man?"

"That's him, and he's the one who's leading the enrichment sessions. I couldn't face him, Lillian, and you know why. I was afraid he'd humiliate me, or even worse, say something to Sam. You know the man can't be trusted to tell the truth—and I speak from woeful experience. Instead of enriching our marriage, I was afraid he'd end it."

"Oh, law, I do remember!" Lillian cried. "I had to come get you outta that church, an' you 'bout died on me from the shame of it all."

Etta Mae was looking from one of us to the other, entranced with what she was hearing. "What happened?"

"He led me on, Etta Mae, deliberately led me on to make a fool of myself."

"You mean he hit on you?" Etta Mae was wide-eyed at the thought. "And you were a recent widow? Why, that's awful."

Grateful to at last have somebody who understood, I said, "And that's not even the worst of it. He was trying to get proof that my mind was going and that I wasn't capable of handling Mr. Springer's estate. It was all a conspiracy between him and the pastor." I shuddered at the memory. "Now do you see why I had to get out of going to that meeting? And why I couldn't tell Sam?"

"Hm, I guess," she said. "But I think Mr. Sam would understand."

"I know he would," Lillian seconded. "He likely go over there an' knock that fool to kingdom come, too."

"Well, I just couldn't bring myself to tell him. Too embarrassed, humiliated, ashamed, whatever. It was easier to be too sick to get out of bed. But I didn't expect to be starved to death while I was doing it." I looked from one to the other, drawing them in. "Now listen, we have things to do to make sure that Etta Mae stays out of trouble, and I can't do them piled up in bed. On the other hand, I'd just as soon that Sam keep on thinking that I'm not yet at my best, so I'll need your cooperation."

Etta Mae frowned. "Well, I don't know if I can do that."

"Me neither," Lillian said.

"I am not asking either of you to lie," I said, and fairly sharply, too. "All I'm asking is that you *skirt* the truth. If he asks how I'm doing, just say, 'Better,' which is the truth, and I'll be even better when we find out what Francie Pitts is up to."

Etta Mae stirred in her chair, wafting fragrant waves as she moved. She seemed unhappy with being less than truthful with Sam, so to distract her, I asked, "What is that lovely scent you're wearing, Etta Mae?"

"Oh, do you like it?" She immediately smiled, pleased that I'd noticed, which to be honest, I could hardly help doing. "It's Shania Twain by Stetson, and I had to go to three drugstores before I found it. It's a romantic mixture of wildflowers and vine-ripened raspberries, and I just love it. And her."

"Very nice," I said, proving that one can skirt the truth while being courteous and sensitive to the feelings of others. I hoped Lillian took note.

Chapter 17

But Lillian kept murmuring half under her breath—just loud enough for me to hear her grumbling on about "messin' with Mr. Sam's head" and "anybody what play like they sick likely get bad sick, they don't watch out."

I went on eating as if I hadn't had a meal in days, which was a fact. After a while, I put my napkin by my plate, poured a final cup of coffee and mentally thanked the Lord for the good health I enjoyed.

Then, unable to ignore Lillian's running commentary any longer, I said, "Lillian, what would you have me do? You want me to admit to Sam that Dr. Fowler and I had a . . . what? A *tryst* in the bridal parlor of the church? Don't you know that would embarrass me to death? And make Sam think I couldn't be trusted alone with a man?"

"All I know," she said, "is Mr. Sam a decent man an' he don't need to be tole no stories. An' what you gonna do if that Dr. Fowler tell him 'fore you do?"

Well, of course, that had been my concern all along, and Lillian had put her finger on it. "I was kinda hoping that Dr. Fowler wouldn't find out who Sam is, and if he didn't see us together, he wouldn't. I'm trying to stay out of his sight, Lillian. But I want you to know that I've considered long and hard about telling Sam everything that happened. You know, just laying it all out for him and telling him the whole truth. And I may still do it, because I can't help but think that if Sam heard *my* side of it, he wouldn't believe a word out of that man's mouth."

"That's what you oughta do," Lillian said, "so why don't you do it?"

"Because I'm embarrassed! And you would be, too, if it'd happened to you." I closed my eyes as the horror of that day—the details of which not even Lillian knew—returned in full force, that day when I'd completely misconstrued Dr. Fowler's advances and Pastor Ledbetter had walked in on us and that redheaded pseudo-Romeo had called me a *nymphomaniac.* Can you believe it? *Me,* the most respectable and upright of women. It hardly bore thinking of, much less admitting to my darling Sam and seeing the love-light dim in his eyes.

With effort, I put those images out of my mind and stood up. "Etta Mae, let's go see if I can get in to visit Francie. I'm anxious to hear what she has to say."

Etta Mae had her eyes downcast, studying the tabletop, and I realized that she'd been uncommonly quiet during the last several minutes. She managed a smile and said, "I guess I won't go. I'd better get on home and start looking for work."

"Why, you have work. Right here, looking after me."

"No'm, if you're not sick, you don't need me."

I sat back down and reached over to put my hand on her arm. "Etta Mae, I do need you. Didn't you hear what I said? I have to keep on feeling under the weather so Sam won't know I'm just avoiding Dr. Fowler."

She glanced up at me. "I thought you'd decided to come clean."

"Not quite yet," I said, "and Lillian, you see the problem, don't you? We need to keep Etta Mae here, and the only reason she'll stay is if she has a job. So I have to keep on needing her, but don't worry—I'm going to start feeling better a little bit every day."

Lillian grunted, but because she liked Etta Mae and wanted to help her, she didn't give me an argument.

"That's decided, then," I said. "Etta Mae, you're still on the payroll, so run get ready. I need you to drive me to the hospital. I intend to tackle whatever story Francie's telling, but all that bed rest has left me too weak to be driving."

She hesitated, then grinned at me. On her way out of the kitchen, she said, "We've been through too much together to give up on you now. I'm game if you are."

She'd barely gotten upstairs when the telephone rang. Motioning to Lillian that I'd get it, I picked up the receiver and answered.

"Mrs. Murdoch?" an authoritative voice asked. "Lieutenant Peavey here. I'm trying to locate Miss Wiggins. She was told not to leave the county, but she's not at the trailer park. Have you heard from her?"

My heart started pounding and my eyes fluttered. I looked around the room, trying to come up with an answer. "Um, well, not recently, Lieutenant." Which was the truth, depending on how one defined *recently*.

To keep him from asking more pointed questions, I went on talking. "I do know that she lost her job, thanks to you and your unwarranted suspicions, so she may be out trying to find another one. And may I ask why you are looking for her again?"

"A few more questions have come up."

"Then I suggest that you speak with her attorney. Binkie Enloe Bates can take care of them for you. And I'm sure she'll bring Miss Wiggins in if she deems it advisable. Call her, Lieutenant, that's my advice."

Grunting in agreement, Lieutenant Peavey hung up, and I whirled around to stare at Lillian. "That lieutenant's after Etta Mae again. What should we do, Lillian?"

"Call Miss Binkie," she said without hesitation.

"Of course, that's what I'll do." And I did so right then.

"Binkie?" I said, as soon as the receptionist put me through, which was right away as she normally did whenever I called. "Lieutenant Peavey's looking for Etta Mae. What should we do?"

"Is she with you?" Binkie asked.

I looked around the room. "Not at the moment, exactly."

"Will you see her anytime soon?" Binkie knew how to put me on the spot.

"Well, I might. What should I tell her, if I do?"

"Tell her to come directly to my office. I'll call the lieutenant when she gets here and let him know she's available. If he wants her to come in, I'll accompany her and be right beside her during any interrogation."

"Good, I'll pass that along when I see her. But Binkie, you've got to find out what's going on. Why do they want to question her again? What has that woman told them? Who else are they questioning? It's not just Etta Mae they're looking at, is it?"

"I can't answer your questions, Miss Julia, because I haven't been able to interview the victim. But Etta Mae does need to come in. I don't want them thinking she's left town and have every law enforcement officer in the state looking for her. That wouldn't do her any good."

As soon as I hung up, I went to the foot of the stairs and yelled for Etta Mae to hurry and come down.

"You have to get to Binkie's office right away, Etta Mae," I said as soon as she appeared. "The deputies are looking for you, and it sounds as if they've already been to your trailer."

"Oh, Lord," she wailed. "They're going to arrest me, I know they are! What am I going to do!"

"Now, hold on, Etta Mae. Binkie's going with you to talk to them, and she'll tell you what to say. Or not say, however it turns out. Come on now, or they'll put one of those bulletins out on you."

"Oh, my goodness," she said, trembling from head to foot. "I didn't hurt that woman, Miss Julia. I didn't do anything to her. How can she say I hit her and choked her and stole her bangle bracelet?"

"I don't know, but I intend to find out. Let's go. I'll drop you at Binkie's office on my way to the hospital."

"But you're too weak to drive."

"I'm getting stronger by the minute and, believe me, I am going to get some answers before this day is over."

Before we got out the door, I'd had another thought. "Lillian, turn off the stove and come with us. Depending on what happens, I may need some help."

I didn't have to ask twice, for Lillian was always ready to be a part of whatever was going on, although she could never refrain from constantly warning about the dire consequences of whatever it was. And right away, even before she'd got in the backseat of the car, she started cautioning me against driving too fast, telling me that she could drive and to pull over if I began to feel dizzy.

I just nodded and proceeded on, pulling up in front of Binkie's office. "Now, Etta Mae, you just put yourself in Binkie's hands. She'll take care of you, and you go on back to the house when you're through. We'll meet you there and maybe I'll have something to report on the alleged victim. Lillian, give Etta Mae your house keys, please."

"I probably won't need 'em," Etta Mae said, holding her hands between her knees. "I'll probably be in jail."

"You better not be," I said, putting my hand on her trembling shoulder. "They have no reason to incarcerate you, and I want you to go in there with a positive attitude. Answer their questions the way Binkie tells you to, and hold your head up high. You mustn't act guilty, Etta Mae, because you're not."

"*I* know I'm not, but they don't." A shudder ran across her shoulders. "Nothing ever works out for me, and this probably won't, either."

Lillian unsnapped her seat belt and scooted up to the edge of the backseat. She put both arms around Etta Mae and said, "They put you in jail, an' me an' Miss Julia come down there an' get you out. We don't care how much bail money it take, do we, Miss Julia?"

"You can count on it," I said, although Lillian was being awfully free with my checkbook. "You won't spend one night in jail, I promise you. Now you go on in and just remember, you have Binkie and Lillian and me, plus Sam and Lloyd, on your side."

We sat, with the car idling, for a few minutes, watching as Etta Mae went into Binkie's office. "Lord, Lillian," I said, "that poor girl is just whipped. She's expecting the worst, and that's often what we get when we do. I wish I could give her some self-confidence. That would do more to put Lieutenant Peavey off his game than anything else."

"No'm, what put him off would be findin' out who conked that lady on the head, an' look to me like whoever got that bangling bracelet be the one what done it."

"You're absolutely right. Let's go see what we can get out of Francie Pitts."

Chapter 18

We almost didn't get in to see her. I'd stopped by the hospital gift shop and purchased a small, barely blooming plant, then, with Lillian in tow, went to the reception desk. We were told that there was no patient by the name of Mrs. Pitts, which at first set me back on my heels.

"Oh, I mean Mrs. Delacorte," I said, correcting myself. "I forgot that she'd remarried."

"We do have a Mrs. Fran Delacorte in Room 302," the gray-haired pink lady said, "but she can't have visitors."

I'd expected that, so I smiled and said, "I know she can't. We'll just leave this plant with the nurses."

The pink lady turned her attention to another visitor, who was drumming his fingers on the counter, so I grabbed Lillian's arm and said, "Come on, Lillian, before she tells us to leave it here."

When we stepped off the elevator on the third floor, I looked down the hall and saw not one soul, not even at the nurses' desk. What good fortune for us that so many patients were needing care and attention.

"Hurry, Lillian," I said. "Help me look for Room 302."

"That lady downstairs say no visitors," Lillian said.

"That lady downstairs," I replied, striding down the hall, "is a volunteer and has no authority whatsoever."

Room 302 turned out to be only a couple of doors from the elevator, so our luck was holding. Ignoring the NO VISITORS sign, I tapped on the door and opened it, sailing past the straight chair in the hall, where magazines had been left on the seat.

"Francie?" I called softly, tiptoeing toward the bed, where a lumpy body lay with one foot uncovered and elevated on a pillow. Another pillow was rolled up under her neck to keep her bandaged head upright. An ebony walking cane, elaborately decorated with gilt swirls, was hooked over the drawer pull of the bedside table, indicating to me that she wasn't completely bedridden. "Francie," I whispered, "it's Julia Springer, now Murdoch. Remember?"

She turned to look at me, and I declare, I wouldn't have recognized her if I hadn't known it was her. The orange hair that had been her distinguishing mark had turned rusty with gray, and tufts of it stood out around the large bandage on the back of her head. Her eyes looked swollen and, in fact, her whole face could've used some help. She had certainly let herself go, but then, not wanting to be unfair, I reminded myself that she had endured a terrifying assault and couldn't be expected to make appointments at the beauty parlor.

"Of course I remember you," she said, glaring at me. "My mind's still working, no thanks to that doctor who flies in and out before I know it, and the nurses are just as bad. You wouldn't believe what I have to put up with."

"Aren't they treating you well? I've always thought the nurses here were quite professional."

She groaned and shifted in the bed. "I'm not talking about

just the nurses. I had to demand, *demand,* mind you, police protection in case that crazy woman tries to get at me again. So now I have someone right outside my door to watch out for me. It's a comfort when nothing else is."

I didn't mention that her police protection had apparently taken a coffee break. Or perhaps a bathroom break. But while she was talking, I took the opportunity to peer closely at her neck. There was not one bruise or any discoloration that I could see from the alleged attempted strangulation.

"I came to see how you're doing," I said, not wanting to hear any more complaints about our fine hospital. "We're all distressed over what happened. Oh, and this is Lillian. You remember her, don't you? Put that plant on the bedside table, please, Lillian. Now, Francie, is there anything we can do for you?"

"I don't need anything right now," she said, stirring under the covers and wincing as she did so. "Except for some better nursing care. A person could die around here before anybody even knew it. I asked for a back rub hours ago, and they keep putting me off. If I wasn't injured so badly, I'd go home and hire my own help."

Well, that certainly reassured me. Francie couldn't be in critical condition if she was thinking of going home. In fact, all the complaining she was doing just reminded me of her normal manner: nothing was ever good enough.

"Of course," Francie went on, "the person I would've ordinarily hired is the very one who tried to kill me and stole the gold bangle bracelet my third husband gave me. So I can't hire *her,* can I?"

"Well, since you brought it up, it sounds as if you know who attacked you. Did you actually see who did it?"

"No, I didn't *see* her," she said, petulance dripping from her voice. "And that deputy has asked me the same thing a dozen times. Like I told him, she came up behind me and hit me on the head, knocking me to the floor. I was out for I don't know how long, and when I came to, she was rummaging around on my dressing table, looking for my bracelet. I heard bottles and jars clinking together, so I started screaming, and that's when she came over and grabbed me up so that I was strangling and choking like you wouldn't believe. I thought I was going to die, Julia. You'll never know how awful it was. My whole life flashed in front of my eyes, then I blacked out again and didn't come to until Evelyn got there. And if she'd gotten to work on time, none of it would've happened. I let her know it, too."

"I'm sure she hates that it happened, Francie," I said. "And we're all sorry you had to go through such a terrible experience. But tell me, how do you know it was a woman when you didn't see anybody?"

"I *didn't* know it," Francie said indignantly, as if I were slow to understand, "until that kitchen girl came in here Sunday with my lunch tray. When she took the cover off the plate, I nearly threw up. *Collards,* Julia! Have you ever heard of serving collards to a *sick* person? They reek to high heaven!" Francie switched her head from side to side on the rolled-up pillow under her neck as if she were still trying to escape the odor. "They give you wind, you know."

Not me, they don't. I won't eat them. "That certainly sounds ill advised," I said, while Lillian murmured, "Law, law," under her breath.

"Anyway," Francie went on, "those collard greens brought it all back, and I had a nurse call the deputy so I could report it."

I blinked in surprise. Report a serving of collards? Maybe

Francie's head injury was worse than I thought. Still, that explained why the deputies waited three days to question Etta Mae, but it didn't explain what she had to do with collards. "But," I persisted, "you didn't actually see who it was?"

"I didn't *have* to see her," she said, "I could *smell* her."

"*Smell* her?" My eyebrows went straight up to my hairline.

"Yes, and that's how I know it was that little twit who was supposed to be looking after me. See, Julia, while I was lying on the floor, there was this terrible odor that just filled the room, but I didn't know what it was. But when the lid came off those collards, I knew right then that it had been her perfume. And *cheap* perfume, at that. Very distinctive and foul smelling, and I called the lieutenant to tell him I'd identified it. I'll never forget it as long as I live. Just thinking about it turns my stomach."

Lord, I had to restrain myself to keep from defending Etta Mae's choice of scent. Although I wouldn't have chosen it for myself, it wasn't all that bad. Etta Mae's perfume was quite sweet and flowery, in fact, with an undertone of raspberry flavoring—nothing at all like collards, which have a pungent odor all their own.

But what was I thinking? Choice of perfume wasn't the problem here. The problem was that Francie had identified Etta Mae solely on an olfactory basis, and I had to get to a telephone.

"We better be going, Francie," I said, stepping away from the bed. "We don't want to tire you. But please call me if I can do anything for you."

"I'm not up for telephone conversations, Julia. You'll have to check with the floor nurses and see if I've left word that I need anything. But right now my head aches so bad I can't think.

And Julia, they *shaved* that place on my head. Had to, they said, to put a bandage on, but I don't believe it. They could've done it without *ruining* me. Now I'm half bald and look like a *monk,* but they don't care." She lifted her hand and pointed at Lillian. "Before you go, have your woman straighten these sheets for me. They get so bunched up, but tell her not to touch my toe. I am just in agony from it."

Mortally offended at Francie's referring to Lillian as my woman, it was all I could do to hold my tongue. The least she could've done was to address Lillian directly and ask for her help. But that was Francie for you. And that was Lillian, too, who carefully smoothed the sheets and stayed far away from the red, swollen, gout-afflicted toe resting on a pillow.

Francie did not thank Lillian for her efforts, just said to me, "Come back anytime, Julia. It's good to talk to an old friend, but on your way out, tell a nurse to bring me some fresh water."

I took Lillian by the arm and got out of there before Francie sent us on a water run. As I closed the door behind us, a deputy sheriff jumped up from the chair that had been vacant when we went in.

"What're you doing in there?" he demanded. "That lady's not supposed to have visitors."

"Oh, don't mind us," I said, indicating Lillian's white uniform. "We were making care arrangements for when Mrs. Delacorte goes home. Besides, you weren't at your post when we came in, but don't worry. I won't mention it when I see Lieutenant Peavey."

I turned Lillian with me and we headed toward the elevator. "Hurry, Lillian, I've got to find a telephone."

"They's some down in the lobby, but who you got to call?"

"Binkie, and right away, too. I'll tell you this, I am going to start carrying a cell phone in my purse from now on. I never thought in this small town I'd need one before I could get home to my own phone. But I do now."

Lillian peppered me with questions all the way down to the lobby, but I put her off. My head was so full of what I had to tell Binkie and Etta Mae that I had to hold it in. Besides, we weren't the only ones in the elevator who didn't need to hear our business.

"Just listen," I told her, as we found a public phone and I at last found a quarter in the bottom of my pocketbook. As soon as Binkie came on the line, I said, "Is Etta Mae still there?"

"I can't talk now, Miss Julia," Binkie said hurriedly. "We're on our way out. Lieutenant Peavey wants us at the sheriff's office. I'll catch you up with everything later on."

"*Wait!* Wait, Binkie, this is important. Don't take Etta Mae down there till she's had a bath. Go to my house and tell her to get in the shower and wash herself *good.*"

"What're you talking about?" Binkie screeched. "We have to go. The lieutenant's waiting for us."

"Please, Binkie, just do it. We'll meet you at the house, and I'll explain. Call the lieutenant and make up an excuse. Tell him, I don't know, tell him her monthlies have started. No, don't say it like that, just hint around that it's a lady thing and he'll be too embarrassed to ask for details. Binkie, please, trust me on this. Get that girl in the shower. Make her wash her hair and change clothes. Lillian and I'll be there in a few minutes. Oh, and, Binkie, while she's washing, I want you to go around the house and hide every perfume bottle you can find."

Chapter 19

"You drive, Lillian," I said as we hurried out of the hospital and into the car. "I'm too nervous to get behind the wheel."

On our way to the house, Lillian said, "I don't know what collards got to do with it, but that sick lady sayin' she smell Miss Etta Mae's perfume—is that why you tell Miss Binkie to make her wash it off, 'fore that lieutenant smell it, too?"

"Exactly," I said, noting again how quickly Lillian could put two and two together, often faster than I could. "I just hope Binkie's making her do it."

"She is. Look, they already here." Lillian had turned the corner on Polk Street and was pointing at Binkie's car parked by the curb at our house.

We hurried into the house to find Binkie sitting at the kitchen table. She didn't look happy. "Okay, let's have it."

"Oh, Binkie," I said, collapsing beside her. "You won't believe this. But first, where's Etta Mae? You didn't take her to the sheriff's office, did you?"

"No, but not because I didn't want to. It was Etta Mae who insisted on doing what you wanted, even though neither of us knew why. She's in the shower now, and I think if you told her to jump off the roof, she wouldn't hesitate."

"She's a good girl," I said with some satisfaction.

"Well, it certainly put me in a bind. I tell you, when a lieutenant in the sheriff's department says he wants to talk to a client, I don't normally fiddle around. So what's going on?"

"Well," I began, then proceeded to tell her how we had gone to the hospital and seen Francie.

"You mean you just walked in?" Binkie couldn't believe how easily we'd gotten in, especially because she'd been kept out.

"We hit it at the right time," I assured her. "Nobody was around." Then I told her what Francie had told us. "So, see, Binkie, the only thing the lieutenant's going on is Francie's nose. And to me, that's not evidence of anything except a warped sense of smell. You know as well as I do that some things smell nice to some people, while the same smell is awful to others. Just think of that musk that some men splash all over themselves. I have to hold my breath around them, but they think women love it." I paused to see how Binkie was taking my explanation. "And that's why I didn't want Etta Mae going into the sheriff's department smelling like she did this morning. Lieutenant Peavey might not like wildflowers and raspberries. He might think it was the foul odor that Francie claims she smelled—like collards, would you believe?"

Binkie lay her head on her arms, which were crossed on the tabletop. "Lord, lord," she said. "This is one for the books. Well," she went on, raising her head, "you were right, but you don't know how close I came to marching Etta Mae right down there, raspberries and all."

"Well, here's the thing, Binkie," I said, "it's pretty clear that Francie smelled *something*. I just don't believe it was Etta Mae.

So what could it have been? Or *who* could it have been? And I'll tell you another thing: I think Francie's recall of a particular odor is mighty poor evidence to be going on."

"It is," Binkie agreed, "which is why Etta Mae hasn't been arrested. But they're looking at her; there's no doubt about that. Not just because of Mrs. Delacorte's recall of an odor, but because she has positively identified it as coming from Etta Mae." Binkie tapped her fingers on the table, thinking. "However, I get the feeling that Lieutenant Peavey's not all that convinced of his victim's veracity. Or let's say her ability to remember the details of the attack."

"Good for him!" I said. "He ought to tread carefully where Francie Pitts, now Delacorte, is concerned. And here's another little item, Binkie. You might not know this, but I heard that the Coral Gables police—that's in Florida—are looking into her next-to-last husband's death, and they've questioned her about it. That should make the lieutenant think twice before believing a word she says."

"Really?"

"Just ask LuAnne Conover. She's the one who told me. And Arley Hopkins told her, and Arley lives out at Mountain Villas, just as Francie does, and she knows what goes on out there."

"If that's true," Binkie mused, frowning with thought, "it just might save Etta Mae's bacon, or at least confuse the issue. I'll look into it."

Etta Mae slipped into the kitchen then, looking somewhat diffident and unsure of herself. She was wearing jeans again, but freshly pressed ones, and a short-sleeved sweater I hadn't seen before. Her hair was full and shiny, recently washed and bouncing with curls.

"Come over here, Etta Mae," I said, "and let me look you over."

I walked all around her, delicately sniffing for any whiff of fruity or flowery odors. She turned as I turned, wondering what I was doing.

"I think she's fine," I said to Binkie. "But you and Lillian come see what you think."

They did, as Etta Mae endured their examination with a puzzled look on her face. "I took a bath," she said, "just like you told me. Didn't I get clean?"

"What do you think, Lillian?" I asked.

"She jus' smell like soap to me."

"Binkie?"

"I think she's fine. You have to get right up close to her hair to smell anything, and that just smells like apple shampoo."

"That's what I used," Etta Mae said, looking more and more concerned as tears began to fill her eyes. "Didn't I get clean enough?"

"Of course you did," I said, patting her shoulder. "You're always clean. The problem is, well, you tell her, Binkie. I don't think I can go through it again." I sank down into a chair, realizing that I'd about expended every ounce of energy I had. A couple of days in bed can sap you good.

So Binkie explained the problem to Etta Mae in a few concise words, like the lawyer she was. I was gratified to see some fire come back into Etta Mae's eyes.

"You mean she said I smell bad? Why, I wear Shania Twain by Stetson! And no way does Shania smell like collards, I don't care what that woman says. She's crazy!" Etta Mae was outraged, and I wouldn't have been surprised if she'd stamped her booted foot on my kitchen floor. "So that's what they were doing," she went on, frowning in thought. "When they had me in there before, those deputies kept walking around behind me, leaning in and sticking their heads over my shoulders, asking their questions. They were *smelling* me!"

"Calm down, Etta Mae," I said. "Now that we know what they were doing and why, all you have to do is stay away from any and all perfume. In fact, I recommend that you leave off all cologne, eau de toilette, talcum powder, and scented deodorant for the duration. I'd watch the shampoo, too."

"Come on, Etta Mae," Binkie said, snatching up her purse and car keys. "Lieutenant Peavey's waiting for us, so let's get it over with."

"You think he's going to put me in jail?" As quickly as Etta Mae's outrage had flashed up, it died out as she faced the prospect of more questions by the lieutenant.

"He'd better not," I said firmly. "You're going to come out of there smelling like a rose. Well, maybe not a rose, but you know what I mean."

After they left for Etta Mae's second interview, I looked at Lillian, hoping for some reassurance. "What if they still think she did it? What if they believe Francie and don't believe her?"

"You got to put yo' trust in the Lord and Miss Binkie," Lillian said. "Don't do no good settin' around worryin'. An' if you ast me, that lady in the hospital don't sound too verasible, jus' like Miss Binkie say." She put a pan on the stove and went on. "I got to start dinner, but what you want for lunch first? Or you got somewhere else for us to go?"

"No, I've done all I can do for today. Anything for lunch is fine. A sandwich, whatever. I can't eat with worrying about Lieutenant Peavey sniffing around Etta Mae."

The telephone rang then. I answered it and heard Mildred Allen's voice.

"Julia," she said, "I'm having a few people over tomorrow night, about seven-thirty, just for dessert, and I hope you can come. I know it's last minute, but I think you'll enjoy it."

"Well, I don't know, Mildred. I've not been feeling well lately, and I'm not sure I should be out late." I turned away from Lillian, who was frowning at my continuing reliance on a made-up illness. "I'll have to check with Sam, anyway. He might have something planned."

"That's fine if he does," Mildred said. "I'm just inviting the ladies for a change. Everybody's buzzing about Francie Pitts and what happened to her, so I thought a nice little get-together would be fun and maybe instructive. We can discuss safety precautions for women. And I might have a surprise for everybody, too."

I could read between the lines as well as anybody, and what Mildred was proposing was a nice little gossip session. I couldn't resist that because who knows? I might pick up from LuAnne or Arley or somebody else a few tidbits that would be of help to Etta Mae, and Binkie's defense of her. And who could resist a surprise? The image of a tanned and muscular self-defense instructor sprang to mind—just the sort of surprise that Mildred would love to spring on us.

"In that case, Mildred, I'm sure I'll be able to make it."

Chapter 20

After lunch, I took the opportunity to put my feet up for a while, but I couldn't turn my mind off. It was filled with images of Etta Mae, even then undergoing interrogation with sharp-nosed deputies just waiting for the least whiff of an odor—either foul or flowery, it didn't seem to matter. By the time Lloyd came home from school, she and Binkie still had not returned, so I began to worry about Etta Mae being jailed on an assault and battery charge, or even an attempted murder charge. I could just picture her scared little face peering out from behind bars.

"Hey, Miss Julia," Lloyd said as he came into the living room, where I was resting. "I'm gonna call Mama now—she said for me to. You want to talk to her?"

"I certainly do. I know she's been calling you off and on, but I'd like to know how she's getting along. Your new step-daddy, too."

If I had let myself, I could've been hurt because Hazel Marie hadn't called me, but I put it down to her unwillingness to admit she was enjoying her honeymoon. Every time I thought of her announcement that being married to Mr. Pickens was going to be in name only, I had to laugh. He'd put up with that for about two minutes, if I knew him. No, they'd spend their week, or however long it took, at the Grove Park Inn in Asheville making plans for their life together. At least I hoped they would, for I wasn't all that convinced that Mr. Pickens would be able to stand a settled married state because he'd never managed to before. Of course, his current married state came with one inherited child and two more on the way, which should be enough to settle anybody down.

When Lloyd called down the stairs to tell me his mother was on the phone, I picked up and said, "Hazel Marie? How are you feeling?"

"Oh, I'm feeling fine," she said, and it pleased me to hear the lightness in her voice. "We're having such a good time, though J.D. won't let me do too much. We took a walk around the grounds this morning, and we're both going to the spa this afternoon. Did you know they have a spa here? It's beautiful and so soothing. We got massages yesterday, and J.D. said it was the next best thing he'd ever had."

"My word," I mumbled, then said, "But how are *you* doing?"

"I've not had any trouble at all. In fact, I think the earlier problems I had were all in my mind. Well, not all of them, but you know what I mean. But I did want to tell you, Miss Julia, before we left, Dr. Hargrove recommended that I see an obstetrician over here, just in case, you know. So I went and J.D. went with me, and he got to see the sonogram and everything. And he's just been so careful of me ever since. Isn't that the sweetest thing?"

"Yes, it is," I said, hoping that sweetness would last. Not that Mr. Pickens was ever *un*sweet to her; I don't mean that.

But he could get his mind set on other things, like his work, and take off without a backward glance. But maybe seeing two little beings that he'd created swimming around on a sonogram screen had straightened him out.

"When will you be home?" I asked.

"Maybe this weekend," she said. "We have so much to do, getting settled and all, that we can't stay away too long. But J.D. wants me to have a good long rest, so I'll let you know when we'll be there."

"That's fine, but consider this while you're resting: what about my asking Etta Mae to help us when the babies come?"

"Oh, I'd love it! But I don't see how she can. She already has a job."

"Not anymore, she doesn't. We'll tell you all about it when you get home. But in the meantime, think how nice it'll be to have her here around the clock while you recover and those babies are up half the night." I smiled to myself at the thought. "You can tell Mr. Pickens that I have his welfare in mind."

I hung up, thinking, So far, so good. It certainly sounded as if their marriage had started off well, and I could only hope that it would continue in the same manner. It is such a toss-up, you know, as to how two people will get along. You never know, when you marry somebody, just what you're going to get. You might think you're getting one thing and end up with something entirely different.

Etta Mae and Binkie came in a little later, both of them looking pleased with themselves. And, I was happy to note, Etta Mae in particular seemed to have gained a renewed sense of confidence that things were working out for her. It's amazing what a good lawyer can do for you.

"I think I might be out of the woods, Miss Julia," she said, bouncing as she sat on the sofa. "You should've seen Binkie. Almost every time Lieutenant Peavey asked me a question, she'd say, 'Don't answer that.' But Binkie," she said, turning to her attorney, "there were some I wanted to answer. I wanted to tell them exactly what happened."

Binkie smiled. "It wouldn't have helped. They'd just bounce more questions off whatever you said. We gave them your schedule and the time line you made out for everything you did last Thursday, and that's all they need to know." Then Binkie laughed. "Miss Julia, you should've seen what they did. The lieutenant sat across from us, but he had a young deputy standing behind Etta Mae, and he kept leaning over, sniffing around her. He must've been selected for his sense of smell, but he reminded me of a dog in heat. Oh," she said, giggling, "sorry for the crudeness, but I almost laughed in their faces."

"My goodness," I said at the picture her words brought to mind. "Well, I guess we did a good thing by getting you descented, Etta Mae. And if I were you, I'd put Miss Shania Twain back in her box and keep her there until this mess is settled."

"Oh, I will," Etta Mae said. "It comes in a beautiful pink box. The bottle, I mean. Not the perfume."

Sam came in then and Lloyd wandered downstairs, so we had to recount our day's activities for them. Sam and Binkie had a quiet conference together, discussing legal angles for Etta Mae's continued freedom of movement. Sam seemed pleased with the outcome of the latest interview she'd had, and so was I, because she wasn't in jail.

Etta Mae had sat quietly while her case was being discussed, her head swiveling from one to the other of us as we spoke. Then, in a lull, she said, "I just thought of something. Miss Julia, didn't you say that Mrs. Delacorte told you that she heard the person who attacked her rummaging around on her vanity table? I mean, while she was lying on the floor after being knocked out?"

"Yes, she did," I said, nodding. "And went on to say that that's when the woman—and she was sure it was a woman— was looking for her gold bracelet."

"I thought that's what she told you," Etta Mae said, frowning, "and it doesn't make sense. Because she was already complaining about her bracelet being gone when I was making her bed. And that was when I first got there."

"You sure about that, Etta Mae?" Binkie asked.

"As sure as I'm sitting here. Mrs. Delacorte all but accused me of taking it, but I didn't let it bother me. I just laughed it off, because she was forever misplacing things and accusing me or Evelyn—you know, her sitter—or the trashman or a neighbor of stealing them. Then in a few days, she'd find whatever she'd lost. She never apologized to any of us, though. So I figured the bracelet was just more of the same and didn't give it much thought." She sighed. "I sure wish I had now."

I sat straight up, struck with a new possibility. "What about that, Binkie? Could we be dealing with *two* crimes and two separate perpetrators?"

"Either that," Sam chimed in, "or we're dealing with a confused victim who doesn't remember what happened or when. She's conflating two separate events that may have nothing to do with each other."

"Binkie," I said, "tell Lieutenant Peavey."

She nodded. "Don't worry, I will. And by the way, he confirmed that the attack did take place between the time Etta Mae said she left and the time that the sitter got there. It was the sitter who found her on the floor and called nine-one-one. The call was registered at twelve-fourteen p.m., and the first responders got there at twelve-twenty-six. They reported no signs of illegal entry or of a struggle. The dishwasher was running in the kitchen, along with a television that had the sound turned down. In other words, everything in the house seemed normal, except for the victim. They noted that she was conscious, but somewhat incoherent."

"I think she's still incoherent," I said, "or more likely, knowing her, she's told one story and can't or won't back down. But Binkie, that surely lets Etta Mae off the hook, doesn't it? She got here for the luncheon that day about fifteen or twenty minutes past twelve. They ought to see that she couldn't have attacked Francie and been here at the same time."

"Well, the problem is," Binkie said, glancing at Etta Mae, "we don't know how long Mrs. Delacorte lay there alone. Etta Mae tells me that she left about eleven o'clock, so if the sitter didn't get there until after twelve, that leaves a full hour that we can't account for. And Etta Mae can't prove she left at eleven."

"Well, on the other hand," I said, with some asperity, "can this Evelyn person prove she'd just gotten there when she called nine-one-one?"

"Actually, no," Binkie said, "but she does have a grocery receipt that proves she bought something from Ingles at eleven-twenty-eight."

"That leaves her plenty of time to get to Francie's house and hit her over the head," I said, eager to put somebody besides Etta Mae in the line of fire. "After all, how long does something like that take? I just hope they're questioning her, too."

"They are," Binkie said. "According to her statement, she drove straight from Ingles to the house, which only took her five or ten minutes; went in the back door to the kitchen; put up the groceries; then started the dishwasher, which she'd forgotten to do earlier. Then she went in to check on Mrs. Delacorte. That's when she found her on the floor."

"Yes," I said, "but that fiddling around in the kitchen could've taken fifteen minutes or more, depending on how efficient she is."

"She's not efficient," Etta Mae said. "She kinda shuffles along on her own time."

Binkie winced. "That could put the attack closer to the time you left, Etta Mae, rather than near the time Evelyn got there. Except one of the deputies noted that the dishwasher was just ending the wash cycle when he got there, so that pretty much confirms her story."

"I just wish," Etta Mae said softly, "that I'd waited till she got there; then none of it would've happened. But I stayed a half hour longer than I usually do. My time with Mrs. Delacorte is supposed to be from eight-thirty to ten-thirty, Mondays and Thursdays, and Lurline gets really upset if we stay longer than we're supposed to. Her clients are on contract, so she can't charge them for overtime. And, Miss Julia, I was so anxious to get to your party that I was on pins and needles, 'cause I had to run home, take a shower and change clothes, then drive from Delmont to be here on time. And even then, I was late."

"It's perfectly all right, Etta Mae," I assured her. "You were hardly late at all, and I still think that Lieutenant Peavey would do better to concentrate on that Evelyn rather than you."

"Yes'm, except Evelyn's been with Mrs. Delacorte for years and I haven't. She even moved up here with her from Florida, and Mrs. Delacorte bought a house for her. And she's pretty old and kinda frail, and ought not even to be driving, so I don't think he figures she'd be up for attacking anybody."

"Well," I mumbled, half to myself, "you never can tell what old people can do. They can fool you sometimes."

When Lillian announced dinner, we urged Binkie to stay but she had to get home to her own family. Etta Mae walked her to the door, thanking her profusely and hugging her, and Binkie assured her that she would push for more information on Mrs. Delacorte come the morning.

As we walked into the dining room, Sam asked how I was feeling. "You've had a busy day, Julia. You shouldn't have done so much."

"I felt fine all day, but I will admit to being a little tired now," I told him, and it was the truth. I had hardly any appetite and wanted only to crawl into bed, which I did as soon as Etta Mae agreed to remain with us a while longer. Actually, I was glad she was staying, because Lillian's portentous warning seemed to be coming true. My pretense of being sick might well have laid the groundwork for a true illness.

Chapter 21

As it turned out, all I'd needed was a good night's sleep, which I got, and I arose the following morning ready to face the world again. The first thing on my agenda was to think up something for Etta Mae to do. With no job to go to and a patient who required no care, namely me, she needed to be kept busy so she wouldn't fall victim to despair.

Of course, when Hazel Marie came home, Etta Mae would have her hands full. But the interim had to be filled with enough tasks and chores so that Etta Mae would feel she was serving a real need. I didn't want her to think she was a charity case.

I needn't have worried. By the time I got downstairs, she and Lillian had the morning mapped out. The two of them were going to go to Etta Mae's trailer and clean it from top to bottom after the ravages it had suffered at the hands of the Delmont deputies. They even seemed to be looking forward to it, although Etta Mae was a little awkward about accepting Lillian's help.

"What am I supposed to do?" she whispered to me when Lillian stepped out of the kitchen. "I've never had a cleaning lady before."

"And you don't have one now," I said. "Listen, Etta Mae, she's offered to help because she likes you and wants to help. The two of you are friends, and you'll both pitch in and have that place clean in no time."

"But do I pay her?"

"No, you'd offend her if you offer. Just accept her help the way you'd accept mine or that of any other friend. Now just go on and have a good time. Lillian," I said, as she came back into the kitchen, "take whatever cleaning supplies you want with you."

"Yes'm, I'm planning to."

"One thing's for sure, Lillian," Etta Mae said, "we won't need any silver polish."

We laughed at that, and I was pleased that Etta Mae seemed more comfortable with the thought of Lillian's help. And even though I knew Lillian would not have accepted any payment, just as I had told Etta Mae, I planned to add a little to her weekly check, simply because I appreciated her good heart.

As they started out the door, loaded down with cleansers and dusters and first one thing and another, Etta Mae turned back. "Oh, Miss Julia, I forgot to invite you. Would you like to go with us?"

Lillian started laughing—either because of Etta Mae's issuing a formal invitation or because the idea of my cleaning a house was so unlikely. For whatever reason, though, I assured Etta Mae that cleaning her trailer was one invitation that I had to regretfully refuse.

⌒

It was pleasant having the house entirely to myself for a change, although I soon grew tired of my own company. With no one to talk to, thoughts of Francie Pitts and her false accusations against Etta Mae filled my head. The woman had to be wrong. Etta Mae would never injure a living soul, much less her own patient. She was a feisty little thing, there was no doubt about that, but in all the tight spots we'd been in together I'd never gotten a hint that she could turn violent.

Still, I couldn't help but recall her flushed face, tousled hair, trembling hands and gasping breath as she arrived at my house last Thursday for that fateful luncheon. Those symptoms could have been the aftereffects of a loss of temper and control that had led her to bash Francie's head in. I had to admit that whenever I'd been around Francie, I'd often felt the urge to slap her face. So given Francie's usual regal ways, I could hardly blame Etta Mae if she had hauled off and let her have it.

But, of course, I didn't mean that. I was prone to let my thoughts run away with me. Etta Mae did not do it. She had left Francie in good health at eleven o'clock, just as she said she had. Either somebody else came in between that time and the time the sitter got there or the sitter got there early and did the job herself. That was the more likely story. Anybody who'd worked for Francie for years could easily have reached the end of her rope last Thursday and decided to shut her up, even for a little while. I didn't care how feeble this Evelyn was supposed to be—anybody could walk up behind a person and have the strength to bring a weapon crashing down. And that brought something else to mind—where was the weapon? And what *was* the weapon?

I started to the phone to call Binkie, having realized that the nature of the weapon could possibly lead to the wielder of it. The doorbell stopped me, so I turned around and opened the door to Emma Sue Ledbetter, Pastor Ledbetter's meek and long-suffering wife.

"Why, Emma Sue, what a nice surprise," I said. "Come in. I'm glad to see you."

"Oh, Julia," she said, following me into the living room as I indicated the sofa. "I apologize for barging in on you like this, but you're the only one I know who'll understand. I know you will," she went on, taking a handful of Kleenex from her tote bag, "because you didn't go either."

"What are we talking about, Emma Sue?"

"That blasted marriage enrichment program!" Emma Sue practically spat the words out, taking me aback because she ordinarily had nothing but good to say about everything and everybody. "I know you were sick, and so was I, but we can't keep getting sick every Monday night, can we?"

"Well," I said, playing for time, as I realized that Emma Sue may have seen right through me. "I guess we can't. But I really was sick, Emma Sue." And that was the dead-level truth, for I recalled with a shudder the cold trembling down my back and the clutch of nausea in my throat when Dr. Fowler's name jumped out at me from the church bulletin Sunday morning.

"Oh, I was, too," she said, nodding with conviction. "Sick to my soul. Body, too. But Julia, I don't want to go to those sessions even though I guess I'm over whatever I had. But I came to ask if you're going to the next one."

"I don't think so," I said, "I figure that because I've missed the introductory session, it wouldn't be fair to the group to come in later on."

"*You* might be able to get away with that," she said, with a despairing sigh, "but I can't. Larry says that because he's the pastor, he has to be there, and because I'm his wife, I have to be, too." She sniffed, then gave up on that and blew her nose. "We both *have* to be there. 'How will it look,' he said, 'if we don't support a church program?' And I said, 'Well, how will it look if we *do*?' Everybody will think our marriage is in trouble, Julia, and besides, I'm already supporting every program and activity in that church, and I simply cannot take on another one. Especially one like that. It'll tear me up, Julia, knowing that everybody in the congregation will be worried about the state of our marriage. Pastors and their wives have to be so careful, you know, not to give offense or stir up trouble." Emma Sue stifled a sob. "But Larry doesn't see it that way. He's convinced that Dr. Fowler can make a good thing even better, and we ought to take advantage of it, while at the same time set an example for everybody else.

"And I'll tell you something else," she went on before I could get a word out, "but you can't tell anybody, Julia, not even Sam, because I know you tell him everything. Promise me you won't."

"I promise I won't," I said.

She really started crying then, pitifully, with tears streaming down her face. "I think Larry's unhappy with me. I think he's come to the age where he's wondering if there's not something better. Men do that, you know. All the books say so, even the Christian marriage manuals. So I think Larry wants us to go to Dr. Fowler's sessions so I'll learn how to be a better wife. And I'll tell you the truth, Julia, I'm not perfect, but I'm doing the best I can already."

"Of course you are, Emma Sue," I said. "Nobody could do better. And you shouldn't be made to feel guilty if you don't want to spend your Monday evenings in the company of that so-called expert on marriage. What're his credentials, anyway? Anybody can hang out a shingle, you know, and just because he has a PhD doesn't mean he knows how to kindle anybody's embers."

I stopped then, remembering with burning shame that he'd once kindled mine. But that was an aberration on my part, one I had to live with but never repeat.

"Yes," Emma Sue said, wiping her face with a fierce swipe of the wad of Kleenex, "and you don't know the half of it." She leaned toward me and whispered, "He's not even married himself, and never even *been* married. So what does he know? Doodley-squat, that's what."

"Really!" I was surprised, though I guess I shouldn't have been, considering his actions in the bridal parlor. "I didn't know that. I just assumed that he'd had some practical experience on the subject."

"And that's not all," Emma Sue hissed. "He lives with his *mother*! And always has, all his life, and he's no spring chicken. She's on up there in age, too, I understand, but still. I think that's more than a little strange, don't you?"

"Well, I certainly do. How can he have the nerve to counsel married people? And Emma Sue, listen to this." I found myself leaning toward her, as I realized that I had a fellow traveler in a common cause. "You know what he's going to talk about, don't you?"

"Making marriages better?"

"Huh!" I almost snorted. "Just read that bulletin and listen to what the pastor must've told you about the meeting we missed. It's all about S-E-X. Think about it. Stirring the embers? Rekindling your relationship? Putting sparks back into your marriage? It's all about," I dropped my voice, "*passion.* And if he's never been married, what does he know about it, I ask you."

"Why, Julia, I do believe you're right." Emma Sue's eyes glazed over as she thought about it. "I wonder if Larry realizes that. I don't think he'd approve at all."

"Well, I'm just telling you that Dr. Fowler—or Dr. *Fred,* as he wants to be called—may use euphemisms, but that's what it comes down to. And I'm here to tell you, I am not going to sit in a group and be embarrassed to death while he talks about private matters in public. Or tries to get *us* to talk about them."

And I determined then and there that that was exactly what I would tell Sam. Why should that mama's boy put me in bed with an upset stomach that I didn't even have just so I could get out of having to look at him? And why should I have to tell untruths to my husband to keep from meeting the man again?

"Me, either," Emma Sue said, looking resolved and decisive. "Larry can't want me to be around talk like that. When he understands what Dr. Fowler's really talking about, he'll not want me hearing a word of it. Thank you, Julia. I feel a hundred percent better."

Chapter 22

Well, goodness, I thought, if Emma Sue spread that word around, it might start a mass migration of wives out of the Monday-night sessions. Not that there'd been all that many to start with.

But as I walked her to the door, she suddenly turned and said, "If you're right, Julia, and that's what Dr. Fowler's going to talk about, I don't know but that I might not mind hearing some of it. But only," she quickly qualified, "if no men were involved—including him. I mean, a women's group led by a woman. And called something else, like, oh, I don't know, Reaching Your Full Potential or something. I expect none of us knows everything there is to know about marital sparks and embers and such."

"That's probably true," I said, although I'd learned a gracious plenty since I'd been married to Sam. Where he'd learned it I couldn't say and wouldn't ask.

"I'll speak to Larry about it," Emma Sue said. "He'll think it's a splendid idea when I tell him how inappropriate it is for wives to hear what you said Dr. Fowler has in mind."

"Well now, Emma Sue," I cautioned, "all I'm doing is interpreting Dr. Fowler's figurative language. I could possibly be wrong, so why don't you wait until the pastor hears for himself what the sessions are about. That way, it'll be *his* idea that you not attend. Then you could suggest a women's group if you want to."

"Oh, Julia, you are so wise. It would absolutely be best for Larry to make that decision on his own. So instead of pushing myself as I always do on Mondays—the weekends, especially Sundays, are so full for us, you know—I'll just give in to fatigue as I've longed to do so often and let him go one more time by himself. The Lord does want us to take care of ourselves, and he'll forgive me because he knows I need the rest."

"I'm sure you do, Emma Sue," I said, opening the door for her. "You push yourself too hard, always doing for others and rarely for yourself."

She stepped out onto the porch as I held the screen door. She looked back at me through welling tears of gratitude. "Not everybody understands like you do, Julia. I get so tired sometimes that I can hardly put one foot in front of the other. Well, I have to be going. Thank you for listening and, oh, I forgot to ask. Are you going to Mildred's tonight?"

"Yes, I'm planning to. I wonder what her surprise is."

"Oh, me, too. I'm so looking forward to it. Well, I'll see you there." She waved and walked with a sprightly step down the walkway to her car.

⌣

When Lillian and Etta Mae returned from their cleaning mission, the first thing Etta Mae did was to call Binkie to learn if there'd been any developments that morning.

"I just can't get my mind off it, Miss Julia," she said to me as she waited to be connected. "All day, every day, it's the only thing I think—oh, Binkie, hi, it's me. Did you get in to see Mrs. Delacorte?"

Lillian and I listened to the one-sided conversation, which consisted mostly of "uh-huhs" and "ohs" and "okays." When Etta Mae hung up, her face told the story—there was no good news.

"Mrs. Delacorte won't talk to her," Etta Mae said. "And apparently she doesn't have to. All Binkie can get is the statement she made to the deputies. And she just got that, so she hasn't read it all yet." Etta Mae slumped down in a chair. "I don't know what I'm going to do. It just keeps on and on."

"Don't give up on us, Etta Mae," I said. "My limited experience with all things involving the law tells me that it's always slow. Seems as if everything is long and drawn out, unnecessarily so, in my opinion. So you just have to ride it out and stand firm on the fact that you have been wrongly accused."

"I think," Lillian pronounced, "she need something to eat. Everybody feel better then. What y'all want for lunch?"

We discussed the options and ended up with sandwiches made from leftover roast beef. Etta Mae undoubtedly felt better with a full stomach, but she didn't look much better. Sadness and worry pulled at her face, and she wasn't the happy and eager young woman I was accustomed to.

"Why don't you go take a nap, Etta Mae?" I urged. "You've been busy cleaning all morning, so run up and lie down for a little while."

"Binkie's going to call back after she studies that statement. I don't think I can rest till I hear from her." Then, with a wan smile, she went on. "Besides, I don't ever take naps. Always too busy."

"Well, you're not too busy today. Here," I said, handing her the newspaper, "go up and at least lie down. Read the paper, and if you get sleepy during that, as I expect you will, you can nap awhile. I'll listen out for Binkie."

It was another couple of hours before Binkie called back to say she was on her way over with Francie's statement. I had to wake Etta Mae from a deep sleep, bring her downstairs and give her a cup of coffee.

When Binkie arrived, she handed Francie's statement to Etta Mae and said, "Read it, and tell me what you think." Etta Mae did, passing each sheet of it to me as she finished it.

Instead of a statement, it consisted of several statements, each given at a different time. Francie's first semicoherent interview was conducted in the emergency room, where she'd been taken after Evelyn had discovered her on Thursday. Francie told the deputy that she'd been "mugged and strangled," although the doctor's notes indicated no signs of injury to her throat and neck. That was the extent of the first statement, because the deputy noted that the victim was unable to provide further information, saying, "I don't know," "I can't remember" and "Leave me alone, I'm dying."

The next interview took place Friday morning in the hospital and was conducted by Lieutenant Peavey. That time, Francie said she didn't know who had assaulted her, just that she had attempted to get out of bed by herself to see if Evelyn had arrived. According to her, she'd stood up and taken a few steps, then "there was this awful pain on the top of my head as something crashed down on me, and I heard a crunching sound like my bones had shattered, and a blackness darker than night descended on me, and that's all I remember." There was no mention of either strangulation or theft of a gold bracelet.

Saturday afternoon, when her doctor noted that her vital signs were normal and she was fully coherent, Lieutenant Peavey visited Francie again. This time, the statement she gave was precise and detailed. And different. According to her, she'd been left alone Thursday morning and decided to get out of bed, although she had "strict orders to stay off that toe." But she was hungry and thought she could hop to the kitchen. "If I fell and hurt myself," she was quoted as saying, "it would serve them right for leaving me alone." I rolled my eyes at that.

Then, according to her, before she got out of the bedroom, that "awful pain" struck, which indicated to her that somebody had to have been in the room already—"right next to my bed, just waiting to take me unawares." Again, according to her, she awoke on the floor, hardly able to move as she listened to her attacker plundering about on her vanity table. At that point, Francie started screaming for help, so the attacker rushed over, drew back her head by the hair and commenced to choke her. It was then that she passed out again and awoke only when those "rough technicians flung me on a stretcher and brought me to the hospital, half dead and terrified out of my mind."

The last statement, taken again by Lieutenant Peavey, had been given early Sunday afternoon. It was then, and only then, that Francie recalled a "terrible and sickening odor" that she attributed to cheap perfume. "So," she was quoted as saying, "I knew then that it was that little twit of a home nurse who was supposed to be looking after me and who left me by myself, then came back because she wanted my bracelet. Her name is Etta Mae Wiggins. No one but her would wear such cheap perfume, and I'd smelled it before, so I know it was her. She nearly killed me, and after all I've done for her, too."

Etta Mae put her head on the table in despair. "Shania Twain by Stetson is not cheap. And I don't wear it all the time, only on special occasions, like for the lunch party." She raised her head. "I don't even *like* bangle bracelets, and I'm not a little twit, either."

"You most certainly are not," I assured her. "This thing," I went on as I flapped the pages of the statement in front of Binkie, "speaking of odors, smells to high heaven. It gets richer and more specific by the interview."

Binkie nodded. "Yes, but the prosecutor will say that's because Mrs. Delacorte's memory returned gradually. He'll use the head injury and resulting concussion as the reason for a temporary loss of memory."

"Well, I think," I said, "that she's making more than half of it up. She's been lying in bed in that hospital, building up an imaginary event and adding more and more to it, just for the attention she gets. I tell you, Binkie, the woman cannot be believed. Why, she told us one time about being accosted by a gang of drug dealers in Panama when she was on her way to a diplomatic luncheon. She said she just drew herself up and told them that she was a lady and unaccustomed to dealing with trash. And if you believe it, which I don't, they apologized and let her go. That, Binkie, is the kind of tall tale she can tell."

"Yes, well," Binkie said with a long sigh, "maybe so. But we have to deal with her statement. It's all we have because Etta Mae can't prove where she was between eleven o'clock and fifteen or so minutes past twelve that day when she arrived here."

"I was in my car for about twenty minutes," Etta Mae said with a stubborn look on her face. "Driving home. Then I was in my single-wide, taking a quick shower, changing clothes and redoing my makeup, then in the car again driving here to Miss Julia's. I may not be able to prove it, but that's what I was doing."

"Wait just a minute," I said. "Maybe you *can* prove it. Binkie, can you get Francie, maybe through one of the interviewers, to describe what Etta Mae was wearing that morning?" I turned to Etta Mae. "What *were* you wearing?"

"My usual uniform," she said. "A light blue scrub suit, Easy Stride running shoes and a navy cotton cardigan because it was chilly early that morning."

"Good!" I said. "Because you weren't wearing that when you got here. So—"

"So," Binkie finished for me, "what we'll do is time the distance from Mrs. Delacorte's house to your single-wide, Etta Mae, then time it from there to Miss Julia's house. What's left will be how long it took you to get out of your uniform and into the clothes that Miss Julia can testify you were wearing when you got here."

Joy bloomed on Etta Mae's face. "That's it! I *can* prove it, can't I? I didn't have time to do it." Then reality set in and she said, "What if Mrs. Delacorte says she doesn't remember? What if she says I was wearing something different?"

"Don't worry about that," Binkie said. "I'll get Lieutenant Peavey to ask her, along with other questions, and she won't think it's important enough to say anything but the truth. Besides, she won't be able to describe what you wore to the luncheon. And you also visited another client earlier, didn't you? We'll get that statement, too, and confirm what you had on." Binkie looked at me. "Can you describe in detail what she was wearing when she got here? And Etta Mae, not one word to her now or later to help her remember."

"Of course I can," I said, then frowned. "And it certainly was not a scrub suit. It was, well, a dress, dark in color. Oh, and long sleeves and a deep décolletage—I remember that in particular. And she had a large tote bag, maybe navy blue? Or black? And high heels." I smiled with relief. "How's that, Etta Mae?"

Binkie held up her hand. "Don't answer that. And whatever you do, don't correct anything. We don't want any hint of collusion here. Come on, Etta Mae, let's go time how long it took you to do all that driving. Then we'll see the lieutenant and get it on record. He'll want to talk to you, too, Miss Julia."

Well, Lord, I hoped I'd come close enough in describing Etta Mae's luncheon attire to convince Lieutenant Peavey of her innocence. Because, frankly, the main thing I remembered was all that bosom she'd had on display.

Chapter 23

I wanted to go with them, but Lloyd came in from school, then Sam arrived, so I stayed to catch them up with the latest developments.

"So," Sam said when I finished, "the lieutenant will have the victim, Francie Pitts Delacorte, saying that Etta Mae was wearing a light blue scrub suit that morning and still wearing it when she left at eleven, and a witness, you, Julia, testifying that she had on a dark, long-sleeved dress one hour and fifteen minutes or so later, which should prove that Etta Mae did leave and go home during that time. So let's say it takes twenty minutes to drive from Francie's house to Etta Mae's trailer and another twenty minutes to drive here from the trailer. That eats up forty minutes of the hour and fifteen, leaving about thirty-five minutes unaccounted for."

"She was dressing, Sam, and fixing her makeup. Who's side are you on, anyway?"

Sam grinned at me. "Just thinking like a prosecutor, sweetheart. And like a certain lieutenant. Still, I've never known you to be able to change clothes and put on makeup in thirty-five minutes."

"Yes, and Etta Mae puts on a lot more than I do, so it takes her longer. But seriously, Sam, what worries me is that she was in a real dither when she got here, all rushed and anxious and upset. And it could've taken her less than twenty minutes to get from one place to the other. But of course, it all depends on traffic, and it could've taken her longer. She could've caught the red light in Delmont both ways, and that would've slowed her down."

"Let's wait and see what Binkie says after they time it. To get to Delmont from Mountain Villas, you have to go through downtown Abbotsville and through Delmont, too, because the trailer park is on the other side. I expect twenty minutes both ways would be about right."

Lillian and Lloyd had been listening to this, both as interested as Sam and I were. Lillian brought the coffeepot over for refills, her face squinched up as she thought about our time lines.

After a few minutes, Lloyd said, "But Etta Mae does everything real fast. Driving, dressing, everything. She doesn't waste a minute."

"That's called efficiency, Lloyd," I said, "but you're right. I'm not sure this is going to get her off the hook. If I know Lieutenant Peavey, he's going to think she still could've hit Francie, grabbed a bracelet and got out of there with enough time left to do everything else."

Lillian stood with the coffeepot in her hand, staring off in the distance. "Yes'm," she said, "but where that bracelet at now? I seen her jewel box this mornin', 'cause them deputies strewed everything out, an' I didn't see no gold bangle bracelet. Didn't see much of anything 'cause she don't have much."

"That's a good question, Lillian," Sam said. "The bracelet and the weapon both are missing. Binkie said that Mrs. Delacorte suffered a large flat injury to the crown of her head, but the deputies didn't find anything in or around her house with evidence of having been used."

"What kind of evidence would be on it?" I asked.

"Oh, strands of her hair, probably. Some blood, if it broke the skin, depending on how hard she was hit."

"Well, that's another thing we don't know," I said. "Just how hard *was* she hit? She had a bandage on her head when I saw her, but the way she exaggerates, it could've been a little tap and nothing more."

"She was knocked out, Julia," Sam reminded me with a smile.

"That's *her* story," I said.

Later, Sam and I sat in the living room before supper, wincing at each bang of a basketball as Lloyd again and again hit the hoop over the garage door.

"Sam," I said, "I've been wondering about something. Now, I know this is a delicate subject, and you may not want to answer it. But tell me this—from a man's point of view—what does Francie Pitts have that nobody else seems to have?"

Sam looked at me, raised his eyebrows, then with a half smile said, "In what way?"

I nudged him with my elbow. "You know in what way. I'm talking about how she's been able to get a new husband almost before the last one is cold in his grave. I mean, let's face it, she's neither young nor attractive, and no one would say she has a scintillating personality. She's probably pretty well off, but I doubt she has enough to blind a man to what she doesn't have. So what's her appeal?"

"Speaking for myself, she doesn't have any."

"Well, but she does, or at least she has had to a lot of men. Why, Sam, she's married and buried and married again over and over, with practically no turnaround time. And I'm trying to understand what they see in her and exactly how she does it."

"Well, Julia, some women just have that little something extra."

"I knew you'd know! What is it?"

"My guess is that it's . . ." He leaned over and whispered, "erotic knowledge."

I jerked back and stared at him. "Erotic . . .? No, Sam, that couldn't be it. How would Francie Pitts have that? Where would she get it? And," I went on, frowning, "what is it, anyway?"

"Oh, ways to please a man, I expect. Sensually speaking, that is." Sam picked up the newspaper from the lamp table. "I'm just guessing. Did you see that article about the Methodist church getting a new preacher?"

"No, and don't change the subject. If there's something to know about pleasing a man, I want to know it. I have a man to please, too, you know."

Sam put his arm around me and whispered against my hair. "You please me just fine."

Well, I wasn't too sure about that. Why else was he trying to get me in a marriage enrichment counseling session? Was he hoping that Dr. Fowler had the inside scoop on erotic knowledge and would disseminate it? An image of Dr. Fowler lecturing on explicit sensual matters sprang full blown into my mind. My eyelids fluttered at the thought.

By the time Etta Mae returned, after having dropped Binkie off, Sam and I had moved on to other subjects, although I was still mulling over the apparent hole in my erotic knowledge storehouse and wondering how I could fill it without attending class. Independent study was one option, though I wouldn't know where to start. But one thing was for sure: if Dr. Fowler and Francie Pitts were the only experts in the field available to me, I'd just stay ignorant and hope Sam would resign himself to doing without the frills.

But I had to put aside this fascinating, though worrisome, subject to concentrate on Etta Mae's problem. On her return, she had confirmed that our estimated driving times were pretty much on the money. "Now if I can just convince Lieutenant Peavey that it takes me thirty-five minutes to change clothes and do my makeup, I'll be okay. Mr. Sam," she went on, turning to him, "do you think I ought to demonstrate how I did it? He could sit in my living room and time me, and I'd do everything just like I did last Thursday."

"I don't think that'll be necessary," Sam said, smiling at her. "He has a wife, so I expect he knows how long it takes."

She didn't seem all that convinced, but she put it aside to shower us with thanks for helping her in her time of need. "But I'd better be getting back and begin looking for a job. Miss Julia, if you start feeling bad again, just give me a call. I don't expect I'll be busy anytime soon."

We urged her to stay on, but she said she didn't want to wear out her welcome. She finally consented to have dinner with us, after which she'd pack her things and be off. I hated to see her go but mentally reserved the right to call her back on duty if I needed to be sick again, come Monday next.

When Lillian tinkled the dinner bell, we all went into the dining room and took our places, still discussing how long it took women to dress.

Wanting to put a stop to it, I said, "It all depends on why she's dressing. I mean, what she's dressing *for*. If she's going to a party, as Etta Mae was, then naturally she'll take a few more pains with her toilette."

Etta Mae frowned at the unfamiliar word, and Lloyd got tickled, putting his hand over his mouth as he giggled.

"Toilette," I said sternly, "simply means one's overall grooming. Among other things."

"Yes'm," Lloyd said, his eyes dancing with delight at teasing me. "I'm laughing at the other things."

⌣

When I arrived at Mildred's house later that evening, after seeing Etta Mae off, I was surprised at the number of women she'd invited. She must've been truly disturbed about the attack on Francie to have gone to so much trouble to arrange for a safety demonstration. I walked in along with three others, and Mildred directed us toward her large drawing, room, where rows of folding chairs had been set up in a semicircle facing the Adam mantel of the fireplace.

Smiling and greeting the others, I strolled through the spacious foyer and through the double doors to the drawing room. The front-row chairs were already taken, which suited me fine. If the well-muscled instructor I envisioned wanted to demonstrate some defensive technique with a volunteer, I preferred to watch from the back row rather than be singled out as an assistant.

As I began to sidle to a few empty seats in the back row, I glanced toward the fireplace and nearly lost my breath. Seated there, in a Chippendale wing chair upholstered in blue and gold brocade, was none other than Dr. Fred Fowler, a smug little smile on his face as he surveyed the eager crowd who'd come to sit at his feet.

I was paralyzed with outrage. False pretenses! That's how Mildred had gotten me there, letting me think I'd learn some kind of judo mumbo jumbo to protect myself, then springing on me the very one whom I'd gone to such extreme measures to avoid.

Then, drawing a heaving breath, I regained some sense. Mildred had done no such thing. She knew nothing of my antipathy toward the man nor anything of my previous dealings with him. It wasn't her fault that I was there, but it would be my fault if I stayed.

I turned to edge back through the crowd, my mind set on getting out of there and getting home. Before I could move, though, I felt a steady push behind me.

"Julia," Emma Sue Ledbetter whispered, nudging me along. "I'm so glad to see you. Let's sit together."

"This is not what I expected, Emma Sue. I'm going home."

"No, don't do that. Look, I brought some paper to take notes. Here's a pad for you." Emma Sue handed me a small, yellow legal pad. "I'm going to take down word for word what Dr. Fowler says so Larry will see what he's up to."

I was momentarily confused. "You knew he'd be here? I thought there'd be a self-defense instructor."

Emma Sue frowned at me. "Where'd you get that idea? Larry asked Mildred to have him. He's hoping that when some of the wives get to know him, they'll get their husbands to go with them to the enrichment sessions. Hardly anybody showed up on Monday, you know."

"Oh for goodness' sakes," I said, shuffling my feet as people moved past us. "I'm not feeling well. I've got to go."

"Oh, sit down, Julia," Emma Sue said. "I need you to help me. If we're going to get out of being enriched, we have to get the goods on him."

She gave me a little shove and I moved over to two empty chairs. Sitting down, because she wouldn't give me a way out, I was relieved to find that I was behind Harriet Malone, who was about as wide as she was tall, and she was tall. I couldn't see Dr. Fowler at all. Even better, he couldn't see me.

"Now, Julia," Emma Sue whispered as she handed me a pen, "take good notes and get down everything he says. I hope it'll run Larry up a wall."

Intrigued by this time at the thought of being of one mind with Emma Sue Ledbetter—it was so unusual, you know—I settled down in the safety of Harriet's broad back to await Dr. Fowler's self-incrimination.

A few stragglers were still coming through the foyer, and there was a lot of talking and greeting of friends as those in the drawing room took their time in finding seats. And all the while, Dr. Fowler complacently surveyed his captive audience, his rimless glasses flashing occasionally as he glanced from side to side. I eased my head to one side to look beyond Harriet's shoulder, taking in as much of Dr. Fowler as I could while he was gazing in another direction.

Lord, how could I have ever seen anything in him? Well, of course I'd not *seen* anything, having kept my eyes closed through the whole episode. But there he sat in a brown suit, yellow shirt and striped tie, one leg crossed over the other, exposing a sliver of white shin between pant leg's end and the top of a brown silk sock with a yellow clock up the side. His red hair had lost some luster and thickness in the intervening years, although it had had little of either to begin with. He'd shrunk with age somewhat as well, though he'd barely been my height before, and I wondered how old he was. Seventy-five if he was a day was my guess, and going around the country advising married couples on how to stoke embers. Most unseemly, I sniffed, and quickly jerked back behind Harriet as his gaze swept the room.

At that point, I noticed the two stacks of thin paperback books on a table beside his chair. Thinking at first that he might hand them out to his audience, I was aghast to see three women go to him, pick up books and hand him money. He was selling them! Of all the inappropriate things to do in a private home, this took the cake.

"Look, Emma Sue," I hissed as I elbowed her, "he's selling those books. Does Mildred know that?"

"Larry told her he had to," she said. "He's self-published, you know, and it's one of the ways he makes his living."

"Well, I think it's a tacky thing to do."

"I guess," Emma Sue said, "but I want one. Somebody said they're workbooks. You know, homework for married couples, and they have illustrations, too." She leaned close to me and whispered. "You get one for me, Julia, and I'll pay you back later. It wouldn't do for people to see me buying one."

"Emma Sue! I will not! You can get it yourself if you want one. But I don't know why you would. Illustrations? You know what they'll be, don't you?"

"No. That's why I want one."

My eyes rolled back in my head just as Mildred walked to the center of the room and introduced Dr. Fred Fowler, who would speak to us about the joys of a Christ-centered marriage.

As Mildred moved to the side, Dr. Fowler straightened up in his chair, cleared his throat and cast a small knowing smile on his audience. I scrooched farther down behind Harriet Malone, gritted my teeth and wished I were anywhere but where I was.

Chapter 24

Dr. Fowler started off by telling us that marriage is a sacred covenant designed by God to demonstrate the relationship of Christ and his church. Nothing new there, I thought.

He went on speaking in a soft and persuasive tone so that the sound of his voice curled around us as we all quieted and strained to hear—a psychological trick, I thought to myself, to keep our attention.

He uncrossed his legs and leaned forward. "Art thou bound to a husband? Then you must render unto your husband his due, for the marriage bed is undefiled. Seek not to be loosed, for a wife must not depart from her husband."

He sat back and smiled as if he'd proclaimed a precept we'd never heard of. Unfortunately for him, most of us had. Shocked at how he'd paraphrased and conflated Scripture, I glanced at Emma Sue, who knew her Bible backward and forward. She was staring at him, her mouth open, a look of amazement on her face. Then she bent to her legal pad and began scribbling as fast as she could.

Without looking up, she whispered, "Write, Julia. Get it all down."

I glanced at her notes, then tried to catch up by jotting down what I remembered. But by that time, Dr. Fowler was rattling on with a full head of steam, and I'd missed how he'd gotten there.

"Has your marriage grown stale?" he asked, as if he already knew the answer. "Are the fires dying down? Do you wonder where the passion has gone? Have you ever asked yourself, 'Is this all there is?' Has your coming together become a growing apart? Then," Dr. Fowler said, his voice gaining strength as he rose to his feet, "*then,* you are in the grip of one or more of the insidious marriage busters. And what is a marriage buster? It's anything done, or *not* done, to hurt your spouse."

He sighed dramatically, then resumed in his quiet voice. "I could list twelve of them, but we're limited in our time together, so I'm only going to speak of one, the worst one. And that is refusing your husband the comfort of the marriage bed, or, just about as bad, enduring rather than participating in that comfort. Do you push him away? Are you too tired or too sick? Do you roll your eyes? Make a cutting remark that lessens and deflates him? Your unwilling or lackadaisical response to his needs will bust up a marriage quicker than anything."

Emma Sue leaned close and whispered, "Is he talking about what I think he's talking about?"

I nodded, my mouth stretched so thin and tight I couldn't get a word out.

"There is no other blessing under the sun," Dr. Fowler declaimed, "more to be desired and honored and *practiced* than that of the physical coming together of a man and wife. It is the physical and spiritual communion of two entities. Now I'm going to give you a news flash: men are different from women."

He stopped then and smiled, awaiting the ripple of laughter that a few granted him. "Men are different in their needs and in the frequency that those needs demand to be met. It is the wise wife who recognizes this and who makes herself available at all times and in all ways. But she should not only be available, she should be *enthusiastically* available. And not only enthusiastically available, but—hear me now, for this is one of the secrets to a happy marriage—she should often be the initiator and the instigator of those actions that will stimulate and arouse her husband to a release of those tensions and built-up resentments that are part and parcel of any marriage."

There was dead quiet in the room as we absorbed and parsed his words. Emma Sue was taking notes as fast as she could, mumbling under her breath, "Wait till Larry hears this."

I couldn't respond, but it struck me that Larry just might agree with Dr. Fowler.

The good doctor took up his cause again. "My dear sisters, I know that you may be shocked, you may think it's too much to ask and you may wonder if I know what I'm talking about. But I assure you I do. Study after study has shown that when a married couple makes every effort to conjoin *daily* in that sacred act of coitus, their marriage is strengthened beyond anything the world can do to destroy it."

There was a loud gasp from every mouth in the room. I couldn't tell if it was caused by hearing that unusual word in a public and mixed gathering or by the prospect of a daily ration of it. I was outraged at the thought of both or either one. Recalling an article I'd read of a preacher whose mind was so filled with images of marital congress that he displayed a double bed beside the altar as a show-and-tell item, I wondered if both the preaching and the psychological professions hadn't taken a wrong turn somewhere.

Dr. Fowler waited until the effect of his words had run its course, then he said, "When you get home tonight, take a look at your vitamin bottle. You'll see the initials RDA, the recommended daily allowance. That's my prescription for you, too, and if you follow the RDA of marital intercourse, believe me, you will begin to see the sparks fly and your marriage will be immeasurably strengthened." Dr. Fowler allowed himself a smile at his own cleverness as his gaze swept the room. I ducked lower over my pad.

"Now," he went on, holding up a warning finger, "a word of caution. I've emphasized how important it is to keep your husbands satisfied and content, but you women are in just as much danger if you allow yourselves to become closed off and antagonistic to married lovemaking. You will set yourselves up to become prey to the natural instinct to couple with the opposite sex and therefore become self-made victims of uncontrollable desires that can spring up in the most unsuitable places and with the most innocent of men. It is up to you to constrain and restrain the animal instincts we all possess in both your husbands and in yourselves. I could give you example after example of cases in which a woman has taken leave of her senses simply because, for one reason or another and sometimes through her own fault, she has been denied a suitable outlet. The loss of self-control in a man is bad enough, although often understandable, but when a woman loses control of her emotions, it is a sad and pitiable thing to witness."

I thought I'd faint dead away. Did he intend to give a *specific* example? Was he talking about me? I bowed my head and patted my chest, dread filling my mind to the extent that I feared I'd melt in mortification.

Then, in the midst of the shame that filled my soul, it came to me that he'd referred to many examples. Did that mean he'd been accosted by other women? Had there been others whom he'd led down the primrose path? It was beginning to sound as if Dr. Fred Fowler was an itinerant psychological seducer, and I hoped Emma Sue was getting it all down.

I groaned softly and whispered to Emma Sue, "I'm feeling sick to my stomach."

"Me, too," she murmured, her pen flying over the pad.

"Now," Dr. Fowler said, "Mrs. Allen, our gracious hostess, has prepared refreshments for us, so let's take a short break. Afterward, I will give you, well, let us say, some kindling to restart the fires of your marriage. There are some very simple and easy-to-learn techniques that I guarantee will stoke the smoldering embers of your marriages into blazing flames."

He turned aside, and the noise level began to rise. Chair legs scraped against the floor and people bustled, talking to one another as they prepared to adjourn to the dining room.

Then Dr. Fowler, with Mildred's help, regained our attention. "Please feel free," Dr. Fowler said, "to come up and purchase one of my books. They're only fourteen dollars and ninety-five cents each, and they're handy reference guides. One stack is specifically for women, and the other is for men. You would be wise to purchase one for your husband, as well as yourself. That way you'll both be on the same page." He laughed at his poor joke, and some simpleminded adorers joined him.

I sat still as others around Emma Sue and me stood, preparing to partake of Mildred's offerings. Emma Sue was still writing, her head bent over her pad, while I looked around for a way to get out of the crush without being seen. We were crammed in so close that Emma Sue's knees were right up against the chair in front, blocking that path. Harriet Malone was making no effort to get up, so I couldn't stand until she did. And unhappily, I heard Harriet ask someone to bring her a plate because she thought she'd stay where she was.

I didn't know what to do, for this was the best time to beat a hasty retreat. If I waited until everyone was leaving, Dr. Fowler would most likely be standing at the front door to wish us a good night. Fearing with all my heart a face-to-face meeting, I determined to get myself out of there while the getting was good.

"Emma Sue," I whispered, nudging her, "let's go."

"It's not over, Julia. And I'm staying till it is. I'm writing as hard as I can, but you're making me forget half of what he said." She bent over her pad again and stayed right where she was.

I did the only thing I could think to do. I slid down in my chair and dropped to my knees on Mildred's oriental rug. Then, turning sideways, I began to crawl over Emma Sue's feet. The folding chairs had been placed so closely together with hardly any room between the rows that I had to squeeze past a chair on one side and Emma Sue's skinny shins on the other.

"Julia!" Emma Sue said in a hoarse whisper. "What are you doing?"

"I dropped something," I whispered back. "Move your feet, Emma Sue. I think I'm stuck."

"Well, for goodness' sakes," she said with a dramatic sigh. "Get up from there and I'll help you look."

"I can't. Swing your legs to the side so I can get through."

She did, and I slid past her, still on my hands and knees. Reaching some empty chairs beyond her, but still hidden by people standing between me and Dr. Fowler, I grasped a chair seat to pull myself up. Folding chairs, as I was immediately reminded, are not the sturdiest objects around, for I found myself unable to get enough leverage to rise. Straining as hard as I could, the weakness of my lower limbs prevented me from getting to my feet, and all I could think of at that moment was the spectacle I would make if I had to crawl all the way to the front door.

"Miss Julia?" a voice above me asked. "Are you all right?"

I craned my head up and sideways to see Tina Doland, the bosomy young Baptist soprano, leaning over me, concern on her face.

"Oh, Tina," I sighed in relief. "Give me a hand if you will. I'm down here and I can't get up."

"Did you fall?" Tina offered her hand and I clasped it, at last able to rise.

Quickly glancing around to be sure I was still behind a group of people, I reassured her. "No, I just dropped something. Let me tell you, Tina, it's not the vision or the hearing that goes first. It's the knees. Thank you for your help. I'll be running along now."

I'd just closed the front door behind me, having left without thanking Mildred for the lovely evening, when it opened again and Emma Sue came rushing out.

"Are you leaving?" she asked.

"I certainly am. I've heard all I want to hear."

"Well, I'm going, too. Helen said she'd buy both books for me, so I didn't need to stay." She took my yellow pad and stuffed it, along with hers, into her tote bag, then said, "I kinda hate to leave, though. I was really learning something."

"I don't understand you, Emma Sue," I said, as we walked along Mildred's brick walk. "You said you wanted the pastor to send Dr. Fowler packing, yet you also want to hear what he has to say. Which is it?"

"Well, both. I want to know what he teaches, but I don't want him to teach it, especially in the church. A subject like that, taught so graphically, is simply inappropriate in a church setting with a mixed audience. I mean, it was bad enough tonight with only women there, and I'm sure he toned it down some, but I think there's a time and a place for everything, and in this case, the First Presbyterian Church of Abbotsville is not it."

"I couldn't agree more, Emma Sue. But where we differ is this: I don't want to hear a thing he has to say. RDA, my foot. I've never heard anything so outrageous and unthinkable. Why, the heart attack rate would be off the charts in this town, and I'm not just talking about the husbands." I fumed a while longer, then went on. "There's nothing I'd like better than to see the last of Dr. Fred Fowler, because if all those women go home tonight and start initiating and instigating their husbands' smoldering embers, there's no telling what would happen."

"Oh my," Emma Sue said, stopping to think about it. "And what about people like Miss Mattie and Helen Stroud and a bunch of others I could name? They don't even have husbands to go home to. What're they going to do? It might be that if we allow Dr. Fowler to keep on, why, this whole town could go up in flames, couldn't it?"

Chapter 25

After seeing Emma Sue off in her car, I walked on in the mild evening to our house. It was already past dark, but the street-lights and our porch light made the walk pleasant enough, and because we lived next door to Mildred, it didn't take long.

I drew up, stopping short of my front steps as several random thoughts suddenly came together. Sam had suggested that Francie Pitts possessed some kind of special knowledge that kept her in husbands as fast as she needed them, and it seemed to me that Dr. Fowler had been referring to the same kind of knowledge when he promised to tell us the techniques and methods of pleasing a husband. The question that popped up in my mind was this: how did those two most unlikely people come to possess such erudition? Where'd they get it, or had they discovered it on their own? Or had they learned it through trial and error? Or by experimentation? Maybe Francie had—she'd had so many opportunities—but that wouldn't answer for Dr. Fowler. He wasn't even married. That stopped me cold, until I realized that Dr. Fowler probably had book knowledge, while Francie had gotten hers through personal experience.

Maybe Emma Sue was right to want to know more. Maybe

I should've stayed and relied on Harriet Malone to keep me hidden.

But no, I mentally shook myself. I couldn't risk having another humiliating meeting with Dr. Fred. Not that I feared the same outcome as before—not at all. I had myself well in hand by this time, no longer a pitifully needy widow woman who'd been like putty in the hands of a master manipulator. No, I just didn't want to have to look at him up close.

And to keep that from happening, there was only one thing to do: confess the whole disgraceful incident to Sam. Just lay out all the humiliation and shame that I had suffered and continued to suffer, then throw myself on his mercy.

Actually, though, continuing to think about it as I lingered at the foot of the porch steps, maybe it'd be better not to mention "throw myself" on or at anything at all. He might think I'd done a gracious plenty of that already.

But at least, I reassured myself, once I'd cleared my conscience, he would understand why I was intent on avoiding Dr. Fred Fowler. I would no longer have to think up excuses to get out of attending the counseling sessions or any kind of gathering where he might be.

The only problem, of course, was whether or not Sam's attitude toward me would change. How would he take learning that his wife had at one time been thought a loose woman?

I could've cried at the possibility that I'd be lower in his estimation, but I squared my shoulders, stepped up onto the porch and prepared myself to tell it all—with the possible exception of a few minor parts of the whole.

As soon as I opened the front door and stepped inside, I could hear a news program on the television. Sam, as he usually did, got up to meet me. "You're home early, sweetheart," he said. "How was it at Mildred's?"

"Fine, but Sam, I need to—" Before I could finish the sentence, the telephone rang. "Who could that be? I'll get it. Go on and watch your program, and I'll be in to talk in a minute."

I went to the kitchen so as not to disturb him. When I answered the phone, I was surprised to hear Francie Pitts's voice. "Julia," she said, "they're sending me home tomorrow, and I'm going to need some help. You offered to help any way you could, remember? So I want to borrow your woman for a week or two. Tell her she needs to be here at the hospital early tomorrow morning so she can learn about my medications and accompany me home."

"What?" I could hardly believe what I was hearing. "Are you talking about Lillian?"

"Why, yes, of course. I need her, Julia. That Wiggins girl just won't do, and Evelyn is not up to it. You can do without Lillian for a while, can't you? I mean, you have your health, while I'm bedridden half the time. Besides, I'm just asking you to lend her for a couple of weeks."

I let the wires hum for a full minute as I got myself under control. "Well, first off, Francie, you'll have to talk to Lillian yourself. I can't speak for her. She's not mine to lend, you know. And second off, don't they have nursing care out at Mountain Villas? Won't you have help from them?"

"But Julia, I need *personal* care. I don't want to have to depend on somebody dropping by twice a day to see whether I'm still breathing or not. Give me Lillian's number and I'll talk to her."

I gritted my teeth, gave her the number and hung up. Lord,

what would I do if Lillian decided to work for her? Francie had a way of getting what she wanted, and I had no doubt that she would offer Lillian an exorbitant amount of money. And if Lillian took the job, she'd earn every cent of it by the sweat of her brow.

I was so disturbed by Francie's high-and-mighty ways that I stomped into the living room, fuming to Sam about losing Lillian. After recounting the phone conversation, I said, "You know, and Francie does, too, that you do not take somebody's help away from them. It's just not done. I have never heard of such arrogance. The idea! Oh, Sam, what will I do without Lillian?"

"Lillian's not going anywhere," Sam said. "She has too much sense to get involved with Francie Pitts and too much loyalty to leave a good job for a couple of weeks' worth of work, no matter how much she gets paid."

"Oh, I hope you're right. I almost didn't give Francie her number, but then I thought it had to be Lillian's decision. I couldn't bring myself to decide for her. Although I wanted to, and I wanted to tell Francie where to get off, too."

We went on discussing the matter for some little while, with time out occasionally for me to vent my anger at Francie's nerve. Then before I knew it, it was time for bed and I had not gotten around to offering a confession of my wild and unseemly behavior in the bridal parlor.

⌒

I didn't sleep well that night, tossing and turning and waking occasionally to go over in my mind how to tell Sam about Dr. Fred, and to think of all the cutting remarks I wished I'd made to Francie. I can always think of the perfect comebacks two hours or more after I need them.

But as I walked down the stairs early the following morning, I heard the familiar sounds of breakfast being prepared and Lloyd talking with someone. With a lifted heart, I hurried into the kitchen and saw Lillian right where she always was: standing by the stove, spatula in hand.

"Lillian," I said, walking over to her, "I am so glad to see you. Thank you, thank you so much."

"What you thankin' me for? These pancakes not even done yet."

"Didn't Francie Pitts, I mean Francie Delacorte, call you last night?"

"Yes'm, she did." Lillian flipped a couple of pancakes in the pan.

"And?"

"An' nothin'. She say she need help real bad, an' I say I help her find some if I can. But I don't know nobody want to work for that lady. She mean talkin'."

"Oh, Lillian," I said, leaning my head against her shoulder. "You don't know how relieved I am to hear you say that."

"Why? You think I take a job when I already got one? I know what side my bread's buttered on."

"Well, thank the good Lord for that. No, I really didn't think you'd take it, but knowing Francie, I figured she'd offer you so much you wouldn't be able to refuse. And I couldn't have blamed you, Lillian, but I'd have been sick about it if you had."

"Shoo," Lillian said, as she stacked four pancakes on a plate for Lloyd. "They's not enough money in the world for me to go to work for her. An' you know I don't talk about yo' lady friends, 'cept she don't sound much like a lady to me."

"To me, either. And you can talk about her all you want. She's no friend of mine. First, she accuses Etta Mae of being a thief and causing great bodily harm. Then she tries to steal you away from me. No, she is no friend of mine." Watching as Lillian poured warm syrup over Lloyd's pancakes, I went on. "I'd like a couple of those, too, and Sam's going to want several. I hope you made enough batter."

Lillian cut her eyes at me, then smiled. "I think I been 'round here long enough to know what my fam'ly want 'thout bein' told. Now go on an' set down. You need some coffee to get yo' head on straight."

She was right, and that's exactly what I did. Sitting at the table, waiting for Sam and a plate of pancakes, peace descended around me like a warm cape. Take *that,* Francie Pitts, I thought. And I kept that serene feeling for about two minutes, right up to the time the burden of unburdening to Sam also descended on me.

Chapter 26

Sam came into the kitchen and walked over to the table, wishing everybody a good morning on his way. It was still a marvel to me that he had such an even temperament, even early in the morning. He was never crabby or snappish, but always warm and pleasant. Such a difference, you know, from my first experience with a husband. With Wesley Lloyd, I always had to test the temperature before opening my mouth, and nine times out of ten, I kept it shut.

Sam walked toward his place at the table, stopping beside Lloyd. Putting his hand on the boy's shoulder, he said, "How's it going this morning? You sleep well?"

Lloyd grinned up at him, a fork dripping with syrup in his hand. "Yes, sir, I did. Hope you did, too."

Sam nodded, patted his shoulder, then sat down. As he spoke to Lillian and awaited his plate, I poured coffee for him, thinking of how the atmosphere in the house had changed since Sam came into it. He had a way of making every one of us feel important because, I guess, he had a true interest in us: what we were doing, how we were feeling, what our plans were, and on and on. It is remarkable how one person in a family can so influence, for good or ill, everybody else. I could see it clearly because I had such opposites—Wesley Lloyd Springer and Sam Murdoch—as illustrations.

So I mentally sighed, even as Sam reached over and clasped my hand. Would he change when he heard what a mess I'd gotten myself into? I would certainly stress that it hadn't been all my fault. I'd not gone to the church that day with the intent of making myself of interest to Dr. Fowler. *Dr. Fred,* I contemptuously corrected myself. Far from it. I'd barely known the man, much less thought of him as a possible suitor. It had been the pastor who'd asked me to show the good doctor around the church and sent us off into the empty rooms and hallways by ourselves. And still I'd thought nothing of it. And didn't think anything of it until we reached the bridal parlor and Dr. Fred began his advances. After that, well, I simply can't be held responsible, I don't think.

But I didn't know what Sam would think, yet I had to tell him and suffer whatever consequences there might be. No more pleasant mornings, maybe, or intimate glances or holding of hands or sweet words or warm places in bed. Well, I'd always been one who believed in holding people accountable for their words and actions, and now it was my turn.

"Sam," I began when Lloyd got up to get his book bag. "Sometime today I'd like to talk to you. I'll come to your house if you won't be too busy. What's a good time?"

"We can talk now, if you want to. I'm never too busy for you."

"No, it'd be better later on. I need the walk as well." Actually, I wanted total privacy and I was unlikely to get it here at home. Somebody was always telephoning or dropping by, and at Sam's house there'd be no one there but James, and I could send him to the store.

"Well, you just come on whenever you want," Sam said. "I'll be there . . . No, wait. Tom Hansen's coming by this morning to pick up the letter of recommendation I've written for his son. And Rotary Club meets today, so I'll be gone till after lunch. I can cancel both, though, if the morning's better for you."

"No, that's fine, Sam. Don't cancel either one. I'll come by this afternoon."

We left it at that, and I set about planning the best way to tell him, what to tell him and how much or how little to tell him. I just wanted it all off my conscience, and I wanted Sam to understand why I couldn't go to the marriage enrichment sessions taught by a poor excuse for a human being. And I wanted him to reassure me that our marriage was already abundantly enriched, with no dearth of sparks to keep it alive.

⌒

After Sam and Lloyd left, I spent half the morning worrying myself to death by going over and over what I planned to say. I couldn't sit still; I couldn't get my mind off it, so finally I told Lillian that I thought I'd call Etta Mae Wiggins to see how she was doing.

"Maybe she's heard something," I said. "You know, Lillian, I'm really worried about her. She's lost her job, and I doubt she has any savings. She won't let me help her, so I don't know what she's going to do. I would've kept her on here for a few more days, but she wouldn't have it."

"Well, call her up," Lillian said. "See if that lieutenant been after her again."

"I think I will." So I did, and stood there listening to the phone ring and ring with no one answering. "She's not at home. Maybe she's out interviewing somewhere."

"Call her on that cell phone she got," Lillian said. "The number right there on that notepad."

"Oh, of course. I should've thought of that." But that number, too, rang and rang, and finally I had to leave a message. "Well, I don't know what I'm going to do now."

"You think of something, sooner or later," Lillian said. "You always do."

"Well, come to think of it, I just have. I think I'll go visit Francie."

Lillian turned from the sink to stare at me. "What for?"

"I want to see her bedroom—the crime scene, Lillian, and she should be home from the hospital by now. And I want to meet that Evelyn, who seems awfully mysterious to me."

"What you mean 'mysterious'? You think she know something?"

"I don't know. I just know that she's been in the background of all this, and who's ever seen her? I certainly haven't. All I've heard is that she's old and frail, although those two don't always go together, and that she's worked for Francie for a long time and that she knows how to dial nine-one-one, and that's it." I looked around for my pocketbook. "Anyway, it'll give me something to do. I'll be back by lunchtime."

Thinking that it would be better to have an accomplice when visiting Francie, I called LuAnne and asked if she'd go with me.

"Oh, I'd love to," she said. "I want to see where she lives and what she has. If her house is anything like the clothes she wears, it'll be a sight. But I can't, Julia. Leonard has a doctor's appointment—just a checkup—and I have to go with him. You know how he is."

Well, yes, I did, but I knew how LuAnne was, too. She didn't think Leonard could do anything alone, and by this time, he didn't think so, either. So, getting Francie's address from LuAnne, I took myself off to get the lay of the land.

Driving across town toward Francie's cottage, I detoured a little way to pick up a ready-made fruit basket from the grocery store. It's always nice to have something in hand when calling on someone, especially when dropping in with no prior notice, as I was doing.

I slowed the car and crept past the gatehouse at the entrance to the grounds of Mountain Villas, nodding at the gatekeeper, who did not question my passing. Hm-m, I thought, they have a modicum of security, but it looks as if anybody can just cruise on in. Maybe that's the way Francie's attacker gained admittance.

Obeying the fifteen-mile-per-hour speed signs, I followed the twisting road, reading the side-street names as I went along. Finally, seeing Woodchuck Lane, I turned in, passed a couple of small dark-stained cottages with lots of windows and started to pull to the curb at number eight.

At the sight of a certain familiar car in the driveway, I was so aghast that I let the car jump the curb and come to within an inch of hitting a scrawny Japanese maple.

Jumping out of the car, I ran up the walk and rang the doorbell. Sure enough, my worst fear was confirmed when she answered the door.

"Etta Mae!" I cried, taking in her green scrub suit and white walking shoes. "What in the world are you doing here?"

"Oh, Miss Julia," Etta Mae Wiggins said, looking somewhat abashed. "Well, I guess I'm working for Mrs. Delacorte. But come on in. I know she'll want to see you. I just got her settled on the sunporch."

Etta Mae stepped back, holding the door wide for me. I walked inside the small dark hall and just stared at her. "What *are* you doing? Why're you here? Don't you know you ought to keep your distance? What's Lieutenant Peavey going to think?"

"Well, I just didn't know what else to do. She called me last night and begged me to help her out, and I know she's had a hard time and, well, I need the work. It's just till Hazel Marie gets home."

"Lord," I said, my eyes rolling back so far it almost gave me a headache. "Etta Mae, you are too good for your own good. But," I went on, as I considered the situation, "maybe this will work to your benefit. It'll certainly show the lieutenant that Francie's not afraid of you, and I think it'll undercut any accusation she's made. Although I don't know how you can stand it after all she's said about you."

At that point, a querulous voice called, "Who is it? Etta Mae, who's at the door? Where are you?"

Etta Mae gave me a quick grin, took the fruit basket from me and whispered, "I don't know how I stand it, either." Then she motioned me to follow her down the hall, past a living room filled with dark, heavy Italianate furniture, into a sunroom, where Francie was ensconced in an easy chair with her gouty foot elevated on a footstool. Noticing the fancy walking stick leaning against the arm of the chair, I wondered whether it could've been the attack weapon. So handy, you know. And since it had gone to the hospital with Francie, maybe no one had thought to test it. But no, a slender cane wouldn't have caused a large flat injury such as the one Francie had suffered, so I quickly, but reluctantly, discarded that idea.

"Look who's come to visit," Etta Mae said cheerily. "It's Miss Julia Murdoch, and she's brought you some fruit."

"Hello, Francie," I said, eyeing her face for signs of a cosmetic surgeon's knife. "How're you feeling now that you're home?"

"Oh, don't ask," Francie moaned, swinging her head from side to side, drawing my attention to the fact that instead of a bandage, she was now wearing a green and gold turban that hid both hair and whatever wound she had. "You wouldn't believe how uncomfortable the ambulance was. And did you know those nurses didn't even want to call one for me? Said I could ride in a car, but I guess I know what's best for me. Have a seat, Julia, and take my mind off my problems for a little while. Etta Mae," she said without even looking at her, "put that fruit up. I'm not sure I can eat any of it. I have to be so careful of my diet, you know."

Murmuring, "Yes, ma'am," Etta Mae left.

I took a seat across from Francie with my back to the windows where the sun was streaming in. Deciding to jump right in, I said, "Francie, I'll have to say that I'm amazed that you've hired Miss Wiggins again. Didn't you tell Lieutenant Peavey that she's the one who attacked you?"

"Yes, and stole my bracelet, too. But Julia, you wouldn't believe how hard it is to get help these days. And I'm not even talking about *good* help. Just help, period. Besides, I'm perfectly safe as long as Evelyn's here. She won't get away with another crime, believe you me."

"Well, it just seems strange to me, and I'm wondering if you're having second thoughts. It could've been a stranger, because you know that anybody can just drive right through the gate and go anywhere they want."

"No, no, Julia," Francie said, waving her hand. "Don't confuse me. I know what I smelled, and it was her. But see, having her here now, I can watch her, and so can Evelyn. Better the enemy you can see than the one you can't."

Well, that might work for Francie, but I couldn't see that it did anything for Etta Mae. All she was doing was putting herself in a position to be accused of something else, and I determined then and there to get Etta Mae out of the line of fire. I would simply advance the calendar some few months and go ahead and employ her for Hazel Marie's benefit. After all, who knew when those babies would arrive? I certainly didn't. For all I knew, they could be here any day.

Chapter 27

Pursuant to that intention, I said, "Francie, I hope Miss Wiggins has told you that she's already booked for this weekend and for some time to come. Hazel Marie and her new husband will be back, and Hazel Marie is suffering through a high-risk condition. She'll need constant nursing care, and Miss Wiggins has promised to be there for her. They're longtime friends, you know."

"Who's Hazel Marie?"

"Oh, I forgot that you weren't here through all my trials and tribulations. Well, Hazel Marie is a dear friend of mine, and she and her son have been living with me for some time now."

Francie's eyes glinted with a little interest in something outside of herself. "That's the one that Wesley Lloyd Springer kept all those years, isn't it? I always wondered how you put up with it."

Stung, I shot back, "I didn't know about it, that's how I put up with it. But it seems that you knew, so why didn't you tell me?"

"Oh," Francie said, with an airy titter, as if the most hurtful event of my life were of no importance. "I don't interfere in other people's business. I assumed you knew. Everybody else did. But I don't understand why you'd be so concerned about the welfare of a tramp like that."

I could feel the blood pounding in my head, so enraged that I could've taken up that walking cane and whacked her across the head. Holding myself in, I managed to say, "First off, she is not a tramp, and second off, you don't need to understand. At least Hazel Marie hasn't had serial husbands like somebody I could name."

"Oh, Julia," Francie said, her face screwing up to cry, but not quite managing it. "How could you throw that in my face? I have been grieving for ten years, even longer, and you don't know what it's like to lose a husband."

"Well, I certainly do. I lost one myself." Of course, losing Wesley Lloyd had not exactly thrown me into paroxysms of grief. Nor, as far as I could tell, had Francie suffered excessively from her series of losses. Or if she had, she'd certainly found solace quickly enough.

"But," I said, bringing my temper under control, "that's neither here nor there. The thing of it is, Miss Wiggins has promised to work for us, and because I haven't been well myself and, in fact, got out of my sickbed to visit you at the hospital, I can't wait for the weekend. I need her to come on today. And, of course, there's no telling when, or if, she'll be able to come back to you." Right then, I decided that I'd better delay telling Sam anything. If Hazel Marie and Mr. Pickens extended their honeymoon, I would have to prepare myself for another sickly spell this weekend in order to keep Etta Mae at least through Monday evening, when the second enriching session would be held.

"Well, I don't know how I'll get along without her," Francie whined. "I'm not well, Julia, and I need her more than you do. You've got Lillian, so you can manage perfectly well."

"But," I pointed out, "you have Evelyn, so it's not as if you'd be alone. And there's all this assisted-living help you could have if you'd just call on them. That's what this retirement place is for, isn't it?"

By this time, Francie was squeezing out a few tears and searching the pockets of her voluminous robe for Kleenex. "That's what they say," she said, dabbing at her eyes, "but they don't suit me. I hope you'll pray about this, Julia, and find it in your heart to help a poor, lonely woman who can hardly get from one place to the other."

"I will pray about it, Francie, but I can tell you right now that Miss Wiggins will honor her commitment to me and to Hazel Marie. She wouldn't be worth having if she didn't, and I'd be surprised if you'd still want her. So under these circumstances, you'll have to make other arrangements. And no amount of prayer is going to change my mind."

"Well!" Francie said, discarding her Kleenex on the floor and clenching the chair arms with both hands. "I've just never known you to be so snippy and uncaring. I can't believe you, Julia. I thought you were a more considerate person than this. Call Etta Mae in here and we'll just see. Get her in here right now."

My temper flaring again at being given orders, I rose nonetheless and walked to the door leading to the kitchen. Etta Mae was standing by the counter, preparing a luncheon tray. Out of the corner of my eye, I saw the stooped back of another woman, short and thin, with her head swathed in a turban of some kind—one of Francie's castoffs, from the look of it. She was clad in a loose dress of nondescript color.

Evelyn, I assumed, but because she didn't turn from whatever she was doing, I stood at the door and gestured to Etta
Mae. "Mrs. Delacorte wants you."

As Etta Mae came toward me, I whispered, "Follow my
lead. I'm getting you out of here."

Her eyes widened, then they darted over my shoulder as
we heard another of Francie's peremptory commands to come
right there. We crossed the room together and stood before the
queen.

"Etta Mae," Francie said, glaring at her, "I hear that you've
taken another job, and that you're leaving me high and dry. I
guess you know that I'll have to dock your pay for noncompli-
ance if you leave before I'm ready for you to go."

Etta Mae's face went white. "Well, uh, no ma'am. I—"

"Hazel Marie will be home any time now," I quickly spoke
over her. "And you promised to take care of her, remember? You
did, didn't you?"

"Yes'm, I did, and I want to. I just didn't know if she'd still
need me."

"She'll need you, believe me. I'd like you to come on now
and get things ready for her. Francie," I went on, turning to her,
"Hazel Marie is carrying twins, and she's having a bad time of
it. She needs experienced help, which neither Lillian nor I can
give her. I hope you'll reconsider your threat, because . . ." I had
to stop as a white haze of anger descended on me. "Because if
you don't pay Etta Mae what you owe her, she'll go directly to
her attorney of record and sue you up one side and down the
other. Won't you, Etta Mae?"

"Yes'm, I guess." Etta Mae was trembling beside me. She did
not like confrontations, but then neither did I. But sometimes

you have to stand up for what is right, and that's exactly what I was doing.

Unaccustomed as she was to not getting her way, Francie really let the tears begin to flow. "You're ganging up on me, both of you, threatening me with lawsuits and abandonment. I'll pay you, Etta Mae, you know I will. But I just got home from the hospital, and I've suffered great physical and mental trauma, and I need you. Don't leave me, please, don't leave me. I'll pay you whatever you want. Just stay with me."

Obviously affected by Francie's pitiful plea, Etta Mae looked beseechingly at me, then said, "I can probably stay until Hazel Marie gets home, but really, Mrs. Delacorte, I promised my friend to be there for her."

"Well," Francie said, dabbing at her eyes, "I guess I'll have to be grateful for that. But you think about it, and if you decide to stay with me, you won't regret it. Julia, why don't you see if you can find somebody else for your friend? At least she has a husband, so she's not alone and helpless like I am."

I raised my eyes to heaven because Francie Pitts Delacorte was the least helpless person I knew. She knew how to play upon tender hearts, and Etta Mae Wiggins had one of the tenderest. I could see the sympathy wash over Etta Mae's face, and I knew how deeply she felt obligated to her patients. All very commendable, except for the fact that Francie was taking advantage of those very qualities.

Unfortunately, I wasn't immune to Francie's pleas, either. "All right," I said, "let's leave it at this. Etta Mae, if you insist on staying, then so be it. But when Hazel Marie gets home, we're going to hold you to your promise and expect you right away. And Francie, you'll have to do the best you can. I'm sorry about that, but you do have access to help right here at Mountain Villas. Well," I went on, turning away, "I must be going. I hope you continue to feel better. Call me if you need anything."

That last was said out of habit and good manners, not because I meant it. "Etta Mae," I said, walking away before Francie could get in the last word, "walk me to the door, if you don't mind."

With a nervous glance at Francie, who was staring sullenly at us, Etta Mae followed me out of the room and down the hall to the front door.

"Now listen," I said, as Etta Mae reached around me to open the door, "come by my house as soon as you get off. We need to talk about this. And one more thing, do not, I repeat, do not let yourself be out of Francie or Evelyn's sight for even a minute. I don't trust Francie Pitts as far as I can throw her, and she could very well accuse you of something else if you're off by yourself."

"Yes, ma'am, I'm already staying close to either her or Evelyn. And Miss Julia, you know I wouldn't drop Hazel Marie for anything. Mrs. Delacorte didn't tell you, but she already knew I'd have to leave when Hazel Marie gets home, because I told her when she called me."

I shook my head in disbelief. "That woman! Just be careful, Etta Mae. There's no telling what she might do if she doesn't get her way. Why, I think she'd feel perfectly justified to get you in trouble again just to punish you."

"You think?" A deeply worried look creased Etta Mae's face, as she looked down the hall toward the sunroom.

"Yes, and that's why I want you out of here as soon as possible. You're walking a thin line with Lieutenant Peavey already, although Francie's rehiring you ought to make him reconsider a few things. But before I go, where's Francie's bedroom? Do we have time for me to take a quick look?"

"It's right there behind you." Etta Mae pointed to the first door on the right.

I tiptoed over, pushed the door open a little wider and peeked in. It was a front room, the windows looking out over the yard. In the middle stood a stately canopied bed covered in a floral print both above and below. The same floral fabric draped the windows with side panels and elaborately pleated valances. Tables with large porcelain lamps on them flanked the bed, and a dressing table covered with bottles and flasks and jars stood across the room. A deep pile carpet covered the floor.

"Hurry, Miss Julia," Etta Mae whispered. "She pretends she can't get around, but she can."

"I'm through." I turned back to the front door and started out. "I just wanted to see the crime scene. And I wanted to meet Evelyn, too. Where'd she get to?"

"Etta Mae!" Francie's commanding voice pierced the entire house. "What're you doing? Come in here, I need you."

"I got to go," Etta Mae said, worriedly looking over her shoulder.

"I'll see you at my house as soon as you get off," I said, and left before more trouble descended on either of us.

Backing the car off the curb where I'd left it, I drove carefully out of the grounds of Mountain Villas, coming to a stop beside the gatehouse at the exit.

Beckoning to the elderly guard to approach my window, I said, "Nice day, isn't it? I'm wondering, though, if you were on duty last Thursday."

"Well, let me see," he said, his grizzled face screwed up with thought. "I 'spect I was, because I work five days a week an' ain't had a sick day yet."

"Do you keep a record of who comes and goes?"

He grinned, revealing a few places that needed dental help. "No'm, too many in and out for that. The res'dents wouldn't stand being stopped ev'ry time." Then the light dawned on him. "Oh, you're talkin' 'bout that day when that lady got hurt. I don't know nothin' 'bout that. I already been asked by the cops, an' I didn't see nobody that ought not to of been here."

"Thank you, but I hope you'll keep your eye out for strange people. There's no telling who could slip in here and do a great deal of harm."

"Yes, ma'am, but I hear tell they already know who done it. That visitin' nurse is who they aimin' to catch red handed."

I stared at him, stupefied at what he'd said. And suddenly I had a different view of Francie's reason for rehiring that particular visiting nurse. Far from being an advantage to Etta Mae in Lieutenant Peavey's eyes, it could be a setup to trap her. I thanked the gatekeeper again and went on my way, so strung out with the dire possibilities that I could hardly wait to get home where I could do something about them. Would Lieutenant Peavey be that underhanded? Had he asked Francie to rehire Etta Mae just to catch her in the act?

I was gasping for breath as I drove toward home, so anxious was I at the thought of the lieutenant and Francie Pitts in cahoots to railroad Etta Mae on another trumped-up charge.

Chapter 28

I thought of stopping at Binkie's office and enlisting her help, but that would've taken too much time. Instead I went straight home, hurried inside and picked up the telephone without a word of greeting to Lillian, who turned to watch me as I sailed past.

She started to say something, but I held up my hand as I dialed Etta Mae's cell phone number.

"Etta Mae?" I said as soon as she answered. "I just got home, and you won't believe this, but Hazel Marie and Mr. Pickens are sitting here at the table. They're already home."

Lillian's mouth opened, but I frowned fiercely at her. "Yes," I said into the phone, "we need you right away. Hazel Marie's not feeling well, and we're about to call Dr. Hargrove. She may be in trouble again, so you need to come right on over."

After listening for a moment, I went on, "Just tell Francie it's an emergency, because it is."

I hung up, then turned to face the music. "Lillian," I said before she could get started, "you don't know the circumstances, so just listen before you lay into me."

When I told her what was going on, or rather what might have been cooked up between Francie and Lieutenant Peavey, she calmed down considerably, but not happily.

"I still don't see," she said, "why you have to tell such a big story. What you gonna do when Miss Etta Mae get here an' she see nobody else here?"

"My first concern, Lillian," I explained with as much patience as I could muster, "is to get her out of that house. I tried my best while I was there—*before* I knew what was going on—but she's so loyal to her patients, I couldn't budge her. But now that I know what Francie and the lieutenant are up to, well, it's absolutely imperative to get Etta Mae away from their machinations. That's why I had to tell a little story, because Hazel Marie needing her is the only reason she'd leave Francie."

"Well," Lillian said, still unconvinced, "don't look like Miss Etta Mae gonna 'preciate it when she see nobody here but us."

"Oh, but she will when I explain what those two have up their sleeves. They're trying to trick her into committing another crime, and because she didn't commit the first one, although *somebody* did, I wouldn't put it past Francie to make sure that something else goes missing."

Lillian thought for a minute, frowning as she did so. "But it don't look to me like that lieutenant do such a thing. Why, he a Christian man."

"When has that ever stopped anybody? Especially when actions can be justified as working for some good outcome? See, Lillian, I think Lieutenant Peavey is convinced that Etta Mae is guilty, but all he has to prove it is Francie's nose, and that's not good enough. He has to catch her doing something else so he can get a criminal off the street. That's all he's thinking about, but he doesn't know what he's dealing with in Francie Pitts."

"But Miss Etta Mae didn't do nothin' the first time. How they 'spect her to do something again?"

"I guess because Lieutenant Peavey believes Francie and doesn't believe Etta Mae. And it's a fact that something happened to Francie—she has a bandage on her head to prove it—so somebody did something. But the thing of it is, Lillian, is that Francie is not telling the truth. It may be that she *thinks* she is, but she's not. Now I, personally, don't care for Etta Mae's choice of perfume, but there's no way in the world that it smells like collards. And that's all that Francie's basing her identification on. What she's claiming could ruin Etta Mae's whole life. And that," I summed up with some satisfaction, "is the difference between a big story and the little ones I occasionally have to tell."

We both looked up at the sound of brakes screeching to a stop outside. Hearing Etta Mae's footsteps pounding across the paved driveway, I stood up and headed for the door. Lillian beat me to it, swinging it open just as Etta Mae rushed in, breathless and ready to tend to Hazel Marie.

"How is she?" Etta Mae gasped. "What'd the doctor say?"

Lillian aimed a this-is-your-little-red-wagon look at me and gave me the floor. "Well," I started, but didn't get far because Etta Mae went right past me, heading for the bedroom.

"Wait, Etta Mae," I said. "She's not in there. Come sit down and I'll tell you."

Etta Mae turned around and started for the door. "Good, if she's having trouble she needs to be in the hospital. I'll go sit with her."

"No, wait. Wait just a minute, and let me talk to you." I pulled out a chair for her, but she just stared at me.

"Is it already too late?" she asked.

"No, no. Nothing like that. Look, Etta Mae, I can explain. Hazel Marie's not here. She's still on her honeymoon, and as far as I know, she is perfectly fine."

"But . . .?"

"I know, and I apologize. It's just that I had to get you away from Francie, and that was the only way I knew to do it."

"You mean . . .?"

"Yes, and I'm ashamed of myself for doing it, but when you hear my reason, you'll understand."

"Least," Lillian murmured, "you hope she do."

Etta Mae collapsed in the chair and put her hands over her face. "I thought, well, I thought she was in bad trouble. And I left Mrs. Delacorte crying and yelling and threatening me with jail, but Evelyn was there, so I just left. I thought Hazel Marie really needed me."

Lillian glowered at me. "See what you done? You in it now."

Ignoring her, I sat down beside Etta Mae and took her hand. "Let me tell you what the gatekeeper out at Mountain Villas said they were doing to you."

When I finished recounting what I suspected, I added, "It wouldn't surprise me if Francie hadn't intended to trap you in some way, Etta Mae. I mean, a woman who is a suspect in the death of one of her husbands—and who knows what happened to all the others?—is capable of anything. I wanted you safe, here with us, and I knew the only reason you'd leave would be if Hazel Marie needed you. So I'm sorry for scaring you half to death, but we *are* expecting her and Mr. Pickens anytime now."

Etta Mae buried her face in her hands, then looked up at me. "I can't believe anybody could be so mean as to set me up like that, but I guess it's better not to give them a chance. Thank you, Miss Julia. I've never had anybody look after me like you do."

Lillian just shook her head, then walked around the counter into the kitchen area. She opened the oven door and said, "I 'spect a little apple pie go good right about now."

Etta Mae gave her a weak smile. "It sure smells good, but I'd better go on home and make some calls. Bills are piling up and I need to pay Binkie something, so I have to find work somewhere. Maybe as a temp till Hazel Marie gets back."

"You can find work right here, Etta Mae," I said. "I'll be happy to employ you."

She gave me a sad smile. "No'm, thank you anyway, but I can't accept pay when I'm not really needed."

Lillian lifted the steaming pie out of the oven, set it on a rack to cool and carefully folded the dish towel she'd used to handle the hot pan. Then she walked deliberately back around the counter and stood by Etta Mae.

"You needed here, Miss Etta Mae," she said without a glance at me. "I didn't want to say nothin', but Miss Julia, she not doin' too good. She been actin' puny an' run down all week, an' it already put her in the bed for two whole days. I 'spect, if she jus' hol' her tongue and keep Mr. Sam in the dark a little while longer, she gonna be down again come this weekend all the way past Monday, 'cause she might give something to that

Dr. Fowler, an' she don't wanta do that." Lillian looked me straight in the eye. "You don't, do you?"

"Oh, certainly not," I quickly said, realizing that my mouth had been hanging open throughout Lillian's discourse. "So, see, Etta Mae," I went on, recovering, "you have a job, looking after me. And it'll work out perfectly, because you'll be here to pick right up with Hazel Marie whenever they have a mind to come home."

"Well, I don't know," Etta Mae said, giving us both a serious look, wanting to believe she was needed but suspecting this was another setup, one done for her benefit. "I need the work, but frankly, Miss Julia, you don't seem sick to me. At least not sick enough to need a private-duty nurse. It can get expensive, you know."

Before I could reassure her, Lillian said, "Oh, she sick, all right. You jus' don't know her like I do. I already tole Mr. Sam she need lookin' after, an' he hire you if she won't. An' don't worry 'bout what it cost. If she don't have the money, Mr. Sam do, but she got it."

Well, thank you, Lillian, I thought, but was pleased that she had not only arranged a job that Etta Mae could accept, but she'd also provided me with a reason to defer my confession to Sam.

Chapter 29

With that settled, we sent Etta Mae home to pack a few clothes for the live-in position that Lillian had arranged for her. How Mr. Pickens would take to the idea of his wife having a personal nurse around all the time I didn't know and didn't much care. I was having to juggle the needs of too many people as it was without having to worry about his.

Of course, with Etta Mae here to see to Hazel Marie, Mr. Pickens might realize that he'd been released from husbandly duties and decide to take off on another out-of-town job. Hazel Marie wouldn't be happy if he did, nor would Lloyd. But to tell the truth, the house was about to get crowded, so a short respite from Mr. Pickens's ebullient presence might put us all in a better frame of mind.

I brought myself up short, realizing that I was thinking ahead when I needed to concentrate on the here and now. And the here and now was full of Etta Mae's troubles and my own with Dr. Fowler. Or more to the point, with Sam learning about my troubles with Dr. Fowler.

Because I'd made a point to arrange a visit with Sam that afternoon, I knew he'd be expecting me. So, toward the end of the afternoon, I walked the four blocks between our houses, noticing as I went the red leaves of the dogwood trees along the way. They were among the first to turn—harbingers of our beautiful fall colors, although it was hot as blazes on the sidewalk.

I strolled along, wondering what I could talk to Sam about now that Lillian had proposed that I might have to be sick again to justify the renewal of Etta Mae's job. Of course, if Hazel Marie and Mr. Pickens were to come home over the weekend, I wouldn't have to worry about keeping Etta Mae—she'd have her work cut out for her. She'd know that it wasn't simply make-work.

But if they didn't get back, and in order to keep up the pretense to Etta Mae that I was unwell, I might have to have another bout of bed rest—something I wasn't looking forward to. On the other hand, it did offer a reprieve from the confession I'd intended to make to Sam. I wasn't sure that my logic made sense, but if I could keep avoiding Dr. Fowler long enough, even if it meant malingering, Emma Sue might be able to get rid of him.

Then, with him gone for good, I wouldn't have to tell Sam anything. A good wife does not trouble her husband unnecessarily, I assured myself, and felt quite virtuous for it.

So what was I going to tell him today? Here I'd practically made an appointment to talk with him, and I had nothing to say. Well, I could say that I just wanted to go over again what we'd gone over a dozen times already, that is, Etta Mae, Francie Pitts, and Lieutenant Peavey. But I declare, we'd about talked that out. What else was there to say?

Well, he didn't know about the gatekeeper's theory. I could tell him that and string out the possible consequences long enough to make my appointment worthwhile. Except I hadn't known of that nefarious plan when I made the appointment.

Maybe I could discuss Hazel Marie and the new babies with him, but we'd gone over all those ramifications many times before. I couldn't think of anything new or worrisome enough to warrant a special consultation.

My steps were slowing as I got within a block of Sam's house, knowing that he would see right through me if I went in and began to ramble about things we'd already talked to death. Of course, I could tell him that I simply wanted his company, that I missed him during the day, and tell him that I craved time alone with him. Well, except for James, who'd have to be sent somewhere if I used that line.

And, of course, I could simply ask Sam what he felt was missing in our marriage and what I could do to rectify the situation. Without seeking outside help, that is. I'd thought earlier about suggesting we renew our vows, but my word, we'd said them twice already. How many times would it take to satisfy a restless husband?

Then it came to me—*Evelyn*! Of course and absolutely, she needed to be discussed. Who was she? What was her full name? Where did she live? Finding out about her was right up Sam's alley. He knew how to track people, so it was the perfect reason to disrupt his work by paying a visit to his office. My steps picked up considerably now that I had a purpose and a perfectly legitimate reason to consult with him.

This time, I strode across Sam's broad front porch, intent on walking right inside. He was expecting me, so there was no need to ring the doorbell and wait to be admitted, even though I generally hesitated to barge in. So I reached for the screen door to open it and found it latched on the inside.

Tapping my foot impatiently, I rang the doorbell, then

heard James yelling from down the hall. "Hol' your horses. I'm comin'."

"Why, Miss Julia," he said, smiling broadly as he unlatched the door and held it open for me. "I didn't know we have the pleasure of your comp'ny today. How you doin'?"

"I'm fine," I answered, "and hope you are, too. Sam's expecting me, though I'm surprised he didn't apprise you beforehand of my intended visit. And James, yelling down the hall to hold your horses is no way to greet guests." For some reason, James brought out the worst in me, but he hadn't seen it all yet.

I went right on setting him straight. "I want you to get out here and look at these windows. With the sun shining on them, you can see a dusty glaze on every one of them. They all need a good washing, so get a ladder and everything else you'll need and start on the north side."

James's smile fell away. "Right now?"

"Yes. Put your hand to the plow and get to it. A task put off is a task undone."

"But Miss Julia, I washed them windows back in the spring, an' I don't never wash 'em but oncet a year."

"This year's different. We've had a dry and dusty summer."

Before I could further encourage him, Sam opened his office door and looked out into the hall. "Sorry, I was on the phone. How are you, sweetheart? Come on in here. I've been waiting for you."

"Be careful on the ladder, James," I said. "I'll come and check your work before I leave." Then, walking toward Sam, I felt my heart lift at his welcoming smile.

We went into the large front room that now served as his office, and Sam closed the door behind us. "What was that all about?" he asked.

"Oh, just putting James to work washing windows. He gets away with murder around here, Sam. Idle hands and all that, you know."

Sam laughed. "I know, but he keeps things halfway decent. Now, come sit down and tell me what's on your mind. You're feeling all right?"

We sat together on the leather sofa as it crossed my mind that this was the time and place that I'd planned to make my confession and throw myself on his mercy. Thank goodness, I no longer had to do that.

"I'm fine. But let me just catch you up with the morning's developments first. I went out to Francie's cottage at Mountain Villas because she came home from the hospital this morning. Now, don't frown at me, Sam. I wanted to see how she was and also see if she'd changed her story again. And I wanted to see the crime scene, too."

"Well, that's interesting," Sam said, "because I saw her, too, a little while ago. I'd just come out of the Skytop Hotel, where we'd had the Rotary meeting, and heard somebody calling, 'Yoo-hoo, Sam! Sam Murdoch, is that you?' I looked around, and there she was, sitting in the passenger seat of one of those old long Cadillacs. I walked over and spoke, and she told me she was waiting for her companion to pick up some things at the dry cleaner's. Then she went into this long account of her troubles, but she didn't say a word about your visit. Just that she'd heard that you'd been ill and she hoped I was managing all right because she knew how disheartening it was to have a sick spouse."

"I guess she does!" I said, infuriated that Francie had been discussing me with Sam. "She's had enough of them. But I'm surprised she was out and about. She sure acted helpless enough this morning. But you won't believe who she'd hired—Etta Mae! I tell you, Sam, it shook me to see her there and to learn that Francie had practically begged her to come to work for her. And at first I thought it was a good thing. I mean, surely, rehiring the very one she's accused of attacking her would undermine the accusation she's made, wouldn't it?"

Sam nodded. "I'd think it'd tear a few holes in it."

"That's what I thought, although I did try to get Etta Mae to leave, reminding her that she'd promised to look after Hazel Marie. Well, anyway, we left it that Etta Mae would work on until Hazel Marie gets home, but you won't believe what I learned from the gatekeeper as I was leaving."

"What?"

So I told him. "Now, it looks to me, Sam, as if there's mischief afoot, and it's all been cooked up between Francie and Lieutenant Peavey."

"Well, I don't know, Julia. That could be seen as entrapment, and I don't believe Peavey would be involved in something like that. But I do think it'd be better if Etta Mae steered clear of Francie until this is settled. Let's encourage her to find another job."

Quickly gathering myself to switch subjects before I let on about how I'd gotten Etta Mae out of Francie's clutches, I said, "Oh, I agree, and I'm working on it. But listen, I've thought of something that we've all let slide. I think we ought to look into this Evelyn person. That's what I really wanted to talk to you about, because it came to me sometime in the night that she's the mystery person in all this. Who is she? Where is she from? And all that. So I want to know if you can find out about her."

Sam looked a little skeptical, but he said, "I guess I could try, but I'm sure the lieutenant has that information already."

"I expect he does, so it's even more important that we have it, too." I sat up and turned sideways to look at him. "You and Binkie could work together on it. She needs to know every-thing about everybody involved in that alleged attack. If it comes down to a criminal case, Sam . . . I mean, if Etta Mae's formally charged, if that's what you call it, then Binkie ought to have every smidgen of information she can get."

Not getting the enthusiasm I'd hoped for, I went on. "Look, Sam, at this point, there're only three people we *know* about who're involved: Etta Mae, Francie and this Evelyn. Now, even though I think it was somebody we *don't* know—anybody can go in and out that gate—nonetheless, those three are all we have to work with. We know that Etta Mae is innocent, so that leaves the other two. Frankly, if there hadn't been some kind of trauma to Francie's head, I'd suspect there'd been no attack at all. But it was enough to keep her in the hospital for four days, so something happened. That leaves Evelyn, and we don't know a thing about her."

"Well, there's always the possibility that Francie simply fell when nobody was there, hit her head hard enough to knock her out and just assumed it was an attack. Have you thought about that?"

That stopped me, because, like the lieutenant, I'd simply taken her word for it, especially because Francie had added a few flourishes, like hearing somebody clinking the bottles and jars on her dressing table and emitting a foul odor that lingered in her mind long enough to be associated with a helping of collards.

"Why," I said, in some wonder that I'd not given credence to that possibility before, "it could've happened that way, couldn't it? And as I've always said, Francie has a way of dramatizing everything that happens to her. And being brutally accosted in her own home, robbed and strangled—of which, I remind you, there was no evidence—certainly makes a better story than tripping over your own feet and knocking yourself out. And, of course, she does have that gouty toe, so it makes sense that she wouldn't be steady on her feet."

"I think we've solved it, Julia. That's probably what happened, and absent any further evidence than Francie's sense of smell, Lieutenant Peavey will think so, too."

"I hope you're right," I said, but not sure he was. "Just in case, though, will you look into Evelyn? For my own peace of mind if nothing else?"

"Sure, I can do that. I'll talk to Binkie and see what she already has, then ask around a little."

"Oh, thank you, Sam. Now," I said, getting to my feet, "I better check on James, then I need to get on home."

Sam stood up, too, then put his arm around me. "Is that all you wanted to talk about? Isn't there something else you want to tell me?"

"Well, my goodness," I said, forcing a smile while fear coursed through me that he'd guessed—or worse, *known*—my original intention. "I've said an awful lot. Wasn't it enough?"

"I thought you might've made a special trip over here to tell me you love me."

I laughed then, in great relief. "I do love you, Sam Murdoch, more than you know." And that was the honest truth, if I'd ever told it.

Chapter 30

"Oh, by the way," I said, turning back to Sam as we walked out onto the porch, "Hazel Marie and Mr. Pickens will be home any time now, so I've asked Etta Mae to come on over so she'll be here when they get back."

Sam smiled indulgently. "You're still looking after Etta Mae, aren't you?"

"I guess I am, but really, Sam, Hazel Marie may need more help than we can give her."

"I'm hoping she won't need a professional nurse."

"Well, I am, too," I said, "but Etta Mae's not exactly a nurse. She's more of a helping hand, a companion, you might say. I'm really concerned that Hazel Marie will start doing too much and get in trouble again. And because Etta Mae desperately needs a job, Lillian and I thought this would be a good way to put her to work and keep an eye on Hazel Marie at the same time. It'll only be until this thing with Francie is settled and she can get her old job back.

"And Sam," I went on, avoiding his eyes as I lingered in the shade of the porch before heading home, "I don't want to worry you, but the other night at Mildred's—right when Dr. Fowler was talking—I had a bad turn. I thought I was going to be sick, but I never got sick, just a sickly kind of feeling. It may have been some leftover symptoms from the bug I had the first of the week. And actually, Emma Sue had a little spell, too. We were both down with whatever it was at the same time, you know. So anyway, that's another reason I asked Etta Mae to stay over."

"I'm worried about you, Julia, and so is Lillian. She kind of hinted around that you've not been yourself lately. I wish you'd go on and see Dr. Hargrove."

"I'm going to. It's time for my annual checkup, anyway, which Lillian's been reminding me of. I'll make an appointment for, maybe, Tuesday." That was in case I had to be ill Monday night.

Sam took my arm, saying sternly, "See that you do. And if you don't, I'm going to put you in the car and take you myself."

James suddenly popped his head around the corner of the house, calling out, "I'll take her, Mr. Sam, anytime you want me to."

Sam started laughing as I murmured, "Oh, for goodness' sakes." Then, in a louder voice, I said, "James, pay attention to what you're doing. You fall off that ladder, and it won't be me who's going to the doctor."

I turned back to Sam. "Now everybody in town's going to think I'm on my last legs. Make him keep on with the windows, Sam. Well, I better get on back in case Hazel Marie calls. She usually does about the time Lloyd gets home from school. Will you be coming soon?"

"Not too much longer. I still have a few things to wrap up.

But listen," Sam said, thinking of something else, "you never did tell me how it went at Mildred's last night. What did you think of Dr. Fowler?"

"Oh, don't ask," I said, waving my hand as if the man were of no consequence. "He talked about the most inappropriate things, although Emma Sue kept whispering to me so much that I couldn't hear half of them. But I'll tell you, Sam, she is up in arms about him and his enriching sessions—now that she knows what *enriching* means. She wants the pastor to close him down, but on the other hand, she's fascinated with what he's teaching." I smiled at him like a conspirator. "She got Helen Stroud to buy his books for her because she doesn't want anybody to know she has them."

Sam smiled, too. "Emma Sue's a caution, isn't she? But if she's so interested, why does she want to stop the sessions?"

"Because the church is not the place for such talk, and I'm inclined to agree with her. The things he said, Sam, you wouldn't believe. And what he recommended! My word, the man is out of his mind. I didn't tell you, but Emma Sue and I left before he finished. It was just too much."

Sam laughed. "If that's the case, I can't wait till Monday. He didn't get into details with us, so I have something to look forward to."

"Oh, you," I said, trying to make light of what was heavy on my heart. "And if he does, you just keep in mind where you are: in the Lord's house, listening to the most graphic and infelicitous discourse on his ideas of what a marriage should entail. *And,*" I said, drawing myself up in indignation, "he doesn't even know what he's talking about because he's not married himself."

"Well," Sam said, putting his arm around me, "maybe that's why we ought to be there. To straighten him out, because we know all about it. Don't we, sweetheart?"

"Shh, Sam," I cautioned, unable to keep from smiling, "James'll hear you."

Sam laughed. "Maybe we'll teach James something, too. Anyway, we'll go together Monday night and find out whether Dr. Fred can tell us one thing we don't already know."

"We'll see." I turned away and started down the steps. "Don't work too late. Hazel Marie and Mr. Pickens may be coming in, and, of course, Etta Mae'll be there."

That evening at the dinner table, there were only Sam, Lloyd, Etta Mae and myself. Hazel Marie had called earlier in the afternoon and, as I had expected, said they would stay at the Grove Park Inn until Sunday. I didn't blame them. Why come home on a Friday when you could have the weekend for another massage or two?

Etta Mae was noticeably subdued and anxious now that she'd committed herself to staying with us to look after a patient who was off gallivanting around. She'd had time to think about Lillian's claim that I needed looking after, and she wasn't buying it. At least not totally.

When she'd come in that afternoon and gotten her bag unpacked in the sunroom, she'd tried to fulfill her duties by suggesting I lie down and take a nap.

"You need to rest, Miss Julia," she'd said. "You're probably just run down and a little anemic. I'll ask Lillian if she'll fix you some calf's liver for supper."

"Don't you dare," I told her. "I don't need a special diet, and certainly not calf's liver. Look, Etta Mae, there's nothing wrong with me except that I have these little spells now and then. So when I have one, you can jump in and prescribe all you want to." I was walking one of those fine lines again, juggling Etta Mae's need for a justifiable salary, Lillian's claim that I was puny, Sam's expectation that I'd be going to an enriching session or to a doctor and my determination not to do either one without telling him why.

Lillian had just come in to clear the table before serving dessert, and Etta Mae slid out of her chair to help her.

"I'll do it," Lloyd said, jumping up with his own plate in hand. "You sit down, Etta Mae. Miss Julia doesn't want guests to do anything."

"Well," Etta Mae said, hesitating, "I don't mind helping. I could scrape the plates and stack them. Wash 'em, too, if Miss Lillian wants me to."

"Both of you set back down," Lillian commanded. "I don't need no help, nor want it neither. You jus' get in my way, though I thank you for the offer."

They sat, with Lloyd grinning and Etta Mae looking chastened for committing what might have been a social blunder.

"Don't worry, Etta Mae," Lloyd said, leaning toward her and cutting his teasing eyes at Lillian. "She'll put us to work sooner or later. She'll work our fingers to the bone."

Lillian laughed as she picked up Sam's plate. "I see them bony fingers where you been workin'."

Sam leaned back in his chair, smiling at the byplay. Then he sobered somewhat and said, "While we're all here, I have something to say and I want you all to listen good." He turned a serious look in my direction, then glanced at the others. "As you know, Julia wasn't well earlier this week, and ever since she's been having these little episodes. I'm worried about her, and I want us all to keep an eye on her."

"Sam—" I started but stopped as he held up his hand.

"That's why I'm here," Etta Mae said, looking a little sprightlier as an immediate need for her services was confirmed. "Lillian's worried about her, too. I'll watch her, Mr. Sam, and keep on doing it even when Hazel Marie gets home."

"Good," Sam said, laying his hand on my mine and looking me in the eye. "Now, Julia, you keep putting off seeing the doctor, but that has to stop. I'm making an appointment for you the first of the week. But the next little twinge you have, you are going right then. I don't care if it's the middle of the night, and I have to take you to the emergency room. We are going to find out what's wrong." He squeezed my hand, then looked around at the others. "I'm putting you all on notice. Keep your eye on her, and let me know anything that happens."

They all nodded, their faces sober and serious, taking to heart everything he'd said—even Lillian, who was the one who'd started it in the first place.

Then Lillian had the nerve to glare at me as if she'd had nothing to do with worrying him to death. "You hear what he sayin', don't you?"

I was the one who nodded this time, for what could I say? Either I was sick or I wasn't. If I wasn't, I'd be going to Dr. Fowler's class, and if I was, I'd be going to Dr. Hargrove's office. One would immediately recognize me as the woman on the green velvet love seat, and the other would have me on an examining table without a stitch of clothes on.

Chapter 31

Saturday morning, and another beautiful fall day as the sun turned the yellow leaves of the trees to gold. If I'd been into walking, I'd have gotten' out and enjoyed it. That's what Etta Mae was doing, only running instead of walking. But before she'd left on her run, she'd insisted that I sit still to have my vital signs checked.

"We're going to do this every morning and evening," she said as she wrapped a blood pressure cuff around my arm. "And I'll keep a record of it so we can chart your progress. Your doctor will be able to see, for instance, if your temp goes up in the afternoon. That could be the case, you know."

Then she'd gotten bossy enough to tell Lillian what I should eat and shouldn't eat. And to add insult to injury, she'd asked me questions about my constitutionals. And wrote it all down! It was a great relief to see her put on her running shoes and leave the house.

So, while hoping that Hazel Marie would soon be home and divert Etta Mae's attention from me, I sat with Lillian at the kitchen table and talked with her. She'd come in for a little while, even though it was a Saturday and I'd told her she didn't need to.

"I got to change them sheets on Miz Pickens's bed," Lillian said, "then I go on back home."

"Why, Lillian, you just changed them when they left, and nobody's been in the bed since."

"Yes'm, but that bed been layin' there gettin' all musty smellin'. If they comin' home tomorrow, they need clean sheets. 'Sides, Latisha wanted to come see Lloyd, an' it easier to come to work than play playhouse with her all day."

I laughed. "Well, she's well entertained now, with Sam taking both of them to the boat show. I just hope they don't come home with one of those noisy motorboats."

"No'm, Mr. Sam won't do that. Maybe one of them trollin' boats, though, for when he fish."

"It's a good thing he kept his house, then. He can just park it over there. I declare, Lillian, what with my car and Sam's car and Hazel Marie's and yours, and now Etta Mae's, where're we going to put Mr. Pickens's?"

She'd gotten up to head for Hazel Marie's bedroom, but on her way out of the kitchen, she turned around. "I hate to say this, but I 'spect we don't have to worry much about that. Mr. Pickens liable to be gone most of the time on one of his 'vestigatin' jobs. An' Miss Hazel Marie not gonna be too happy 'bout that."

"I know, and it worries me, too. Still, the man has to make a living. Just think of all the mouths he'll have to feed."

She laughed and went on to the linen closet to select the sheets she wanted. And just as the door swung to behind her, the telephone rang.

"Julia? Is that you?" Emma Sue Ledbetter asked, as if she'd expected somebody else to answer.

"Yes, Emma Sue. How are you?"

"Much, much better, I'm happy to say. I just had to tell you that I've done what we agreed had to be done."

My heart lifted. "You got rid of Dr. Fowler."

"I certainly did. When I told Larry what that man talked about at Mildred's the other night, he was just as outraged as you and I were. See, Larry thought he was going to teach that passage in Ephesians—you know, the one about the husband being the head of the household and the wife being submissive to him. He didn't know Dr. Fowler was going to get into the *specifics* of submission. So he agreed that such things shouldn't be discussed in a church setting. Anyway," Emma Sue said, after stopping to take a breath, "he prayed and prayed about it, because there're lots and lots of couples in our church who need to hear these things. I tell you, Julia, you wouldn't believe who they are, but, of course, Larry doesn't confide in me— pastoral confidentiality and all that. But I'm not dense. When somebody keeps calling him here at home at all hours of the night, crying and sobbing, needing to talk to him, well, I can put two and two together. And Julia, the two biggest problems in any marriage are money and, well, you-know-what." Emma Sue couldn't bring herself to say the word.

"In-laws?" I asked innocently.

"No, Julia, not in-laws and not children, either. Dr. Fowler's subject, the thing we've been talking about. Do I have to spell it out for you?"

"No," I said, almost laughing. "I was just teasing you."

But Emma Sue didn't take too well to teasing, so she ignored me.

"Anyway," she said with a patient sigh, "there's so much about it on television and in the movies these days. I mean, it's just glamorized and glorified everywhere, and Larry says that modern couples have this idea that everybody knows more about it than they do, so they're eager to hear what they're missing out on, which is exactly what these sessions supply. So Larry and I are of one mind. In spite of Dr. Fowler's subject matter and the graphic way he teaches it—Julia, you ought to see his books—we think there're plenty of people who need to hear it, and hear it from a Christ-centered point of view. Just not in the church."

"How're you going to manage that?"

"Why, they're just going to meet somewhere else. Larry's decided to ask Mildred if she'll let them meet at her house every Monday evening. She has that huge drawing room, you know, and Larry thinks with the spurt of interest that's come about, we'll fill it up."

"Well, that seems a good solution, and Mildred is known for opening her home for worthy causes." Actually, which I didn't mention, that solution could work out well for me. Sam might not feel as obligated to go, because the classes would no longer be under the auspices of the church.

"But I tell you, Emma Sue," I went on, "I was hoping we'd seen the last of Dr. Fowler. He just doesn't appeal to me at all."

"To me, either, but I admit that he has some fascinating things to say, I mean, to read, because I'm not going to those meetings, regardless of where they have them. I told Larry that it wouldn't do to have everybody in the church wondering about the state of our marriage, and I'd just study those books and follow the instructions. I figure that I can stoke the marital embers just as well as somebody who hears it in person."

"I wish I had your excuse," I said, thinking for the first time ever that there might be some benefits in being a minister's wife. "Sam never worries about what people think of him. He'd just laugh if anybody wondered about our marriage and say it was none of their business."

"Well, we can't do that. There are twelve hundred church members who make everything we do their business."

"I know, Emma Sue, and it's a shame. I don't know how you stand it sometimes."

"I just try to do the Lord's work, Julia. That's the only thing that gets me through. And speaking of the Lord's work, do you know where Francie Pitts lives?"

"Francie? Why, yes, she lives on Woodchuck Lane out at Mountain Villas—number eight, I think. Why? Are you going to visit her?"

"I thought I would. She's had a hard time, I understand, and she was a member of our church at one time. After losing so many husbands and getting attacked the way she did, she may be ready to return to the fold. Monday's my day to visit newcomers anyway, so I thought I'd drop by. Of course, she's not exactly new, and she hasn't exactly come to church recently, but she's just gotten out of the hospital, so I think she qualifies for a visit."

"I expect she does," I said, but hesitated as I wondered how to warn Emma Sue about Francie's propensity to cast blame where none should be, namely, at Etta Mae Wiggins. "But let me caution you, Emma Sue. Francie may still be suffering the ill effects of that attack. I know for a fact that she's thrown around some wild accusations that the evidence does not bear out. So be careful about believing everything she says."

"Oh?" Emma Sue's interest perked up. "What's she saying?"

"It doesn't bear repeating, although you'll probably hear it. Just take whatever she says with a grain of salt."

"You know I will, Julia. We must all properly discern the word of truth. And since I do pastoral work, too, I take confidentiality seriously. Well," she said in a wrapping-it-up tone, "I must get busy and get some things done. Oh, and Julia, I'm going to look through Dr. Fowler's books one more time, then I'll pass them on to you. But I want them back. I might need them for future reference."

"Has the pastor read them?"

"Well, he sorta skimmed them until he got to the illustrations, which is when he decided they weren't appropriate for the church." Emma Sue paused, then went on. "Julia, if you'll take it in the right way, I'd like to ask a favor of you."

"I'll do whatever I can, except visit Francie with you. What is it?"

"No, it's not that. It's, well, I hope you won't be offended, but I wish you'd stop referring to Larry as the pastor and calling him Pastor Ledbetter."

"Well, my goodness, Emma Sue. I'm showing respect for him, because I can't call him Larry. That's too familiar and presumptuous on my part." Besides, which I didn't say, he had never corrected my use of his title in all the years he'd been our pastor. It seemed to me that if he wanted the church members to be on more familiar terms with him, he'd have said some-thing. "But," I went on, "I wouldn't want to offend either of you. So what should I call him?"

"It would really help me if you could bring yourself to call him just Larry, at least when you're talking about him to me. You see, Julia. Oh, this is so embarrassing, but Dr. Fowler's book has opened my eyes to some of the things that reduce a woman's, well, I guess you'd call it willingness. And as soon as I read that, I realized that one of the things that really puts me off is knowing that I'm in bed with, quote quote, *the pastor.*"

I was shocked that Emma Sue would evoke such a graphic image in my mind. But she did, and she was right. Being in bed with the pastor would certainly put *me* off. But then, so would being in bed with just Larry.

But I said, "I'll do my best, Emma Sue. It's an ingrained habit, though, so I may slip up now and then. Just overlook it if I do."

When we hung up, I stood by the phone a minute, wonder-ing if it would work. If Emma Sue could think of her husband as just a man named Larry, and not as the dignified pastor of a Presbyterian church, would her embers be more likely to burst into flame every time he took his pants off?

I didn't like thinking of either possibility and wished she'd never brought it up. As far as I could see, there wouldn't be a nickel's worth of difference between his two personas, but for me, thank goodness, there didn't have to be.

Chapter 32

"Lillian," I said, as she pushed through the swinging door and came back into the kitchen. I was still bemused by Emma Sue's revelation of the difficulty of being in bed with her pastor. "Lillian," I said again, "have you ever thought of your pastor as a regular man? I mean, like he's a husband?"

"No'm, not mine."

"Oh, I'm not talking about your pastor in particular. I'm just wondering about men of the cloth in general. I'd think it'd be a little disconcerting to be married to a man who puts on a pastoral robe and stands up in a pulpit to deliver the word of God, and then go home with him and, you know, be his wife."

She studied me a minute. "I tell you the truth, Miss Julia. It never cross my mind, 'cept for oncet a long time ago when we had this young preacher come for the summer. I thought about him takin' off that robe all summer long."

I laughed. "Well, you were young then. But I was just thinking it would be hard for a pastor's wife to switch back and forth. You know, from being a member of the flock, so to speak, to being, well, let's say, an equal partner at home."

"I figure they not so equal," Lillian said in a way that made me realize that she had thought about it. "I figure a big man in church be a big man at home, an' his wife be a little mouse in both. But Miss Julia, if it worryin' you, jus' look at the Reverend Morris Abernathy at our church. He don't do his switchin' at home, he do it in the pulpit. He give out the word of the Lord strong and sure up there, but oncet he come down, he jus' a sweet little ole pussycat. Everybody love him to death, includin' Miz Abernathy, and that say a lot for a man, whether he a preacher or not."

Lillian wasn't entirely following my line of thought, but I couldn't bring myself to be more explicit. I agreed that the Reverend Mr. Abernathy was an exceptional person, which he assuredly was, and let it go at that.

⟋

Later that afternoon, after Sam and the children got home from the boat show—without a boat in tow, I'm relieved to say—he took my hand and led me out to the back garden. Etta Mae was occupied with making lists of all the baby things that Hazel Marie would need, from cribs to Handi Wipes, and I was happy that she had something to do besides study me for stray symptoms.

"Won't be long now," Sam said, looking up at the trees that edged the yard. "We'll be out here raking our heads off."

"I'm not looking forward to that," I said. "I hate to see the leaves fall. Not because of the raking, but because it means winter's not far behind. Another year, Sam."

"Yes, a good year passing with another good one on the way." He took my arm and edged me toward a garden bench beneath the arbor. "Let's sit awhile. We don't get many chances to be alone."

I smiled as we both swept a few leaves off the bench and

sat down. "I know, and it'll be harder when the new couple gets back."

"True," Sam nodded, putting his elbows on his knees and leaning forward to survey the yard. "We'll just have to make time for us. I don't want us to grow apart with all the demands on our time."

"Me either. We may have to make dates to meet out here in the yard just to get away."

"That's a good idea," Sam said, straightening up and putting an arm along the back of the bench. "If it gets too hectic, you can come over to my house and have lunch. James can fix something and we'll have that time together."

"That sounds good, and it'll give James something to do. Of course, we'll have to eat in your office with the door closed or James'll add his two cents' worth about everything we say."

We laughed, then sat in companionable silence as we watched a few leaves float down around us.

"By the way," Sam said, "we saw Ledbetter at the boat show this morning, and he's had second thoughts about Dr. Fred."

"Yes," I said, carefully. "Emma Sue mentioned something about that. She was up in arms about the church's sponsoring him, and when she showed his books to the pastor, well, I think that about did it."

"I guess she got to him then, or the books did. He told me that upon consideration, he felt that the subject matter could be viewed as inappropriate in a church setting. I got the feeling that he'd been on the verge of canceling the whole thing, but after Dr. Fred spoke to the women at Mildred's the other night, there's been an outpouring of interest. His office phone has rung off the hook with people wanting to attend."

"My goodness. You'd think that because they'd missed the introductory session, they'd be too far behind to show up for the second one." At least, using that excuse had been my plan.

"No, not at all. In fact, Ledbetter said Dr. Fowler is thrilled that so many want to come." Sam smiled wryly. "It might be that the church is paying him by the head."

"Oh, surely not." I smiled, content to discuss Dr. Fred Fowler without the fear of meeting him. "Emma Sue said something about moving the sessions out of the church, which, if they're not going to cancel them entirely, seems more appropriate to me. By having them in a private home, people won't feel an obligation to support the church. They'll only go if they want to."

Sam nodded in agreement. "That's the hope, anyway. He's already spoken to Mildred about having them because she has that large room. But," Sam said, flicking a yellow leaf off his shoulder, "she and Tonya are going to Atlanta to shop for a few days. I told him I'd check with you, but we could probably have the meeting this Monday. Is that all right? It'd just be the one Monday. Mildred will take them after that."

I felt my face drain of color. Have Dr. Fred here? Where I couldn't avoid him or hide from him? Lord, I thought, strike me down right now.

Then, mentally shaking myself and licking my lips to be able to speak, I said, "Of course it will. It's your house, too, and you can invite anybody you want to." Including, I thought, the last man on earth I want to see. "You know, though," I went on, choosing my words with care, "we'll have a full house already. The Pickenses will be here and Etta Mae, too."

"That's right, and it's the main reason I made the offer. Etta Mae's had her problems with marriage, to say nothing of Pickens and his several stabs at it. We talked about how beneficial the sessions would be for him and Hazel Marie, remember?"

Beneficial for them, but not for me—and not for Sam, either, if he but knew it. But I nodded in agreement, a mental picture of stirrups on an examining table waiting for me. There was nothing for it but to resign myself to facing either Dr. Hargrove or Dr. Fowler, and at that point I didn't know which was the worst.

We'd barely gotten back inside when the phone rang, and it was Emma Sue again.

"Julia," she said, sounding excited, "I know I'm worrying you to death, but I just had to tell you. Larry told me about seeing Sam at the boat show and how kind he was about offering your house for Monday night. I'm so glad, because I want you to tell me all about it. I mean, you could take notes again so I'll know what he says without having to be there."

"Well, I don't know—" I started, but she had the bit in her teeth.

"But that's not all. Guess who may be there, too."

"Who?"

"Francie Pitts, would you believe?"

"*No!* Why would she come? She's not even married, although who knows? She could've found another one in the last couple of days."

"Now, Julia," Emma Sue said, "that's not very nice of you. She's more to be pitied than censured, and we should all extend the hand of fellowship to her."

I just hated it when Emma Sue took a lecturing tone with me. As many times as she'd cried on my shoulder and begged for my advice, you'd think she'd stop doing it.

"Anyway," Emma Sue went on, "what I really wanted to tell

you is that when Larry and Sam were talking at the boat show, Sam mentioned that he'd seen Francie downtown. And immediately, the Lord laid her on Larry's heart, and you know how he gets when the Lord does that. I mean, when the Lord gets ahold of him, that man doesn't sit around. He *acts*! He went straight to the B and B where Dr. Fowler's staying, and they got down on their knees together so they'd know what to do. And you know what they did?"

"I have no idea, Emma Sue, and I'm almost afraid to ask."

"Why, they went right over there to see her—both of them. Well, of course, they called first, and she was so grateful. Just pathetically grateful, Larry said. She told him that nobody at all had had the kindness to visit, and—"

"Wait just one minute. *I* went to see her! Doesn't that count? I declare, Emma Sue, the woman wouldn't know the truth from a hole in the ground."

"Well, I'm just telling you what she told Larry. She said she was all alone without a friend in the world."

"And that's about the first truthful thing she's said."

"Now, Julia," Emma Sue said. "You might've had some problems with her, but you should learn to put them aside. She has suffered terribly, you know, physically and emotionally."

I couldn't help it. My eyes rolled back in my head.

"So," I said, bearing up as best as I could, "how did the pastor's, I mean Larry and Fred's, visit go?"

"Oh, Julia, you shouldn't call Dr. Fowler by *his* first name. You don't know him that well."

I was getting tired of all the admonishments Emma Sue was ladling out. Besides, she was unaware of just how well I did know Fred Fowler.

"I stand corrected, Emma Sue," I said, a trifle tartly. "You'll have to forgive me. I got carried away trying to remember who rates a title and who doesn't. But tell me about their visit."

"I can't. They're not back yet. They must've found loads to talk about and, of course, they'll spend some time in prayer with her. I expect the poor thing's lonely. But Julia," she cautioned, "even when they get back, I can't tell you what was said. Pastoral—"

"Confidentiality. Yes, I know. But is she really planning to come here Monday night?"

"Oh, I think that was the whole purpose of their visit. Naturally, Larry told Dr. Fred about her marital history, and he said that Dr. Fred said he'd never heard of any woman who needed his lessons more than she does. So he's real anxious to meet her and try to guide her to either choose healthier husbands or to be content in whatsoever single condition she's in. As he says he is." Emma Sue stopped to take a breath, which she needed. "Oh, Julia, wouldn't it be wonderful if Dr. Fowler—and remember, it was *Larry* who brought him here—could lift that poor soul out of her misery and reach her for the Lord? Dr. Fowler could teach her so much."

I wasn't too sure of that. In fact, I wondered if Francie couldn't teach him a thing or two, especially because he'd apparently had such poor personal luck with women, seeing that he'd lived a lifetime without a wife. But recalling what Sam had said was probably Francie's secret weapon in attracting husbands, all I could think was Lord help us all. Put those two together with their combined store of erotic knowledge, and there was no telling what kind of combustible material would flare up.

Chapter 33

After hanging up the phone, I stood there fuming over Francie Pitts's putting on the poor-little-me act during a pastoral visit. Then I began stewing because I'd gotten trapped into having both her and Dr. Fred as guests in my home. And if I hadn't watched myself, I could've turned my wrath against Sam for putting me in the position of hosting them, especially Dr. Fred. But being the clear-eyed woman I am, I had to shake my head and give a rueful laugh, for I'd been the one who'd put myself in that position the day I lost my head in the bridal parlor.

But it wasn't funny, and I didn't know what to do about it. I didn't want either one of them in my house or anywhere around me. What I did want was for Francie to go back to Florida and Dr. Fred to go back to his mother.

There was only one thing to do, and my shoulders began to slump as I realized it. I had to confess to Sam, with no fooling around this time. Then, even if he pulled away from me, at least he'd know why I couldn't bring myself to face that hypocrite of a Christian psychologist. And he'd know why I couldn't sit and listen to the man's high moral lectures on Christian marriage when I knew without a doubt that he had, with malice aforethought, led me on to make a fool of myself.

I left the kitchen and headed for the living room, where Sam was watching a ball game on television. Lingering in the dining room, I could hear Lloyd and Etta Mae playing some kind of video game upstairs. I glanced at the dining room table that Lillian had set for supper before she and Latisha left. She'd put a pot roast with vegetables in the oven, telling me it'd be ready when we were.

The house was filled with the aroma from the oven, but I doubted I'd be able to eat any of it after baring my soul to Sam, and his stomach would probably be so turned that he'd be unable to eat either. So, I sighed, Etta Mae and Lloyd would enjoy it, and there'd be enough left over for Sunday.

The voices of Lloyd and Etta Mae drifted downstairs as they laughed and talked, having a good time together. I declare, there was something pleasantly childlike about Etta Mae, the way she could lose herself in the moment, whatever that moment happened to contain.

I was stalling, lingering there in the dining room as I worked up enough courage to face Sam. I knew I was putting off the inevitable, yet I went around the table, aligning knives with forks and centering plates on the place mats. Maybe Sam was engrossed in the ball game, maybe this wasn't a good time to disturb him and maybe I was looking for an excuse to wait a day or so.

I considered getting sick again. If so, I'd have to start feeling bad fairly soon. I knew a weak spell would work just as well as it had the first time, because Sam was already worried about me. And this time, because Lillian and Etta Mae would know what I was doing, they'd likely help me carry it off. Except . . .

Except it saddened me to the depths of my soul to conspire in pulling the wool over Sam's eyes. He'd been so concerned, and still was, about my health. I hadn't meant to worry him so, and I certainly hadn't meant to be threatened with a full-body examination in a doctor's office.

Well, I thought as I heard the announcer proclaim halftime, this was as good a time as any to get it off my chest and over with. I straightened my shoulders, took a deep breath and walked purposefully into the living room.

"Sam, do you have a minute?"

"Always," he said, as he hit the mute button on the remote. "Come sit with me and tell me what's on your mind."

I sat gingerly on the sofa beside him, but not close to him. I kept myself perched on the edge, turned so I could see the expression on his face when I told him what I had to tell him.

"Well," I began, then looked away because I couldn't bear to see the moment his face fell. "It's like this, Sam." I stopped, my eyes darting around the room, afraid to come out with it. "I hate to say this because I know it means a lot to you. And you'll be disappointed in me, I know, and I'm just so sorry that it's come to this."

"What has it come to, sweetheart? And how in the world could I be disappointed in you? You keep me hopping. I never know what's going to happen next."

"And you don't want to know this time. It's just so awful, Sam, and I thought I could get around it without telling you. Not," I quickly added, "that I wanted to keep anything from you. I just didn't want to upset you, but now, with all those people coming here Monday night, which means I'll have to greet them and offer refreshments and smile and be friendly and listen to Dr. Fred talk about private matters right out in public, well, there's nothing for it but to just . . . confess."

"Confess what, honey? Tell me and we'll fix it."

"Oh, I wish we could, but it goes against the grain of everything I stand for in this town. And I know people will talk, and Pastor Ledbetter will think I'm awful, and there's no telling what LuAnne and Emma Sue will say."

"Listen, now," Sam said, taking my arm and urging me closer. "It can't be that bad. Are you not feeling well? Is that it?"

"I feel all right—just sick to my soul for doing this to you."

"That's sick enough," he said, beginning to rise. "Let's get you over to the hospital. I'll call Dr. Hargrove to meet us there."

"No, wait. Really, Sam, I'm not sick that way. It's just that it makes me ill to admit this to you, because it puts you in a bad position." I clasped his hand, working up the nerve to tell him. "I guess the only thing to do is just say it straight out."

Sam looked at me, frowning with concern, as I took a deep breath, blew it out and looked him straight in the eye with all the courage I could muster. I bit my lip, felt a tremor in my hands, then said in a rush, *"I don't want to have that meeting here Monday night."*

There, I'd said it. I stared at him, waiting for his response.

"You don't?"

I shook my head and looked away. "No."

"Okay."

"What?"

"Okay. We won't have it. I'll call Ledbetter and tell him to find another place. To tell the truth, honey, I was about to suggest we back out, too. A lot's going on in the next few days with Hazel Marie and Pickens coming home and you not feeling well, so having a bunch of people in is just too much."

I kept staring at him, unable to believe that it'd been so easy. I'd expected him to ask *why* I didn't want to have it, at which point I'd planned to spill the whole sordid mess. Instead, he'd supplied an answer himself. Thank you, Lord, I thought, and sagged onto Sam's shoulder. Saved again!

"Well," Sam said, as he hung up the phone after passing the news to the pastor, "he wasn't happy about it, but he knows you haven't been well—apparently Francie asked about you when he and Dr. Fowler visited her, and Emma Sue mentioned it, too. He'll announce the change tomorrow during the service."

It struck me as odd that Francie had expressed interest in my well-being, first to Sam when she saw him on the street and again to the pastor when he visited her. She was generally so wrapped up in her own woes that nobody else's seemed to count.

"I'm really sorry, Sam," I said, dropping Francie from my mind. "Ordinarily, I'd love to have it here, but I really don't think I'm up for it right now." Of course, I wasn't up for it now and never would be, but not because of being sick.

What I needed to do from this point on was to let Sam see me gradually feel better, which would reassure him and, in the process, stave off a visit to the doctor. Then, with the sessions settled at Mildred's, I might manage to avoid Dr. Fred entirely.

"I know you're not," Sam said, running his hand along my arm, "and I should've known better than to suggest it."

"Did the pastor say where they'll be meeting?"

Sam laughed. "I think it's going to end up back in the men's Sunday-school room at the church. Emma Sue won't like it, and neither, I think, will he in his current state of mind, but it'll just be the one time. Mildred will be back for the rest of them."

⌒

A low front had moved in during the night, so Sunday morning dawned gray and drizzly. I dressed slowly, dreading the church service for fear that I'd run headlong into Dr. Fowler, who would certainly be there drumming up business. I'd have to do some quick stepping between Sunday school and the service, when people milled around greeting one another, to stay out of his line of sight.

Hearing Etta Mae, Sam and Lloyd in the kitchen preparing our usual light Sunday breakfast, I quickly finished my toilette and hurried downstairs to do my part.

Just as I pushed through the door into the kitchen, I sneezed, not once but three times.

Sam set the milk carton on the table and came over to me. "All right, back to bed. You're not going anywhere."

"Why, Sam, it's just a little sneezing fit. I feel perfectly fine. Besides, it's allergy season."

"Maybe so, but you don't need to be out in this damp weather. I want you to stay home. At least put your feet up and rest."

"Well," I said, as if reluctant to miss Pastor Ledbetter's sermon, "if you think it best." But I was thinking, what a reprieve, and completely unplanned!

Etta Mae walked over and eyed me carefully. She was dressed in a short skirt, a simple blouse and sling-back heels—bare legged, though. It was her churchgoing attire, I assumed, because plans had been made the night before for her to accompany us to the service. She hadn't been enthusiastic about it but had acquiesced easily enough.

Knowing that a realistic sneeze can hardly be manufactured on demand, Etta Mae showed some concern. "I'll stay with her."

"There's no need for that," I said firmly. "Because it's raining, I will stay home, but I'm not going to bed. I'll put my feet up and read the paper. It'll be nice to have a little peace and quiet around here."

Lloyd laughed. "Better get it while you can, Miss Julia. Mama and J.D. will be home today, and I can hardly wait. They've sure been gone a long time."

"I'm looking forward to seeing them, too," I said, and sat at the table and proceeded to eat the cold cereal and warm muffins that the three of them had prepared. I didn't want any comments on a lack of appetite that might've indicated the need for bed rest. Still, the sneezing fit would work beautifully if I needed another excuse to stay home Monday night.

After they left to walk across the street to the church, I sighed with pleasure at being alone in the house. I took another cup of coffee into the living room with me, separated the pile of advertisements from the newspaper and settled down in one of my Victorian chairs by the fireplace to enjoy catching up with the world.

The world not being all that exciting, I think I dozed off for a while, but came alert at the sound of a car door closing. Hazel Marie and Mr. Pickens! I jumped up and went to the front window. Parked at the curb was a long Cadillac painted a garish Florida color—some sort of orangey bronze—and limping up the walk with the help of a cane was Francie Pitts Delacorte.

"My word," I said aloud, "what is *she* doing here?"

I thought of pretending I was at church and just not answering the door. But curiosity got the best of me, and I hurried to see why she was ringing my doorbell.

"Why, Francie," I said, as I opened the door and took in her filmy dress in muted fall colors, her rakish hat trimmed in the same, her Prada pocketbook hanging on one arm and her rubber-soled flat shoes, one with the top cut off for her gouty toe. "What a surprise. I didn't know you were able to be out and about."

"I'm really not," she said, with a long-suffering sigh. "But I had to come, Julia. I'm not one to sit at home when a friend needs a comforting hand."

"Oh? Well, do come in." I stepped back to allow her to enter, then led her into the living room. "Have a seat, Francie. You're obviously feeling better, and I must say you're looking well."

Forgive me, Lord, I thought, for telling such a story on a Sunday. LuAnne had been right about Francie's heavy-handed makeup application, for it looked caked on—a far cry from the pallor of her hospital stay. She was even wearing blue eye shadow—at her age, too. Hazel Marie would've been aghast.

As Francie settled herself in the chair I'd vacated, spreading out her full skirt and smoothing it over her knees, I studied her face for signs of surgical scars from her alleged face-lift. There were none that I could see, but her face was certainly smooth and wrinkle free, with just a hint of stretching around the mouth and more than a hint of a wide-eyed stare.

"Would you care for coffee, Francie?" I asked.

"No, dear, I'm just fine visiting with you." She glanced around, leaning over to see into the dining room across the hall. "Where is everybody? They didn't leave you alone, did they?"

Aha, I thought, she's here to talk Etta Mae into coming to her again. I settled back into the sofa, pleased to have discovered her purpose and determined to nip that in the bud.

"They're all at church," I said. "But Francie, I have to tell you that Hazel Marie will definitely be home today. So Etta Mae is fully employed."

"I could care less about the Wiggins woman." Francie put her pocketbook on the floor, then adjusted her cane against the chair arm, making sure that it wouldn't fall over. "I'm concerned about you. They shouldn't have left you alone, but that just goes to show how much I'm needed. Now," she said, as I started to interrupt, "don't pretend otherwise. I know you don't want the rank and file to know your condition, but there's no need to pretend with me." She glanced toward the front door. "When will church be over?"

"A little after twelve," I said, then frowned at her. "But Francie, I don't know what condition you're talking about. I'm as well as I can be."

"Of course you are, dear. And we'll keep it under wraps as long as possible. But I want you to know that you can depend on me. I've had so much experience with sickness of all kinds, and caring for you will be no problem at all." Francie looked at her watch. "Sam went to church, too?"

"Yes, he always does. But truly, Francie, I don't need any help. I have Lillian and Etta Mae and Hazel Marie, to say nothing of Sam and Lloyd, and that's if I *needed* any help. Which I don't, and I don't understand why you think I do."

"Why, Julia," she said, leaning toward me with a worried look on her face, "it's all over town that you are quite ill, and what's a friend to do but be with you in your time of need?"

"But I assure you . . . ," I started, but, hearing the sound of footsteps on the porch and of Etta Mae and Lloyd talking and Sam's soft chuckle, I rose to greet them, hoping that Francie would take the hint and leave. "There they are now."

"Oh my," Francie said, followed by that tittering laugh. "I expect they'll be surprised to see *me* here." She smoothed her skirt again as she sat up straight, arched her back and turned sideways as she crossed her ankles.

Watching as she arranged herself, I saw an avid look of anticipation on her face as she turned toward the door. Posing, I caught myself thinking, and wondered why she thought Etta Mae would be impressed with the picture she made.

Chapter 34

After the greetings were over, Etta Mae and I went to the kitchen to put lunch on the table, leaving Sam and Lloyd to entertain Francie. She'd made no move to leave, even though it was clearly mealtime, so I had no option but to invite her to stay and eat with us.

"Nothing fancy," I said, hoping she'd take the hint. "Just leftovers."

"Oh, I'd love to have lunch with you," she'd almost gushed. "It's so seldom that I'm in such pleasant company."

Etta Mae helped me put a few things on the stove to heat, or rather, I helped her because she was so handy. We could hear the sound of voices from the living room, but not the words.

"I'm kinda surprised to see Mrs. Delacorte here," Etta Mae said, broaching the subject carefully.

"You and me!" I shot back. "You know what she wants, don't you? She wants you to leave Hazel Marie and work for her. I don't know what she's doing, staying on for lunch. Anybody with any manners would know it's time to leave. Especially having dropped in with no warning at all." I slammed a pot on the stove, working up a full head of steam at Francie's gall.

"Well, I'm not going to work for her," Etta Mae said, as she began slicing tomatoes. "She just doesn't know when no means *no*. I think she wants me back so she can accuse me of something else, like that gatekeeper said."

"I wouldn't put it past her. How would you heat up these rolls, Etta Mae?"

She glanced over from the counter where she was working. "Wrap 'em in tinfoil and put 'em in the oven. They'll heat up without getting too brown." She finished the tomatoes, then took several cucumbers from the refrigerator. "I wish she wouldn't keep on after me. It worries me because I haven't heard a word from Binkie, and I don't know if I'm still number one on Lieutenant Peavey's hit parade or not."

Before I could tell her that no news probably meant good news, Lloyd pushed through the swinging door into the kichen. "Y'all need any help?"

"I don't think so, honey," I said, "but thank you anyway. What've you been talking about in yonder?"

"Oh, I don't know. I didn't do much talking. Just listened until it got boring. That lady's telling Mr. Sam about Florida and how wonderful it is. I kept wanting to ask why she moved back here if it's all that great."

"Good question!" I said, as Etta Mae laughed. "In some ways, she's to be pitied, Lloyd. She's had a hard life, although she's brought a lot of it on herself. Anyway, we're almost through here, so you can go back out if you want to. You're sweet to think of helping."

"I didn't exactly think of it," he said, leaning on the counter to watch Etta Mae. "That lady told me to."

I turned from the stove where I was stirring the beans and

met Etta Mae's eyes. Our eyebrows went up at the same time. What was Francie up to?

"Well," I said, "you run right back out there and tell them they can come to the table."

He grinned, snatched up a cucumber slice and put it in his mouth. "Yes, ma'am."

When he left, I turned to Etta Mae. "That beats all I ever heard. She sent Lloyd out so she could play on Sam's sympathy and make him feel sorry for her. I expect she hopes he'll help her get you back. I'm beginning to think that the woman is just plain evil."

"She's just used to getting her way," Etta Mae said. Then, with a frown, she went on. "You think Mr. Sam won't want me here? He might think Mrs. Delacorte needs me worse than Hazel Marie does."

"Not a chance. He's not all that eager to tend to twins, even if they're not here yet. Besides, where you work is your business, and he's not going to interfere in that." I picked up a platter of pot roast and vegetables. "Let's get this on the table and get it over with. Hazel Marie and Mr. Pickens will surely be home in a little while, and I want Francie gone long before that."

"I can't wait to see them," Etta Mae said, as she took the rolls out of the oven and put them in a napkin-lined basket. "I bet Hazel Marie's getting as big as a house."

⁓

"Your table is lovely, Julia," Francie said as she took a seat on Sam's right. "I don't know how you do it, with all you have going on."

Because there were only the five of us, I'd seated everybody at one end of the table—me on Sam's left, Etta Mae to my left to keep her away from Francie and, unhappily but necessarily, Lloyd across from Etta Mae and next to Francie.

The meal transpired pleasantly enough, for Sam was as always the genial host. He had the innate ability and courtesy to draw out any guest, asking pertinent questions and express- ing sincere interest in whatever opinions, plans or experiences the guest offered. Francie glowed under his attention, dominat- ing the conversation as she responded to him. Sam attempted to include the rest of us, but his expertise failed to elicit satis- factory responses, mainly because Francie constantly drew the conversation back to herself.

As the meal drew to a close, Etta Mae whispered, "You stay right here. I'll fix the pound cake." And as soon as she stood, Lloyd was up like a shot, eager to clear the table and go to the kitchen with her.

The two of them served toasted pound cake slices with ice cream and chocolate syrup, a simple dessert that Francie consumed in minutes, in spite of her constant flow of words. We heard all about Florida: its scenery, its ocean breezes, its lovely beaches, its wonderful shops, its wealthy residents and on and on. Then we heard about her sorrowful experiences, especially the trying time she'd had with her sick husband—or husbands. I was never able to determine which one, or ones, she was speaking of.

The one matter that she didn't bring up was the recent theft and assault she'd suffered. I kept waiting for her to mention it, hoping for some small sign that she'd moved away from her accusation of Etta Mae. I mean, how could she sit placidly and companionably across the table from someone who she believed had physically injured her?

She couldn't; nobody could, which indicated to me that Francie knew that Etta Mae was not guilty of anything. But did she bring it up? Did she apologize, even in a roundabout way? No, she didn't. In fact, she ignored Etta Mae completely, which might've indicated some animosity toward her. But then, she ignored Lloyd, too, and she couldn't have had anything against him.

Well, the fact of the matter was, she ignored me for a good part of the time, and when she did take notice, it was to refer obliquely to the sad state of my health. And though it tightened my mouth to do it, I held my tongue, because I might have to use that excuse again, come Monday night.

Finally, the meal was over and we rose from the table. Surely, I thought, Francie would leave. Her unannounced visit had lasted more than two hours, and that was long enough for anybody without a suitcase. And thank goodness, she'd not brought one of those.

Lloyd hopped up, saying, "I'll do the dishes." And Etta Mae immediately said, "I'll help."

I nodded, thanking them, knowing that they preferred the busyness of the kitchen to Francie's boring monopoly of the conversation.

But at last, Francie began to indicate that she was preparing to leave. First, she excused herself to go to the powder room—the ladies', she called it, as if I had gender-separated bathrooms in my home. But before that, she'd had to swish into the living room for her pocketbook, walking delicately in front of Sam to retrieve it. When she came out of the "ladies'," she'd refreshed her makeup and reseated her hat.

I'd about had enough of her company, so when she returned,

I handed her the walking stick. "We've loved having you, Francie. There's nothing better than catching up with old friends. And this was the perfect time for it, too, because Hazel Marie will be back this afternoon, and there'll be no time for visiting from now on."

From the quick glare she aimed at me, I knew she understood what I was saying. But that didn't stop her from suggesting that I lie down and rest. "You're very pale, Julia. I fear you've overdone it, what with working in the kitchen and all."

I fumed, because she'd not offered to help, yet here she was criticizing me for preparing the food she'd eaten.

"Sam," she said, turning to look up at him, "you must see to it that she takes care of herself. We want our Julia to stay mobile as long as she can. It's ever so much better that way for all concerned."

"Francie . . . ," I started, then restrained myself as Sam smiled and winked at me. If he could see through her, then I didn't have to bother.

Having collected her cane and pocketbook, Francie turned toward the door. "Sam," she said, taking his arm, "walk me to the car, if you will. I'm still not too steady on my feet, having just gotten out of the hospital, after suffering such trauma as you wouldn't believe."

"I'll be happy to," Sam said, as he opened the door and escorted her out.

I watched as they went down the walk, Francie walking ever so slowly and leaning slightly on Sam. She continued to talk the whole way and kept him stooped over her car after she'd climbed in and closed the door.

As Sam finally walked away from the car to return to the

house, I quickly took myself to the living room and sat down. Pretending to have been engrossed in the newspaper, I looked up when he came in.

"That woman can talk, can't she?" he said, as he picked up the remote control. "You feel like watching a football game, sweetheart?"

"Not especially, but you go ahead. What was she talking about that kept you so long?"

Sam sat on the sofa beside me and clicked on the television. "Same thing she talked about the whole time she was here: her feelings, her problems, how she'd go back to Florida if it weren't for her duty to stay here." He flipped through several channels, bypassing golf, thank goodness, and settling on football. "I never did find out what that duty was, but she told me she felt it was her calling."

"My goodness, maybe the prayer vigil Pastor Ledbetter and Dr. Fowler had with her is paying some dividends. Which is too bad if it results in her joining our church. I'm not sure how much more of Francie Pitts I can take."

Sam smiled. "I know what you mean. But she does seem concerned about you, and that makes her easier for me to take." Sam put his hand on my knee and left it there.

Chapter 35

Sam didn't seem too wrapped up in the game, so I ventured another question. "Did Francie have anything to say about Etta Mae? She completely ignored her at lunch."

Sam laughed and cocked an eyebrow at me. "Advised me to lock our bedroom door at night. She thinks Etta Mae might attack us in our sleep."

"Oh, for goodness' sakes!" I cried. "Sam, that woman's out to ruin Etta Mae. Even if Lieutenant Peavey's looking elsewhere, which I hope to goodness he is, Francie's determined to punish her in some way. You might not have picked up on this, but the reason Francie showed up here today was to inveigle Etta Mae into working for her again, so she was trying to get you to fire her." The blatant nerve of the woman just frosted me good. I sat up and stared at him to be sure he understood the seriousness of the matter. "She *knows* Etta Mae needs to work, and if we let her go, she'd have to take whatever she could get. And after Francie gets through spreading such rumors, nobody'll hire her. Then Etta Mae'd have to work for Francie, which would put her right in line to be set up again and put in jail. Francie Pitts is a malicious woman and that's all there is to it."

Sam pulled me back against the sofa so that I was leaning against him. "It doesn't matter what she's trying to do, sweetheart. Etta Mae's safe here with us, and it looks as if we'll need her for a long time to come. Anyway, Binkie seems to think that they're looking in a different direction, so as long as Francie has no opportunity to make more accusations, then Etta Mae is safe from that, too."

"I hope you're right," I said, sighing. Then sat up with another thought. "Have you found out anything about Francie's maid or companion or whatever she is?"

"Evelyn? Not much. She doesn't have a record that I can find, but there's only so far I can go in looking. Her address is on Spring Street, that little lane off the boulevard, so I drove by to see it. It's one of those small houses built by some local volunteers to rehabilitate the area."

"Don't you have to show need to get one of those houses? How would Francie manage that? Because I heard she bought it."

"Evelyn must've bought it herself, because you're right. There're strict requirements on who gets the houses."

"Yes, and some way or another, Francie has worked it so she can take credit for it. That woman!"

"I did find out her name. Oh, man, look at that tackle!"

"What?" I glanced at the television and saw a pile of bodies on the screen. "Oh yes, that's something, isn't it? So what is it? Her name, I mean."

"Plemmons. Evelyn Plemmons. Seems her previous license was from Coral Gables, Florida, which makes sense because you said that's where Francie had been living. Anyway, she's sixty-four years old, has gray hair and blue eyes, and stands five feet four inches. That's all the information I could get."

"So she's a little old lady," I said, then realized with a start that she was younger than I was—not by much, but some. Still, she *sounded* old. "I mean," I hurriedly added before Sam could laugh at me, "somebody said she was old and frail, and Francie implied that Evelyn wasn't able to do much."

All of a sudden we heard feet running overhead and on the stairs as Lloyd came bounding down like a thundering herd. "They're home! They're home! Miss Julia, Mama's here!" he yelled, as he flashed past us and out the front door.

Etta Mae came down the staircase behind him, but much slower, standing back as if she weren't sure of her place. Sam and I hurried to the door to welcome the newly wedded couple. At my first glimpse of Hazel Marie as she met Lloyd with open arms, I thought, no, she wasn't quite as big as a house, but she was well on her way. Twins in a small woman don't have any room to grow except outward, and that's what they were doing. And thank goodness, the evidence of their growth was covered by a loose maternity top, and not one of those stretched-out T-shirts some women wear that aim their bulging navels at you like a headlight on a train. It's enough to make your own stomach revolt.

"Hazel Marie, honey, you look wonderful," I cried as she came into the house. "So rested and well. Welcome home, but where's your husband?"

"He's unloading the car," she said, smiling broadly. "I'm so glad to be home. How is everybody? Mr. Sam, it's so good to see you. And Etta Mae!" Hazel Marie hurried over to hug her friend. "How did you know I'd be home today?"

"Well . . . ," Etta Mae began, but stopped because she didn't know where to begin in recounting all that had happened in the past week.

"Etta Mae's here to help us out," I said. "I've been feeling run down, and we knew you'd need an extra pair of hands, so she's working for us."

"Oh, that's wonderful," Hazel Marie said, but she looked a little dazed at the thought of having a baby nurse before having any babies.

Mr. Pickens came in lugging a pair of suitcases, with Lloyd right behind him with an armful of boxes and packages.

"Well, we're back," Mr. Pickens said, putting down a suitcase and shaking hands with Sam. "I hope you can stand us for a while."

"Oh, we can stand you, all right," Lloyd said, his face alight with pleasure. "We sure have missed you."

After the newlyweds had gotten settled in the downstairs bedroom, which Sam and I had vacated when Hazel Marie had been ordered to stay off the stairs, we sat around the kitchen table eating leftovers and catching one another up with all that had happened. Hazel Marie told again about the massages they'd had and about the walks around the hotel grounds they'd taken and about Mr. Pickens's house in Asheville, which, I was relieved to hear, they did not plan to live in.

"Not much is selling these days," Mr. Pickens told Sam. "So I told the agent to put it up for rent."

Then Hazel Marie, still not understanding Etta Mae's presence, asked her about her job as a Handy Home Helper, so that gave us the cue to tell about Francie Pitts and her accusations, plus the dreadful anxiety that Etta Mae had been under as a leading suspect.

Mr. Pickens cast a worried look at Etta Mae. "Can I do anything to help?"

"You certainly can," I said before Etta Mae could open her mouth. "You can find out who actually attacked Francie, because we know it wasn't Etta Mae. She just happened to be at the wrong place at the wrong time, or almost at the wrong time, because she was long gone before anything happened to Francie."

"Why don't I talk to Binkie tomorrow?" Mr. Pickens suggested. "See if she needs me for anything."

Etta Mae ducked her head, unaccustomed to such concern from someone she hardly knew. "Thank you," she murmured.

Mr. Pickens glanced at Hazel Marie and took her hand. "I'm supposed to go to Birmingham to look into an insurance fraud case, but if Binkie thinks I can help, I'll put it off for a few days."

"Oh, J.D.," Hazel Marie said. "Don't talk about leaving."

Lloyd, who'd been avidly following the conversation, quickly changed the subject. "Mama, have you thought of what you're going to name the babies?"

Hazel Marie immediately perked up. "I've thought of a million of them. But we don't even know if they're boys or girls or one of each. J.D. went with me to see the obstetrician that Dr. Hargrove recommended, and they let him see the sonogram. We couldn't tell what was what, but the doctor could. But we said we didn't want to know, so we don't. We want to be surprised, don't we, J.D.?"

"It'll be a surprise, all right," Mr. Pickens said, and I could imagine just how big a surprise it was to him already.

"But you've thought of some, haven't you?" Lloyd persisted. "Tell us what you might name 'em."

"Well," Hazel Marie said, her face glowing at the thought of what was to come. "If at least one of them is a girl, I'm going to name her Apple."

There was dead silence around the table as we considered the chosen name, and only a few of us were able to glance at one another.

"Apple?" Lloyd asked.

"Yes," Hazel Marie said, "I just love the name. And that's what Gwyneth Paltrow named her little girl, and ever since I heard about it I've wanted to name mine the same thing."

We all continued to sit without comment, although Mr. Pickens had to turn his head and look out the window. Finally, when he'd gotten himself under control, he said, "Honey, you might want to rethink that."

"Why?" Hazel Marie asked. "Don't you like it?"

"Mama," Lloyd said, a delighted grin on his face. "Think what her whole name will be."

"What?" Hazel Marie said, frowning. "Why, it'll be Apple . . ." She stopped as a distressed look crossed her face.

"Apple Pickens!" Lloyd cried, laughing. "I love it, but I don't think she will. I'll be taking up for my little sister for the rest of my life."

We were all able to laugh by this time, but Hazel Marie looked crestfallen at how unsuitable her favorite name would be.

"Don't worry about it, honey," Mr. Pickens said, as he put an arm across her shoulders. "We'll think of something even better. And think of this: they may both be boys."

"Oh, I hope they are," Hazel Marie said, clasping his free hand and kissing it. "And I hope they're as sweet as you."

"Yuck," Lloyd said at this lovey-dovey display of affection.

"And," Mr. Pickens added, smiling at him, "boys just as fine as their big brother."

"Double yuck," Lloyd said, grinning as his face reddened with pleasure.

Chapter 36

Fairly early the next morning, on the dreaded Monday, a phone call came in for Etta Mae. After speaking for a few minutes, or rather, nodding and agreeing, she hung up with a distraught look on her face.

She turned to the three of us—Lillian, Hazel Marie and me—who were lingering at the breakfast table after the men had left. "That was Binkie," she said, as she slumped into her chair. "Mrs. Delacorte's bracelet has turned up."

"Why, that's good," I said, trying to encourage her. "At least now they know you didn't have it. Where did they find it? Or did Francie have it all along?"

Etta Mae shook her head. "No, it was turned in to the sheriff by a pawnshop owner, the one on the Asheville highway."

Not knowing that there were any pawnshops in town, much less more than one, I nodded as if I did. "Well then, that's one thing they can take off the books against you. Although I never did think it was all that important—compared, I mean, to the *alleged* physical attack."

Lillian, who'd been contemplating the matter, spoke up. "When you go to pawn something, the pawn man take down yo' name an' address an' all kinda things, an' he give you a ticket for when you come back to pay off an' get yo' belongin's back. So that lieutenant ought to know by now jus' who did the pawnin'."

"My goodness, Lillian," I said. "I didn't know you knew how to pawn something."

"I know lotsa things," Lillian said, laughing. "Like anybody do that can't make it till payday."

Hazel Marie, who'd been sipping a glass of orange juice, said, "My granddaddy used to pawn things all the time. He had an old railroad watch that he must've pawned a dozen times, over and over."

Etta Mae nodded knowingly. "Mine, too. But Binkie said that the problem with this is that the bracelet wasn't pawned. It was sold outright, so the pawnbroker didn't have to keep any records. And he didn't, so he doesn't know who sold it."

"You mean," I said unbelievingly, "that he bought that bracelet within the last few days and can't remember who brought it in? That's ridiculous."

"No," Etta Mae said, as she turned her coffee cup around and around in its saucer. "He wasn't there at the time. It was a nephew he'd left in charge over the weekend while he took some time off, and Binkie said the nephew's pretty sure it was a woman who brought it in."

"That's all?" Hazel Marie asked. "You'd think he'd be able to give some kind of description, wouldn't you? But how did the pawnbroker or his nephew know the bracelet was stolen?"

"Binkie said," Etta Mae said, "that the sheriff always puts out a list of stolen property, which goes to all the pawnshops. When the owner got back, he looked at the transactions his nephew had made, and there it was. That's when he reported it to the sheriff, bright and early this morning."

"But they don't know who brought it in?" I asked.

"No." Etta Mae shook her head. "So Lieutenant Peavey's going to do a lineup to see if the nephew can identify somebody. I'll be in it."

I almost came out of my chair, thinking of Etta Mae lined up with a row of criminals. "They're going to put you in a lineup? They can't do that, can they? What did Binkie say?"

"Yes, ma'am, they can. But it's not a real lineup like on television. I don't even have to be there. They'll just use my picture along with several others and see if the nephew can pick me out." Her hands trembled as she picked up a spoon and stared at it.

Hazel Marie reached over to put her hand on Etta Mae's. "You don't need to worry. He can't pick you out because you were never in there."

"Not recently, anyway," Etta Mae said, her face coloring with what I thought might be shame. "I've pawned a couple of things in the past, back when I was really up against it, so he might recognize me."

"Oh, Lord," I moaned under my breath. Then, with a start, I spoke up. "If whoever brought the bracelet in brought it in over the weekend, it couldn't have been you, Etta Mae. You were here all weekend, and I know for a fact that you weren't out of our sight either Saturday or Sunday."

"Yes, ma'am, I know it, too. But I went home Friday to pack a few clothes, remember? So I guess it'll depend on which day of the weekend it was, and whether Friday is part of it."

"Well, yes, I guess so, but Friday is never considered part of a weekend unless you're talking about a *long* weekend. Then it is. Either that or a Monday." I stopped, realizing that I was getting off the track. "But what are we doing trying to think up an alibi? You didn't do it, and that's all there is to it."

Etta Mae looked at me through a sheen of grateful tears, and I thought again of how I'd like to wring Francie's neck for putting her through this.

"Well," she said, getting to her feet, "I better get ready and go on. Binkie wants me in her office about ten. I think that's when the lieutenant will let her know if the nephew identifies me. If he does, well, I guess I'm in for it."

"I'll go with you, Etta Mae," Hazel Marie said.

Etta Mae started shaking her head, as Lillian and I both said, "No, you won't."

"You got to rest," Lillian went on. "You don't need to be in a sheriff's office or a lawyer's. 'Sides, you need to unpack them suitcases in yonder, so I can put in a load of washin', an' if anybody goin' with Miss Etta Mae, it be me."

"No, it won't," I said, standing. "I'm going with her."

"No, wait," Etta Mae said, smiling in spite of herself. "Thank you all, but Binkie said to plan on staying awhile. Regardless of whose picture he picks out, she wants us to go over everything again. So I'll just call you when I hear something."

That being determined, we all set to our various tasks, even though that left me with little to do. It was just as well, though, because after Etta Mae left and Hazel Marie was handing her soiled lingerie and Mr. Pickens's used underclothes to Lillian, I got another phone call from Francie.

"Julia?" she said when I answered. "Have you heard that my bracelet has turned up? From a pawnshop, would you believe?

And that lieutenant won't even let me have it. Says it's evidence, and he has to keep it until the case is closed, of all things."

"Why, yes, I suppose he does. But I'm pleased that it's been found. I know how much it means to you."

"Well," Francie said, a snippy tone in her voice, "apparently it didn't mean much to anybody else. The pawnbroker only gave the Wiggins woman seventy-five dollars for it, and Julia, it's solid eighteen-karat gold. That's an insult."

"Francie, I'll remind you that it hasn't been determined that Miss Wiggins was the one who pawned it, and I wish you'd stop accusing her."

"Oh," she said in an offhand manner, "it's only a matter of time. But listen, Julia, is Sam there? I need to speak with him. Oh, and by the way, how're you feeling this morning?"

"I'm fine, and no, Sam's not here."

"I really need to talk to him. Where can I reach him?"

"You can't," I said, my mind racing ahead trying to figure out why she'd want to speak to him. I certainly wasn't going to give her the phone number at his house. "He's gone for the day and won't be back until late."

"I bet you know where he is, though, don't you?" Then, without moving away from the phone, she shouted, "Evelyn! I told you not to do that. Can't you ever do anything right?" And in a normal tone, she resumed her conversation with me. "Now, Julia, just give me the number where I can reach him. I'm sure he'd want you to."

Before I could think how to respond, she took off on Evelyn again, but this time her tirade was muffled as she covered the phone. All I could hear was the vicious sound of her voice and the occasional sharp exclamation aimed at Evelyn. But don't you just hate it when somebody interrupts a conversation to berate a child or a pet or to carry on with somebody else? It's so rude, you know. It just left me standing there, waiting for her to get back to me. I mean, *she* had called me, and if she'd needed to tend to other matters, she should've postponed the call.

"Whew," Francie said, speaking again into the phone. "I tell you, Julia, I don't know what I'm going to do with that woman. She drives me to distraction. Now, where were we?"

"I'm not sure, Francie. You called me, remember?"

"Oh, of course. I need Sam to come over. I have a couple of lightbulbs that need replacing and Evelyn can't reach them. But Sam's so handy and he did offer help if I needed anything."

A flash of white-hot anger ripped through me. Sam might've been handy, but he was no handyman at her beck and call. "Francie," I said, and sharply, too, "you can call the maintenance people out there where you live. That's what they're there for and what you're paying for. Sam doesn't have time to be replacing lightbulbs for you."

"Oh, Julia," she said, with a little titter, "you misunderstood me. The lightbulbs are just a while-you're-here matter. What I really need Sam for is to advise me on some legal problems that have come up from when I lived in Coral Gables. The family of my next-to-last husband is trying to make waves."

"Sam no longer practices law," I snapped, just so irritated that she would impose on him. "He's retired and has other things on his mind. I'd advise you to hire a practicing attorney if you need legal advice."

"Well," she almost huffed, "I can see that you're no help. Perhaps we're feeling a little under the weather today?"

"Maybe *you* are, but I'm feeling fine."

"I understand," she said, as if she were soothing a child. "Don't worry about it. Just tell Sam to call me when he gets in. Can you remember to do that, dear?"

If the phone hadn't been made of hard plastic, I would've squeezed it to death. "I think I can manage to remember. So nice to talk to you, Francie, but I have to hang up now. I'll be late for a meeting."

And I did hang up, in spite of the fact that it was rude of me to end a call that I had not placed. But if we're comparing levels of rudeness, mine hardly placed.

I remained standing by the phone, gritting my teeth while thinking of a million other things I wished I'd said. Hazel Marie wandered into the kitchen, took one look at me and stopped.

"Are you all right?"

"That woman!" Then I proceeded to tell Hazel Marie what Francie had wanted and how, even worse, she had assumed the right to call on Sam for whatever she needed, from legal advice to home maintenance.

Hazel Marie smiled. "Sounds like she has a crush on him."

I turned so quickly I almost put a crick in my neck. "A what?"

"A crush. You know, after what you told me about her and all her husbands, maybe she's after him now."

"But why? He's married."

"Huh," Hazel Marie said, "that wouldn't stop some women. Besides, you said she keeps thinking you're sick and offering her help." Hazel Marie pulled out a chair and sat down. "I've known of a couple of cases where a best friend tended to someone who was dying, then right after the funeral, up and married the widower."

The sickening light dawned, and all I could do was collapse onto a chair next to Hazel Marie. "That's it, Hazel Marie. That's what she's doing. She's after my darling Sam and can't wait to see me in my coffin." I clenched my fists, angered by the unmitigated gall of Francie Pitts. "And for all I know, she's capable of hurrying me into it." I reared back and straightened my shoulders. "But I'll tell you this, she is not going to find it easy, and I don't care if she does have some kind of secret erotic knowledge. I'll fight fire with fire if I have to."

Chapter 37

Hazel Marie frowned. "She has what?"

"Secret erotic knowledge. That's what Sam said she probably had to get all those husbands, when it's obvious that she has nothing else to recommend her."

"How would Mr. Sam know that?"

"It was a guess, Hazel Marie!" I said, more sharply than I'd intended, because I was wondering the same thing. "He doesn't know for sure. How could he?"

Yes, I thought, how could he know? But there it was: it wasn't possible that Sam would have personal knowledge of Francie's secret knowledge—he hadn't known her long enough. But he knew enough to feel that something was missing in our marriage, else he wouldn't have been so eager to attend those blasted enrichment sessions. Lord! He was searching for something that I didn't have, but Francie did.

"Miss Julia," Hazel Marie said with a far-off look in her eyes. "You could ask J.D. about that, because I think he has some of it, too."

"Some of what?"

"That secret stuff you mentioned. I'm pretty sure he knows all about it."

"Hazel Marie, honey, I'm not about to discuss such a subject with Mr. Pickens. I'd never hear the last of it and never live it down, either. No, I've got to go about this some other way, though I don't know what it'll be."

"I don't think you have to worry about Mr. Sam," Hazel Marie said. She put her hand on my arm and smiled. "He's so in love he can't see straight."

"No, he's not." A pain like a knife thrust ripped through my heart, and I covered my face with my hands. "Oh, Hazel Marie, I hate to say this, but Sam's so unhappy and I don't know why. Except it has to be because of me."

"I don't believe that for a minute." Hazel Marie spoke so firmly, I had to look up at her. "No way in the world is that man unhappy because of you or for any other reason. And I don't see how you'd even think so."

So I told her. I told her about Sam wanting us to go to Dr. Fowler's marriage enrichment classes and how I couldn't. Hazel Marie already knew a little because she'd been around during my first encounter with the man. "So, see," I went on, "why would Sam want us to go to those classes if he was happy with the way things are? I tell you, Hazel Marie, it's a clear wake-up call to me that Sam feels something is lacking in our marriage. Why would he want us to go get enriched if he didn't feel impoverished?"

"Maybe it's just what he said," Hazel Marie said. "He wants to support the pastor. I don't think you need to look for anything else."

"But Hazel Marie, the wife is always the last to know, and

I'm afraid that his wanting to get me to those classes is an indication that something is wrong. I'd be a fool to ignore it, and under any other circumstances I'd just go and be done with it. But I can't, not with Dr. Fowler there, because if Sam learns about that little episode, I might as well head out for Reno. Or for a quiet divorce downtown. Because that will give him the excuse he's looking for."

"Oh, Miss Julia, you can't believe that!"

"Well, I don't, but that's what I'm afraid of. And now you say that Francie Pitts is just waiting in the wings, so that's another thing to worry about. Wanting to go to those classes is clear evidence to me that Sam is restless, and she's just waiting to pounce." I grabbed a napkin to mop up the tears that had been waiting to spill out, for the more I thought of all that had happened, the more I'd convinced myself that our marriage was on the rocks.

"You're making a mountain out of a molehill," Hazel Marie said. "I don't for a minute believe that Mr. Sam's unhappy about anything, and as for Francie, don't make me laugh. From what you say about her, he wouldn't have her on a silver platter."

"Well, Hazel Marie, when you look back at how we got married, you have to admit that Sam might have a hard time *feeling* married. Remember? We eloped to Pigeon Forge and ended up before a defrocked preacher who had no legal right to marry anybody. Then, in order to rectify that, we got remarried by the Reverend Morris Abernathy. Now, I know that Lillian's pastor is as legal and as qualified to marry people as they come, but a wedding ceremony in an empty classroom at the high school after a beauty pageant? What kind of wedding is that? I don't wonder that Sam feels he's missed out on something. I sometimes feel that way myself."

"Well, that's easy to fix," Hazel Marie said. "Why don't you just get remarried? You can renew your vows—you know, like you told everybody that J.D. and I did. Only you and Sam really would. And you could have a big reception with all the trimmings, invite everybody and have the kind of wedding every woman dreams of. I'd love to help. It'd be like having my own real wedding, although," she quickly added, "I'm happy with the one I got, considering how slippery J.D.'s been all these years."

"I don't know, Hazel Marie," I said, cringing at the thought of such a public spectacle, yet thinking at the same time that it would be a small price to pay to ease Sam's mind.

"Think about it," Hazel Marie urged. "And feel Mr. Sam out. It might be just the thing to put a little fire back into your marriage. If that's what's missing, I mean."

"Well, that's just the thing. If it's fire that's missing, I sure haven't noticed. Yet Dr. Fowler's classes are all about how to stoke the embers and stir up the flames, so maybe that is the area that concerns Sam." I wiped my face, shuddering a little for discussing such intimate matters with Hazel Marie. Or with anyone, for that matter. What happens in the bedroom ought to stay there, in my opinion. Yet the longer we'd talked, the more desperate my situation seemed, and at least Hazel Marie had suggested something I could do other than just worry about it. "Well, it's something to think about, Hazel Marie, and I will. But I'll tell you, after all the other times I've been through it, I've about memorized those vows."

Etta Mae knocked on the back door, then walked in, looking edgier than usual after her visit to Binkie's office. Hazel Marie and I both looked at her, just as Lillian came into the kitchen.

"What happened?" We all said at about the same time, bringing a tiny smile to Etta Mae's face.

She dropped into a chair and said, "Well, he didn't identify me."

We all, in our various ways, expressed relief and gratification that the pawnbroker's nephew had such an excellent memory.

"Actually," Etta Mae went on, "he couldn't identify anybody in the pictures they showed him. And Lieutenant Peavey wouldn't tell Binkie whether he'd even hesitated over any of them. I just wish he could've identified one of the others. But he didn't, so I guess everything's still up in the air."

Lillian and I did our best to reassure her and tell her that surely the nephew's inability to point at her picture proved her innocence. I don't think she was convinced and probably wouldn't be until the real culprit was revealed. I can't say that I blamed her, for Francie's accusation—the only lead the lieutenant had—still hung over her head.

Hazel Marie had been quiet for several minutes, then with a knowledgeable tone that surprised me, she said, "You know what they do, don't you? They put your picture in with four or five pictures of people they know—probably women deputies or clerks in the office, like that. The thing about it is, Etta Mae, there wasn't anybody but you in that lineup that they're even looking at." She glanced around at us. "J.D. told me how they do it."

"Well, my word," I said, flaring up, "you'd think they'd put some real suspects in the lineup. What good did it do to go through that rigamarole when we know that the one person they suspect is innocent? I think they should've put Evelyn's picture in it, and maybe the gatekeeper's, the trashman's and so forth—anybody who had access to Francie's cottage."

Lillian said, "I thought that nephew 'membered it was a woman that hocked it."

"Oh," I said, "that's right. Well, I guess they should've used pictures of wives and girlfriends of those people. Or," I went on with a sudden flash, "even Francie's picture, because I don't trust that woman as far as I can throw her."

Hazel Marie patted my arm. She knew that I suspected Francie, but for far more than the theft of a bracelet.

When we'd talked out the open-ended results of the lineup, thrashed through the ineptitude of the sheriff's department and eaten lunch, Hazel Marie asked Etta Mae if she still felt like doing some shopping. Etta Mae looked tired and drained from her unproductive morning, but she quickly agreed.

"She don't need to be on her feet too long," Lillian cautioned, with a knowing look at Hazel Marie. "Miss Etta Mae, don't let her be traipsin' all over the place. You know how she like to shop."

Etta Mae gave her a quick grin. "I sure do, but don't worry. She just wants to look at cribs, then we'll be home."

"That's right," Hazel Marie said. "I'm just looking today to see what they have. Then I'll get J.D. to go with me to see which one he likes."

"Lots of luck with that," I said, smiling, as Lillian laughed at the thought of Mr. Pickens judiciously studying a lineup of baby beds, then, after careful consideration of each one, pointing out his choice. It wouldn't surprise me, though, if he opted for a dresser drawer and a pillow. Make that two dresser drawers and two pillows.

Chapter 38

"Lillian," I said as they left for their shopping trip, "something's got to be done to help Etta Mae. But for the life of me, I can't think what it could be." But something else was niggling at the back of my mind, something that might take care of the other problem that was troubling me.

"It all work out in the long run," Lillian said. "You don't need to be messin' 'round in it."

"Oh, I agree. I just want to give it some thought." And to that end, I went into the living room so I could think by myself without anybody taking the wind out of my sails.

As concerned about Etta Mae as I was, it was Sam who had me in mortal turmoil. Inadvertently, Hazel Marie had opened my eyes to the danger that he was in. Everybody knows that the most constant of husbands can have his head turned, and Sam's innate kindness would allow him to put up with Francie until she had him where she wanted him. I didn't doubt that Sam was faithful—he might be unhappy, but his own high moral standards would keep him faithful. So on those grounds, as opposed to the moral standards of Wesley Lloyd Springer, I trusted him completely. But I didn't trust Francie Pitts.

So did that give me license to fight fire with fire? I thought it did, and to that end I went back to the kitchen and told Lillian that I was going to pay a visit to LuAnne Conover. But just as I started for the door, the phone rang.

As soon as I answered it, Emma Sue Ledbetter began talking. "Julia, I just got back from visiting Francie Whatever-her-name-is, and I'm so upset I can hardly stand it. Something is really, *really* wrong with her."

I could've told her that to begin with, but I just said, "I know."

"No, Julia, I don't think you do. She's had some medical problems, I know, but I think she has some sprirritual problems, too. You know that woman who stays with her? That housekeeper or whatever? Well, you wouldn't believe how ugly Francie talked to her, and I mean with me sitting right there listening to it all. Francie yelled at her, called her a moron and an idiot and just *berated* her like I've never heard before. Why, I wouldn't talk to a dog that way, much less a person. And she didn't even apologize to me, just acted like it was something everybody does and I'd understand. But I didn't and I still don't. I tell you, Julia, the whole thing scared me. It was like she has a demon, a demon of anger, and she could turn it off and on without thinking a thing about it. And you know what the worst thing about it was?"

"No, what?"

"That woman is her *cousin*!"

"Really! I didn't know that. But I've heard Francie lay into her, too, and it's not a pleasant thing to witness. And to think that she's a relative!"

I listened as Emma Sue went on telling about her visit, but my mind was engaged with this new information. Evelyn was

Francie's cousin—did that mean anything, and if so, what?
It seemed obvious to me that Evelyn had to be dependent on
Francie—financially speaking, at least—else why would she put
up with such abuse? And maybe she was emotionally dependent on her as well and had been so beaten down that she could
no longer stand up for herself. I'd heard of cases like that.

Finally, after agreeing with Emma Sue that the pastor
should be informed—especially because Emma Sue had convinced herself that a demon was involved—I was able to end
the conversation.

After hanging up, I turned to Lillian. "Lillian, do you believe
in demons?"

She frowned at me, wondering where that had come from.
Then she said, "I b'lieve in the devil, so it wouldn't surprise me
if he have some helpers flittin' 'round. Why?"

"Oh, I was just wondering. Emma Sue believes in them, but
I think they could just be a good excuse for people who can't
or won't control themselves. They can blame their faults on
somebody else."

But with the greater knowledge of Francie's personality that
Emma Sue had given me, I had no hesitation in going on to
LuAnne's to put my plan in motion.

⌒

It was unlike me to drop in on a friend without calling first,
though goodness knows people did it to me often enough. But I
still wasn't sure that I could follow through on what I'd decided
to do. I wanted to be able to back out before I got there, and if I
did, I'd just turn around and go home.

I didn't back out. In fact, I was even more determined to see it through when I saw who else was visiting. Parked in front of the Conovers' condo was Francie's bronze Cadillac, and I nearly broke my neck hurrying out of the car and up to the front door. The woman was everywhere.

When I rang the bell, LuAnne greeted me with a gush of welcome. "Julia! Come on in! You'll never guess who's already here, and I thought this was going to be a long, boring afternoon. We're out on the screened porch where we can enjoy the view. It's not too cool yet, though it will be when the sun goes down. Come on, Francie'll be so glad to see you."

I followed her through the small rooms crowded with furniture from LuAnne's previous home, out onto the screened-in porch. And, of course, there was Francie, hat—this time a cloche—and all, in the most comfortable chair with her foot elevated on an ottoman. She was wearing rubber-soled earth shoes, one of which had been hand customized for comfort.

"Look who's here," LuAnne said to Francie. "We might as well have a party."

"Oh, Julia," Francie said, her brow knitted with concern. "Should you be out by yourself? They really should take better care of you. I must talk to Sam. I know ever so many little things that would make life easier for you."

Before I could answer, LuAnne stared at me. "Are you sick? Julia, why haven't you told me? Here, sit down. What would you like to drink? Something hot? Cold? What can I get you?"

"LuAnne," I said, as firmly as I could manage. "And you, too, Francie. I am not sick, and I don't know where you got the idea that I am. I think you're projecting your problems onto me, Francie. I mean, you have been ill, and still are if that shoe you've had cut off is any indication."

"Oh, now, well," LuAnne dithered, leading me to a chair. "I'm sure Francie didn't mean anything. Let's talk about something else. Who's going to Dr. Fowler's class tonight? Are you, Francie?"

Francie waved a languid hand. "I don't think so. Dr. Fowler personally invited me, you know. Dr. Ledbetter, too, but I'm a single woman, and I have to be careful not to start tongues wagging. It wouldn't look good for me to attend a class meant for married couples."

I had about gotten myself under control by this time, and I coolly decided I would do what I'd come to do. I didn't particularly like myself for it, but I didn't see that it could cause any damage and, who knows? It might do some good.

So I said, "If they both invited you, knowing that you're single, then they want you there. And you might enjoy it."

"Are you and Sam going?" Francie asked, her eyes squinching up at me.

"We haven't decided yet. Hazel Marie and Mr. Pickens are home, so we might just visit with them tonight. Then again," I went on, my intent to get her there in mind, "Sam may go by himself. That's what he's been doing."

LuAnne chimed in then. "You won't be the only single person there, Francie. I'm trying my best to get Leonard to go without me. And I doubt that Emma Sue will be there, but the pastor will be. Oh," she said, jumping up, "what am I thinking! That coffee's perked by now. I won't be but a minute."

"I'll help you," I said, and followed her to the kitchen, knowing full well that Francie would not stir from her chair.

As LuAnne began to prepare cups and saucers on a tray, I said as casually as I could, "We really should encourage

Francie to go tonight. I heard that Dr. Fowler has taken a personal interest in her, and she'd be foolish to pass that up, single as she is."

LuAnne stopped pouring coffee, an avid look on her face. "A *personal* interest? Does that mean what I think it means?"

"Oh, I wouldn't want to start any rumors. I just know that he visited her on Saturday—with the pastor, I might add—and has been burdened by her situation ever since."

LuAnne's eyes sparkled. "Wouldn't *that* be something? Does she know he's interested?"

"It doesn't sound like it, because she's not planning to go to his class tonight. But don't say anything, LuAnne. What I heard may not mean anything. I wouldn't want to get her hopes up. Although," I mused, "I heard that he'd been in prayer about her all day yesterday. That could mean something."

I figured by that time that I'd accomplished enough and noted with satisfaction that I'd not embellished one thing. I could leave the rest to LuAnne, who'd never kept a secret in her life. So I lingered awhile, had coffee on the porch, listened to Francie talk about Florida, her recent hospital stay, the dearth of good help and her toe until I could stand it no longer.

Rising, I said, "This has been nice, but I must be on my way. Thank you, LuAnne, and Francie, it was good to see you again."

LuAnne, protesting that I needn't rush off, followed me to her front door. Then she leaned close and whispered, "You think Dr. Fowler is really interested in her?"

"That's just what I heard, and it may not be true. But we know she's looking, and if he is, too, well, one never knows, does one? I wouldn't say anything, you know, *definite,* if I were you."

"Oh, I wouldn't do that, but maybe just a little hint?" LuAnne giggled. "I think it'd be so romantic to get those two together."

⌒

On my way home, I continued to congratulate myself on how well I'd handled the matter. LuAnne would take care of the rest, for I'd probably not gotten out of sight before Francie knew that she had a secret admirer. I could sit back now and watch Francie switch her attention to a bird in the hand.

When I went into the kitchen, all was quiet, if you discounted the radio playing gospel music and Lillian singing along.

She stopped as I walked in. "Where you been so long?"

"Just talking," I said, reaching for the telephone. "I let the time get away from me. Have you heard from Sam? Is he still at his house?"

"Yes'm, he was." She turned from the sink, where she was peeling potatoes. "But it won't help to call him now 'cause he won't answer. He tole me he have a meetin' downtown an' won't be home till suppertime."

"Well, my goodness," I said, hanging up the phone in exasperation. "Every time I want to talk to him, he always has something to do and I have to wait. But I'll tell you this, he better not be volunteering us for anything else. I don't care who asks him to."

"You won't have to do no waitin' this time 'cause you got to go to the doctor. Mr. Sam, he tole me to tell you to go right on to Dr. Hargrove's soon as you come in. The doctor gonna work you in, an' Mr. Sam, he say he don't mean maybe."

"*What?* I don't have time to go to the doctor. What does

he mean by making an appointment for me? Just because I sneezed a few times yesterday, he thinks I need a doctor. I'm not sick, Lillian, and you know it. Why didn't you tell him I'm not?"

Lillian closed her eyes and shook her head, her mouth in a thin line. "Uh-uh, not me. I don't tell him nothin' that have to do with you. You can do yo' own tellin'. But if I was you, I'd go on and see that doctor. Mr. Sam, he firm about it."

There was nothing for it but to do it and get it over with. There was still that enrichment class that was due to start in a couple of hours, and with all my running around that day, I would be hard pressed to pull another sickly spell. Maybe Dr. Hargrove would tell me I needed to slow down or not go out in the night air or something.

Ungraciously, I grabbed my pocketbook and flung myself toward the door. "Well, I'll go to please him, but I don't like it. I'll be back in a few minutes."

I fumed all the way to the doctor's office, so put out that I'd brought this on myself, pretending to be sick just to avoid Dr. Fowler. I was reaping what I'd sown, but it didn't make me feel any better.

And Francie hadn't helped, going on and on about my poor health, getting Sam even more worried than he needed to be. The only bright spot was the possibility that I'd turned Francie's avaricious gaze in another direction.

Chapter 39

It was after five by the time I reached Dr. Hargrove's office, and I was hoping he'd given up on me and gone home. So I confidently breezed into the empty waiting room, apologized to the receptionist for being so late and asked for an appointment later in the fall.

She looked up over her glasses, frowning. "He's waiting for you."

Just then, a nurse opened the inner door and stood aside. "Doctor's waiting for you, Mrs. Murdoch."

"I heard," I said, and, firming my shoulders because I was trapped, I followed her down the hall to the doctor's inner office.

And indeed, he was waiting, surprising as that may sound to any number of patients who've done their share of waiting for him. He closed the medical journal he'd been reading and rose from a chair behind his desk when I entered. "Come in, Miss Julia. Sam tells me you've not been feeling well. Have a seat and tell me what's going on with you."

"Not one thing. And I'll tell you right now, I am not going to undress and crawl up on a table. I have neither the time nor the inclination for it. Sam has gotten himself so exercised over a few sneezes and a thirty-six-hour bug that he's taken entirely too much on himself."

Dr. Hargrove's eyebrows went up at that, but he seemed to take it in stride. "Well, since you're here, why don't I at least check your throat and listen to your chest. That'll put his mind at rest, then we'll sit down and have a little talk."

Put that way, I did sit down because I was tired. What I'd been up to that afternoon had taken a lot out of me. Propping my pocketbook on my lap, I said, "As long as I can sit right here, I'll open my mouth and two buttons. That's as far as I'm willing to go."

With a smile, he used a tongue depressor to look down my throat, then, sliding a stethoscope bell inside the bodice of my dress, he listened intently. He had some trouble running his hand from the collar down the back of my dress, but he managed it without demanding I come out of my clothes.

"Everything looks and sounds fine," he said, laying the stethoscope on the desk, which is a sign of self-confidence in a physician. He didn't need to draw attention to himself by wearing it around his neck. "Now," he went on, resuming his seat behind the desk, "catch me up with what's going on. How's Hazel Marie? She back from her honeymoon? And Lillian, how's she doing? Tell her I'd like to check her blood pressure again." He glanced up at me, real interest on his face. "And Lloyd? He's turning into a fine boy, isn't he?"

"Oh, he's growing up, Dr. Hargrove," I said, smiling.

"And you? How is your life these days?"

He spoke so softly and so kindly, as if he truly wanted to know, that I nearly broke down. I felt something give way in my chest and before I knew it, I was turning myself inside out, telling him what had happened to Francie Pitts and how convinced I was of Etta Mae's innocence and how I was trying to prove it because Francie was either lying through her teeth or totally confused. "And she's basing her whole accusation on nothing more than smelling Etta Mae's perfume. Shania Twain by Stetson it was, and Dr. Hargrove, it doesn't smell bad at all. Quite nice, actually, but Francie's convinced that it smells like collard greens, because that's what she had for lunch in the hospital and it reminded her of what she'd smelled after she got hit on the head. Can you believe such a thing? And a young woman's life is about to be ruined. It's no wonder Sam thinks I'm ill. I'm just anxious, that's all. And I think that's enough to be anxious about without worrying about him."

Then, hardly taking a breath, I found myself spilling out how concerned I was that Sam was unfulfilled in our marriage. "He's going to that enrichment course at the church, Dr. Hargrove, and I notice that *you're* not going. At least, nobody's said you were there, and I don't blame you. I'm not going, either, but that doesn't mean that it's not worrying me to death that Sam is. It is just shattering to me that I'm happy and he's not. That means that I don't have a clue as to what he's thinking, and I've been in that situation before, as you well know, and I don't want to go through it again. Oh, Dr. Hargrove, will you talk to him? Find out what I'm doing wrong, and I'll change it if I can. I'll do anything except go to that enrichment thing because, believe me, the answer is not there. Or maybe you could find out whether I'm just wrong for him, in which case I'll have to fold my tent and crawl away."

By this time, the tears were flowing while I searched frantically through my pocketbook for a Kleenex. Dr. Hargrove pushed a whole box across the desk, revealing his preparation for all contingencies.

"You certainly have a lot to be anxious about," he said, his face grave and his voice filled with empathy. "Things haven't been easy for you, have they?"

I shook my head, dabbed at my eyes and sniffed to get myself under control. How comforting to be listened to and understood, I thought.

He went on comforting. "I'll be glad to talk to Sam, maybe even the two of you together. I'm not a counselor, but I am a listener. If he's willing, we can meet a few times and try to get to the bottom of what's troubling you."

"It's not *me* who's being troubled! It's *him*. He's the one who's feeling deprived or impoverished or whatever he's feeling. I have everything I ever wanted in a marriage, and it's just doing me in that Sam doesn't feel the same way."

"We can talk about that. He may just need an opportunity to express his feelings. But I'll have to tell you, Miss Julia, I've never gotten a hint that Sam's unhappy. Just the opposite, in fact."

"You don't know him like I do," I said, clasping a wad of damp Kleenex in my hand. "Anybody who'd go to a counselor who bounces from one church to another dispensing secret erotic knowledge based on a warped view of the Bible has to be at his wits' end." I sniffed again and wiped my face. "If we did come talk to you, you'd stay away from such as that, wouldn't you? I mean, you wouldn't involve Dr. Fred Fowler and his teaching, would you?"

He smiled. "No, I think we could manage well enough on our own."

"So do I." I stood then, feeling relief and some optimism that all was not lost. I had an ally in Dr. Hargrove, and I was glad that I'd come even though it'd been Sam's doing to start with.

"Thank you, Dr. Hargrove. You've been very kind, but I must be getting home. And you, too. Your dinner will be waiting. I'll let you know when, or if, Sam is willing to come talk."

He opened the office door for me, then put a hand on my arm and said, "Wait just a minute, Miss Julia. Something you said earlier has triggered something in the back of my mind."

He walked over to a bookcase and pulled out a thick medical book. Flipping through the pages, then back again, he finally settled on an article that took a while for him to read. I was about to get restless, anxious to be on my way and just a little bit testy that he was doing research on my time.

"Ah," he said, finally straightening up from the book. "I thought so." He looked at me and smiled broadly. "When you mentioned that Shania Twain perfume, it rang a bell. A patient came in not long ago who was wearing it, and my office help went crazy over it. That's all I heard for days, Shania Twain this and Shania Twain that. It got so the whole office smelled like a cosmetic counter because they all went out and bought it. But I'll tell you this, it does not smell like collards."

"It certainly doesn't. But what's the point?"

"The point is something called dysosmia. You said the Pitts woman reported smelling a foul odor after she was hit on the head? Well, it happens that way sometimes. A head injury can produce dysosmia, a condition that distorts the sense of smell. It can cause a person to hallucinate a foul or unpleasant odor. That could be what happened to your friend."

"She's no friend of mine!" I said, then, as what he'd said began to sink in, I went on more calmly and with some wonder. "She was *hallucinating*? All this turmoil from hallucinations? That would be just like Francie Pitts, and poor Miss Wiggins has had to suffer for it. But how that woman could confuse perfume and collards is beyond me. Goodness knows, collards smell to high heaven when they're cooking, but I'm not sure you could call it foul, exactly."

"Well, I could," he said, laughing. "But here, read it yourself—a blow to the head can distort the sense of smell." He held the open book out to me. "And apparently, there doesn't have to be another odor to stimulate it—the foul odor is dredged up by the brain itself."

I scanned the page, stopping on the few sentences in plain English that I could understand, and, sure enough, there it was as plain as day: an explanation for the odor that Francie had smelled, and it hadn't needed a whiff of anything else to set it off. It had come out of her own head, and furthermore, there was not a single solitary mention of Miss Twain. Or Mr. Stetson, either.

Chapter 40

Hurrying across the parking lot to my car, it was all I could do to contain myself. My nerves were so on edge that I felt jittery all over and had trouble getting the key into the ignition slot. I could hardly wait to get home and tell everybody, so full of what I'd learned that I wanted to speed through the streets to get there. Finally, an explanation for the mysterious odor that had assailed Francie's nose, on the basis of which she'd accused Etta Mae and caused her to be suspected and interrogated, when all the time it had been concocted in her own head or sinuses or wherever. An olfactory hallucination, would you believe! I was sure that Francie wouldn't believe it, but when scientific proof from a medical textbook was placed before Lieutenant Peavey, I had every reason to believe that he would. I mean, collards, of all things!

It was amazing that the answer had been sitting in a book on an office shelf all along, and none of us, including Lieutenant Peavey, had known it. After all, that's what having an education means—not that you know everything, but that you know where to look for it. So it wouldn't surprise me if

Dr. Hargrove hadn't supplied the very thing that would completely clear Etta Mae.

It was as if the skies had cleared and the sun was shining
to have that problem taken care of, leaving me with only Sam
and Dr. Fowler to deal with. And with that thought, I noticed
that the skies weren't all that clear, and that it was, in fact,
later than I'd thought. Dusk was falling and night wasn't too
far behind.

I sped down Harding Street, passing the front of the church,
and turned right along the side to get to my house on the far
corner of Polk. Streetlights were already on, as they were timed
to do on an overcast fall evening.

Running over in my mind how I'd tell Etta Mae what
I'd found, then how I'd present it to Binkie and Lieutenant
Peavey, I patted the pages that Dr. Hargrove had copied from
his book, which were on the seat beside me. Proof positive
that there'd been more to meet the nose than Francie had
claimed.

As I drove past the side of the church, I caught a glimpse of
a certain flashy car parked in front of the Family Life Building.
I almost stood on the brake, so unnerved that I could barely
catch my breath. Francie's car! Who could miss it? There wasn't
another like it in all Abbotsville, and there it was parked not a
hundred yards from my front door. I hadn't been able to turn
around the whole day without running into her.

But what was she doing here? Visiting Sam? Creeping in
to see him when I wasn't there? What was she telling him? I
knew, oh yes, I knew. If she wasn't trying to entice Etta Mae
to work for her, she'd be playing on Sam's concern about my

health—worrying him to death with intimations of my down-hill slide and assuring him of her eagerness to nurse me and comfort him. Of all the sneaky, underhanded things to do, that took the cake.

Well, I was not going to stand for it. The woman needed taking down, and I had the means to do it. Deciding to forgo parking in my driveway, so as not to announce my presence, I pulled in behind Francie's car on the side street.

Fully intending to walk across the street and show up at home before Francie knew I was on the premises, I noticed lights on in Pastor Ledbetter's office and suddenly changed my plans. I took myself straight to the back door of the church and went in. Francie might be making herself alluring to Sam, but I'd just thought of a strategy to outflank her.

I walked purposefully through the large Fellowship Hall, located under the sanctuary, toward the pastor's office, my footsteps echoing off the tiled floor. I assumed the pastor was working on his sermon or perhaps gathering himself for the enrichment meeting, which I noted from my watch was only an hour or so away.

I hurried through Norma Cantrell's dim office, glad that it was after hours and I didn't have to contend with her officious gatekeeping. Not wanting to interrupt if the pastor had some-one with him, I tapped on his closed door and waited for him to respond.

He did, opening the door himself, and seemed somewhat taken aback to see me.

"Why, Miss Julia," he said, "what brings you here? You're a little early for Dr. Fowler's meeting."

"I didn't come to see or hear Dr. Fowler. I have a matter of some import to share with you, Pastor, and I think when you hear it you'll be just as concerned as I am."

"Well, come on in. I was just going over a few things, but they can wait. Have a seat and tell me what's on your mind." He quickly went around his desk, covering the booklet he'd been studying with a stack of papers, but not before I saw an illustration that made my eyes water. He'd been looking at Dr. Fowler's graphic depictions of how to stoke the marital embers.

I filed that away for future reference because I had more on my mind than the pastor's study habits. Besides, he might learn something that Emma Sue would appreciate.

"Pastor Ledbetter," I began, perching on the edge of a damask-covered wing chair, "I know, because Emma Sue told me, that you and Dr. Fowler have been having prayer with Francie Pitts Delacorte, and counseling her, too, for all I know. But I have just come into possession of some information that you should have before you get too deeply involved with her."

"Why, Miss Julia, any soul that seeks help from the church should receive it. It surprises me that you would not rejoice with us that Mrs. Delacorte is right before recommitting her life to the Lord. She will make a fine member of our congregation. She's so outgoing, so eager to be a part of our church family, and it is my privilege to be called upon to guide her more deeply into the faith."

"Even though she has a demon?"

"What?" His eyes bugged out at my quiet comment. "A demon? Miss Julia, that is a dangerous allegation and should not be thrown around lightly."

"I'm only quoting your wife, although she's planning to tell you herself. I would never have thought of such a thing on my own—I'm not even sure I believe in them—but when Emma Sue speaks, I listen. She knows her Bible, and if anybody can recognize a demon, it would be Emma Sue. Now, I thought Francie was just mean and self-centered, but Dr. Hargrove has pointed out to me that most likely she's suffering from hallucinations. Although he's never treated her, he recognizes her symptoms. So whether it's from dysosmia, as he says—here, you might want to read this article," I said, handing the copied pages to him, "or a demon, as Emma Sue thinks, or just plain meanness, as I think, it doesn't matter. The woman is dangerous, and you and Dr. Fowler are playing with fire." I nodded my head for emphasis, then added, "And I'm not talking about playing with the specific embers that *he's* concerned with."

Pastor Ledbetter stared at me, then scanned the pages I'd handed to him. He cleared his throat and began to speak. "I hardly know what to say." His eyes darted around, then he thought of something. "These could be libelous accusations, Miss Julia, and we must tread carefully. We tamper with demons at our own peril, although demonic activity has been misdiagnosed as hallucinatory in the past. There's apparently a fine line there. But I've seen no evidence of such activity in or around Mrs. Delacorte." He rubbed his hand across his mouth, studied the papers a little longer, then said, "I can't, however, discount Emma Sue's perception of the situation. She is, as you say, keenly sensitive to such matters. So I must admit that you've given me food for thought."

"Well, while you're at it, think about this: what kind of people have hallucinations? Crazy people, that's who. And I've been suspecting Francie was crazy for some time. Just look at what she's already done: fingered my friend Etta Mae Wiggins as a thief and an inflicter of great bodily harm at a time when the young woman was miles away in Delmont, spewed invective at a person in her employ who might even be a relative, buried five husbands and been questioned about the demise of at least one of them, put it about that I am on my last legs with absolutely no basis in fact—she just made that up—and now she's so deluded that she thinks Sam will have her in my place. That, Pastor, is what you're dealing with, and if you and Dr. Fowler continue to woo Francie into this church, don't say you weren't warned."

He swallowed hard, then murmured, "I didn't realize . . . And you say that Emma Sue thinks . . . ? Well, I'll discuss this with Dr. Fowler. He knows more about demons than I do."

I got to my feet, ready to leave, having done what I'd come to do. "I wouldn't be surprised," I said, and saw myself out.

I left the pastor to his ruminations and proceeded through Norma's office and out into the dark Fellowship Hall. It was large and empty with only one light on near the back door, which was where I was headed, intent on rescuing Sam from Francie's clutches. But as I walked across the expanse, I realized I was hearing the murmur of voices coming from the corridor on the opposite side of the Fellowship Hall, the corridor that led to the two-story addition of Sunday-school rooms. My nerves froze in their tracks when I recognized Francie's tittering laugh floating out of the darkness of the corridor. Without a conscious thought, I practically leaped into the alcove where folding chairs were kept for the Wednesday-night covered-dish suppers.

What was she doing here? I'd thought she was at my house, playing up to Sam. She had no reason to be wandering through empty rooms on a Monday night, especially because Dr. Fowler's enrichment session wasn't due to start for another hour. I wondered if the pastor knew, but if he did, wouldn't he have mentioned it when we discussed her in his office?

Strange, I thought, as I pressed against the wall, waiting for her and whoever she was with to walk across the Fellowship Hall. I wanted to see who'd brought her in and find out, if I could, why. Well, I might as well be honest and admit that I was pretty sure I knew who she was with. I could just picture how she'd gone to visit Sam and been put off her stride at finding so many people in the house. My eyes narrowed as I thought of how she must've talked him into walking her across the street and into the church, where they'd be alone.

I didn't like it; I didn't like it one little bit, but what could be done about it I didn't know. So I waited and waited, but nobody came, and I began to wonder if I'd had an auditory hallucination. But no, I heard that laugh again, almost like an echo emanating from the bowels of the building.

Then, across the way, the pastor stepped out of his office, closed and locked the door and proceeded across the width of the Fellowship Hall, heading toward the corridor and the men's Sunday-school room, where Dr. Fowler's meeting was to be held.

As he passed the alcove where I was hiding, I leaned out and hissed, "Pastor!"

"Whup!" He jumped a mile and dropped a book. Then he emitted what sounded like a strangled expletive. "What? Who is it? Come outta there." Then, as I eased out, he visibly relaxed and just as visibly tightened with anger, something that usually happens when you've been scared half to death. "Miss Julia!

What're you doing here?" he demanded. "What's the matter with you?"

"Nothing, but keep your voice down. Did you know that Francie Pitts is back there in the Sunday-school rooms?"

He frowned and looked toward the corridor. "What's she doing?"

"I have no idea, but she's laughing and talking with somebody. Maybe whoever it is is showing her through the building." I couldn't bring myself to say that I thought it was Sam—in fact, I was hoping against hope that it wasn't. But the whole thing reminded me that I had done some completely innocent showing around some years back when the pastor himself had asked me to escort Dr. Fred Fowler through the church. And with a shudder, I recalled what had happened as a result of that tour. "Maybe it's Dr. Fowler."

Although if that was the case, I had to concede that Francie was a mighty fast worker. She'd only heard of Dr. Fowler's interest that very day, and already she'd pounced.

Pastor Ledbetter frowned even more, a worried look crossing his face. "I don't think so. Dr. Fowler was still at the inn where he's staying when I spoke with him on the phone. That was right before you came in. He didn't mention coming over this early. Besides, I would've heard him come in." He gestured toward the back door where I had entered. Because all the other doors were kept locked after hours, the back door provided the only access to the pastor's office, the Fellowship Hall, the upstairs sanctuary, as well as the Sunday-school rooms in the new addition.

"The only other entrance," the pastor went on, explaining what I already knew, "is the side door next to the men's classroom, where we'll be meeting, and it stays locked except when there's a service of some kind. I was on my way to unlock it and turn on some lights."

My concern about Sam eased off. If the door was locked, he couldn't have gotten in. "Then who could it be? Who could've gotten in without your hearing them or through a locked door?"

A flash of apprehension swept quickly across his face, and his eyes widened. He swallowed hard and whispered, "Emma Sue said a *demon*?"

"Yes, she did, but surely not here, Pastor. A demon wouldn't dare enter this place. So put on the armor of God and buck up. We're not dealing with the supernatural. We're dealing with someone who knows how to get into the building and bring that woman with him."

"You're right. Of course you are." He withdrew a large hand-kerchief and mopped his face. "It's somebody who has a key to the side door. Dr. Fowler, for one, and a few of the elders and those who have authority to look after the building. It's some-one who knows Mrs. Delacorte and wants to show her what First Presbyterian has to offer. Let's just go see who it is."

Having recovered his own authority, he started off down the corridor. But not before hurrying me along for company. I complied with a heavy heart, for I knew only two people who met the criteria he'd just listed: Dr. Fowler, as he'd said, and Sam, who, as I knew, often checked the church during the week. I was sickened at the thought of encountering either one off somewhere in a dark corner with Francie Pitts.

Chapter 41

As we walked down the corridor, Pastor Ledbetter hit every light switch we passed, leaving no dark corners anywhere. We reached the end of the corridor and turned left into a short connecting hall that led to the side door. The pastor tried it, found it unlocked and grunted with chagrin that somebody had entered the church without his knowledge.

Then he leaned through the door of the men's Sunday-school classroom, the first room from the side door, and switched on the light to be sure it was empty. The room was the largest in the building, which was the reason it had been designated for Dr. Fowler's sessions, despite the fact that, so far, he'd not come close to filling it.

"Nobody's here yet," Pastor Ledbetter said, which I had also noted. "But we'd better look around. I'm beginning to think that the door was inadvertently left unlocked, so anybody could've come in—vandals or tramps or somebody like that."

"I'm sure it was Francie I heard. She has a distinctive laugh."

"An empty building can distort sounds, Miss Julia," he said in a patronizing tone. "I can't imagine that Mrs. Delacorte would be so presumptuous as to come in without letting me know. It's probably somebody looking for a handout or a place to sleep."

"In that case," I said, dutifully following him as he strode toward the dark end of the cross corridor. "Shouldn't we call the sheriff?"

"Not at all. I'll just find whoever it is and offer a few dollars for a meal. This sort of thing happens all the time." He'd obviously overcome his earlier apprehension and was now determined to sort things out on his own.

That lasted just long enough for us to approach the elevator, the one that old Mr. Stenson had insisted we put in for all the members who used walkers, in spite of the fact that it ran the building fund over budget. Just as we got to the elevator, we became aware of a rumbling sound, heard a ding and saw the light above the door come on.

Pastor Ledbetter looked at me, and I looked at him. We waited as the door jerked, then began to slide open. My heart almost stopped, for neither of us had pressed the call button. Pastor Ledbetter took a step back, almost colliding with me, as we waited, neither of us moving, until the door was fully open. Then we waited some more. *Nobody was in it.* I gasped, and Pastor Ledbetter took a sharp breath.

"Who sent it down?" he asked, his voice catching in his throat. "Did you punch the button?"

"I didn't go near it. It was somebody else."

"I'm going to see," he said and started to enter the elevator.

"Wait, Pastor," I said, putting out my hand. "Let's take the stairs. The way that thing's acting, I don't want to ride in it."

"Good idea. We should check the stairwells anyway."

So up the stairs we went, Pastor Ledbetter snapping on lights so that the building was being lit up like a Christmas tree. But the more light the better, as far as I was concerned. My joints were having enough trouble climbing those stairs without stumbling around in the dark.

We came out on the second floor, walked the halls, stuck our heads in empty classrooms and walked on into the main building, which housed the sanctuary and the choir room. We found nobody anywhere, nor any sign that anybody had been there.

So we retraced our steps to search the rooms along the cross hall, both of us puffing by this time. Finding no one, even though we looked in every classroom, closet and supply room, we headed for the more public areas of the building. Perched on a small incline, the front part of the Sunday-school building was at street level, and that was the part that had been spe-cifically designed as a chapel for small funerals and weddings. It, too, had an exterior door, a narrow portico and a walkway leading out to the sidewalk. And right next to the chapel was that infamous, though elegantly decorated, room where bridal parties gathered to await the ceremony.

I realized as I tried to keep up with Pastor Ledbetter that it was the first time I'd been near the place since that humiliat-ing episode a few years back. In fact, I'd deliberately avoided it, not wanting to be reminded of what had happened. I'd had no reason to be there, and plenty not to be.

And all this while, I was becoming more and more agitated for fear we'd find Sam in a compromising position with Fran-cie Pitts. The woman would stop at nothing to get what she wanted, and it was plain that she wanted Sam in spite of my efforts through LuAnne to aim her toward Fred Fowler. It was entirely possible that Sam had not one impure thought in his head, intent only on Francie's spiritual welfare, but she could turn on him the way Dr. Fowler had turned on me, overwhelming him with that secret knowledge of hers. Trotting along behind Pastor Ledbetter, I could've cried at the thought.

"Unless we've walked right past him," Pastor Ledbetter said, looking to the right and the left, "he's got to be here somewhere."

"Pastor, it's not a him. It's a her, but a him might be with her."

"Well, now, Miss Julia, let's not jump to conclusions. I can't imagine you can identify someone by a laugh, especially in a building of this size." He veered off to jerk open the door to a storage room, seemingly having regained his confidence. But he hadn't regained it totally, for he still wanted company. "Let's be sure nobody's hiding in here."

I followed him, whispering, "I think the chapel is the place to look. Somebody could be hiding among the pews or behind the pulpit."

"Not yet," he said decisively. "We'll go there last. I want to make a lot of noise so we'll herd whoever it is into the chapel and, hopefully, on outside. That way, we'll avoid a scene in the church."

I nodded agreement, as I surveyed the five-branched candlestands and other stored objects used for weddings. But I was wondering how easily a demon could be herded. If Emma Sue was right, we were dealing with fire, and for that reason I made sure to let Pastor Ledbetter take the lead.

So intent was he to search the supply and storage rooms that I just stood in the doorways and watched, which allowed me to keep an eye on the hall as well. I had a fear of someone or something sneaking up behind me.

Then I heard something: a scuffle of sorts and a muted laugh. And, Lord help us, a moan.

"Pastor!" I whispered, clutching at his sleeve.

He whirled away from his inspection of a collection of mops and brooms. "What!" he said in a fierce whisper.

"I heard something. Listen!"

He stood stock still, a look of concentration on his face as he listened intently. "I don't hear anything."

"Just wait, because I did."

Then we both heard it: a garbled voice and a thump against a wall.

"The bridal parlor!" Pastor Ledbetter said, and off he took, muttering to himself. "I'm not going to have this. I simply am not. There're valuable things in there, and I'm not going to have them stolen. My patience is at an end."

Oh, Lord, I thought, as I scurried to keep up with him. Please let it be a tramp or a thief. Or let it be just Francie in the throes of a hallucination. Or, because by this time I was seeing the end of my marriage, let it even be a demon; I didn't care. Just don't let it be Sam.

Although, and I almost stumbled as the thought came to me, if it was Sam, I wouldn't have to worry about confessing my own little set-to in the bridal parlor. He'd be begging for my forgiveness, instead of the other way around.

Then shame washed over me at having thought of such a thing, and I went back to praying that it wasn't Sam. Please let him be home reading or watching television or getting ready to come to Dr. Fowler's meeting—anywhere but in that room.

Just as Pastor Ledbetter reached for the doorknob, the door sprang back and Dr. Fred Fowler rushed out. A breath of relief rushed out of me, and I felt like singing the "Hallelujah Chorus." Who would've thought I'd be so happy to see him? Even so, I stepped back out of his line of sight, not at all eager to renew our acquaintance.

I needn't have bothered, for he had a more urgent problem on his hands, and he looked it. His hair, rusty and gray, was tousled, his eyes wide and staring out of crooked glasses, and the knot in his tie was halfway down his chest. His shirt was unbuttoned, too.

"Larry!" he screamed, coming to an abrupt halt as his face screwed up in shock at seeing the pastor. Then, quickly recovering, Dr. Fowler practically threw himself on him. "Just in time, Larry, you got here just in time."

"What's going on here?" Pastor Ledbetter demanded, pushing Dr. Fowler away.

"You have to understand," Dr. Fowler pleaded, his hands scrabbling against the pastor. "She's crazy, and I'm a PhD, not a physician. I don't have the tools to deal with her."

And then there was Francie, standing in the doorway. She smiled at us, tittered and straightened her dress. Her hat, I noticed, was on the floor behind her, and her hair looked the worse for it.

"Why, Pastor Ledbetter," she said, just as calm and collected as you please. "And Julia. You really should be home resting, dear. Fred and I have been wrestling with my spiritual problems, and he's been ever so much help."

"Seems you've been wrestling with more than that," Pastor

Ledbetter said. He shrugged off Dr. Fowler, who'd scurried behind him and was nudging up against his back.

All this while, Dr. Fowler had taken no notice of me, mainly because my initial shock at seeing him had made me step back into a corner. And I guess he had enough to handle without bringing up a previous wrestling match.

"It was innocent, Larry," Dr. Fowler pleaded. "I promise you, it was innocent. Until, until something just came over her. I am just done in. I can't get my breath. I need to lie down. Cancel the meeting, Larry, I can't go on."

"I certainly will cancel the meeting," the pastor said, his mouth in a firm line. "And you, Mrs. Delacorte, need to go home. The church, after hours, is no place to wrestle with anything. And Fred," he went on, turning to him, "you go to the inn. We'll discuss this tomorrow."

"Well!" Francie retorted. "I guess *I've* been told off. All right, I'll go, but you can bet I won't darken the door of *this* church again!" And she tossed her head and began swishing her way toward the elevator.

"Wait, Francie," I called, so pleased with her banishment that I forgot to stay hidden. "You forgot your hat."

"Bring it to me tomorrow," she said without slowing down. "I know when I'm not wanted."

"You don't know the half of it," I said, half under my breath but not caring who heard me.

Pastor Ledbetter put his hands on his hips and gazed, somewhat scornfully, at Dr. Fowler, who stood trembling and, by this time, leaning against the wall. If I hadn't personally known how manipulative the man could be, I might've felt sorry for him, in spite of the fact that I was seeing more than I wanted to see of white chest hair. But he'd just met his match in Francie, who, unlike me, didn't have a smidgen of shame in her. Dr. Fowler was left holding the bag, and I didn't think Pastor Ledbetter could whitewash a second such episode with a widow woman in the bridal parlor.

"Larry," Dr. Fowler said, suddenly straightening up and speaking more authoritatively than he had any right to do. "You have a severe problem here. You should take note of Paul's letter to Timothy concerning idle widows who wander from house to house, carrying tales and stirring up trouble. A series of classes on the proper conduct of widows is required to get this church back on track. I'll be glad to take that on for you." He slid the knot of his tie up to his collar, even though his shirt was still gaping open. With an effort to sound calm and in control, he added, "I have some experience along those lines, you know."

Pastor Ledbetter just stared at him, a look on his face of stunned disbelief at Dr. Fowler's presumption. Then he turned to me and said, "Miss Julia, I think I owe you an apology for a past error in judgment."

Chapter 42

Well, he certainly did, and he made one of sorts, though it humbled him to do it.

Then Pastor Ledbetter motioned Dr. Fowler and me toward the elevator. "The two of you can go on home. I'll stay and cancel the meeting. In the meantime, Fred, you need to spend some time in prayer. I'll meet with you in the morning in my office."

We got in the elevator, each taking a different corner, and rode down in silence. I studied Dr. Fowler, marveling at how the mighty had fallen. He continued to ignore me, and I wondered if he didn't remember or even recognize me. That was probably it, and here I'd been suffering agonies of shame and regret for years over a terrible lapse of common sense.

When we stepped out of the elevator on the ground floor, we heard voices and laughter coming from the men's classroom, where people had begun to gather.

Pastor Ledbetter said, "I recommend that you both go out the main door, so you can avoid meeting anybody. I'll tell the group that you're incapacitated, Fred, and won't be able to continue the classes."

"But Larry," Dr. Fowler declared, "I'll be able to complete the series. Just let me get myself together tonight, and I'll pick right up next week. What I have to say about enriching marriages is too important to let fall by the wayside."

I didn't think that Pastor Ledbetter's face could get any grimmer, but it did. "This church," he said, "has had all the marriage enrichment it can stand. The series is canceled."

And with that, he stalked off toward the men's classroom to send the group home. I turned down the corridor, hurrying to get away from Dr. Fowler and go home, too. I wasn't quick enough, though, for Dr. Fowler was right behind me, and he hadn't forgotten who I was.

"Mrs. Springer," he called in a loud whisper, for he wasn't eager to draw attention to himself from the group who'd gathered to hear his lecture. "Julia, wait, we need to talk."

I kept on going. "My name is Julia Murdoch—Mrs. Murdoch to you—and we have nothing to talk about."

"But you can help," he said, drawing abreast and falling in step as we approached the Fellowship Hall. "All you have to do is tell Larry how easily these things get out of hand, and I am not to blame. Explain to him how widowhood creates a longing for intimacy and how, for some unknown reason, I seem to—I don't know—just inflame lonely women."

Walking into the dark Fellowship Hall, I came to a dead stop and turned to face him. "*For some unknown reason?*" I cried. "Let me tell you something, *Doctor* Fowler. *You* are the reason! Now, I grant you that you may've bitten off more than you could chew with Francie—she's a different kettle of fish. But you took advantage of me, and you know it. You deliberately led me on to make a fool of myself. Maybe you did it to help the pastor get his hands on the Springer estate, or maybe you did it to have an example to cite and laugh about in your classes, I don't know. But I do know this: I wouldn't help you out of this mess if you were the last man on earth."

Dr. Fowler's shoulders slumped, as he said in a sad and dejected voice, "You're a hard woman."

"You better believe it," I said and stomped off toward the door. Then I thought better of it and turned back. "Let me give you some advice: get yourself married. That way, you'll have a little authority when you teach your classes, and it might keep you out of all the trouble you seem to have with widows." Then, with sudden inspiration, I went on. "And Francie Pitts Delacorte is the perfect woman for you. She *likes* being married. She has lots of experience with it and she's actively looking for a husband." I knew, because she was looking at *mine*. "And furthermore," I whispered, leaning toward him, while looking around to be sure we were alone, "she is well-to-do, and not only that, she has secret erotic knowledge. Why, Dr. Fowler, she could completely transform your ember-stoking classes."

I declare if a spark of interest didn't flare up in his eyes, turning soon into a gleam of speculation. "You don't say," he said.

"I certainly do, but I'd get a move on if I were you. Francie gets married at the drop of a hat, and right now she's between husbands. You should call her." Then turning to head toward the door, I added, "Maybe you could pick right up where you left off in the bridal parlor."

Lord, so much had happened in the past hour that I had to take myself in hand to recall the reason I'd been anxious to get home. Hurrying to my car, I went over in my mind all that

Dr. Hargrove had told me about dysosmia, that strange reaction to a blow on the head. I'd left the copied pages with Pastor Ledbetter, so I hoped I could recount the information closely enough to convince whoever needed convincing.

Getting in my car to move it off the street, I noted with satisfaction that Francie's car was gone. I clicked my tongue, just so put out that the woman had no shame. If it'd been me who'd been caught wrestling with Dr. Fowler in the bridal parlor, I'd . . . well, it had been me at one time, and I still cringed at the thought.

I drove the few yards to my driveway, got out and went into the house. The kitchen was clean and quiet, but I could hear voices in the living room. Just as I started to go there, Etta Mae pushed through the swinging door.

"Miss Julia!" she said, then almost ran to me. "Where've you been? We've been so worried. Are you all right?" Then, lifting her voice, she called, "Hazel Marie! She's home."

They all—Hazel Marie, Mr. Pickens and Lloyd, but no Sam—trouped in, exclaiming over my late arrival. After assuring them that I'd been both unavoidably and constructively detained, but that I was perfectly all right, I said, "I'm about to starve."

Etta Mae immediately went to the oven and brought out a plate that had been kept warm. "Sit right down and eat. We ate hours ago."

"Sorry I'm late," I said again, "but I'm glad you went ahead without me." Then, glancing around, "Where's Sam?"

Hazel Marie said, "Why, he went to that enrichment meeting at the church, but he almost didn't go, he was so worried about you. The last we knew you were supposed to see

Dr. Hargrove, and he was afraid he'd put you in the hospital or something."

"I believe I'd have called if that'd happened," I said somewhat dryly as I took a seat at the kitchen table.

"That's what we told him, and he finally decided to go on because he thought you might meet him there."

"Huh," I said, picking up my fork. "Not likely. Besides, he'll be back any minute because those classes have been canceled." I began to eat.

So far, Mr. Pickens hadn't said a word, just stood there with both hands resting on a chairback, those sharp, black eyes boring into me. "Is it safe to ask what you've been up to?"

"Well, my goodness," I said, somewhat smugly, "why would you think I've been up to anything?" But I could hardly wait to tell them what I'd found out both in Dr. Hargrove's office and in the church. "Let's wait for Sam, then I'll tell you. But Etta Mae," I said, unable to stand it any longer, "your worries are all but over. And that's all I'm going to say until Sam gets here."

"Would you like a roll?" Hazel Marie asked, passing the basket.

"Thank you, I believe I would." Then, glancing at Etta Mae's anxious face, I decided to take pity on her and give her some relief. "Well, the first thing that happened—Sam made me an unscheduled appointment with Dr. Hargrove. I can tell you that because he already knows it."

At the sound of the front door opening and closing, I stopped. Lloyd ran out of the kitchen, calling, "That's him now. I'll get him. Don't tell anything till I get back."

"Julia," Sam said as he appeared in the room. "Honey, where've you been? I've been worried sick."

"You shouldn't have been," I said, somewhat tartly. "You knew I was at the doctor's because you made the appointment." Then, because pity was engulfing me all around, I took some on him. "I'm sorry I worried you, Sam, but I got waylaid over at the church. Come sit beside me, because I have some interesting news."

By this time, they'd all gathered around the table and, between bites, I began to tell them almost all that had happened since I'd left home that afternoon. I left out my visit to LuAnne because I didn't believe that was germane to the subject. Although I could assume that LuAnne had happened to mention to Francie that Dr. Fowler had more than a passing interest in her, and that might have sparked her interest in him, which may have led to the wrestling match in the bridal parlor.

But as I say, I left that out and proceeded to explain Dr. Hargrove's discovery of a certain article on dysosmia. After defining that unusual reaction to head traumas, I had to wait for it to soak in.

"You mean," Etta Mae exclaimed, "that she didn't smell *anything*? That it was all in her head?"

"I never heard of such a thing," Hazel Marie said in some wonder. "It's kinda scary to think you could smell something that's not even there."

"Well," I said, "it's a settled fact that nobody was cooking collards in Francie's house."

Mr. Pickens took Hazel Marie's hand, then he said, "Peavey wasn't interested in collards. He knew that was unlikely. It was the Delacorte woman's linking an odor to Etta Mae that he was going on—regardless of how it smelled. Although he told me that he couldn't understand it. He kinda liked your perfume, Etta Mae."

Etta Mae smiled, but it was a little strained.

Sam put his arm around my chair. "Well, Julia, you and Dr. Hargrove may have solved one problem. I hope so, anyway. But I declare, woman, you've run me a merry chase." He patted my back, then turned to Mr. Pickens. "J.D., you think this medical explanation will cut any ice with the lieutenant?"

"I'm thinking it will. At least he can put that aside and concentrate on who really attacked the woman. Perfume and collards were red herrings anyway."

"Oh, me," Etta Mae moaned, "that means he'll still be looking at me. The pawnbroker's nephew can't say who pawned her bracelet, and I can't prove I wasn't there."

"Well," I said, putting aside my fork, "just hold on, Etta Mae. There's more coming." And I went on to tell about the search for unauthorized personnel that had been conducted throughout the church by Pastor Ledbetter, with me in tow. "That's why I'm so late getting home. We walked all over that church, looking in every room, closet, hall and stairwell in the place. And let me tell you just who we found. You won't believe it."

They almost didn't, but it was too delicious not to. Hazel Marie had to know every little detail: what Francie looked like when she stepped out of the bridal parlor, what Dr. Fowler said, how Pastor Ledbetter reacted and what he would do about the enrichment classes.

"I'm sorry, Sam," I said, turning to him, "but it looks as if they're over." And with a certain amount of vindication I couldn't hide, I went on. "I know you're disappointed, but the pastor is simply outraged at finding Dr. Fowler conducting a laboratory class instead of a lecture."

Sam and Mr. Pickens laughed, and Sam, to my surprise, said, "Serves him right. Actually, it serves both of them right. Ledbetter for bringing in somebody who stirred up trouble once before, and Fowler for putting his theories into action."

I stared at Sam, wondering how much he knew of the trouble Dr. Fowler had stirred up once before. Of course, he might not have been referring to the specific trouble the man had stirred up for me, but it was certainly not the time to ask questions, with everybody sitting around listening.

"So, Etta Mae," I concluded, to put her mind at ease and to get off the subject of Dr. Fowler, troublemaker extraordinaire. "Francie Pitts Delacorte has shown her true colors everywhere. How anybody could believe a word out of her mouth after all she's done is beyond me, and Lieutenant Peavey will have to take that into account."

And if he didn't, I thought to myself, something was brewing in my mind that just might make the lieutenant sit up and take notice.

Chapter 43

Sam and Mr. Pickens discussed Dr. Hargrove's suggestion that Francie could've suffered from dysosmia until I'd about heard enough of it. Sam said he'd feel more confident if Dr. Hargrove had ever treated Francie, while Mr. Pickens wanted to see the medical book for himself. They talked it up one side and down the other, becoming more and more intrigued with the possibilities the diagnosis offered.

"Only thing is," Sam said, after we'd carried the conversation as far as it would go, "the only way to duplicate what might've happened is to hit Francie over the head again and see if she smells anything." He laughed and stretched. "I don't imagine Lieutenant Peavey will try it, though."

"After the way she's treated Etta Mae," I said, "I'd volunteer to do the hitting." Then, feeling somewhat fatigued from all that traipsing through the church, I excused myself and went upstairs to bed.

When Sam came up, he was still chuckling about Dr. Fowler and Francie. I was all but asleep, but not close enough that I couldn't pose a question.

"You're not disappointed about the classes?"

"Not a bit," he said, climbing into bed and putting his arm around me. "I have better things to do with my Monday nights."

⌒

Tuesday morning, and in fact most of the long day, was spent waiting to hear from Etta Mae or Binkie or Sam or Emma Sue or somebody. Things were going on that I knew nothing about, and it made me edgy and unable to settle on anything. I didn't know how Lieutenant Peavey would react to hearing about dysosmia or what he was interrogating Etta Mae about or what Binkie was doing to protect her or what Emma Sue would think about Dr. Fowler and Francie—demon activity or aged hormones run amok.

By lunchtime, with no word from anybody, I began to think of something else that could be done. I didn't share it with Lillian or Hazel Marie, knowing they'd say it was too risky. But it continued to run through my mind in spite of the fact that Hazel Marie talked about stretch marks while we ate.

By the time she'd decided to take a nap, I'd made up my mind. I went upstairs out of their hearing and dialed Lloyd's cell phone number. I knew he wouldn't answer because to do so during school risked losing his phone to the principal. But I could leave a message, which I proceeded to do, knowing that he would check as soon as the bell rang.

"Lloyd?" I said, as if he would respond. "Don't walk home today. Look for me in front of the school. I have a little project I want you to help me with, okay?"

I thought the day would never pass. All I could think of was how I could accomplish my plan and how, if I did, it would surely get Etta Mae off the hook. When it was almost time for school to let out, I picked up my pocketbook, told Lillian that I had a little shopping to do and left.

⌒⌒

Crammed in with a long line of other cars, I had several minutes to wait outside the school, but at last the doors opened and hundreds of young boys and girls streamed out of the building. I saw Lloyd craning his neck looking for me, but it took a while before the line moved and I could ease up to where he stood, cell phone in hand.

Opening the door and slinging his book bag onto the backseat, Lloyd asked, "Hey, Miss Julia. What's up?"

"You have film in that phone?"

"Film?" He gave me a frowning look. "No'm, it doesn't need film. Why?"

"We're going on a photo shoot—I think that's what it's called. Only it has to be done in secret and under cover. I want you to take a picture of three people, up close and full face, if you can get it. But none of them can know you're doing it. Can you manage that?"

Lloyd grinned. "Depends on whether they're expecting it or not. See, if they don't know what I'm doing, I can pretend to be texting somebody while they talk to you, then I'll just tilt the phone—like this—and get 'em."

"That sounds easy enough," I said with some relief as I headed away from the school grounds. "But we can't get caught doing it or it won't work. Not," I hurriedly said, "that we'll be doing anything wrong, but these people might not appreciate being taken unawares."

"Okay," he said, giving me another grin, but this one with a tinge of conspiracy in it. "Who're we gonna capture and why?"

"The why is for Etta Mae. Lieutenant Peavey put her picture in a lineup, but she was the only suspect in it! That doesn't make sense to me. I want to give the witness some real suspects to look at."

Well, of course, then I had to explain to Lloyd what all had gone on, and after doing so, he wholeheartedly agreed that it was only right to give that nephew some choice in the matter. How in the world could he be expected to identify a thief out of a bunch of women clerks and deputies?

"Whose pictures are we taking?" Lloyd asked again. "I need to get myself ready for some surreptitious aiming." Laughing, he fiddled with some buttons on his phone. "That was one of our spelling words. I've been waiting for a chance to use it."

I smiled, immensely proud of his intellect and his aptitude for all things electronic. "First, I want a picture of the gatekeeper when we get to Mountain Villas, which is where we're going. I don't really suspect him because we're looking for a woman, but it'll give you some practice. Then I want a picture of a woman we're going to see and then another one of her companion-housekeeper-sitter."

"Is that one person or three?"

"Three people in all, but only one companion, although she's a combination of things. And Lloyd, take as many pictures of each one as you can. I want to get clear pictures of their faces."

"I hate to tell you this, Miss Julia, but the resolution won't be too good. These phones aren't the best cameras in the world."

"Just so they're recognizable; I don't think it'll matter."

I glanced at him as we neared the gate at Mountain Villas. "Where can we get them developed?"

"I'll e-mail them to myself, then print 'em out at home."

"Well, my goodness," I mumbled, as I pulled to a stop at the gatehouse and put my window down.

When the grizzled gatekeeper shuffled out to the car, I greeted him and asked if he knew if Mrs. Delacorte was at home.

He leaned down to the window—just as I wanted him to—and said, "I don't pay no mind to who goes, just to who comes in, so no, ma'am, I can't tell you."

Sneaking a glance at Lloyd, hoping he'd gotten a good shot, I thanked the gatekeeper and proceeded on.

As soon as the street curved so that we were out of sight of the gatehouse, I pulled to the curb.

"Did you get him?"

"Just look," Lloyd said, and held up his phone so that I could see a perfect image of the gatekeeper, bad teeth and all, framed by the window as he peered in at us.

"That's wonderful," I said. "And he didn't suspect a thing. You did it so well that I didn't even notice, and I knew what you were doing. Now," I went on as I eased away from the curb, "let's see you do the same thing with these other two—they're the important ones."

"No problem. I think I'm suited for this kind of work."

I glanced worriedly at him, wondering what nefarious career I was encouraging him toward.

But it was too late for second thoughts, so I said, "Now, Lloyd, listen for a minute. You know it will be rude for you to be standing around with your thumbs working away on that thing while I visit with these women, but I want you to pretend that you don't know any better. In fact, I may even scold you a little for it, especially if one of them takes note of what you're doing. But if you get a good picture of each of them, it'll be worth a little playacting in the long run. I just don't want you to think it's a normal way of doing things."

"Oh, I don't think it's normal," Lloyd said, grinning, "but it sure is fun."

I pulled to the curb in front of Francie's cottage, neatly avoiding the listing Japanese maple, glanced at the Cadillac in the carport that proved they were home and said, "Don't have too much fun. You're going to law school, remember?"

Chapter 44

We got out of the car and went up the driveway to the walk that spanned the front of the cottage to the small stoop. I could see that the front door was open, probably because we were having a warm and beautiful autumn day, although a full-length glass storm door kept the nice breeze out.

When we were halfway across the walk, I stopped Lloyd with a hand on his shoulder. "Wait," I whispered, as a loud voice emanating from inside the house went on and on, getting shriller and more hateful by the minute. It was Francie's voice, and even though the words were indistinct, they were said in the same tone I'd heard her use with Evelyn and Emma Sue had also heard.

My hand tightened on Lloyd's shoulder as the thought crossed my mind that Emma Sue might've been right: a demon was loose in that house. Then I shook myself. Basically, it was Francie's vicious temper, call it whatever else you will.

"Lloyd," I said, "that's one of the women I want you to get, and the other one is the woman she's yelling at. But let's wait a minute till she runs out of steam. I don't want to get in the middle of it."

"Me, either," he said, but then he began easing toward the stoop, with me right with him. "I never heard the like. Let's see if we can find out what brought it on."

We reached the stoop and stood there for a few seconds, peering through the storm door while waiting for Francie to get whatever it was out of her system. I could see a short way down the center hall, but the glare prevented me from seeing into the sunroom at the far end, whence came the flow of abuse.

Then we heard a metallic *wha-ang*, and Francie's voice came to a sudden stop. Lloyd jerked back in alarm, and his eyes widened as my mouth dropped open.

"What was that?" he whispered.

"I don't know, but it sure put a stop to her, didn't it?"

"Reckon anybody got hurt?"

"I don't know," I said again, while images of mayhem flashed through my head. "Something could've fallen. Or maybe somebody threw something." Or maybe, which I didn't say, somebody really stopped Francie.

Lloyd said, half under his breath, "Maybe we ought to go."

I considered it, I really did. But I don't like leaving a job half finished, and besides, somebody could be lying inside injured and in need of help. "No, let's see what's going on."

And I walked boldly across the stoop and rang the bell, as if we'd just appeared on the scene with no knowledge of anything amiss. Out of the gloom of the hall, Evelyn appeared, scuttling toward the door in a gray sacklike dress, her head bound in a lopsided purple turban.

"Yes?" she murmured as she reached the door.

"Good afternoon. Miss Plemmons, is it? Or do you prefer

Evelyn? I'm Mrs. Julia Murdoch, a friend of Francie's, remember? I visited with her the other day, and we've just dropped by to see how she is. Oh, and this is Lloyd. May we come in? We can't stay long."

Without a word, she unlatched the door and pushed it open for us, and I got my first close-up view of her face—wrinkled, uncared for, without expression and with hooded eyes. Tired, it seemed to me, more than anything. Deep, bone-weary fatigue, etched not only on her face but also on her slumped shoulders and her entire bearing. It didn't help that the turban she wore was cockeyed on her head, the knot skewed around to one side with strands of gray hair straggling out from around the edges.

"She's in the sunroom," Evelyn mumbled, turning away as if it didn't matter one way or the other whether we followed her or not.

We did, though, and turned left toward Francie's chair when we reached the room, as Evelyn, without a word, veered right toward the kitchen.

I hurried over to Francie, trying to appear bright and cheerful to give her no hint that I'd heard the aforementioned commotion.

"Francie, how are you?" I said, my eyes glancing around to see if a vase had been thrown or a walking cane wielded. The only damage I saw was on the edge of a side table, where a long sliver of veneer was missing.

I pretended not to notice and turned to Francie. "I hope you don't mind our dropping in like this. This is Lloyd, my . . . Well, we were out this way, and I thought I'd come by to see how you're doing. Last evening must've been traumatic for you, and I was wondering if you've heard from Dr. Fowler. He was so concerned about how the situation might've appeared to the pastor and eager to correct any false impressions. You should've heard him. Everybody says he's thoughtful that way, and, you know, Pastor Ledbetter was a little short with you. I expect he regrets that today."

I was rambling because Francie wasn't responding. She sat, enthroned in her chair, her foot with its gouty toe elevated on an ottoman. There was a stunned look on her face. Lloyd edged to my side, his thumbs going a mile a minute, but she took no notice of him.

"Are you all right?" I asked, leaning down to look closely at her. "Can I get you anything?"

"No. No, I'm fine," she said, stirring a little as if she were coming out of shock. "Although I could be dead for all anybody cares." Then in a lower voice, she asked, "Where's Evelyn?"

"In the kitchen, I believe. You want me to get her?"

"No, leave her alone. Oh, Julia, I'm so glad you're here. You wouldn't believe . . . Listen," she whispered, reaching up and grabbing my hand, "I need to talk to Sam. Where is he? I need to see him right away."

"Francie," I said, heaving a sigh of exasperation, "I've told you. Sam is not a maintenance man. You'll have to have someone else replace your lightbulbs. Why don't you call Dr. Fowler? He seems fairly handy."

"I'm not thinking about lightbulbs," she snapped, her voice rising as she shifted in the chair. "I need to see Sam, and I mean *today*."

I reared back. "I'll pass the word along," I said through tight lips.

"You need to do more than that. This is urgent, Julia, and all you have to do is tell that boy with you to call him up."

Lloyd looked up, his thumbs momentarily stilled, his eyes wide at being singled out. He glanced at me as I gave a little shake of my head. Then, with his quick grasp of the situation, he nodded and said, "Yes, ma'am, I'll call him now."

We waited while he punched a few buttons, put the phone to his ear and gazed off into the distance. Francie watched avidly, then demanded, "Hand it here. I want to talk to him."

Lloyd ignored her, continued to listen to whatever the phone was doing, then shook his head. "Nobody answers, not even the answering machine. He may be downtown."

Francie sagged back into the chair. "I can't stand this! Nobody is ever where they ought to be. I need him! Julia, go find him for me. I . . ."

She stopped abruptly, looking past my shoulder at Evelyn, who had come silently in, holding a tray. But a tray the likes of which I'd never seen. My eyes widened as I realized that it was a Teflon-coated cookie sheet, but one that was warped at one end. Balanced on it was a plate of cookies.

She took the plate of cookies off and put it on the table beside Francie. Without a word, she stood for a second, holding the warped cookie sheet in front of Francie, then turned and went back into the kitchen. As she passed Lloyd, he turned his phone toward her, a movement that she paid no attention to. The whole episode unnerved me.

"Well, ah, Francie, I guess we'd better go. Lloyd has homework and I can see this is not a good time. I'll try to reach Sam for you, but if I don't, maybe you should look for another attorney. As I told you, he's no longer practicing anyway."

Francie hunkered down in her chair and gave me a brief nod, seemingly lost in her own thoughts. Or sulking, one of the two.

I put my arm around Lloyd's shoulders and soldiered out of the house as fast as I could go. We didn't say a word until we were in the car and the engine turned on.

"What happened in there, Lloyd?" I asked as I steered the car around the circle that led us to the main road of Mountain Villas.

"I don't know, Miss Julia, but something did. That lady acted weird."

"Which one?" I asked with a nervous laugh.

"Well, both of 'em, come to think of it. That fat lady in the chair? I think she was the one yelling at the other lady before we went in, and the other one, that gray lady, she gave me the creeps the way she came up behind me with those cookies." He took his bottom lip in his teeth, thought for a minute, then went on. "And did you see that tray she had? It looked like something you bake cookies on, not serve 'em on."

"It was a cookie sheet, all right. And did you see the way it was warped? Of course, a really hot oven can sometimes do that, except that one looked actually dented."

I drove out of the gated confines of Mountain Villas, raising a hand to the gatekeeper as we passed. Lloyd and I were silent as I maneuvered the car through the traffic, but my mind was replaying the scene we'd left. One thing was for sure, I wanted to find Sam and tell him as soon as I could, not that I wanted him to rush to Francie's side, but something strange was going on and he'd know what to do about it.

After a couple of stoplights held us up, Lloyd, in a musing kind of way, said, "Miss Julia, have you ever read that story about a woman who killed her husband with a leg of lamb she took out of the freezer?"

"Why, no, I don't believe I have." I glanced at him with a smile. "What brought that to mind?"

"Well, that cookie sheet did. Because in the story, after she killed her husband with the frozen leg of lamb, she put it in the oven and cooked it. Then when the police came, she served it to them and they ate up the murder weapon."

"I declare," I murmured. Then, with sudden understanding, I almost threw up my hands. "It was Evelyn! And that warped cookie sheet was right there in front of our eyes!" I veered out of the traffic and pulled to the side of the road. "Lloyd, you are the smartest boy in the world. They said Francie had a blunt-force injury from something large and flat, and Sam said the weapon would have evidence on it. But a weapon was never found. I bet that thing went in the dishwasher and was clean as a whistle when the deputies got there."

"Yes'm," Lloyd said, wiggling with excitement, "and did you see how that fat lady got real quiet when Evelyn walked in and just held it in front of her?"

"It certainly subdued her, didn't it? It was a threat, Lloyd, and I think what we heard before we went in was Evelyn's demonstration of what would happen again if Francie kept on at her. Honey, we've solved the whole thing, or rather, *you* have. Now all we have to do is get them to admit it, and Etta Mae'll be free of any suspicion whatsoever." Then as I sat there thinking, I remembered our reason for visiting Francie. "Did you get their pictures?"

"I sure did, good ones, too, because they weren't paying any attention to me. I'll print 'em out and show you."

"And I," I said, "will find Sam." But not for Francie, at least not for the reason she wanted him. I pulled back into a lane and headed for home. "On second thought, we may need Mr. Pickens more. This case calls for a professional now, although I think we've done a pretty good job on our own."

Chapter 45

We arrived home full of excitement and ready to lay it all out for everybody. Lloyd immediately ran through the kitchen and up the back stairs to print out the pictures he'd made, with Lillian calling after him to come to the table. I was taken aback to find that supper had been served early to accommodate Sam.

"Where is he?" I demanded. I couldn't believe they hadn't waited for us—that was the second night in a row—and Sam was off somewhere again.

"That pastor call a meetin' which Mr. Sam say is to decide what to do 'bout that man you don't like. He think they gonna get rid of him."

"That's the best news I've heard all day. Except the pastor already decided that last night. I guess he wants to make it official, but I declare, Lillian, I need Sam here."

"He say he won't be long, so you an' Lloyd go on in to the table. They all still settin' in there."

And so they were—Hazel Marie, Mr. Pickens and Etta Mae—and none of them looking too happy. Lillian brought in a glass of iced tea for me and milk for Lloyd, still grumbling about his flying off upstairs without eating.

"He'll be down soon," I told her, as I took in the long faces around the table.

"What's going on?" I asked. "You look like you've had bad news."

Nobody said anything for a minute, then Etta Mae sighed. "Yes'm, at least I have. Lieutenant Peavey wants to interview me again in the morning."

"What for? He should know by now that you had nothing to do with it. Mr. Pickens," I said, glaring at him, "didn't you tell him what happens when a person gets hit on the head? You could've called Dr. Hargrove, you know, if the lieutenant had any questions."

"That's exactly what he did," Mr. Pickens said. "But the problem is not what the woman smelled or didn't smell. The problem is still who hit her, and Etta Mae is one of the ones who had access. Looks like he's reinterviewing everybody."

"Then I guess we'd better get something done tonight," I said as Lillian set a filled plate in front of me. "Don't despair, Etta Mae. We have one more matter to take care of and you can see the lieutenant without a care in the world."

Mr. Pickens's eyebrows went up, as he sat sideways in his chair, one leg crossed over the other, an arm resting on his empty place mat. The other arm, I noticed, was draped across the back of Hazel Marie's chair. Etta Mae sat for a few minutes, then with a deep breath, she rose to help Lillian clear the table. Clearly, she was not reassured by what I'd said, but I didn't go further, hoping that Sam would come in and I'd only have to tell it once.

As Lloyd came bounding into the dining room, his face beaming and his hands full of photographs, I said, "Mr. Pickens,

Lloyd and I would like to have the benefit of your forensic expertise, if you don't mind. Lloyd, did you get everything printed out?"

"Yes, ma'am, I sure did, and I got Etta Mae's picture, too—one I took the other day—so there'd be no question about it. And Miss Julia, I thought of something else. To be completely fair, we ought to have some other pictures in the lineup that are about the same age as the ones we suspect. So I put Mama's picture in 'cause she's about Etta Mae's age."

"Thank you, son," Hazel Marie said, laughing. "I think."

"And," Lloyd said, his eyes shining with eagerness, "I got one of you, Miss Julia, when you weren't looking, because you're about the age of those other ladies."

"Of *me*? My word, Lloyd, I don't want to be in a lineup, and besides, it's not polite to bring up a person's age."

Mr. Pickens had his usual amused look on his face, but then he straightened up. "Lineup? What've you two been doing?"

"Police work, Mr. Pickens, if you must know. Sit down, Etta Mae, and listen. Between us, Lloyd and I have just about cleared up this mess. All we need is for Mr. Pickens to take our pictures to that pawnbroker's nephew so he can identify the real culprit, and we need Mr. Pickens to do it because he has some professional authority. Then he can present it, along with what Lloyd and I heard and witnessed this afternoon, to Binkie and to Lieutenant Peavey."

Mr. Pickens was sitting straight up by this time, gazing across the table at me with those black eyes. He seemed none too pleased to learn that we'd been encroaching on his territory.

"What've you done?"

"Let me tell 'em, Miss Julia," Lloyd said as Lillian guided him firmly to his place at the table.

"You better eat something 'fore you dry up and blow away," she said.

"Yes, ma'am, I will, but look, J.D. Look at these pictures. We've got a real lineup now, but Miss Julia and me think it was that Evelyn woman, 'cause we heard her crash down that cookie sheet, but we didn't know what it was at the time, and when we got inside, that other lady acted real scared, telling us we'd come just in time and wanting me to call Mr. Sam to come help her. And then, *then* that Evelyn woman came in and served cookies on the very *same* cookie sheet—we know it was the same one because it was dented—and she just kinda stood there, like she was warning the other lady what could happen again, so when I told Miss Julia about the leg of lamb, why, we just figured it all out, because it was in the dishwasher, not the oven, when the deputies came."

Hazel Marie peered at him. "What?"

"Take it a little slower, son," Mr. Pickens said, "and tell us again."

Between the two of us, Lloyd and I went through the events of the afternoon again. "So," I summed up, "what we have to do now is take those pictures to the pawnshop and see what that nephew says. He'll identify Evelyn; I'm sure of it just from the way she acted. And Francie knows the truth now, too, so she'll have to recant her accusation of Etta Mae. And if she won't, well, I have a few cookie sheets in my kitchen, too.

"But Mr. Pickens," I went on, leaning toward him, "we need to get these pictures to the nephew tonight—pawnshops stay open late, don't they? I mean, with Lieutenant Peavey still breathing down Etta Mae's neck, we should get this thing settled."

All this while, Etta Mae had been looking from Lloyd to me, listening to what we were saying, an expression of hopeful wonder on her face. Hazel Marie jumped up and hugged her.

"Oh, Etta Mae, it's over now. The lieutenant will have to believe it, but J.D.," she said, turning to him, "Miss Julia's right. You need to get to the pawnshop before it closes. Let's all go right now."

"Hold on just one minute," Mr. Pickens said as my heart fell at his stern look. "Let me see those pictures. It'd be just like somebody I know to send me off half-cocked." He shuffled through them, giving each one his full attention. Then he set the gatekeeper's picture aside, saying, "What's this doing in here? We already know it was a woman."

"That," I told him, "was just a practice shot. Please, Mr. Pickens, go do it now. There's no reason in the world for Etta Mae to go through one more night like she's been doing."

"All right," he said, getting to his feet, to my great relief. "It won't be legitimate, but Lieutenant Peavey can conduct a more official lineup tomorrow. And," he said with a quick smile at Etta Mae, "conduct a few different interviews than the one he'd planned."

"I'll go with you," I said, hopping up.

"No, you won't." Mr. Pickens glared at me. "I don't want to make it any more off the books than it already is. Besides, Sam will be here before long, and if I'm not mistaken, you have a few fences to mend, what with gallivanting all over the place and nobody knowing where you were."

He gave Hazel Marie a quick kiss and left, taking our picture lineup with him. I was tempted to follow him but decided I could leave it to him. We looked around at one another: Etta Mae with hope lighting up her face; Lloyd with his eyes gleaming with excitement; Lillian unsure of what had happened; and Hazel Marie frowning as she thought about it.

"Tell me again," she finally said. "What did a leg of lamb have to do with it?"

"That's what I want to know," Lillian said. "Y'all don't even *like* lamb."

We heard voices outside and feet shuffling at the front door. Then Sam stuck his head in and called that he was going with Mr. Pickens. I almost got up to go with them but felt too tired to make the effort. I thought to myself that if the menfolk couldn't close the case after everything had been handed to them on a platter—or, shall we say, on a cookie sheet—I'd get some rest and pick right up after them in the morning.

So I went to bed, then couldn't go to sleep for wondering what was happening. As tired as I was from the busy afternoon, to say nothing of the past several days, I sat up in bed and waited for Sam.

I even tried reading the latest issue of *Guideposts* but couldn't concentrate enough to get anything out of it. Hearing Sam and Mr. Pickens come in downstairs, I immediately put it aside and awaited the latest news. But, of course, Hazel Marie and Etta Mae had waited up for them, and I could hear the murmur of conversation downstairs. When I could stand it no longer, I threw off the covers, intending to join them to hear what had taken place. Then I heard Sam's footsteps on the stairs.

He'd barely gotten in the bedroom before I asked, "What happened?"

"Well," he said, laughing as he sat on the bed beside me, "I thought Pickens was going to strangle that nephew. The boy is as nearsighted as anybody I've ever seen, and he hemmed and hawed over the pictures of Francie and Evelyn. He couldn't make up his mind because they were both wearing turbans, and that was the only thing he definitely remembered. According to him, the woman who sold him the bracelet had what he called a funny kind of do-rag on her head."

"My word," I said. "Francie would have a fit at having her custom-made turban called a do-rag. But what about Etta Mae's picture? Did he say anything about that?"

"Didn't give it a second glance. Anyway, we went from there to the sheriff's office, called Lieutenant Peavey and waited for him. That's why we were so long. So Peavey went with us back to the pawnshop, and by that time the nephew had decided it was Evelyn. I don't know how well he'll hold up to give testimony, but it hardly matters. Once Peavey homes in on Evelyn, I think he'll get the truth. He'll want to talk to you and Lloyd, as well."

"About time," I murmured, then said, "So tell me what happened at church tonight. What did Pastor Ledbetter have to say about Dr. Fowler?"

Sam started laughing again. "I'll tell you the truth: if you hadn't already told me what really happened with Francie, I wouldn't have heard about it tonight. Ledbetter went on and on, putting the best face on it he could, but what it came down to was Dr. Fowler had to withdraw for personal reasons.

Which, I noted with interest, were never clearly defined. So the enrichment classes are canceled, and nobody seemed that upset about it."

"But Sam," I said, putting my hand on his arm, "are *you* upset?"

"Me? With football on Monday nights? I should say not." He put his hand on mine. "Why? Were you planning to go?"

"Oh goodness, no. Our marriage is as enriched as it can get as far as I'm concerned. But Sam," I said, almost choking on the emotion I was feeling, "if you don't feel that way, we can find another counselor, one with some sense this time, or I'll read a book, or I'll even ask Francie to share some of her secrets, even though it would about kill me to do it. What I mean is, well, I'll do anything to make you happy."

Sam frowned and looked carefully at me. "What is this? I'm already a happy man. I don't need, or want, anything else."

"Well, but you wouldn't have gone to those classes if you hadn't felt something was missing, and, I declare, Sam, I don't know how to stoke our embers any higher than they are, but if you'll just tell me, I'll try my best to do whatever it takes."

"Honey, I told you. I only went because Ledbetter asked us to. I thought it'd be something you and I could laugh about, because there wouldn't be a thing Dr. Fowler could teach us. I thought you'd enjoy the irony of an unmarried man who lives with his mother trying to teach new tricks to a couple of old hands like us."

"Oh, Sam," I said, trying not to cry but doing it anyway, "I couldn't enjoy anything with that man around. I've spent all this time trying to stay out of his way, afraid he'd say something that would turn you against me. You don't know what I've suffered, and I could just stay quiet and not tell you now because he's leaving, but I have to. I can't stand keeping it from you, so here it is." I stopped, took a rasping breath and whispered, "Pastor Ledbetter caught Dr. Fowler and me in the bridal parlor, too."

Sam stared at me for a minute, then he said, "You mean that time they were after the Springer estate? Sweetheart, I know all about that. Ledbetter told me in detail at the time."

"He *did?*" I sat straight up in bed and glared at him. "You mean you've known all along? I can't believe this. Then why did you think I'd want to be anywhere around Dr. Fowler? And," I said, flopping back on the pillow, just so undone, "how could you marry me, knowing all that?"

"Why, sweetheart, that just made me more eager. I like a feisty woman, or haven't you noticed?"

"It never made any difference to you?"

"Look, I knew what Ledbetter and Fowler were doing and what they were after. But I *didn't* know that you were still troubled by it. I should've figured it out, though, and I'm sorry about that. All I knew was that if Fowler made a move toward you, I was going to cut him off at the knees."

"Oh, Sam," I said, trying to decide whether to laugh or to cry. "Maybe we need a class on communication skills, but then again," I went on as he stretched out beside me, "maybe not."

A while later, I said, "Sam?"

"Hmm?" He was a little out of breath.

"Hazel Marie thinks we should renew our vows."

His head rose up off the pillow. "You mean they've expired? I thought we had a lifetime subscription."

"Well, *I* do. I just want to be sure that you do, too."

"How can you not be sure?" Sam said, smiling as he smoothed back the hair from my face. "Look at me. I'm the happiest man you'll ever meet. Besides, we've gotten married twice already."

"I know, but the first one didn't take, so we can't count that. Anyway, I just want you to know that I do love and honor you, and I promise to try to obey you, and I will do all three for the rest of my life. And if you ever begin to feel impoverished, like something's missing and in need of anything at all, I promise to do whatever it takes to make your life as happy and as full as it can possibly be." I put my hand on his neck and smiled up at him. "There now. I've renewed my vows. Are you feeling enriched?"

"More than you know," he said with the sweetest smile.

Chapter 46

Not only did Evelyn own up to hitting Francie and taking her bracelet, she told Lieutenant Peavey she'd do it again if she had to. We got all the inside information from Mr. Pickens, who got it from the lieutenant and from what he called general cop talk.

According to what he heard, Evelyn had said, "If you had to live with that woman, you'd do worse than me. At least I didn't kill her, though I thought about it many a time." And all during her confession, she'd not expressed any remorse or even any concern as to what would happen to her. She was as calm and self-assured as she could be. In fact, Mr. Pickens said that all the deputies were just shaking their heads at how little the whole affair seemed to affect her.

At one point, when her court-appointed attorney told her how many years she could expect to be sentenced to serve, she'd said, "I'm tired of living with Francie anyway."

She's getting a psychological evaluation as we speak, and I just hope whoever's doing it has better qualifications than Dr. Fred Fowler.

Francie, of course, was outraged when the truth came out, although she'd gotten a good idea of what the truth was from seeing that dented cookie sheet waved in front of her face. Arley Hopkins told us that Francie kept saying over and over to whoever at Mountain Villas would listen to her that Evelyn had bitten the hand that fed her. "I took her into my home, held her to my bosom, and she turned on me. Just *turned* on me. That's gratitude for you, isn't it? She didn't have a nickel to her name, and I took her in because she was a relative, after all, and she *attacked* me in my own *home*, sent me to the hospital, and now she doesn't even have the intestinal fortitude to face me and say she's sorry. I hope they put her under the jail."

We haven't heard anything more about the Coral Gables police, but if I were Francie, I'd be careful about flinging the word *jail* around. Arley's on the lookout, though, and she'll let us know if some official cars from Florida show up.

But the next thing that Arley told us was that Francie had been keeping company with a certain gentleman at Mountain Villas who had suddenly gained a new lease on life. Arley said the residents out there are amazed because he's dashing around in his scooter chair with a lecherous glint in his eyes. She said the women scatter like a flock of birds when they see him coming. And the word is out that he's buried three wives to Francie's five husbands, so if they marry, an enterprising resident plans to take wagers on which one will bury the other. My money would go on Francie if I were a gambling woman.

But things might change, because I just got a call from LuAnne, who'd just talked with Arley, who told her that Dr. Fowler had been seen at Mountain Villas yesterday looking into reserving a place for his mother. And what's more, he'd visited Francie and had stayed long enough to have lunch with her. And what's even more, Francie had played bridge later that

afternoon sporting a new bracelet that she made sure everybody noticed. "A friend gave it to me," she'd said with a coy
titter, "as an indication of his honorable intentions."

Arley said that a certain gentleman in the scooter chair was
noticeably toned down at dinner last night, not even trying to
pinch the ladies or look up anybody's dress. So Francie must've
cut him off after realizing she'd had a better offer. But can you
imagine her and Dr. Fowler married to each other—she for
the sixth time and he for the first? It boggles the mind to think
about it, and I could almost work up some sympathy for him—
if I didn't know him so well.

⌣⁀

And wouldn't you know, Francie's not said one word to or about
Etta Mae. And talk about no remorse, Francie goes on her merry
way with no thought of the damage she did or the anguish that
young woman suffered from being a suspect. But Etta Mae's
doing all right now; she's even gone back to wearing Shania
Twain by Stetson, and every time I get a whiff of it I think of
collard greens. I can't help it; the connection, if not the smell,
is just there, that's all. And one time, Etta Mae confided that
she did the same thing, but she had to use it up because she
couldn't afford to throw out a perfectly good bottle of perfume.
"But as soon as I use it up," she'd said, "I'm going to try Jessica
Simpson's Dessert." No telling what that'll smell like.

As soon as the newspaper reported that Evelyn had been
arrested, the owner of the Handy Home Helpers was on the
phone begging Etta Mae to come back to work. I told Etta Mae
she should show some reluctance to work for someone who was
so quick to fire her, and she did, but not much. But that little

bit gained her a salary increase that emboldened Etta Mae enough to negotiate a six-week leave of absence when Hazel Marie has those babies. So we can count on her being back in the house when we need her most, and that suits me fine. The more I think about it, the less eager I am to be up half the night changing and feeding infants. The Lord knew what he was doing when he gave children to the young.

And Hazel Marie, bless her heart, is enjoying these months, sitting around and getting bigger by the day. Oh, she walks, or rather waddles, every day, but I don't know how long that's going to last. From the looks of her, she's going to need a crane to get up and down before long. But happy? That woman *is* happy. No, a better word is *serene*. I've never seen a woman so completely satisfied with being married. Of course, it took her long enough to get that way. Every time I look at her there's a blissful smile on her face, and in spite of my doubts as to his qualifications as husband material, I have to give the credit to Mr. Pickens. He's as caring and attentive a husband as anyone could ask for, although that hasn't stopped him from taking off for days at a time to pursue his investigative career.

Nor has it stopped him from teasing me. Every once in a while, he'll look sidewise at me, shake his head and say, "Dysosmia. Who would've thought it?" Or something like, "Baked any cookies today?" I think he's just put out that Lloyd and I showed up both him and the sheriff's department.

⌒

So it looks as if everything's been solved, and we've settled down to await the advent of whatever Hazel Marie's carrying. Lillian says that at least one of them is a boy because she's carrying it low, but the way she's filling out looks to me like she's carrying both high and low. Maybe that means something. The doctor thinks we'll have New Year's babies, maybe even for Christmas because twins tend to come early. Lloyd says he figures it'll be a holiday regardless of when they come, so it doesn't matter to him. He's been busy making a list of names for his mother to choose from—some of them make Mr. Pickens laugh and my eyes roll.

⌒

And Sam? Why, Sam's a happy man, I'm finally convinced of it. I'd just projected my own insecurities onto him and let myself get in a swivet because of them. See, I know a little psychology, too. Because Sam was never in doubt as to the state of our marriage, he's just gone right on being his own darling self, while I, well, I'm positive that Hazel Marie was right. Renewing our vows was all it took—even if I did most of the renewing and did it not at an altar but in our bed, which, come to think of it, may be the best place for any kind of renewing, enriching or stoking of embers.

⌒

So I'm sitting back and letting life roll on, smiling to myself on occasion at how well things worked out. Hazel Marie got married, Etta Mae got out from under suspicion, Evelyn got arrested and Francie got Dr. Fowler, which means that he'll get what's coming to him.

Sam is feeling fully and completely enriched these days, and justifiably so, because I'm seeing to it myself.